TRULY, MADLY, DEEPLY

ERIKA KELLY

TRULY, MADLY, DEEPLY

Erika Kelly

ISBN: 978-1-955462-18-1

Cover image by Sara Eirew Photographer and Designer
Cover design and Formatting by Serendipity Formatting
Editing by Sharon Pochron
Editing by Olivia Kalb Editing
Proofreading by Karen Hrdlicka

Titles by Erika Kelly

Have you read the Rock Star Romance series? Come meet the sexy rockers of Blue Fire:

MORE THAN A FEELING

Sign up for my newsletter to read the EXCLUSIVE novella for my readers only! You'll get two chapters a month of this super sexy, fun romance! #rockstarromance #surprisepregnancy #forcedproximity. Also, get PLANES, TRAINS, AND HEAD OVER HEELS for FREE! I hope you'll come hang out with me on Facebook, TikTok, Twitter, Instagram, Goodreads, and Pinterest or in my private reader group.

Here are all the places you can find me:

https://linktr.ee/erikakellybooks

Dedication

This book is dedicated to Superman.
Thank you for always being there. You're my favorite person,
and I wouldn't want to do life without you.

Acknowledgments

- To Superman, thank you for always putting down the paper when I need to talk about my stories. They wouldn't be nearly as good without your input!
- Thank you, Sharon Pochron, for being my truest friend.
- I couldn't do any of this without Erica Alexander. Thank you for always being there for me.
- Thank you to Melissa Panio-Peterson for being so steadfastly on my team.
- Melissa Martin, you make my life easier —thank you!
- I lucked out when I found Christian Sarlo of the Penn State University hockey team. He's not only a great player, but he gives outstanding help with all the hockey lingo and situations. He is endlessly patient and generous with his advice. Any mistakes are mine.
- To Karen, thank you for taking on this project and making my book better! You're awesome!
- Thank you, Olivia, for your great insight. As always, you made the book better.
- A big shout out to Laetitia Treseng for helping with the recipe conversion—that was incredibly kind of you!

- And thank you to the readers, bloggers, reviewers, and all my author friends who make this job so richly rewarding and worthwhile.

Thank you

We've created a recipe book for you! Ten fabulous pastry chefs contributed their luscious recipes. Use the QR code to get your copy!

Lee Ruocco of SweetAddictionFix.com
Fran Costigan of @goodcakesfran
Michal M. of Badolina Bakery and Café
Jean-Philippe of Oui Pastries Glasgow
Chef Nate of the French Kitchen
Manuella Mazzocco of Cooking with Manuela
Rebecca Blackwell of ofbatteranddough.com
Monique Polanco of Peaches 2 Peaches
CJ Cheyne of Oui & Si in Philadelphia
Angelina of Angelina Italian Bakery

Aim your cell phone camera at the QR code below to get links to the recipe book, the bonus scene, and all the places you can find me!

https://linktr.ee/erikakellybooks

Chapter One

"Can I get a more serene look?" the wedding photographer asked.

"Sure. Let me just grab a piping bag and fill some pâte à choux." Grace Giordano laughed. The billowing of whipped cream inside the flaky crust, the scent of sugar and butter, the swirl of tempered chocolate...yeah, that would get her serene real quick. "Sorry, but I'm literally walking down the aisle in twenty minutes. I don't think I can fake it." She held out her hand. "Look, I'm shaking." But she'd try. She closed her eyes. *Serene, huh?* She tried to think of her honeymoon, but the only images that came to mind were the glorious pastries she hoped to find as she wandered the streets of Paris.

"Ooh, that's good. Hold on to that expression right there." The woman fired off some shots. "You must be thinking about Ian because you've got this dreamy look."

Well, not exactly.

Grace tried to hide her smile. *Is it bad that I'm dreaming of whipped cream and not my fiancé?*

"Okay, hang on." The photographer lowered her arm. "Let me change my lens, and we'll get a few more."

Turning to face the mirror, Grace barely recognized the woman staring back at her. The fancy updo, the elaborate make up, and her great-grandmother's high-necked, long-sleeved wedding gown (*that I'm wearing in summer!*) made her look like a bride in one of the antique photos hanging in her parents' living room.

Most days, she wore leggings and Renzo T-shirts, and her only make-up came in the form of flour dusting her cheeks.

What does serene even mean? A woman at peace with herself, who was exactly where she wanted to be, living the life she'd always wanted. *Hm.* She was marrying the boy from down the street, she worked in the family bakery she adored, and she'd lived in the same neighborhood all her life except for college.

What could be better than that?

She stuck a finger under the collar of the dress. "I must have the neck of a linebacker because this thing is way too tight."

The photographer looked up from her camera bag. "You have a lovely neck. Now, come on. Give me a smile that says you know all the delicious things Ian will do to you tonight."

"You do know Ian and I have been together for fifteen years, right?" She regretted the words the moment they came out. "Oh, that sounded bad. I love him. I do. I only meant we've been together so long—"

The woman held up a hand. "Been married thirty-three years. I get it."

"Oh, wait. I know exactly how to get the expression you're looking for." She grabbed her phone off the dresser and sorted through her playlists. When she found the right Lorelei Calloway song, she hit play.

No matter how many times she heard it, this song had the power to change her emotions. From the very first note, the haunting melody stirred her, and the romantic lyrics made her swoon.

The photographer lowered her camera. "Oh, I love this one."

"I know, right?" Holding her bouquet, Grace turned back to the mirror and let the poignant melody carry her away.

And then, she started singing along.

"Are you kidding me?" The photographer gawked. "You sound *just* like her."

Yep. And Grace had capitalized on it. "Believe it or not, I used to sing in a tribute band."

"Actually, you know what? You look like her, too."

"Biggest compliment ever."

"Oh, gosh. Look at the time. I have to do the mother-of-the-bride shots. You want to text your mom, get her back here?"

"Sure." She'd left to pay the chamber trio a while ago. Something must've distracted her. "Let me grab her." Setting the bouquet down, Grace headed for the door.

"Hurry. Showtime's in fifteen minutes."

Still humming the song, she headed down the hallway, the layers of her satin and lace dress swishing with every step. She followed the voices and found her mom and the cellist at the top of the stairs.

"That's not possible," her mom said. "I have more than enough in my account."

Owning a bakery meant her parents worked twelve hours a day six days a week. The fact that it was a family business, employing all the aunts, uncles, and cousins, meant money was tight at the best of times.

Which was why Grace had begged her parents not to pay for this wedding. She'd have been happy eloping with the boy who was already like a son to them. But her parents had insisted. She was their only daughter, and it was their duty and pleasure to host a party celebrating her joyful union.

They'd compromised by hosting it at her childhood home on Duff Island. Friends and family would provide food, and the only cost came from the flowers and landscaping on the lawn that sloped prettily down to the ocean.

After all her parents had done to make this a special day, Grace wouldn't let the cost of a chamber trio stress them out. "Hey, Mom. It's time for mother-of-the-bride pictures. Why don't you let me handle this, and you go get your glam on?" She reached for her mom's phone.

"No, you're not paying for the music that walks you down the aisle at your own wedding."

She gave her mom a look. *Let's not make the musician any more uncomfortable than she already is.* Besides, the amount wouldn't make a dent in Grace's account. She'd been saving since she was a little girl. What had started out as a silly fantasy of owning her own bakery had turned into a possible down payment on a house.

Reluctantly, her mom handed the phone over. She waited as Grace logged into her bank account and transferred the money. "There you go." She smiled at the musician. "I'll see you out there in ten minutes." But just as she went to log out, she noticed a flash of red. *It didn't go through. What the hell?* She showed it to her mom. "That's not possible. Hang on." She checked her bank balance. "One hundred dollars?"

What in the world?

"That's what's in mine." Her mom clasped her hands together so tightly the knuckles turned white.

Fear sent a sting through her body. "What's happening?"

"Listen, it's your wedding day." The musician backed away. "We can settle up tomorrow." She smiled and then headed down the stairs.

"I'm so sorry," Grace called. "We're going to pay you." But really, she didn't know that.

Because all their money was gone.

Gone.

With a vise around her lungs, she couldn't take a full breath. Once the woman was out of sight, Grace turned to her mom. "What's happening? How are both of our accounts empty?"

"I don't know. Could there be a glitch in the system?"

"That doesn't make any sense. Oh, my God." She couldn't believe it. She was so shaken, she couldn't think.

"Hang on. Check your most recent transfers."

"Right. Of course." Grace tapped the screen, and when she saw her fiancé's name, the bottom dropped out of her world.

"What? Grace, what is it?" Her mom grabbed the phone back. Reading the name, her forehead creased. "I don't understand. Did he need it to pay for the honeymoon?"

"You think our week in Paris is going to cost a hundred and fifty thousand dollars?"

Shock and confusion gripped her mom's features. "Why would he do this?"

She didn't know, but she'd sure as hell find out. "Mom, how much did you have in your account?"

"Not much. Don't worry about us."

"Don't worry? My fiancé *stole* from you. Tell me how much."

"We had fifteen grand."

"Thank you." Lifting the weighty skirt, she hightailed it down the hallway to her oldest brother's bedroom. She barged right in and addressed the six groomsmen. "Everyone out." Their surprised expressions broke through the anger. *This isn't their fault.* "Sorry. Could you please give me a moment alone with—" She couldn't say his name. Couldn't even look at him.

Fortunately, she didn't need to because the men filed out and shut the door.

Alone with her fiancé, she rushed over to him. "What have you done with my parent's money?"

Ian had grown up a few houses over, so she'd known him most of his life. When his mom's business blew up and they got rich, they moved into a mansion, but they'd never left the island. They were good people. They respected their roots and valued friendships.

Loyalty, honor…that's how Ian was raised.

She knew everything about him. She'd seen his every expression…except this one. He was tortured. Okay, something had happened. Maybe it wasn't his fault. "Talk to me." She'd at least give him a chance. "Explain."

He tipped his head back and shouted, "*Fuck.*"

Fear unlike anything she'd ever known snaked up her spine and wrapped around her throat. What had he done? "We're supposed to walk down the aisle in eight minutes. Make it okay for me to do that."

He whipped around. "What are you talking about? Of course, we're getting married. Baby, I'm going to fix this. You just have to give me a few days. I swear, I'll put everything back. But we're leaving town tonight, and I had to settle some debts."

"Debts? Since when do you have debts?"

"Look, things didn't go the way I'd planned. I had a sure thing, and…" He shook his head like he couldn't believe his misfortune. "I don't know how it went so wrong. But you have to trust me. I've always paid you back, and I'll do it again."

Again? "Wait." Her mind fought to hold on to something in this conversation that made sense, but she couldn't get any traction. He might as well have been speaking a foreign language. "You've done this before?"

"Yeah. But see, you didn't even notice because I've always put the money back."

She gazed into his familiar brown eyes, but for the first time, she was looking at a stranger. "Are you telling me that you logged on to my laptop and hacked into my account… to pay your debts?" She took a step back. "Who are you?"

"Don't be like that. I—"

"No. Don't tell me what to be. I've known you most of my life, and the Ian I grew up with would never drain my parents' bank account."

"It's not like that. I would never steal from you guys. It's temporary. I swear. I'm going to fix everything after the ceremony."

"You're talking to me like I'm irrationally angry at you for not taking out the garbage. We're talking about theft. You get that, right?" He didn't, though. She could clearly see that. "You stole from my *parents*. They went to your basketball games. They went to your graduations. My dad bakes a cake for you on Founder's Day because of some inside joke. They've treated you like a son, and you hacked into their bank account?"

"I know. I'm sorry. I feel like shit. But I swear to God, I'll put every penny back. I just need a little time."

"How?" But she already knew the answer. "The only way you can pay back a hundred and sixty-five thousand dollars is by gambling." The sum was so enormous, she grew worried for him. "Ian, do you have a problem?"

He jammed a hand into the pocket of his suit pants and lowered his gaze to the worn rug. His chest rose as he inhaled deeply. "No. It's fun, and I've made a lot of money."

"And lost it." A sharp pain hit behind her eye and turned into a throb. "All of it."

"I'm sorry, baby. I am."

"That's it? That's all you've got—you're sorry? You've been using my savings account as your own personal playground, and you don't seem to understand just how wrong it is. You're only sorry because you got caught." The pain behind her eye escalated, and she rubbed her temple. "God, how am I just finding out about this?" Because it was a savings account that she never touched.

"You know I've always bet on games."

"Yes, for fun. When you had money to burn. How did it blow up to *this*?"

"Because I want us to have a good future. I want to be able to buy a house and raise our kids."

"Bullshit. My savings was more than enough for us to buy a house. Besides, we'll *earn* the money we need. We both work."

"Come on. Neither of us is going to get rich off our jobs. With the economy the way it's going, I can't meet my quotas at work. I could get fired. They've already announced that layoffs are coming over the next year."

"Stop. Just stop trying to justify stealing from me." The

shock had worn off, and now she just wanted facts. "How did you do it? How did you get into my parents' account?"

"Your passwords are saved, so when your mom's making dinner or everyone's outside…" He hunched a shoulder.

"Ian." She was unbearably disappointed. The neckline of her dress clutched her throat, and she wanted to rip the buttons off. But she couldn't, of course. It had been in her family for generations. She would've been the fourth Donato to wear it. "You're like a son to them. They trusted you enough to leave their laptops open when you're around, and you betrayed them."

"Shit. I had a big loss, and I had to pay them back. If you don't—"

"Jesus, Ian. *Them?* Who did you borrow from? The mafia?"

"No, no. It's nothing like that. But you have to understand. I work in finance. If anyone finds out about my gambling, I'll lose my job—I'm in *wealth management.* No one would ever hire me again."

"Okay." She'd heard all she needed. "I get it." There was nothing left to talk about.

"You do?" He reached for her. "Thank—"

"No." Her hand flipped up to ward him off. "Don't misunderstand what's happening here." Was he out of his mind? "I *get* that my parents work their hands to the bone keeping Renzo's going—not for themselves, but for all the aunts and uncles and cousins and grandparents who make it their livelihood. I *get* that I'm the kid who babysat and walked dogs after school instead of playing a sport or joining a club…or having friends. I'm the woman who got up at three in the morning six days a week to make croissants and turnovers but still sang in a tribute band on the weekends so

I could build up a savings that you wiped out in the click of a button." She headed out.

"Wait, where are you going? We're still getting married, right?"

It wasn't sinking it. She needed to make herself very clear. "Two things are going to happen. I'm going to walk away from you because I can't stand to look at your face, and two, you're going to put the money back into my parents' account. I don't care how you do it, but I want it done." Standing in the doorway, she looked at this man she'd loved since she was a teenager. This man who'd broken her heart and healed it a dozen times.

A man who'd betrayed her in the most unforgivable way.

And she knew without a shred of doubt that it was over. "Goodbye, Ian." Weighed down by the heavy dress, Grace hurried back to her bedroom. Thank God, it was empty.

Well, of course, it's empty. I'm supposed to be walking down the aisle right now.

All those people. Anxiety gripped her, and she went to the window. Her stomach twisted at the sight of the wedding arch covered in stunning pink peonies, her favorite flower. Everyone she'd ever known sat in folding chairs they'd painstakingly adorned with ribbons and a spray of baby's breath.

Romeo stood as officiant. He was not only the brother closest in age to her, but he was also Ian's best friend. *He'll be devastated when he finds out.*

Well, she had to do it. She had to tell everyone the wedding was off.

But wait. Ian's boss and coworkers were there, too. If she made the announcement, everyone would want to know why. The truth would spread. She might be done with him, but he'd never be able to pay her parents back if his career was ruined.

Her chest hurt with all the emotions thrashing around. It was so hard to think clearly. She had only one instinct, one incessant voice drumming at the back of her mind.

Go.

Get out of here.

Run.

She grabbed her purse and suitcase and hurried down the hallway. As soon as she got clear of the house, she'd text her mom, ask her to let everyone know, and that the bride and groom would return the gifts.

At the bottom of the stairs, she stopped to catch her breath. She had to slow down. *Where am I even going? Think.* Voices in the kitchen propelled her toward the door.

None of this made sense. Ian wouldn't do this. He just couldn't. If he came over and saw her dad mowing the lawn, he took over—even if he was dressed nicely. He always cleaned the kitchen after her parents cooked a meal.

How could the same guy who helped unload delivery trucks for the bakery at six a.m., making him late for work, be the same guy who hacked into their laptops?

I can't breathe.

She had to unbutton the back of the dress, but before she could set her luggage down, she heard the chamber trio launch into *Canon in D*. Any minute now, her mom, her bridesmaids, *someone* would come looking for her. They'd ask why she was running, and what could she say? She couldn't lie to them. It just wasn't her nature.

I have to get out of here. I have to think.

Throwing open the front door, she slammed into a hard body. "Oof." The air left her lungs, but before she went down, two very strong hands gripped her biceps.

"Whoa. Where's the fire?" a deep voice asked.

The first thing that hit her was his scent. Expensive, intensely masculine—it fired up a vague, oddly sexual sensation. But then, she gazed into the blue-gray eyes of the most breathtakingly handsome man she'd ever seen. Jaime Dupree. He was one of Ian's oldest friends, and yet, she barely knew him.

Growing up, Ian's family spent two weeks every summer on a dude ranch in Wyoming. This guy's family owned it.

"I…uh." She needed to get past him, but his big, muscular body blocked her way. "Can you…?"

"Looks like I missed something." He glanced down at her suitcase. "Or did we skip to the honeymoon?"

Her fiancé had always been obsessed with Jaime. Where Ian was a clean-cut New Englander in boat shoes, Jaime was a bad boy with messy dark blond hair, scruff, and cowboy boots. He was a hockey player—a goalie, if she remembered correctly—with battered hands and big skates. He was wild and uninhibited, a total free spirit who did the kinds of things Ian didn't have the balls to do. Crazy things like rappelling off granite mountains and heli-skiing on glaciers.

Something happened to Jaime ten years ago, though. A BASE jumping incident where his friend got hurt and could no longer play hockey. After that, Jaime stopped his extreme adventures. A daughter came into the picture. His former coach passed away and left him a whole-ass hockey team. Play-time ended.

He still looked like a bad boy, though. Very bad.

"No. It's not that." *I can't breathe.* She set down her suitcase. "Can you unbutton me, please?"

His gaze flicked to the back of the house, where he had a clear view out the sliding glass doors to the wedding party and all their guests. When his attention came back to her, he said, "Turn around."

She got the strangest shiver at his commanding tone and found herself instantly obeying. Once she had her back to him, he gently brushed aside the strands of hair that had fallen from her bun. His touch was light as a silk scarf, and it teased her skin.

"How many do you want me to undo?"

"Just enough so I can breathe." The fabric bunched across her back as he wrested the lace-covered buttons free of their tiny hole. Heat from his broad chest made her tingle as if she'd just come in from the cold.

"There you go." His fingertips brushed the bare skin between her shoulder blades. "Looks uncomfortable."

"Yeah. It's itchy." His nearness made her uneasy, so she turned back around and reached for the suitcase. "Anyhow, thank you." She needed to get past him, but he wouldn't budge. "I'm sorry, but can you excuse me?"

"Where you headed?"

"I don't know."

"I was sent to look for you." He studied her. "Ian said you might run."

"Did he tell you why?" She realized how belligerent she sounded, and that wasn't fair. Her fiancé's bad behavior wasn't this man's fault. "I'm sorry. I'm not myself right now. But yes, I'm leaving. Though I don't know what he expected you to do about it. Drag me by my hair?"

Those sensuous lips split into a naughty grin, his teeth extra white against all that facial hair. "Do you *want* me to drag you by your hair?"

"Okay, heartbreaker." It was starting to come back to her now, how Jaime affected her. A memory popped up out of nowhere. The one time he'd come back east to go sailing with Ian, she'd been waiting at the harbor. Her breath caught just looking at him standing shirtless at the bow. Her boyfriend was lean, but Jaime—God, the man was big, muscular, and imposing. When Ian introduced them, they'd hugged, and she remembered the way his bare skin smelled after swimming in the ocean and drying off under a hot sun. "Listen, there's nothing you or anyone can do to make me go through with this wedding, so can you just let me go, please?"

Still, he didn't budge. "What do you want me to tell him?"

She wasn't about to air their dirty laundry. "Nothing. He knows."

The smile faded into a look of concern. "You're seriously not going to marry him?"

She visualized walking down the aisle, toward the man she thought she'd known inside and out. But her brain kept flipping to scenarios of Ian's gaze darting around to see if anyone was near, silently opening her parents' laptop, and transferring money out of the account.

She could see her mom in the kitchen making dinner for whoever happened to be visiting that day. Her dad was likely checking someone's tires or grabbing his screwdriver to fix a bicycle. "My parents are the best people I know."

He watched her carefully before giving a slow nod. "Yes. They're good people."

"How could anyone hurt them?"

"I don't know. *Has* someone hurt them?"

One hundred and fifty thousand dollars. Fifteen thousand of her parents' hard-earned money. Seven grand for this wedding. The amount was unfathomable. "I have to go. I have to think." She had to make sense of this. She moved around him, hurrying down the porch stairs and along the slate walkway.

Now what? Where do I go? She couldn't fit the strap of her purse on her shoulder because of the puffy sleeves. *Dammit.* Sun burning the top of her head, her body prickled with perspiration. Her skin itched, and she wanted to scream, but that would just draw attention.

A wall of heat came up beside her, and Jaime pulled the luggage handle out of her hand. "Where we going?"

She looked up and down the street. Nobody was home, of course. Her neighbors were sitting in her backyard, waiting to see the little girl who used to have a lemonade and cookie stand exchange vows with the boy who used to deliver their newspapers. Her friends were here, and they'd all grown up with Ian, too. None of them could give her a ride.

"Did you know he gambled?" She tried again to hoist the purse strap onto her shoulder, but it flopped right back down to the crux of her elbow.

"Yes." He said it carefully, his tone cautious.

"Did you know because you gamble, too, or because he borrowed money from you?"

"I don't fuck around with money. It's too hard to come by. But yeah, he's borrowed some."

She startled at the way he said fuck—almost giving it a growl—and it sounded so *sexual* she momentarily got distracted. But she snapped out of it. "And he hasn't paid you back?"

"Not yet."

"But you think he will? You believe him?"

"Has he borrowed from you?" He relieved her of the purse.

The relief was palpable. "Do you know anyone at his work?"

"No. I live in Wyoming."

Good. Then, she could tell him. If she didn't talk about it, she'd explode. "He *stole* from me." She didn't know what reaction she'd expected, but it wasn't complete stoicism. If it weren't for the muscle in his jaw, she'd think he didn't care. "*And* my parents." Tears sprang so quickly, her eyes burned. "He cleaned out our accounts. One hundred and seventy-two thousand dollars." Saying it out loud hardened confusion and panic into anger.

"Are you sure?"

"He admitted it. Even worse, he said he's done it before, but he's always been able to put the money back before I noticed."

He had no reaction other than the arch of one eyebrow.

Of course, he'd side with Ian. He wasn't her friend. "If you think for one minute that I can forgive him, that I can walk down the aisle and pledge my future to him—"

"I don't."

"Well, good. Because I can't even look at him, let alone marry him." But she couldn't involve this man. It wasn't fair. His loyalty was to Ian. "I'm just...I'm going to get a cab. I need some time. Thank you for..." Her whole body shook. "For letting me vent."

Carrying her luggage with her purse on his shoulder, he took off toward the street. When she just stood there, he dangled a rental car key off his finger. "Last chance to tell me where we're going."

"As far as you can take me."

Chapter Two

Jaime couldn't concentrate.

Every time the runaway bride wiggled her ass on the leather seat, tried to cross her legs in that ridiculous dress, or dug a finger under the sleeves to scratch herself, she made a loud rustling sound.

Worse, each movement kicked a soft, floral scent into the air that just really fucking appealed to him.

But he had work to do. This little detour back home caused a serious twist in his plans. With his daughter in mind, he intentionally arranged his schedule to pack in as many meetings as possible. The less he traveled, the better for his family. So, while he'd come for the wedding of an old friend, he also had appointments he now had to reschedule.

Exhibition games started in two months, and the Renegades weren't at the level they needed to be now that Cole Montgomery, the best forward in the league, had joined them. They had a decent goalie, but he'd screwed up his ankle on vacation with his family a week after the season ended. Even though he was getting the care he needed,

Jaime knew it could take up to six months for it to fully heal.

But it didn't matter. Now that they had Cole, they needed a goalie who matched his ability. Ross LaRoux was their only hope of becoming competitive. So, Jaime would go home for the day and then fly back out. He wouldn't miss the meeting with Ross's agent.

He shot off a text to his GM.

Jaime: You crunch those numbers?

GM: Working on it. You know we won't have enough for him.

Yeah, he did know. They'd carefully curated this team, offering nice contracts. That was when the idea of Cole joining was out of the question. Then, the asshole fell in love with his now-fiancée and two little girls and wound up asking for a trade.

But damn, it was hard to focus when Grace looked so lost and freaked out. And what was with that hideous dress? It looked like one of those family heirlooms. Which was nice, he supposed. Like him, she valued family. Traditions. She was loyal.

Family first, always.

In the past, he'd only caught glimpses of her. A picture on Ian's phone, a smiling woman on social media, the pretty girl waiting at the harbor when their boat docked. He'd never paid attention because she'd been Ian's girlfriend.

Fuckin' Ian. What had he done? He'd always been a good guy. He'd never come off as entitled or snobby. To Jaime's knowledge, he didn't lie, cheat, or steal. When had he gotten in so deep with gambling?

The runaway bride's thumbs tapped across her phone's keypad. She'd been at it from the moment they'd boarded. Was she apologizing to each of her three hundred guests for bailing on the wedding? She seemed like the kind of thoughtful person who would do that.

Right then, she glanced up.

And caught him staring. His cheeks went hot.

"I'm being rude." She lowered the phone. "I'm so sorry."

"Nah." He waved his cell. "I'm working, too."

"Well, it's not work." Her teeth sank into her plump bottom lip. "My phone's blowing up. Everyone wants to know what's going on, but what can I say? If I tell the truth, Ian loses his job. And then, how's he ever going to pay my parents back? But the thing is, what harm are we doing by *not* telling everyone? What if he tries to steal money from other people?" She sucked in a breath. "What if he already has? Oh, God." When she closed her eyes, her lips parted, and she looked so damn upset. "I don't know what to do."

The situation sucked, and it wasn't her fault. "Hey." He shifted across the aisle to sit next to her. "You ran for a reason. You don't have to talk to anyone right now. You can turn off your phone and just take some time for yourself."

"But they deserve an explanation."

"Sure, but that's Ian's job. He did this, not you. And you deserve some time to come to terms with all this." *Christ, those sad eyes.* He'd thought they were brown, but they had flecks of green, amber...whiskey... And seeing them through a sheen of tears about killed him. He barely knew her, but he wanted to slay anyone who hurt this beautiful, sweet woman.

"I should've stayed. I took the coward's way out, and I left my mom with a mess. That's not fair to her."

"Again, if anyone should deal with the mess, it's the man who created it."

She gave him a soft smile. "Okay, but I could've at least helped my mom clean up."

He didn't know anyone who would think about other people an hour after finding out their fiancé had cleaned out their bank account. "Look, I'm not going to tell you what to feel, but your mom has three hundred helpers. The least of your concerns is folding the chairs and freezing the casseroles. They'll manage without you just fine. And if you lay out your options, isn't it best to take some time to get your head on straight? Your future's just been turned upside down."

"Oh." Briefly, she squeezed her eyes shut. "Wow. I hadn't even gotten there yet." She leaned against the headrest. "I never considered a life without Ian in it. He's just always been there." She sighed. "I really do need to think."

He took in her lush raspberry lips, delicate features, and the silky hair that refused to cooperate with the harsh bun. How the fuck could Ian have screwed this woman over? Later, when they landed and she wasn't around, he'd talk to him. He'd find a way to recoup her losses.

"I may be saying the obvious here, but you know you're not stuck with me, right?" she asked. "I really appreciate you letting me hitch a ride, but I don't want you to think you're in any way responsible for me."

Well, he kind of was. Where was she going to go when they landed on the airstrip? "Do you have plans? Know anybody in Wyoming?"

"No. But I'm sure there are hotels." She looked past him, out the window. "Motels."

"Tell you what. I've got some rental cabins on my property. I bought them in an attempt to turn our finances around, but it didn't work. It wasn't profitable, and the guests were nothing but a liability on a working ranch. So, I've got eleven of them, sitting empty. You're welcome to stay in one."

"Really? You don't mind?"

"That's what they're for." He'd gone all out with luxury details, and now, they only got used when they had guests in town or the annual family reunion.

Well, and for him, of course. He hadn't thought of that when he'd made the offer. But he'd put her in the one farthest from him and Kinny.

"Well, thank you. Then, I'd love to take you up on that. But don't think you need to entertain me."

"I don't."

Adorably, she went on. "A bed, a bathroom, a kitchen… I'm all set. Besides, it's just for a few nights."

"Sure. No skin off my nose. I'm just a ride and a place to crash. Once we get there, you're on your own. I've got a meeting in New York the day after tomorrow anyway."

Her brow furrowed. "What do you mean? You're going back to the East Coast?" She set her hand on his forearm. "Wait. You weren't planning on going home after the wedding?"

"No, but it doesn't matter. I'll take any excuse to go home and see my girl." He was sure all parents felt the same way, but he never fully relaxed unless he was with her.

Grace tried to tug up her sleeves, but they were too tight. "Ugh. This dress."

"You want to change?"

"More than I want to breathe."

"Here." He got up. "Let me grab your suitcase."

"I can get it. What I really need help with are the buttons." She stood, showing him her back.

"Sure thing." The tiny lace-covered dots went all the way down to the rise of her perfect peach-shaped ass. The fabric hugged it, accentuating each ripe cheek, and an unwelcome tug of lust hit his groin. *What the fuck's wrong with you?* Picking up where he'd left off at her house, he reminded himself she'd been a couple of minutes short of becoming Ian's wife.

His body's response was not just inappropriate but completely out of left field. He'd never been attracted to wholesome women. His reaction didn't make sense.

When he got halfway down her back, the fabric fell off her shoulders, and she sighed. "Thank you so much. This dress must weigh a hundred pounds. I don't know how my great grandmother managed to walk down the aisle in it. She was a little slip of a thing."

Without thinking, he brushed his fingertips across her back, and goosebumps bloomed on her skin. "Shit. Sorry. It's just…you've got red marks all over."

"It's the lace. It's been driving me nuts." Holding the top of her dress to her chest, she headed to the closet and pulled out her suitcase. "You mind if I change right here?" She slipped behind a partition.

"Not at all." Pissed off with himself, he sat down and went back to work. His GM had come back with some numbers for his pitch to the agent. Ross LaRoux was the highest-paid goalie in the league, and the Renegades couldn't afford him. They had to come up with a different angle— and it had to be more than Cole Montgomery.

Fabric swished, and he could imagine it lowering, exposing her sexy, lacy lingerie. He knew exactly what it looked like because he'd gotten a peek of that deep purple satin. Also, it sucked, but he knew exactly what her curves looked like.

Several years ago, he'd gone sailing with Ian and his buddies. When they'd stopped at Duff Island, Grace had met them at the dock wearing a bikini top and white shorts. He remembered slim, toned legs and voluptuous breasts.

Shit. Fuck.

Her tits had jiggled when she'd waved at them.

And that smile.

Fucking dazzling.

He heard a whoosh of heavy fabric hitting the floor. And then, as if he wasn't stirred up enough, she moaned. "Oh, thank God. I love this dress. Well, I mean, you know, for the sentimental value."

Stop thinking about her tits. "I figured it was passed down. What would you have chosen for yourself?"

"I wouldn't have. I wanted to elope. My parents can't afford a wedding."

He realized it was more than her scent and body that got him all worked up. She had an incredibly sexy voice. Sensuous, but with an edge. The kind he'd hear when he took her up against the wall.

Seriously, what the fuck, Dupree?

You're not taking Ian's fiancée up against a wall.

Annoyed with his body's reaction to this woman, he pulled out his phone and sent a text to his mom.

Jaime: Kinsley okay?

Mom: Ask me one more time. One. More. Time.

Jaime chuckled. **Like you wouldn't have checked in when we were little.**

Mom: I would've enjoyed my very rare time away. And

since I've raised six rascals, I think I can handle your sweet little girl.

Kinsley was sweet. No doubt about that. But she had a hard time curbing her impulses. When she got a wild hair up her ass, nothing stopped her from taking off.

Mom: I don't know why you worry when we've got a whole crew on her. Enjoy the time off. And you're supposed to send me pictures. You know I only get to host one tiny, sad wedding in my lifetime.

He hadn't told her about the runaway bride. He should since Grace was staying on the ranch a few nights.

But first, he'd play a little.

Jaime: Because Abby's a tiny, sad person? Or is it her future husband who's tiny and sad?

Mom: Oh, stop. Your sister's magnificent. It's sad for me because I pushed out five bruisers, and only one girl. And tiny because I only get to throw one big party in my lifetime.

Jaime: Your annual gala isn't enough? You want to throw some wild parties, Mama?

Mom: Well, yes, actually. I would! Can I throw you an extravagant wedding?

Jaime: If I ever get married, then yes, it's all yours.

An easy promise to make since he didn't think marriage

was in the cards for him. He'd never met a woman who'd knocked him sideways.

Mom: Let the matchmaking begin!

Jaime: Oh, hell, no. Don't even think about it.

Mom: I know, I know. All right. Have fun. I'm sad you'll be missing the event this year but glad you're standing up for Ian on his special day.

Oh, she was going to love this.

Jaime: Not gonna miss it. On my way home right now.

Mom: Are you serious? You're coming home just for my charity ball?

He could tell her yes, but he never lied to his mama.

Jaime: That's not the reason, but the timing works, so I'll be there.

Mom: Yay! I'm going to grab your tux right now and get it pressed. TTYL.

Right then, a text came in. *Ian.*

Ian: Hey, man. I asked you to go look for Grace. Not run off with her.

But Jaime was in no mood to fuck around.

Jaime: Is it true you drained her and her parents' bank accounts?

Three dots floated and disappeared. It happened a few more times.

Whatever hope Jaime held on to that Grace might've misunderstood what happened flamed out with his friend's inability to respond.

Jaime: That's some fucked up shit.

Ian: You think I don't know that? It was a bad situation, and I had to take care of it before I left town. I never thought they'd notice. I don't know why they were checking their bank accounts ten minutes before the ceremony.

Jaime: That's what you're worried about?

Grace was right. He didn't get it at all.

Ian: No, of course not. This shit's killing me. But you know how it goes in gambling. You win big, and you lose big, but you always manage to stay ahead. Usually, I can pay it back, no problem, but on this one, I got in over my head. And if I didn't pay them back, they'd have gone to my boss. But don't worry. I'm going to pay everyone back.

Jaime: You stole from more than the Giordanos?

Ian: Yeah, I borrowed from my parents, too.

That was all it took to lose all respect for his old friend.

Jaime: Say it with me so I know you understand what you've done. I STOLE from my own parents. I STOLE from my fiancée's parents. And I STOLE from the woman I planned on spending my life with.

Ian: What do you mean *planned on*? It's not over. It's never over with me and Grace. I'll pay everyone back, and she'll be fine. She's the most forgiving person you've ever known.

Jaime: That's funny. You've known her most of your life, and I've known her an hour, and I can already see you don't get her at all. She's all about family and loyalty. And with this betrayal, you've just cut yourself out of her tribe.

For good. He had no doubt.

Ian: Come on, man. You've been in my shoes. You almost lost the ranch.

Jaime: I have never been in your shoes. When my parents told me they had to sell, I gave up hockey. And then, I bought a bunch of cabins to bring in rental income. When that failed, I did a ton of research. And then, I figured out that we could sell bull sperm. So, see, I didn't have to steal from anyone. I had to sacrifice and wait until one of my ideas panned out.

The closet door clicked shut, and Grace returned wearing a bright yellow and white sundress. She'd relieved her dark hair of the bun, and now it tumbled down to the swells of her breasts. "I feel a thousand times better."

She was so pretty, so fresh, he couldn't even speak. He just stared at her.

Her smile wilted. "Everything okay?"

"Yeah." He sounded gruff. Annoyed, even. He tried to brighten his tone. "Great." But then, he just sounded fake. *Fuck my life.*

"What can I get y'all to drink?" Marty, the flight attendant, stood between them in the aisle.

"Oh, just water for me." Grace gave him a beaming smile. "Thank you."

"Honey, you just ran from your own wedding. Now, I don't want to stick my nose where it doesn't belong, but you must've had a good reason. Getting out of a bad situation's a good reason to celebrate. How about we toast with a nice, cold glass of champagne?"

"That sounds like a good idea." She beamed a smile that would melt the heart of the coldest man. "Unfortunately, I don't think I'm ready for that just yet."

Marty gave her hand a squeeze. "Oh, honey. You're shaking. What can I do? How about a mug of chamomile tea? Maybe a slice of cake?"

Neither the booze nor the tea registered on her happiness meter, but the last suggestion made the needle go wild. "What kind of cake?"

Marty smiled. "You know how everything happens for a reason? Well, I just took the team back from a baby shower in Montreal for one of the wives. They brought a bunch of leftovers but forgot all about them, so I'm stuck with a whole platter full of yummies. Let me show you what I've got." He gave Jaime a bored expression. "Don't worry. I'll get your water and salad." Marty jerked a thumb in his direction. "This one's no fun at all."

Jaime feigned offense. "I'm fun."

"No booze, no dessert, no snacks." Marty headed off to the kitchen area. "It's like you're punishing yourself or something."

"You don't like dessert?" Grace asked.

"I just don't care about it," Jaime said. "There's nothing new under the sun, you know?"

"No. I don't think I do." Clamping her hands on the armrest, she lifted up and crossed her legs under her before sitting back down. "Explain."

"How many doughnuts can you eat before they all start to taste the same?"

She stared at him with an incredulous expression. "Are you serious with me right now?"

"What? Ice cream, pie, cake… I've had it all."

She nodded. "Yes, I can see how that would happen once you hit your nineties. And you're how old again?"

He found himself fascinated with the snark that came out of that soft, sexy mouth. "Twenty-eight. Same as you."

"Well, I'm no world traveler, but there are as many ways to make tiramisu as there are chefs. And personally, I can't wait to try every single one. That's the whole reason I'm going to Paris—" That brief moment of vibrancy while talking about dessert died at the memory of her lost honeymoon.

"You can still go." Man, he hated to see her so sad.

"To Paris? No, we didn't pay for the hotel in advance. We just have reservations. I'm not going to spend what money I have left on a trip like that." She grabbed her phone. "I'd better cancel it right now."

"If it helps, losing the people who matter most to you…

it's the kind of thing that changes a man." After Booker's accident, he hadn't talked to his friends in ten years. It was their former coach's funeral that forced them together again.

But from that moment on, he'd worked hard every day to be a better man. To make better—safer—choices.

"If you're suggesting I'll get back with him, you can forget it. I've not only lost respect, but I can't trust him. It makes me sick to my stomach to think of him sneaking around, hacking into our accounts, and stealing our money. No, there's no hope for our relationship."

"I'd be the same way. I get it."

"Now that I'm calming down a little, I can see how things escalated over time. He lost two thousand dollars on last year's Super Bowl game. At the time, I remember thinking, God, I wouldn't even put a quarter in a slot machine, you know? I'm just not cut out for it." She turned thoughtful. "That was a sign, wasn't it? Losing a hundred bucks in a poker game isn't in the same ballpark as two grand."

"No, it's not."

"How did I not notice? But I guess that's the whole problem. We're so used to living separate lives, we stopped paying attention to the details."

It'd be so easy for him to fix the problem. "Listen, I'm going to loan Ian the money—"

"Absolutely not. No. If you fix the problem, he's just going to keep on gambling. He has to do this on his own."

"Where's he going to come up with money like that?"

"He'll get a bonus this year."

Did she not know how much Ian made? His bonus wouldn't cover even a quarter of it. "I'm not sure it'll be enough."

"But eventually, right? After he has enough experience,

he'll go work with his mom. He's supposed to take over her portfolio one day. That's the plan."

"You really think she's going to give him access to her clients after this?"

Fear widened her eyes, and her jaw went slack. "Oh, my God." She clasped her hands together and squeezed. "I'll never get my money back." Popping out of her seat, she paced the length of the jet.

He wanted to help her. He wanted to reassure her, but she didn't want his money—and what else could he offer?

Giving her time alone, he tried to get back to work, but he couldn't concentrate.

Could he get her the money without her knowing? Give it to Ian and let him find a way to give it back? If she asked, Ian could say—

Perfect. Just what she needs. Another liar, deceiver, and manipulator. *Yeah, no.* He wouldn't do that. He'd respect her wishes.

She worked for the family bakery on Duff Island, so he couldn't imagine any scenario in which she could earn that money back. Could he offer her a job?

Fabric swished, as she made her way back, and she dropped down into her seat. "He'll never be able to repay me, so he'll just have to focus on what he owes my parents."

"What about your savings?"

Her features collapsed into pure sorrow, and a single tear slid down her cheek. "It's gone. There's nothing I can do."

Fuck. He crossed the aisle and sat beside her. "I'm sorry." *I can fix this. I can put it all back.* But that wasn't what she wanted to hear, so he kept his mouth shut.

She tipped her head onto his shoulder. He probably should keep his filthy hands off her, but she seemed to need the contact, so he slid an arm behind her, bringing her in

ERIKA KELLY

closer. He was too aware of her silky hair on his hand, the feminine scent of her that woke him up in a startling way, and the warmth of her body. "I'd like to help. If there's anything I can do…"

"No, no. I appreciate it, but really." She exhaled in a huff and sat up. "I saved it once before. I can save it again."

"At least let me pay your parents back."

"No. Thank you. Honestly, he has to do that. And if it means he has to take on extra jobs, then so be it. Let him bartend at night or work at the yacht club on the weekends."

He couldn't imagine Ian ever working at the fancy club where his parents belonged. "How were you able to save that much?" As far as he knew, she'd only ever worked for Renzo's.

"Oh, gosh, I did everything." She swiped the tears away. "Let's see. It started when I was ten and sold lemon squares in front of our house. I babysat, I walked dogs…you know, odd jobs like that."

"That added up to a hundred and fifty grand?"

"No, the biggest earner was the tribute band I sang in."

"You sang in a *band*?" He tried to picture her in torn fishnets and dyed black hair, a smear of red lipstick, but it just didn't work. She was too…sweet.

She laughed. "Why is that so hard to believe?"

"I just can't picture you rocking out."

"Well, we're not talking Alice Cooper. There was no face paint involved."

"What kind of music? Like Pat Benatar kind of shit?"

She shook her head.

"Stevie Nicks?"

Smiling, she waved her hands at him to stop. "Don't even try. You won't guess it."

"So, tell me."

32

She tipped her head back and groaned. "Okay, but you can't make fun of me."

Oh, this is good. He liked seeing her playful. "I mean, I *can*."

"But you won't because I've had a traumatic day." Her spirits rallied, and she flashed him a smile so bright it awakened a part of him that had been unused for a very long time.

It was scary and a little thrilling. "You don't know my family, but that's not exactly a solid reason for me to go easy on you."

"Brutal."

He gave her a chin nod. "Hit me."

"Fine." She made a big show of reluctantly giving in. "Lorelei Calloway."

"Why would I make fun of you for that? Everyone loves her."

"She sings from the heart, about love and trust and happy ever after, and for some reason, you don't strike me as the kind of guy who'd like that kind of music."

"What's that supposed to mean?"

"Oh, come on. You've got this bad-boy vibe. With your ink and your scruff, and all that…messy hair. You're more one-percenter than you are Hallmark hero."

"I'm nobody's hero, that's for sure. But I have a daughter, and I want her to find everything Lorelei sings about."

Her features softened.

"What?" Had he said something sappy?

"That's just incredibly sweet."

Dismissing it, he hunched a shoulder. *Doesn't every parent want what's best for his kid?* "But no, I don't listen to country music, so I'm not a fan." He thought about it for a moment, remembering his sister dancing around the kitchen to one of the artist's songs. "Or maybe she's pop. Either way, not my thing."

"See, that's what I love about her. She doesn't fit into any one box. In the beginning, when she was just starting out, everyone told her to find her lane and stay in it, and she was like, 'Isn't the point of art to use our own unique voices? That's the only thing that differentiates us.' She even produces her own albums. She hires people to come in and work with her, but everything about her music is authentic, and I love that."

"So, you made a lot of money singing her songs?"

"Not *a lot* a lot." She gestured around the jet. "Not by your standards."

"Hey, man. I didn't earn any of this. I inherited the Renegades from my former coach who passed away last year. This plane is just part of the package. And there are three other guys who have a stake in it, too. Right now, they're silent partners, but one day, I hope they'll decide to do this with me."

"What could they possibly be doing that they wouldn't want to own a hockey team and live like this?"

"Well, one's coaching the team, and the other's our newest forward." Anxiety gripped his chest—he had to get Ross—but then, he forced himself to let it go. *I'm working on it.* "But I'm sure when they retire, they'll step in."

And maybe then, he'd be able to let go of the guilt. It would mean they'd all moved on and that they were in good places.

That his friends forgave him.

"Anyhow, what were you saving all that money for?" he asked. "What was the objective?"

"When I was ten, the goal was to open my own bakery. That was why I ran the lemonade stand."

"Are you talking about franchising Renzo's? Opening one in New York?"

"No." She flashed him a bittersweet smile. "I was just a kid wanting to do things differently. When we were little, my brothers and I would make sand pies. Of course, they would throw them at each other, but for me, it was about decorating them with flowers and seashells. It was art. And I got this idea in my head that I could do that, make pretty pastries for the family bakery. But my parents were like, 'Hun, nobody around here wants fancy stuff. That's not our clientele.'"

A picture was forming, and it sucked. Here was this bright, sunshiny woman, who had to dim her light to be part of the family business.

"Don't get me wrong, I love Renzo's. I love our history. But it's veered away from the original concept."

"Which was?"

"You don't know the story?"

"Just that you deliver turnovers to the people docked in the harbor."

"Oh, it's so much more than that. You want to hear it?"

"We've got two more hours till we land." He shifted back in his seat, stretching out his legs. He couldn't think of the last time he'd enjoyed a woman's company like this. "Give it to me."

"Okay, so, it all began eighty years ago when my great-great-grandfather came to America."

Jaime loved the pride shining in her eyes. He felt the same way about the history of the Dupree Ranch.

"In Naples, he was a bread baker, so when he moved to New York City, he got a job in a hotel restaurant. Well, he fell madly in love with one of the guests and followed her to Duff Island. He wound up opening a bakery to sell his bread, but once they started having kids, he needed to earn more money. He added croissants and turnovers, but it still wasn't growing the way he needed it to so, to get the word out, he started taking his products down to the harbor. And to get everyone's attention, he'd sing."

"What kind of songs?" he asked.

"Italian opera." Her features were suffused with happiness. "But his customers were out there on the water, so he figured he'd better get himself a boat and go to *them*. And it became a hit. People would dock in South Harbor just to hear the singing baker shout, 'Mangiamo!'"

"Hey, no one woke me up with opera when I visited."

"That's because no one in our family's done it since Lorenzo passed away in the nineteen-fifties. We still take the boat out and sell pastries and sandwiches, but no one sings anymore."

"You obviously do."

"Oh, I don't deliver. I'm in the kitchen baking."

"That's a shame."

"What is?"

"You should be out there singing and showing the world your smile."

"Oh, stop." But her eyes held wonder, as if she wasn't convinced of his sincerity.

Trust me. I mean it.

Marty returned with a bright pink bakery box, two glasses, and a carafe of water. "Did I hear you're a baker?"

"I am." When he set the dessert on her tray table, she peered inside. "Oh, I love macarons." She pulled out a purple one and bit into it. "Mm, so good." With a look of encouragement, she offered it to him. "It's blackberry."

He waved a hand. "No, thanks." He'd had them before.

She lifted another pastry out of the box. "Ooh, I love,

love, love a good fruit tart. The creamy custard with the acidity of the strawberries?" She closed her eyes as she took a healthy bite. Her head tipped back, and she moaned. "So good." When her eyes opened, she lifted the treat to Marty.

The flight attendant nipped the edge of it and chewed. "That's good."

"Good? Are you kidding me?"

"Yeah, not a huge fruit fan."

"That's fair." With greedy eyes, she scanned the other contents. "Let's try the chocolate."

Watching her teeth sink into the soft, gooey slice of cake got his dick humming. It made no sense. He had to look away.

But he couldn't. His gaze was riveted on that wide, supple mouth made for giving pleasure. Because those sounds she was making? She'd make the same ones when he licked inside her.

What the hell?

He forced himself to look away.

You're not fucking this woman.

Jesus. What's wrong with me?

Chapter Three

HER EYELIDS FLUTTERED CLOSED. "MM. I'M IN heaven." When they popped open, she was staring at him with pure mischief and seduction. "Try it."

"I'm good."

"When was the last time you had dessert?" she asked.

"No idea. Don't really think about it."

"Look at him getting all grumpy." Marty dug back into the box. "Maybe he'd prefer this one. What is it?"

"That's a dacquoise," Grace said. "It's almond and hazelnut."

"I'll pass," Jaime said. "Really, it's not my thing, but you guys enjoy."

Grace set the box down. In two steps, she was seated beside him with her shiny, dark hair, seductive smile, and her lemon-sunshine dress. "Do you like chocolate?" She lifted the glossy cake to his mouth.

"I can take it or leave it." Why did she affect him like this when she was clearly not his type?

He liked women with tousled hair and smoky eyes, women who'd had a few drinks and were down to party. He liked the kind of woman who ran a hand down his thigh and pressed her mouth to his ear. *Meet me in the bathroom, handsome.*

Yeah, he liked *that* kind of woman.

Not the kind whose eyes lit up over a damn cookie. Who wore pretty sundresses and insisted on repaying her parents before she recouped her life savings.

"Try one bite." She leaned closer.

She was having too much fun trying to convince him to taste the cake to notice that the arm pressed against her side pushed her breasts together, plumping them. He could practically feel the hard bead of her nipple in the palm of his hand and imagine the hitch in her breath when he pinched it.

Irritation rose like a swarm of mosquitoes, and he looked her right in the eyes. "I'm not interested." He got up. "I've got some work to do." Heading to the back of the plane, he dropped into the desk chair.

He opened a contract he needed to look over, but the only thing he saw was the way she'd recoiled from him. He'd hurt her.

As if she hadn't had enough pain for one day, he'd piled on.

And for what? Because he was attracted to her?

That's not her fault.

He just needed to stay away from her.

As soon as they landed, he'd get her settled in a cabin. Tomorrow, he'd spend time with his daughter and hit the charity ball, and then the next day, he'd head back to the East Coast.

By the time he got back from visiting Ross LaRoux's agent, she'd be gone.

There you go.

Problem solved.

Jaime was awakened by the bounce of his mattress.

Apparently, his dad brought Kinny home on his way to work. The commercial herd was calving, so he'd be out early.

The duvet lifted, and cold little fingers tickled the soles of his feet. "Are you up, Daddy?"

"No." He'd had a hell of a time getting to sleep. After they'd landed, he'd stopped at the grocery store to make sure Grace had what she needed for her short stay. He'd helped bring in the groceries and then checked to make sure the place was habitable.

By the time he'd gotten to his parent's house, Kinsley was already asleep. He'd stayed longer with Grace than he should have.

Because he liked her. And it made him realize something. He didn't know the women he fucked. He didn't know the players on his team. Outside of his family, he didn't spend time getting to know people.

"Why are your toes so hairy?" His daughter tugged on the fine strands. "Mine aren't."

"You know why." His voice sounded rough with sleep. "I'm part bear."

She grinned. "No, you're not."

"Yeah. I am." With a roar, he reared up. She tried to scramble off the bed, but he caught her by the legs and dragged her onto his lap. Enfolding her in his arms, he nibbled her neck.

As she writhed and wriggled, she let out a squeal of delight. "Don't eat me, Daddy! Don't eat me!"

"Of course, I'm going to eat you. I'm a bear."

"You're not a bear! You're my daddy."

Tossing her onto her back, he lifted her nightgown and blew raspberries on her belly. "Now, do you believe I'm a bear?"

"No." She giggled as he tickled her.

"Say it. Say I'm a bear."

"You're...not..." She had a hard time catching her breath. "A bear!"

He got out of bed and threw his arms open wide, growling as he towered over her, wiggling his fingers in a threat to continue tickling her. "Do you believe me now?"

Eyes shining, she shrieked, "Yes."

"Say it."

"You're a bear! You're a bear!"

"Okay, then. That's all I needed to hear." Lifting her, he held her close, breathing in the baby shampoo scent of her curly dark hair. "I love you, punkin."

"I love you more." She clung to his neck. "I'm glad you're home."

"Me, too. I'm leaving again tomorrow morning, but I'll be right back after my meeting." When he set her down, he noticed the massive brown stain on her white nightgown. "I see someone found the chocolate milk I hid at the back of the refrigerator." *This girl.* "Why don't you go change?"

"I have to tell you something."

"Oh, so you didn't wake me up just to ask about my hairy toes?"

"No, I woke you up because Joseph's knocking on the door."

"What? Is he still there?"

"Yes."

"Then why didn't you let him in?"

"You said not to open the door to strangers."

"*Kinsley.* Joseph isn't a stranger." He shoved his feet into his gym shoes and took off. Right away, he could hear a banging. "I'm coming." He hurried down the stairs and across the living room. When he flung the door open, he found his ranch manager staring at him with an arched brow. "Sorry about that. Is everything all right?" Dawn turned the sky a watercolor of pinks, purples, and oranges. In the distance, he could see truck lights heading up the driveway and hear the distant lowing of cows in the pasture.

Joseph's gaze shifted behind him and lowered. "So, I'm a stranger now, huh?"

Kinsley's innocent expression cracked as one corner of her mouth started to curl into a mischievous grin. "You could've been pretending to be Joseph. I can't see the porch from the window."

"And you didn't recognize my voice?" The lines around the big, burly guy's eyes creased in amusement.

"It could've been someone faking."

"Bet if I'd offered you candy, you'd have opened it."

"You got candy?" Kinsley stepped forward and held out her palm. "Please, can I have some?"

Jaime clamped a hand on his daughter's shoulder and pulled her back. "Joseph doesn't have candy." He tipped his chin to her stained nightgown. "And you've had your share of sugar already. Now, go and change like I asked."

"Will you have breakfast with me?" she asked.

"Of course. Don't I always?"

"Okay, Daddy." She dashed off.

"And put your nightgown in the laundry room and not on the kitchen floor." He turned back to the ranch manager. "So, what's up?"

"There's someone in Cabin A, and she's raising a ruckus."

"You mean Grace? What's she doing?"

"Don't know her name, but she's got her own rock

concert going on. Got the windows open and music blasting." He shook his head. "Since no one told me about any visitors, I should've gone in and busted her, but I figured I'd tell you first in case it's one of your…friends."

"Since when do I do sleepovers?" His daughter's heart was pure and wide open. No way would he let her get attached to someone who wouldn't stay in her life. "Grace isn't a hookup. She just needed a place to crash for a few nights."

"Is that right?" Joseph chuckled. "Because it sure looks like you went to your friend's wedding and brought back a bride."

He closed the door behind him so Kinsley didn't hear. "How do you know she's a bride? You said you didn't go over there."

"No, I said I didn't bust her. Of course, I went over there. Peeked through the window and saw a wedding gown on a hanger. You steal yourself a bride?"

"Nah. But she pulled a runner, wanted to get away for a few days, so I told her she could stay here."

"Got it. Well, she's waking up the hands, so either you tell her to keep it down, or I will."

"I'm on it." He didn't want Grace getting in trouble for something that wasn't her fault. She didn't know the bunkhouse was so close. In fact, she'd be mortified to find out she'd been putting on a show for the unsuspecting guys.

Joseph turned to go, his boots heavy on the porch. He stopped at the top of the stairs and glanced at him over his shoulder. "That bull's comin' in around noon. Since you're home for the day, you wanna be there?"

Jaime nodded. "Text me when the truck's at the gate."

"Will do."

After he shut the door, he hurried to catch up with his

daughter. "Kinsley? I've got to take care of something, and you need to come with me." He found her in the kitchen in nothing but her lime green underpants. "Can you get dressed, please? Quickly?"

"No, thank you." Kinsley grabbed his phone off the counter where it was charging and typed out a message with her thumbs.

This kid. Way too mature for her age.

"What're you doing?" By the time he caught up with her, though, she'd set the phone back down.

"I asked Grandma to come over."

"You can't just make demands like that." He quickly dialed his mom.

"Morning, sweet pea." His mom obviously thought it was his daughter because she used her soft, sweet voice. "I'm just getting my shoes on."

"No, Mom."

"Oh, good morning, sweetheart." For him, she used her brisk, ranch owner voice. "Give me five minutes."

"Mom, stop. You don't have to come over. Kinsley shouldn't have texted you. I just have one thing—"

"You know I don't mind." She disconnected.

"Kinsley." *Dammit.* "I want Grandma to do less, not more."

"You want her to do less *work*. You don't want her to be less of a *grandma*."

She's got you there. "You can come with me for a quick errand."

"But I'm right in the middle of something."

"At six in the morning?"

"Yes."

As an only child, he worried about her spending too much time alone, but she was industrious, always deeply involved in one project or another. *Whatever.* He had to get going. "I'm going to get dressed." Passing through the living room, he said, "I'll make French toast when I get back."

"Grandma's bringing cinnamon rolls," Kinsley called from the kitchen. "I asked."

"When did you have time?"

"Me and Grandma have our own language. She gets me." Kinsley gave him a teasing smile, and his whole body went warm with affection.

He'd never wanted children. Being the oldest of six had been enough kid chaos for a lifetime, but his daughter was unlike anyone he'd ever known. A true one-of-a-kind, she was bright, creative, loving, kind, generous, and curious beyond measure.

She'd also revealed to him a capacity to love beyond anything he could've imagined. He adored his little girl. She was his life.

If anything ever happened to her—

Fear gripped his chest and squeezed. He forced himself to shake it off.

She's fine. Everything's fine.

As he headed up the stairs, Kinsley called, "And I asked for more chocolate milk, too."

Given this was a working ranch, they'd had to situate the cabins relatively close to the main road. They couldn't have guests traipsing across pasture or grazing land or risk them getting mixed up with bulls, horses, and farm equipment.

The moment he stepped out of his cabin, he heard the music. *Shit.* He thought of the hardworking hands being jolted awake at the sound of a Lorelei Calloway song.

It was a late June morning—still chilly in the mountains

—and he hadn't grabbed a jacket. He stopped to take in the sunrise. As he stood there watching streaks of golden sunlight cut through the violet sky, he took in this land that had been in his family for a hundred and fifty years. He'd always loved it—even while resenting the time it took away from hockey and his friends.

It was the reason he didn't get a contract right out of high school like his friends had.

And then, it became the reason why he didn't get to play at all.

He had no regrets, though. As he took in the stark mountains, the snowy peaks glistening in the growing light, and the thousands of acres of rolling hills, he knew he wouldn't have made a different choice. Even if things hadn't turned out the way they had with Booker, he would still have chosen to stay home and find a way to make the ranch profitable.

Thinking about the accident, he rubbed his chest. He'd long ago accepted the nightmares and the shocks of adrenaline that hit his system when his mind threw out a random memory from that night.

Sometimes, to get his heart rate back under control, he'd remind himself that Booker was alive and one of the top sports agents in the country. And that through it all, Jaime had gotten to keep this ranch. He'd enabled his parents to ease up on their backbreaking work. And he'd finally become a good role model to his siblings.

When he reached her cabin, he gave the courtesy of a knock, but he knew she'd never hear it. Not only was she blasting music, but she was also singing along at the top of her lungs. So, after his first attempt went unanswered, he turned the knob and walked in.

The small but open space was lit up, and even with the

windows flung wide, it was warm. The place smelled like sweet, yeasty bread. Every available surface had trays of… *What is that?* He moved closer to get a better look and found bright yellow lemon bars, red and blue fruit tarts, a variety of pastel-colored macarons, and several glossy chocolate cakes.

Funny, but when they'd stopped at the grocery store on the way home, he hadn't paid attention to her purchases. He'd been too busy talking to her.

Well, and reining in his base instincts. But he'd assumed she'd gotten a few basics like milk, eggs, and butter. Things to tide her over until she went back home. Not yeast, sugar, and *cookie sheets*.

The music ended abruptly, leaving a silence that pulsed and vibrated.

"Grace—"

But she didn't hear him because, apparently, the song hadn't ended. It had only paused before the melody changed to something slow, sexy, and sultry. And somehow, Lorelei Calloway and Grace Giordano's voices merged.

Her eyes closed, her hips swayed, and she picked up the spatula and used it as a microphone, singing a cappella. Her voice was clear as a bell. It was stunning.

And then, the beat kicked in, and she was back to jumping and bouncing and tossing all that dark hair from side to side.

Jesus, this woman. She was so…vibrant and spirited. So happy.

How could anyone cause her harm?

From out of nowhere, a longing hit. He couldn't describe it, couldn't begin to explain it. It just tore through him like a brutal wind, knocking down everything in its path, leaving him raw and exposed.

Forcing him to face an ugly truth. He'd been working so hard to be a better man, to make up for the pain he'd caused, but he hadn't changed one bit. He was still the same irresponsible, selfish asshole he'd always been.

And he knew that because he wanted to fuck his friend's fiancée so badly, he could feel the shape of her ass in his hands and the taste of her mouth on his tongue. He wanted to grab that long hair and yank back her head, pull down those floral pajama shorts, and kick her legs apart with his knee. He wanted to slide his cock into her slick heat.

A fierce desire grabbed hold of him, so beyond anything he'd ever experienced that it scared him.

But he'd managed to control himself for ten years, he could do it now. The selfish impulses might still be there, but he hadn't acted on them.

And he wouldn't now.

He found the speaker and snatched the plug from the socket.

Grace's body jerked, as she spun around and threw the spatula at him. "*Oh.*" Her hand slapped against her chest, and she burst out laughing. "Jaime. You scared me to death."

"Sorry. I knocked, but you didn't hear."

"No, don't be sorry. It's your house. But, boy, I sure kicked your ass with that spatula." She came right up to him, fighting back a smile. "You okay? Did you need stitches?"

Of course, the rubber spatula had landed nowhere near him, so he just grinned. "I'll live."

Taking a step back, she glanced at the clock. "What're you doing up so early?"

"Cold fingers on my toes." Her expression was comical, and he realized how it sounded. "No, not—"

"Hey." She held up both hands. "You're a single man. It's none of my business who touches your toes."

He chuckled. "It was my daughter. She woke me up because the ranch manager was at the door."

It didn't take more than a second for her to figure it out. "Because of me?"

"Yeah. Right behind that row of trees"—he pointed out the window—"is the bunkhouse."

She looked, but of course, she couldn't see anything but woodland. "Oh, my God. I woke everyone up. I am *so* sorry." Color rushed into her cheeks. "Do you want me to go? I can find a motel in town." She looked so worried he could hardly stand it.

"No. You don't have to go anywhere. The guys are fine."

"It won't happen again, I promise."

"I know. Don't worry about it. You can play music. Just not as loud."

"Oh, my God. I feel terrible. I had no idea anyone was around."

"Well, that's on me. I didn't explain anything." He gestured to the trays. "So, what's all this for?"

"Oh. I couldn't sleep last night. I just kept thinking, going over every minute of my relationship. When I spiral like that, the only cure is to bake. It's my happy place. I guess I got carried away."

"You don't make this for Renzo's, right?" She'd said her parents didn't think their customers wanted fancy stuff—and it didn't get fancier than this.

"Oh, no. I do strictly croissants, turnovers, and muffins. My aunt and cousins make the sandwiches and picnic baskets."

"These look professional. Are you trained?"

"I am, actually. Much to everyone's disappointment, I

dropped out of college. It started for a terrible reason but wound up being the best thing that could've happened."

"What was the reason?"

"Ian and I went to different colleges. When he joined a frat, he dumped me. That was our first breakup, and I was sure he'd go wild and sleep with every girl on campus." Her voice trailed off, and she grew contemplative.

"Did he?" He couldn't help reaching out and brushing her cheek. Not just because of the flour but because she was so obviously struggling, and he had no way to comfort her.

She lowered her chin, turning away slightly. "No. He didn't. In fact, we were back together by Christmas. But we broke up a million more times after that over the years. I was just realizing, though, that I stopped caring what he did on our breaks. That really says something, you know?"

As much as he wanted to comfort her, he supposed the point of this getaway was to come to terms with the end of her long-term relationship. "Well, hopefully, you had fun on your breaks, too."

"You bet I did. At first, I was miserable, waiting for *him* to decide whether we'd be together, but then I went to culinary school. I chose the Culinary Institute because it was three hours from Boston and four from home, but once I got into it, I totally stopped waiting. It was like I found myself." She shot him an apologetic look. "Listen to me babbling. You came over here to tell me to turn the music down, and then I go on and on about my relationship."

"Don't worry about it. Isn't that why you're here? To get a fresh perspective on things?" He gestured to a tray. "Have your parents seen what you can do? I can't imagine anyone not liking this stuff."

"Well, thank you. That makes me happy to hear, but no. I gave up trying to convince them years ago. Our customers don't eat Paris-Brest or opera cake. That's a whole other clientele."

He supposed he could see that. Sailors wanted breakfast food. Something quick and not too messy. "So, what're you going to do with all this?"

"I guess I could give it to the hands as an apology."

"You could. But since you need cash, why not try to sell it? There's a farmer's market at the fairgrounds every Saturday." Which was the day after tomorrow.

"I'd love to, but I don't think it works like that. You have to apply for a booth months in advance."

"I can ask my mom about it."

"No, that's okay. I wouldn't even have a way to get there." She raised a hand. "And before you get all sweet and offer to loan me a car, no one's going to give me a one-day pass to sell my baked goods. Now, if you want to point me in the direction of the driveway, I've been known to make serious bank with my lemonade stands."

"Nice idea, but we're off the beaten track out here. The only people who come by are delivery drivers, family, or workers." He checked his impulse to get more involved by heading for the door. "Well, I'll let you get back to it." But once he got there, he realized she'd gone quiet. He couldn't resist turning back around.

She stood at the counter, staring at her phone. Her forehead creased.

He should go. It was none of his business. What could he do to help anyway? She had to get through the breakup on her own. And yet, he couldn't just leave her like this. "Everything okay?"

"No. I mean, yes. Sure." She looked more frustrated than sad or lost.

He gestured to the phone. "Ian?"

"He keeps texting, calling…posting memories on social media. Like, what does he think? That I'll forgive him for stealing from my family? That I'm just going to let it slide?"

"I'm sure that's what he's hoping for. Have you told him where you stand?"

"You bet I have. I told him he's shown me his character. And thank God I found out before I married him." She sounded resolute. The phone vibrated again, and after a quick scan, she flipped it upside down. "There's nothing left to say. The weird thing is I'm not sad that it's over."

"Probably because you're so angry."

"Sure, I'm angry, but honestly? More than anything else, I'm relieved. Isn't that crazy? After fifteen years with a guy, the only emotion I have left is relief that it's over." She picked up her phone and motioned him over. "Come here. Let me show you something."

As he approached, he traced the line of her thin gold necklace down to the pendant that flirted with her cleavage.

"I was going through photos last night." She turned the screen toward him, her silky hair brushing across his arm. "Look. This is from his brother's wedding. Ian and I aren't even touching. And this one? He'd just come back from a trip with his family, and he's hugging me like a sister." Their gazes locked, and standing this close, the connection lit up every cell in his body. "I can't remember the last time he grabbed my ass. Or…or took me up against the wall. I'm a *woman*. I need that. I want it."

Ah, hell. She'd just loaded filthy images into his mind. Because, of course, it wasn't Ian grabbing her ass and slamming her against the wall. *It's me. My* tongue licking a path down her neck, sucking her tits through the thin cotton of her shirt, and then pulling back to watch the nipples bead.

Fuck my life.

Maybe if I'd gotten laid any time in the last month, I wouldn't get hard watching this woman dance.

Tomorrow, when he was in New York, he'd go out with his colleagues. Hit the clubs. Have some fun.

"Sorry." A torrid pink rose up her chest and the smooth column of her neck, fanning out across her cheeks. "I shouldn't be talking like that to you. I don't know what I'm thinking. I guess since I know I'm not your type, I figured I could be real with you."

How did she know that? As far as he knew, she'd never seen him with a woman. *It's not like I date or take selfies.* "You can. It's fine."

"But you're Ian's friend, so I really should find someone else to confide in."

"I *was* his friend. Right up until he admitted what he did."

"He did?" She lowered the phone. "Does he feel any shame?"

"Not really. He just kept insisting he'd pay everyone back."

"Which isn't even the point."

"No, it's not. So, don't worry. I'm on your side, and I have no plans to talk to him again."

She moved away from him, picked up the spatula, and set it in the sink. "Well, you've done more than enough for me. You don't need to be my therapist, too."

"You have any idea what you want to do while you're in town?"

She gave him a sheepish look. "More baking?"

"Have at it. If you need more supplies while I'm away, just ask Joseph. He's the ranch manager, and he'll take care of you. He'll loan you a car, tell you where to go. Whatever you need."

"That's awesome. Thank you."

"You're welcome. I've got to get home before my daughter convinces my mom to bake her cookies after stuffing her face with cinnamon rolls and chocolate milk."

"Ah, a girl after my own heart." With a grin, she tipped her head. "I've got a wicked sweet tooth."

This woman had some weird power over him, because instead of walking out the door, he said, "I don't know if you like getting dressed up, but I've got a charity event tonight." No way could he leave her alone in this little house with no one to talk to and nowhere to go.

"I love getting dressed up. Are you asking me to go with you?"

"Yeah." He shrugged like it was no big deal. Like he didn't have this crazy energy zinging through him and didn't care whether she joined him or not.

"Because I don't want to be a third wheel if you've got a date."

"No date. I didn't think I'd be in town for it, but since I am, and it's important to my mom, I'll go."

"What's the charity?"

"It's called Mercy. My mom started it after we turned our ranch around. It's a fund for ranchers and farmers who're hard hit by the economy, environmental issues, or injury."

"That's awesome. I would love to go, but of course, I didn't bring anything to wear. Other than the wedding gown, I only have a few outfits for sightseeing in Paris."

"Don't worry about that. My mom'll take care of everything."

Happiness sparked in her eyes. "Really?" But it quickly dampened. "No, I don't want to impose on anyone. It's her big night. The last thing she needs is to waste time on some sad runaway bride."

"My mom has five sons and one daughter. Ask her, and she'll tell you she got screwed. Believe me, she'd like nothing more than to play fairy godmother. You in?"

"Well, then, yes. I'm totally in. Thank you so much."

"No problem. Okay, I'll let the singing baker get back to her therapy."

She gave him a funny look.

"What?"

"Nothing. It's just I've known you a total of twelve hours, and you know me better than Ian and my family. I mean, you nailed it in one sentence."

"What do you mean? You don't sing and bake around your family?"

"I mean, sometimes. But I think I've just become wallpaper."

He cocked his head.

"You know how you're so familiar with the wallpaper you've grown up with your whole life that you don't even see it? And one day, you're staring at it, lost in thought, and suddenly, you realize there's a cow in it. And you're like, Mom, why do you have cow wallpaper?"

He chuckled. "Uh, no. I can't say I've had that experience."

"I guess with such a big family, we've stopped seeing the details that make us different from each other."

He only knew he'd reached for her when his hand fully circled her delicate wrist. "Trust me, Grace. You'd stand out in any crowd." She had a light inside of her that glowed.

Her gaze focused on the point of contact. The scent of her—vanilla and sugar cookies—swirled around him, and he stood so close the heat of her body sank under his skin.

When she looked up at him, lightning struck his core, and electricity raced through his body. "I should go."

"Yeah." She sounded a little breathy.

He hurried to the door. "Expect a visitor within five minutes of me telling my mom about the gala."

"Can't wait." She followed him out. "You're like me and my family. I live a few blocks away. If I have kids one day, my mom or dad can just walk over and babysit for me. It's nice, isn't it?"

"I wouldn't have it any other way."

"Thank you, Jaime. You've been really good to me."

"You're welcome." But he didn't look back. If he did, she'd see. She'd know.

So, he focused on the lawn, sparkling with morning dew, and breathed in air scented with freshly mown grass and a hint of manure.

He'd let her think the best of him, the man that worked hard to be responsible and good.

The less she knew about his filthy thoughts, the better.

Chapter Four

As she sat on the bar stool getting her make up done, Grace marveled at how different this world was from her own. From the working ranch to the cozy cabin to the startling mountain ranges that encircled the valley, Calamity felt like an alternate universe.

And she loved it.

Jaime was right. His mom had jumped at the chance to glam her up. She'd even gotten her daughter to join in. They'd just needed a few minutes to get organized and asked her to meet them at the Dream House in an hour.

Last night, Grace had driven past it, of course, but it had been dark. She could only see its size and interesting features —like arched windows and balconies.

She'd been pretty excited to get a look inside, but when she arrived, she'd been shocked to find it only sparsely decorated. "Does anyone live here?" she asked.

"Nope." Abby—the middle Dupree child—brushed powder on each cheek. "Jaime built it for my parents, but they never moved in. He was involved in literally every step of the design process because he wanted it to be perfect for them."

"It's stunning." With its high ceilings and rustic wooden beams, an entire wall of windows that took in the Teton mountain range, and a massive stone hearth, it was the Western version of luxury.

But the centerpiece was the kitchen. Built to accommodate dozens of guests, it was a chef's dream with two of every appliance. "I guess you like to cook?" she asked Kate, Jaime's mom.

"I wouldn't say I like it." Kate was *darling*. Slender, dressed head to toe like a cowgirl from the pearl snap buttons on her shirt all the way down to the snakeskin boots, she was a force to be reckoned with. "Remember, I've been feeding eight people for thirty years. He was just trying to make it easier on me."

"So, why aren't you living here?" Grace closed her eyes while Jaime's sister dusted her eyelids with a glittery shadow.

"I raised six kids in my house. Every nick on the furniture, scratch on the floor, and hole in the wall is a beautiful memory. Besides, what do I need ten thousand square feet for?" Seated at the kitchen table—a banquette that ran the length of one whole wall—Kate let out the top of one of her daughter's evening gowns. It was a perfect fit for Grace—except for the boobs, of course.

"Yeah, but you host all the family gatherings. That was his point in designing a kitchen like this." Abby, an artist who did graphic design for ranch merchandise, smelled of fresh apples and paint.

"Well, I've done it in my house for nearly thirty years. We're doing just fine." The matriarch pointed the scissors in Grace's direction. "I'm going to let you in on a secret. The bigger your house, the less time your family will spend together."

"Unless of course, you're the only daughter." Abby flashed a playful grin. "And then you get a whole bedroom to yourself. A bathroom, too. Meanwhile, the boys were jammed into two bedrooms."

"Livin' the high life, that's for sure." Smiling, Kate continued sewing. "But my point is when you've got eight people living in three thousand square feet, you're forced to watch TV together and eat together. When you share a bedroom, you're forced to learn how to compromise and get along. And before you make a joke"—she eyed her daughter —"the six of you are best friends."

"Well, I'm not sure if that's because we lived in a three thousand square foot house or the fact that Jaime made us get along."

Ooh, what does that mean? Grace was dying to find out more about this man who seemed to switch from hot to cold and back again without warning. One minute, she was convinced she wasn't his type, and the next, he'd give her a smoldering look that made her knees shake.

But it was a waste of time to try and figure him out. After tonight, she'd never see him again. "Sounds like he's got oldest child syndrome." A look passed between mother and daughter, only making Grace more curious. "Enzo's the oldest in my family, and it took him a while to get there, but now, he checks every box on that list." She ticked them off on her fingers. "He's the most responsible, he's a perfectionist, and he's a high achiever. He went to business school and has all kinds of ideas to change the way we run the bakery."

"Trust me, Jaime wasn't always like this," Abby said. "He did a total one-eighty after the accident."

"That sounds a lot like Enzo." Though, for him, it hadn't been an accident.

"So, now, remind me how you know my son?" Kate asked.

Grace was impressed with the subtle way she'd shut her daughter up. She only noticed because, in her family, her mom would've tossed a banana at her and said, *Shut your cakehole.*

"He's Ian Adler's friend."

Kate's gaze snapped up from the dress. "Ian?"

She didn't see any reason to keep the truth from this family that lived two thousand miles away from her ex's business. Unless… "You don't let him invest your money, do you?"

"No," Kate said. "Not that he hasn't asked, but we're more conservative than most. When you've had as many lean years as we've had, you don't take the good times for granted."

"Okay, then, I can tell you the truth. I was the bride, but I didn't marry him. Ten minutes before I was supposed to walk down the aisle, I found out he'd gambled away my savings. I left, and that's why I'm here."

Abby yanked her hand back. "*Ian?* Are you serious?"

"And before you think I bailed instead of helping him, you need to understand he stole my parents' money, too."

"I cannot believe this." Abby set the makeup brush down. "He was my first crush. I used to follow him and Jaime around like a puppy. But you know what he said to me once? I'll never forget it. He said, Abby, you're a great girl, but I've got a girlfriend, and she means the world to me."

"That's very sweet." A couple of days ago, she might've

liked hearing that. "Unfortunately, I don't mean more to him than money."

"Sweetheart." Her mom got up and squeezed Grace's shoulder. "I'm real sorry this happened to you. We always loved having the Adlers out to the ranch. They're good people. This must be hard for them, too."

"This is awful." Abby dropped onto the barstool next to her. "You must be devastated."

"I'm hurt. I'm angry. I'm…God, my entire life savings is *gone.* But to be honest, something's been missing between us for a very long time, and I only noticed when I came out here. I think I just accepted my relationship. But now, it's… how do I explain it? I guess it's hard to think outside of what I've always known, and coming here, the scenery's changed so dramatically, it's like it's opened my mind to a world full of possibilities. This whole experience, the mountains, baking to my heart's content in my cabin…having two fairy godmothers getting me ready for the ball…it's all so good and so much fun. And I guess I just feel…free."

"Well, I'm even happier to do it than I was before." Kate went back to the table.

Abby got back to work, too. "You want false eyelashes?"

"No, thanks. Just mascara, please. If you've got a mirror, I can do it myself." She hopped off the stool and grabbed her make up bag from the counter. "I'm the coastal version of you. I've got four brothers, and we grew up in a small house, too. My whole family works at our bakery, just like yours does on the ranch. I've always loved my life…"

"You just needed to shake it up." Abby reached for the platter Grace had brought over to thank them for their help. "These are the prettiest pastries I've ever seen. No wonder you're so happy. You get to make these beauties for a living."

"Actually, I don't. Renzo's sells croissants, turnovers, and muffins. That's it."

"Oh." Abby seemed confused.

"The sailors who dock in our harbor want something fast and hearty, and the tourists in town want ice cream. Fancy pastries are for the fine dining restaurants."

Abby bit into a slice of marjolaine cake. "Oh, my God. I don't know what this is, but I know you should be making it. This is your calling."

"I wish." Wouldn't that be nice? "But I work for the family business just like you do. Maybe one day I can have a side business or something."

"So, ours isn't really a family business," Abby said. "Jaime's just found a way for all of us to do the thing we love most here."

Grace didn't understand.

"He knew how easy it would be for the six of us to go off on our own, and our parents really wanted to keep us all together. Like, after art school, I could've stayed in New York and gotten a job there, but Jaime found a way for me to do what I love here. He gave me free rein to design the merchandise and the website any way I wanted. He's done that for all of us. When Huck graduates, he'll be a large animal vet for the ranch."

Wow. "Your brother's pretty amazing."

"Oh, he's okay." Abby grinned.

"If any of the kids could bake like you, he'd open a bakery right here on the ranch," Kate said. "Just out of curiosity, couldn't your family hire someone to make muffins and turnovers?"

"Well, I mean, everyone in the family works there. Aunts, uncles, cousins. Everyone has a role, and that's mine."

"But you have a passion for something else," Kate said.

"And it's special. Look at those pretty designs. Even the cakes have tiny flowers on them. I've never seen pastries as fancy as these, and we have some very upscale stores in Calamity. Would it be so crazy to open your own bakery? I think you'd be very successful with a product like this."

"And be cast out of the family business? Are you kidding me?" Grace laughed because it was truly unthinkable.

"But you'll always be part of your family, right?" Kate asked. "You'll just be doing the thing that makes you happy."

The thing that makes you happy.

Oh.

Grace's heart heaved. It was a wrenching so great she could feel the organ rip from the roots. A yearning took hold, so powerful she had to close her eyes and breathe. She could never leave her family, but the message hit deep. "You're right." It came out a whisper. "I should definitely be doing the thing that makes me the happiest." How had she not seen that before?

When she got home, she'd find a way to sell her pastries. She'd talk to her mom. Maybe they could have a separate rack in the bakery for her specialty items.

Yes. This is good.

This is so good.

It wasn't a date. She knew that.

Then why did she have the jitters? And why did she keep checking herself in the mirror?

Jaime said he'd pick her up after getting Kinsley ready for bed. Since the entire family would be at the ball, he'd hired a sitter. He didn't seem to trust anybody with his little girl, because he left nothing for the sitter to do other than read to her until she fell asleep.

Now, Grace waited. She'd never worn a ball gown or this much makeup, and the high-heeled sandals pinched her toes —which was to be expected since she was used to wearing chef clogs— but she loved it and couldn't remember the last time she'd been this excited.

Strangely, not even for her own wedding. Now that she had some distance, she could see the event had been nothing but business for her—organizing, planning, and setting up the yard. It had never been about marrying the love of her life.

That's because Ian isn't the love of my life.

Whoa.

What a crazy thought. *I was going to marry a good friend.*

Because, really, when was the last time her stomach had fluttered around him? How many times had she seen his name pop up on her phone and ignored it to finish talking to someone or run an errand?

Yeah, too many times.

Tonight was the first bit of romance she'd had in ages.

Not that it was a *date*. Jaime had made that clear.

I'll be busy helping my mom.

You might get bored.

The hotel has a driver, so feel free to leave early.

Message received loud and clear, buddy.

Why did he feel the need to even say those things? She might be attracted to him, but she'd never flirted. He was one of the groomsmen at her wedding *two days ago.*

It's not like I'm looking to date. Jeez.

It was fun to play Cinderella, but she wouldn't be losing a glass slipper tonight.

I'd need a prince for that.

Headlights flashed, and tires crunched on gravel. Grace checked the mirror one last time before grabbing the clutch Kate had loaned her and heading out the door.

He was just getting out of a black SUV, and the sight of that gorgeous, rugged man in a tuxedo caused her to lose her step. Since she'd tripped over nothing, it made her burst out laughing. "As you can see, I don't dress up much. Anything more than a two-inch heel, and it's like trying to stand still on a buoy."

"Here." Taking her elbow, he led her to the passenger side.

But his gruff voice was a little off-putting. Did he regret inviting her? She just could not read this man's moods.

After opening the door, he waited until she gathered the shimmery material of the dress and tucked it into the footwell before closing it. Alone in the quiet of the car, the jitters took hold. She probably looked like a girl playing dress-up—she certainly felt that way. In her world, she fit in. Her confidence came from belonging to the Giordano family, to Renzo's bakery. But with Jaime, she felt ordinary. He was so much more than handsome. His physique, his air of authority…he was a man who knew what he wanted and didn't waste time with anything not on his agenda.

No doubt he was used to women who wore designer clothes and got their hair and nails done. Grace spent her summers in bikinis, jean shorts, and flip-flops. If she wasn't baking, she was hanging out with her friends and family. No one she knew went to balls or high society events.

Oh, my God. So what? I'm not his date.

He thinks I need to get out of the cabin, and that's what I'm doing.

With the grace of an athlete, he slid in and fired up the

engine. "I wound up dropping Kinny at my parents' house. She wanted a sleepover."

Well, there you go. He'd probably drilled it in that she'd be on her own because he had plans. She wanted to tease him and have some fun with it, but for some strange reason, it pinched her heart to think of him with another woman.

She wasn't his date, but apparently, she wanted to be.

He slung an arm along the back of her seat. Her first thought was that he was going in for a hug, so she leaned in, got a whiff of his subtle masculine scent, and nearly died when he twisted around to see behind him as he backed out.

Why would he hug you? You idiot. Her entire being shriveled like plastic wrap near a flame. Quickly, she opened her clutch and pretended to be searching for something. She couldn't see anything, though. She was burning up in embarrassment.

She wanted to go back to her cabin, knead butter into dough…fill a pastry bag with whipped cream. She wanted to breathe in the scent of her baking pie crust, aware of the exact moment it was ready. In the kitchen, she was competent. Around her family, she was comfortable.

But apparently, outside her familiar world, she didn't fit. And it was awful.

Then again, maybe she just wasn't used to moody men she couldn't read. *Yeah, that.* Her dad was fiery, her mom was outspoken, and her brothers were blunt and hilariously cutting. At home, she knew where people stood.

But not with this guy. She gazed out the window, counting the fence posts they passed along the driveway. Until it struck her.

Why am I giving him this power over me?

I don't even know him. And I certainly don't know what's going on in his world.

Between his team, his daughter, and the ranch, he had a million balls in the air. Maybe the sitter canceled. Maybe some of his cows had gotten into a fight. *I don't know.*

All she could do was be herself. And if he didn't like her, so be it. She was only here for another day or two.

Feeling better, she turned on the radio. "How about some music?"

"Think you can choose something other than Lorelei Calloway?"

"Now, why would I do that?"

And there you go. She'd broken the tension.

She found the playlist she wanted and spent the rest of the ride belting out her favorite songs.

Grace stood alone at the dessert table.

They're pretty basic. Other than a variety of easy-to-eat petits fours, they had strawberry shortcake in a jelly jar, decadent chocolate chunk cookies, and rich, creamy New York-style cheesecake.

She'd chatted a little bit here and there, met some nice people, and learned that Calamity had a "tiny" population of thirty-thousand full-time residents. She'd laughed because Duff Island had *one* thousand. And while Calamity had a million people living here during peak seasons, her town only tripled in size. So, yeah. She knew about tiny.

Throughout the evening, she'd caught glimpses of Jaime shaking hands, engaging with some people and acting a little more formal with others. He'd been particularly kind to the wait staff, always thanking them and telling them they were doing a good job.

She hadn't seen him with any one woman in particular,

nor had she seen him flirting. He'd just been a dutiful son at his mom's annual charity ball. Maybe the hookup was after?

Whatever. She'd wasted enough time trying to figure out the elusive and mysterious Jaime Dupree. A waiter offered her another glass of champagne, but she'd already had two, so she declined. She planned on baking her butt off tonight and wanted to be sober to really enjoy herself.

After a quick trip to the bathroom to check her hair and fix her lipstick, she wandered over to the auction table and look at the offerings.

A day on Trevor Montgomery's ranch! Fly up to his private cabin overlooking Jackson Hole and enjoy a gourmet picnic for up to six people!

Whoa. Trevor Montgomery lives here? Damn. She moved on to the next item.

A custom couture wedding gown designed by Knox Holliday!

She picked up the lookbook, and her jaw dropped. *Are you kidding me?* She didn't regret wearing her grandma's dress, but she would've loved to wear one of these. With detailed embroidery, lace, beadwork, and crystals, they were stunning.

A four-night ski package at Wild Wolff Village Resort including all meals, champagne, and ski passes!

That'd be fun. Grace checked the bids—*holy moly*! They were already in the high five figures.

Her phone vibrated, and she pulled it from the borrowed clutch.

Jaime: Where are you?

Why? Is it time for me to leave?
Is the hotel's driver waiting for me?

But she had no reason to be bitchy. He'd done nothing wrong. Not only did he invite her, but he'd arranged for her to get all dressed up.

Besides, he'd done an outstanding job setting her expectations.

Grace: I'm at the auction table. Where are you?

When he didn't answer, when she didn't even see three bouncing dots to indicate he was working on a response, she turned to look for him in the ballroom. Crystal chandeliers hung from the ceiling, an orchestra played, and servers dressed in black and white threaded through the crowd with silver platters.

Outside of TV and movies, she'd never seen so much glamour. Everyone was dressed in designer duds, the men in polished black dress shoes and the woman in diamonds and jewels.

And knowing Jaime Dupree was coming for her sent her pulse soaring.

Obviously, nothing would ever happen between them, but she was still in the throes of a silly crush. The butterflies in her stomach grew increasingly restless as she waited for him to appear.

As she scanned the crowd, she marveled at these mountain men. Were they all strapping and handsome?

Wait—was that *Trevor Montgomery?* In a kilt, knee socks, and shiny black boots, it couldn't be anyone else. Lord, the actor was handsome.

And then, her gaze landed on him.

Jaime.

The sight of him hit like a Taser to her chest. In a room where everyone had groomed and polished and scrubbed themselves shiny, he stood out with his scruff and tousled hair. If it weren't for the black tux that hugged his broad shoulders and muscular thighs, he would look like a man who'd just rode in from mending a fence on the back forty. He hadn't even bothered to run a comb through all that dirty blond hair.

He prowled through the room, his impatient gaze flitting, as if looking for his prey.

He found it.

It's me.

A smile of pure relief cracked his features wide open. Someone reached out to grip his hand, but the way he stared at Grace—like she was the first sighting of land after being adrift—had the gentleman turning to look, too.

She didn't know what to do under that scrutiny, so she just waved. Awkwardly.

Never taking his eyes off her, Jaime exchanged a few more words with the guest, dropped his hand, and then stalked toward her.

There was no other way to describe the way he moved.

Her blood went as fizzy as the champagne she'd drunk.

Gorgeous, magnetic, confident… Every head turned as he strode by.

He was the most dangerous man she'd ever seen.

And not because he was the most handsome or the

tallest or the wealthiest in any room. It was his charisma. His power. Everyone wanted him.

But he was completely and totally unavailable. He held himself back from everyone but his family.

Finally, he was in front of her, cupping her elbows. His energy unmistakably said *I missed you.* In another world, he'd hug her so hard he'd lift her off her feet. She knew it. She wasn't misreading this.

"Hey." That gruff, masculine voice plucked a nerve deep inside, making her bones vibrate.

"Hey." God, she was *shaking.*

"Look at you. Not a speck of flour on your cheek."

She burst out laughing. "No. Your sister made sure of that. And why are you acting like this is the first time you're seeing me? You did pick me up and drive me over here."

"It was dark."

And you avoided looking at me.

"Is that her dress?" he asked.

"Yes. Although your mom had to make some alterations."

His attention fixed on her cleavage. "I'll bet."

She swatted him. "Eyes up here, player."

But he didn't smile. And his gaze lingered long enough to make her breasts tingle and her nipples harden. It took a slow journey up her neck, over her mouth, and then to her eyes. "I'm not a player. I'm very honest about what I can and can't give."

Her joints were locked, her throat dry. The men unnerved her. But she didn't like what he was implying. "I didn't ask for anything."

"You didn't have to." He lifted a wavy lock of her hair and twined it around a finger. "I'm sorry I didn't tell you how beautiful you look when I picked you up."

"Yeah, well, you were in one of your moods."

He seemed totally thrown. "I don't have moods."

"Are you kidding me? You're the moodiest man I've ever met."

He stared deeply into her eyes, the muscle in his jaw ticking. Around her, people laughed, sampled hors d'oeuvres, and jotted down their bids, and all the while, Jaime was locked on to her. A whole story unfolded across his features, but unfortunately, she couldn't read a single word.

But his energy...well, anyone could read that. It was sexual, carnal. If they hadn't been in a ballroom, she was certain he'd haul her up against him and kiss the living hell out of her. She could almost feel his hands sliding down her back, grabbing her ass, and lifting her, carrying her across the room, and slamming her against the wall.

Yes, please.

Ooh, this man would be a wild ride. And maybe that was the appeal right there. He was all leashed energy, and some lucky woman was going to snip the bindings and uncage him. And when he let himself go, he'd be thrilling. God, she wanted that.

Sex with Ian had never been exciting. It had been familiar. It had been...well, quick. Only now did she understand how unsatisfied she'd been. This moment brought it all into sharp relief. She needed passion. Craved it. She needed a man who couldn't keep his hands off her, who wasn't gentle.

No, she wanted him to be out of his mind for her.

But just like that, his face went blank. "Only around you."

"*Me?* What have I done? I haven't asked you for a damn thing. You asked *me* where I wanted to go, you offered me a cabin. I'm sorry I woke up the crew, but you failed to explain they were so close." She let out a huff of breath. "Do you think I came here to hook up with you or something? I wish you'd tell me what you're thinking because it's driving me crazy."

"Trust me. You don't want to know what I'm thinking." He looked past her. "You see anything you want?"

"You're my host, so I'm trying to be polite here, but I'm telling you, only my brothers can rile me up the way you do. At least with them, I can get right up in their faces."

He stepped into her space. "But I'm not your brother." He stared at her like he wanted to hike up her dress right there in front of everyone.

The air left her lungs. Her palms went damp. Her legs barely supported her. Because she wanted him to. She wanted his big hands on her ass, squeezing her flesh.

But just like that, he moved to the auction table. "What looks good?"

She let out a shaky breath. It was impossible to keep up with him, so she just had to stop trying.

I like simple men.

Men I understand.

This one's way too complicated. She glanced at some of the offerings. "They're mostly trips. You know, vacation homes." She was glad for the reprieve. Needed the haze of lust to clear. *This is ridiculous.*

"Where do you want to go?" He picked up a brochure. "How about Jumby Bay? It's a private island off the coast of Antigua. Looks nice."

"Me?" Right. Like she could have fun knowing her family was struggling to get the orders fulfilled, the deliveries checked in, or to find someone to cover a sick employee.

"I'm not going anywhere. I can't take any more time away from work."

He continued perusing the offerings. "You like pink diamonds?"

"I wouldn't know. I've never seen one." He better not buy something for her. "Should we dance or something?"

That got his attention. "I don't..." He exhaled in frustration. "Sure. Yeah. We'll dance."

"Oh, my God. Forget it. Don't do me any favors." Sick of his crap, she tried to move around him, but he caught her arm and pulled her close.

Their bodies touched. She saw the scar on his chin. Another bisecting his eyebrow. Also, she'd been wrong about the color of his eyes. They were the blue of a stormy sea. And a whiskey-colored starburst around the black pupil.

This man was a roiling, suppressed ball of sexual energy, and she wanted to pull the pin.

"I honestly can't tell if you want me to take the next flight out of here or if you want to rip this dress off me."

"If I rip this dress, I'll never hear the end of it from my sister. Now, come on. Let me bid on a few things, and then we'll dance."

"Bid away. I'm not stopping you."

He gave her an intense stare that was impossible to read, and it got her all hot and restless and needy, and then he made things worse by clamping a hand at the back of her neck and holding her in place while he whispered in her ear. "All I have to do is look at you, and the world stops. I can't think. I can't breathe. I don't know what it is, but you get under my skin." He leaned in, close enough that his lips grazed her cheek. "But I can't afford temptation right now. And I need you to keep your distance. Do you understand?" His grip tightened. "I'm not the man for you."

Chapter Five

Under his spell, she nodded slowly, even while thinking, *No. I actually don't understand anything you're saying.* She held on to one tiny piece of clarity, though, and it was enough to get her to duck out of his hold. "I'm not going to see you after tonight, so I should probably just let it go, but for the record, don't ever assume you know what's best for me. Do *you* understand?"

He let out a growl that sounded very much like *Fuck*, and his hand lowered to the bulge tenting his tuxedo pants. "You're a vexing woman."

"Given the party in your pants right now, I'm going to assume vexing means sexy, so I'll take that. Now, if you'll excuse me, I'm going to find a nice young man to dance with before I ask the driver to take me home."

For the second time, she started to walk off, but once again, he grabbed her forearm and pulled her back so hard she crashed against his chest. "I'm trying my best here, Gracie."

He'd called her Gracie. And in the kind of rough tone

she'd expect to hear under the covers as he held her wrists together over her head and slammed into her.

"But if I find you with another man, I'm going to start flipping tables. So, before I ruin my mom's event… Do you want to dance with me, or do you want to dance with someone else?"

"You." *Gracie.* It was such a sweet term of endearment. She could barely stand it.

Grabbing her hand, he led her to the center of the ballroom. The other couples were a blur of smiles and glittering jewels, and she barely registered the big band music, because her entire being yearned to be in his arms.

The beat was fast, fun, and retro, and there wasn't a chance she could boogie in these ridiculous heels, so she did a little side to side, swinging her arms and snapping her fingers. Basically, doing what she could to not fall on her ass. Meanwhile, buttoned-up Jaime danced like he was on a Broadway stage. She couldn't believe a man of his size and musculature could move so deftly. He had loose limbs and the agility of a gymnast.

But then, he pulled her up against him, set their clasped hands on his chest, and started slow-dancing with her.

"What're you doing?" She glanced around, self-conscious.

He lowered his mouth to her ear. "You're gonna break your ankle in those heels."

"Not untrue." She breathed in the scent that would forever remind her of her time away from home.

"Did you just sniff me?"

"I did." When he looked at her strangely, she said, "What? You smell good."

"So do you."

"That must be the hair product."

"No, not that. *You.*"

"Trust me." She pulled back. "I don't wear perfume. There'd be no point. I'm in the kitchen all day, so I'm always going to smell like sugar cookies."

"It's not that. I noticed it on the plane. It's something else. Something fresh. Sweet. *You.*"

"You don't even know me, but since you're not being moody, I can thank you for letting me come tonight. It's been fun."

"I shouldn't have left you on your own so much." His gaze shifted somewhere over her shoulder. "Shitty thing to do."

"Not at all. This is your mom's night. You don't have to worry about me." She had so many questions, but none she could ask without being nosy. He wasn't here to be dissected by a woman he'd never see again.

Holding her close, he swayed gently. The heat of his body seared her, and the intensity in his eyes made her restless. She barely knew him, so why did she need his arms around her? What was this unbearable desire to crack him open and discover his secrets?

So, it made sense, when the song finished with a crash of cymbals, she was disappointed to lose her excuse to touch him.

Except…he didn't let her go. He kept her locked in his embrace, in his gaze, and it was like the whole world disappeared. When the band launched into a slow, sultry song, she rested her chin on his shoulder. "Your mom said Kinsley's giving you 'a run for your money.' What did she mean?"

"Just that I was a terrible kid. Constantly in trouble. I don't think there was a day of my life I didn't hear, *Jaime.*"

He said it in a harsh tone. Well, come to think of it, it was more exasperated than aggressive.

That's weird. That's not how his mom or sister described him at all. "And Kinny's like that? I didn't get the impression she was so difficult."

"She's not. She's the sweetest kid you've ever met. But she's curious, so she gets into all kinds of trouble. You can't be mad at her because she's not sneaky or acting out. It's that she wants to understand how things work. She wants to see it and experience it herself."

"Give me an example."

"Yeah, so, if we read about a magic treehouse, I know with absolute certainty she's going to head outside and check every tree, looking for the one that'll transport her somewhere."

"That's adorable." Grace glanced up to see if his expression matched his adoring tone. It did. "I'll bet you sleep with one eye open."

"I do."

It was the strangest thing, this current of excitement running between them. She knew he felt it, too. Knew from the way his grip tightened, and the way his body heated up.

Their chemistry was wild, and she loved it.

The band launched into a new song, but she barely noticed the change in rhythm. She didn't care about anything other than being in his arms. "I remember when you found out about her. Didn't her grandparents come to the ranch?"

"Yeah. That was...something." He grew contemplative. "They showed up with a paternity test, said I'd gotten their daughter Jenny pregnant. I didn't know anyone with that name, so I blew it off. But then, I wasn't really asking for names at that point in my life." He cut her a look that spoke volumes. He thought she'd judge him.

"Ian said you'd gone a little feral after the accident." She said it with a smile to let him know she wouldn't do that.

He seemed to relax. "That's a good description. Anyhow, they said Jenny didn't want to be a mother and had no intention of telling me about her, so they'd been raising Kinny by themselves. After she died, they decided to tell me. They said they loved her and would keep her if I didn't want her, but that they were getting older and finding it harder to keep up. So, I took the test and there you go. My girl was two when she moved in with me."

"I can't imagine. That must've been so hard."

He didn't answer, so she figured she'd let it drop, but then, he pulled her even closer. "She saved my life."

She knew about the accident, of course, and how it had changed him. After his friend had nearly died BASE jumping, he'd pulled out of his contract to play in Canada's junior division. He gave up hockey to help save the ranch. But Ian had just broken up with her for the very first time, and they weren't together, so she hadn't heard any more about it.

Jaime drew her closer. "I love her because she's smart and funny and sassy and independent and so fucking cute I can't stand it, but I also love her for making me pull my head out of my ass."

"I don't know what you mean by that. Ian thought the world of you. He wanted to *be* you. He was always talking about Calamity, how the people here have free spirits, how they can't be tamed."

"Yeah, well, there's being free, and there's being reckless. And it was having Kinsley in my life that made me understand what I'd put my parents through."

His gravelly voice in her ear made her shiver. There was something so dark and dirty about Jaime. If she could strip off that thin veneer of civility, what would he be like? "I think you might be too hard on yourself."

"Not in the slightest. But I'm trying. Every day, I try to be a responsible man and parent."

"Okay, but maybe there's a place for everything."

He stopped dancing and just looked at her. "What does that mean?"

"Just that you can be a good and responsible parent, son, sibling, and businessman, but outside those roles... Well, I'm just saying we all have many facets. We behave a certain way depending on the situation."

"Gracie." A slow grin spread across his features. "Are you trying to tell me there's more to you than a sweet smile and cute pajama bottoms?"

"You'll never know, will you?" She gave him a saucy grin.

He squeezed his eyes shut. "Fuck." He let go of her hand to wrap his arm around her. "You're killing me. You know that?"

"I don't know why. I'm not at all your type, so what do you care what I do when I'm not smiling?"

"I'm trying very hard not to care, Gracie. Very fucking hard."

"And I don't know why you'd think I'm the same person around my parents as I am around my siblings or my friends. That the woman I am in the bakery is the same as the woman under the sheets."

When his hips punched forward, pressing his erection against her stomach, she realized he'd been deliberately angled away from her. "That's enough." He took a step back, lifted their joined hands over her head, and spun her around.

After she found her footing again, they went back to swaying in place. She should let it go—but she wasn't in the mood for that. "I didn't realize you were so prissy."

"Prissy? *Me?*"

She had to stifle a laugh at his reaction. "I referred to sex, and you clutched your pearls."

"Jesus, Gracie. I'm trying to—"

"Be a responsible adult. Yes, I know. But I don't see your daughter anywhere, and you're not in the middle of a negotiation with a sports agent, so maybe on the dance floor with a smoking hot woman, you could loosen up and have a little fun?"

As he held her gaze, his hands traveled slowly, firmly, down her back to the rise of her ass. Her breath hitched, and her body went hot with anticipation. They slid lower, grabbed both her cheeks, and then squeezed. Hard. He pulled her in, sandwiching his cock between their bodies.

Fire flashed across her skin, her knees went weak, and if she wasn't in a crowded ballroom, she'd reach for him. She had to know what he felt like in her hand.

She could see it so clearly, what he'd be like in bed. He'd give her what no one else ever had.

She hadn't understood it before, but she'd only ever been with boys. Even at twenty-eight, Ian was still unformed. Tough experiences had hardened Jaime into a man.

The next song brought a flood of couples onto the dance floor until there was barely any room, but she couldn't take her eyes off him. His palms splayed across her cheeks, fingers nearing the crack of her ass. His fingers curled, fisting her dress, and the pulsing between her legs turned into a throb.

"You don't want my kind of fun." His voice had turned hard.

"Is that you making assumptions about me again?"

"What are you saying, Gracie? You want to fuck me?"

She wasn't sure anything had ever been more exciting than a rugged, powerful man like Jaime Dupree asking her if she wanted to *fuck*.

Flashes of him in bed lit up her mind.

Him kneeing her legs open and entering her with such force her back arched.

Sensation streaked through her.

His big body looming over hers, slamming into her as he grunted, out of control, his long, silky hair shaking with his every thrust.

Those big hands cupping her bare breasts, pushing them together, while he tongued her nipples.

Holy shit. Where is this coming from?

It came from the carnal look in his eyes, the flare of his nostrils, and the heat radiating off his body.

Yes. She wanted to say it out loud, but she didn't know what he'd do. He switched from hot to cold so often, she couldn't bear his rejection. She absolutely did not mean to do it, but she squirmed against him. At the feel of his very hard cock pressing against her stomach, desire exploded in her chest, sizzling all the way down to the soles of her feet.

He lowered his face into her neck. "Fuck."

"Yes, please." Then, she whispered a reminder in his ear. "I leave the day after tomorrow. By the time you come back, I'll be gone." *It's a no-risk situation.*

He jerked back, grabbed her hand, and led the way out of the ballroom.

Anticipation rode through her so hard, she could hardly catch her breath.

Where is he taking me?

What the hell is this man going to do to me?

She couldn't wait to find out.

This woman—*Jesus*. Her tongue stroked luxuriously, like she was savoring a decadent slice of chocolate cake. But even while she took her time to tease and explore his mouth, her body moved restlessly against him. Her palpable desperation to get closer fueled his desire to the point where he wanted to rip the dress off and get to the soft, smooth skin he'd only glimpsed on the plane.

The fabric swished against his pants, and he tried not to groan too loudly since every sound was amplified in the small hotel powder room.

He'd let her go at her pace, of course, but he didn't know how much longer he could take it. He wanted to fill his hands with her breasts and lick every inch of her. Between her breathy cries and plaintive moans, he was harder than he'd ever been.

With shaky fingers, Jaime lowered the pull of her ball gown. Her flushed skin gave off the heady scent of arousal and sweet flowers, causing all the blood in his body to pool in his painfully aroused cock.

Fully unzipped, the dress barely clung to her shoulders, so all it took was a sexy little shrug to send it cascading to the hardwood floor. The dress had its own bra, so she stood there topless in all her feminine glory.

She was the most beautiful woman he'd ever seen.

Jaime shifted around her, so he could look at the two of them in the mirror. From behind, he took in the plump sides of her breasts, the narrowing of her waist, and the flare of her hips. A black thong bisected the cheeks of her perfect ass. He couldn't take it a second more, so he wrapped a handful of that dark, silky hair around his fist and tugged. "Look at you."

As her neck tipped back, her eyes widened with surprise. A second later, they turned sultry. Her response opened a whole world for them.

He had to get a handful of those tits. Cupping the heavy mounds, he pushed them together, letting the nipples peek through his fingers. When he pinched, she shuddered. A surge of need had him unzipping his pants and pulling out his cock. "I'm going to fuck you now."

He'd never wanted anyone the way he wanted Gracie. He was out of his mind with need—but also, there was an unfamiliar tug, a pull toward her. A strange and unwelcome hunger for something he couldn't have with this woman.

And it made him so uncomfortable that he ran a hand down to her pussy. Stroking her folds, his finger slipped inside all that slick heat while his thumb sought the hard nub of her clit. When he found it, her hips pitched back so hard, his cock wedged between her ass cheeks.

A harsh spike of lust had him squeezing her breasts. "You're not a good girl at all, are you?"

"Not when I'm naked, no."

"But you're not really naked, are you?" He took a step back to take in her hourglass shape. Her round ass and toned legs in those high heels about killed him. He yanked the thong, and she gave a sexy little moan. He couldn't wait to sink into all that wet heat. But first, he needed to watch her lose herself in his touch.

As he stroked her slick inner wall, his thumb circled her clit.

"Jaime." Her voice, her features, everything about her was flooded with pleasure. And when she sighed, when she whispered, "Oh, God," he got a hit of wonder.

Because he didn't know it could be this good.

He didn't know he could care this much.

The thong kept getting in the way, so his teeth sank into her earlobe, and he asked, "How important are these panties to you?"

Leaning her head back against his shoulder, her long dark hair falling across her eyes, her lips pouty and pink, she lowered her hands, fisted the thin material, and ripped them off her body.

Fuck, this woman fired him up. "Hold on." He pressed a hand to the middle of her back and pushed her down. His other hand clutched her hip and jerked her back to him.

Neck arched, hands gripping the edge of the counter, she held his gaze in the mirror. "Do it."

He looked at her, so bold and sweet, sexual and genuine. She could be everything to a man. He eased inside her, his cock so hard, so ready for release, he could barely control himself.

Driven wild by her breathy moans, her cries, and the way she rammed back to meet him, he fucked her. He reached between her legs, found her hard little nub, and rubbed. Jesus, she was so wet, so fucking responsive.

His balls tightened. He wasn't going to last. So much pent-up confusion and lust and frustration—it was all coalescing, coming to a head. He bit her shoulder, slid his fingers deep, and caressed the sensitive patch inside her.

"Oh, God. Oh…oh, my God." Her head tipped back, and she cried out. Her body jerked, spasmed, and her knuckles went white on the counter.

Burning up, he shrugged out of his tuxedo jacket and tossed it aside. And then, he drove into her, fucking her hard and fast. Watching her tits bounce and her eyelids flutter closed drove him to the breaking point.

Lost in the unbearably rising sensations, clawing his way to release, he finally broke. He stifled a roar as he drove hard and fast, hitting one peak after another, a never-ending string of orgasms that left him spent and utterly elated.

Unable to catch his breath, he wrapped his arms under her breasts and clung to her, his chest to her back. Tremors continued to rock him, and he held on as if he could somehow keep her.

Keep her? What the hell?

Uneasy, he reached for her dress, waited while she slid her arms through, and then zipped her up.

For several years now, he'd done a great job of reining in his impulses. But this woman proved to be a temptation he couldn't resist.

Thank fuck I'm leaving tomorrow.

And by the time I get back, she'll be gone.

Grace couldn't believe it. She literally could not believe the hot night of sex she'd had.

As soon as he'd dropped her off last night, they'd had a second and then a *third* round. And it had been filthy. Her body still hadn't recovered from being so deliciously used.

She closed her eyes to savor the memories. The rain battering his SUV, the way he'd run around to the passenger side, lifted her carefully out, shielding her with his tuxedo jacket, and then carried her to the cabin—all so she wouldn't ruin her shoes in the mud.

Last night made her understand for the first time that she and Ian didn't have chemistry. They had history, they had affection, but she'd never been out of her mind with lust for him.

And she only knew that because she'd never wanted anyone's touch the way she did Jaime's.

He looked at her like he would die if he didn't get his hands on her, and he'd get this expression, like he was caught between agony and ecstasy, and she *loved* it.

And, seriously, in all her twenty-eight years, she'd never been sore the next morning.

After he'd left, she'd been way too wired to sleep, so she'd baked.

Now, Grace took in the dozens of desserts she'd made. *What on earth am I going to do with all this?* Her phone rang. When she saw her mom's name, she stepped outside to take the call. "Hey, Mom."

"Hi, sweetheart. I'm just calling to get your flight information."

Since Jaime was heading back to the East Coast, the obvious choice would've been to fly with him, but the weird way he'd left last night—forget it. She didn't want to deal with his moodiness. "I'm not sure yet. I have to book something."

"You know you don't have to come home just yet. We hired Eliza, remember? You still have time left on your vacation."

Imagine five more days of sex with Jaime.

The way he'd kicked open the door and set her down, getting on a knee to pry the fancy heels off her feet? *Holy cow.* How thrilling was that? She'd handed him a towel to wipe the raindrops off his face. He'd only given it a quick swipe before he was helping her out of her dress for the second time.

And then, they'd been all over each other. She could still hear the ping of buttons landing on the wood floor as she ripped his shirt open.

Me.

I did that.

A cool breeze fluttered the cotton fabric of her dress, and she stepped deeper into the woods. She smiled so wide she was glad her mom couldn't see her.

But then, she remembered how he'd left. And it all came crashing down. "There's no reason for me to stay any longer."

"Well, good. Because Eliza's croissants aren't nearly as good as yours."

"I'm sure hers are fine."

"I guess. We just worry about you, honey. We need you home, safe and sound."

There was nothing safe about Jaime. He'd been a savage in bed. There was this one moment when he'd flipped her onto her belly, grabbed her hips, and hiked her ass up, and then...he'd spanked her.

Spanked me.

Not hard. It was more playful than anything. *Give me that ass.* He'd said it in his growly voice. But right after, he'd gripped a handful of her cheek like he was so hot for her he couldn't stand it.

But after they'd worn themselves out, his mood had changed. He'd gone from fun and wild to shuttered. Right before he left, he'd said, *I'll be gone tomorrow.*

She'd wanted to say, *Yeah, buddy. I get it.* Did he think she'd start planning their wedding? That she had expectations beyond last night?

She'd gotten exactly what she'd wanted. Hot, crazy sex. The kind she'd fantasize about for years to come.

She wasn't looking to fall in love with some guy from Wyoming. She had a life to get back to. She glanced at the pastries resting on every surface of the cabin. The idea of going back to making muffins...after creating desserts like this? *Ugh.* "I'm coming home, but I'll still take the rest of the week off." Could she stay here that long? What would happen when Jaime came back and saw her?

Then again, she could bake all she wanted in her apartment on Duff Island.

Right. As if her brothers wouldn't stop by, her mom wouldn't ask for a favor, and some crisis at the bakery wouldn't require her to come in.

No, if she wanted a break it had to be somewhere else.

I want it to be here.

She ignored the twist of wistfulness. Because it was ridiculous. She probably only loved it here because she needed a vacation so badly.

Well, and Jaime. He was just so different from the men she knew. All that broody masculinity. That tortured soul thing. Why were women attracted to that anyway?

Do we actually think we can heal men like that?

Oh, hell, no. She was not falling into that trap.

Except…he was also competent and strong. He was a good father, a good son. He was kind, generous…

Okay, fine. She could admit it. *I really like him.* And the way he looked at her—like he wanted to devour her? *Whew.*

No one had ever looked at her like that.

And now, after a few short hours with Jaime, how could she ever go back to another bland relationship?

"Okay," her mom said. "You deserve some time off… As long as you're coming home. You'd have to be bored on a ranch with no one to hang out with. Besides, it's better to be with your family when you're going through something like this. I didn't tell you, but since you're going to find out soon enough… Romeo punched Ian in the nose. I heard it crack."

"He what? *Mom.* Why do you sound so happy?"

"Oh, come on. He had it coming. I loved that boy like a son, and he *stole* from me? It's not okay. Now, I know we

ERIKA KELLY

agreed not to tell anybody yet for the sake of his job—I mean, how else is he ever going to pay us back—but Romeo happened to come home right when Ian was apologizing, and he heard the whole thing. Stormed right over and clocked him. Got him good, too."

"Oh, man." *I really don't want to go home yet.* She wanted to stay in this cozy little cabin and bake her heart out. "That's awful."

"And this is why I always say friends come and go, boyfriends break your heart, and the only people you can count on are family."

"You just said Ian was like a son to you."

"But he isn't a son, is he? And he broke your trust. So, you come home and let us take care of you."

Grace didn't answer right away.

"You're not going to get back with him, are you?" her mom asked, misunderstanding her hesitation.

"Not a chance. But that doesn't mean I wish violence on him." She glanced up at the morning sunlight filtering through the pine trees. "I should go. Let me look at the flights, and I'll let you know as soon as I book something."

"Sounds good. I can't wait to see you, sweetheart."

After disconnecting, Grace went back into the cabin, set the phone on the counter, and took in all the cookie sheets and racks of cooling pastries. She picked up a slice of opera cake, the mirror glaze perfectly shiny.

Clarity hit her in a rush. *I can't go home.*

I don't feel this kind of creativity there, and I need to do more of it.

Because this is my heart and soul, and I can't ignore it anymore.

How do I make it work, though? Ian stole my money, so I

90

can't stay in a hotel. Well, I can't cook in a hotel, either. And, after the way Jaime bolted, she couldn't stay on the ranch.

Unfortunately, she didn't have options here. But maybe it was enough that she'd had an experience that opened her eyes.

"This is really good." The sweet voice came from behind her.

She whipped around to find a little girl sitting on her couch, munching on a chocolate éclair. "Oh. Um, thank you?"

"I love chocolate." The girl had a smear of it on her lips.

With that blond hair and gray-blue eyes, she had to be Jaime's daughter. "You must be Kinsley."

"Yes." She got off the couch and headed for the sink, where she raised both arms.

It took a moment to understand the girl needed to be lifted so she could wash her hands. Grace mobilized, got the water running until it warmed, and then helped her clean up. After she set the girl down, she handed her a clean towel.

"I have to go now." Kinsley started for the door.

Jaime wasn't home, so she didn't know where the little girl was staying. "I'll walk you."

"That's okay." And then, she was gone, swallowed up by the bright sunshine.

Grace didn't think a six-year-old should be alone on this busy, thriving ranch, so she hurried outside. A tractor rumbled along a dirt road, horses trotted inside a corral, and a group of ranch hands baled hay. Actually, it had leaves, so she wasn't sure what it was. "What do you call that stuff?"

"That's alfalfa. It's a different kind of hay."

"Ah, okay. So, who're you staying with while your dad's out of town?"

"Grandma and Grandpa. But Uncle Nash and Aunt Abby and everybody comes over and plays with me."

"Do they know you left?"

"Grandma's on the phone. Can you do this?" The cutie started skipping.

"You bet I can." Grateful for the distraction, Grace joined in and found herself laughing. "You're really good at that."

"I know. I'm really good at sports."

"Oh, yeah? What do you play?"

"I don't play anything. I'm too little. What are you good at?"

Too little? What does that mean? Her brothers were playing soccer at that age. Grace found herself out of breath pretty quickly, but she rallied. "I'm good at baking."

"I know. You're really good. My grandma uses dirty flour for her cookies and raisins instead of chocolate chips."

"Dirty—" *Oh.* "Well, whole wheat flour's better for you."

"It doesn't taste better."

No, it sure doesn't.

"I'm going now." And just like that, the girl unlatched a gate and left.

Grace watched her skip across the grass, jump up the porch steps, and disappear into the house.

That girl's got some serious self-confidence.

I'll bet she wouldn't run back home just because she'd had a one-night stand. She'd take the rest of her vacation days to explore this old western town. In fact, she wouldn't hesitate to ask the ranch manager if she could borrow a car.

Heading back to her cabin, Grace took in the dramatic mountain ranges wreathing the valley. It all felt so big here, so wide open.

And right then, she understood why she loved this place. At home, she fit into a slot. The second child and only daughter. The croissant maker. No matter what interests she pursued, she'd never be more than the role she played in her little world on Duff Island.

Here, she could reinvent herself. She could be anything or anyone.

She had five days left of her vacation. Why on earth would she go back home to play the same part?

She had dozens of pastries. *I want to sell them. I want to see people's expressions when they bite into one of my desserts.* Could she just roll up to the farmer's market and sell out of the trunk of a Buick?

A golf cart drove by. The wagon attached to the back held stacks of wire.

And right then, an outrageous idea struck.

And it infused her whole body with so much joy, she knew she had to go for it.

Chapter Six

Jaime hit the ground running.

Fuck, yeah.

Perfect landing. Once he came to a stop, he checked on his friends.

Two jogged toward him. The other one dangled from his parachute, coming in at just the right speed.

Elation soared through him.

The three on the ground laughed their heads off. What better way to spend this final night together than clear skies, perfect weather, and a BASE jump?

I love these guys.

And you know what? Just because they were going off in different directions tomorrow morning, leaving him behind, didn't mean he'd never see them again. Maybe he could go to Canada and play after all. Maybe he could help his family while he was playing.

Anything's possible. He just had to figure it out. His parents' news tonight didn't have to mean the end of hockey. He'd totally overreacted.

Their parachutes fluttered to the ground, glowing in the

bright moonlight. As one, they glanced up to watch Booker's landing. He was coming in beautifully. It couldn't have gone better—

Until a harsh gust of wind jerked the nylon, and a terrible sensation shot up Jaime's spine. The hairs at the back of his neck spiked.

Turbulence twisted Booker like a rag doll.

The look of terror on his friend's face made Jaime cry out, "No."

His skin went hot at the same time his blood turned ice cold.

And then—

Jaime jolted awake. Skin slick with perspiration, heart racing, he jackknifed up. He had to go. Get out. He yanked the sheets off his body, but he was tangled. Trapped. He pumped his legs, fighting for release. "Fuck."

A glimpse of the glossy black entertainment center and minifridge reminded him he was in a hotel.

Right. He was in New York City for the meeting.

It's okay. Everything's okay.

He covered his face with his hands. His skin cooled, and his pulse pounded wildly in his throat.

When would these nightmares stop? Jesus, no matter how many years had passed, he couldn't get it out of his head. He wanted to go back. Stop himself from sending that text message and just handle the bad news on his own.

So what if he couldn't play hockey? So fucking what?

But he couldn't go back. Couldn't change a damn thing about it.

And he couldn't live with the guilt. It was tearing him apart.

What the hell was he supposed to do about it? How could he make it right?

You can't.

You can never make it right.

Booker hadn't wanted to BASE jump that night. He was packed, ready to report to the Los Angeles Cavalcade the next morning. He hadn't wanted to go out at all.

If Jaime hadn't sent that text, Booker would undoubtedly be a top player in the NHL.

But his selfishness had stolen that dream right out from under his closest friend.

And there was no way to give it back.

And that's why I'm here. If he signed Ross LaRoux, he could at least make it up to Declan and Cole. He'd give them the team they deserved.

So, he threw off the covers and headed for the shower.

Time to put on his game face.

Fresh out of the meeting, Jaime made his way down the hallway of Elite Sports Management, the top agency in the world. He pulled out his phone and checked the messages. Predictably, he had a dozen from his GM. He thumbed the call button.

Without even a greeting, Darren asked, "How'd it go?"

"Exactly as we expected." Navigating the maze of hallways, Jaime headed toward the reception area.

But with all the people striding down hallways and meeting in conference rooms, he found it hard to concentrate on the conversation.

Because Booker worked here.

He could be coming around the next corner.

Which is probably why I had the nightmare.

"You've got to give me something," Darren said.

He knew that. It was why he'd called right away. "He laughed and said Ross would never go for it." He kept his voice low, even though no one was paying attention to him.

"But we've got Cole Montgomery. It's a whole new show now."

"He doesn't care." On edge, he glanced into each office he passed, wondering if he'd see his old friend. "Ross's a loyal guy. He's been playing in Montreal for six years now, and he likes it. Likes the guys. Loves the fans."

"Okay. He'll like our guys. Our guys are cool."

"Yeah, but we just signed a bunch of new players, and it takes a while for the guys to catch a groove. He knows we're not there yet."

"Who do you think he's talking to?" Darren asked.

Since Ross was a free agent, other teams would be making offers. "No idea, but now he knows that come July thirteenth, we're making a play." The free agency market ended August thirty-first. They had time.

"Everyone will be. We just need to know what it'll take for Ross to consider us."

"I think the only clue was what he said about loyalty. Since we don't have the money, that's got to be our angle." As he rounded a corner, he nearly walked into a tall, blond-haired man in an expensive suit. Jaime's heart thundered.

Is it him?

Is it Booker?

It only took a second to see it wasn't. Jaime gave the man a chin nod and carried on.

He doubted he'd still be hung up on this whole thing if he'd had the chance to see his friend after the accident. But as soon as the doors had closed behind the ER gurney, that was it. Booker's parents had kept Jaime and his friends away.

And then, out of nowhere, they'd put their house on the market and moved back to the East Coast.

Leaving no forwarding address.

"That doesn't give me much to work with," the GM said. "We need money, but with the salary caps, it would mean letting go of some of our players. We've hand-picked everyone."

After their coach passed away and Jaime and Declan took over, they'd worked long and hard on a strategy. A way to make their team competitive. But even with Cole on the roster, they had little hope of making the playoffs without a great goalie.

"He threw out a couple of other names, but no one we'd be interested in." The moment the words came out of his mouth, Jaime knew he'd overstepped. As an owner, he left the running of the team to his GM—and he'd hired the very best guy for the job.

He'd only gotten involved because of Cole and Declan. He felt a personal responsibility to get the Renegades to the level that would make it worthwhile for them to have joined.

When the foyer came into view, his gut twisted. It was his last chance to talk to Booker. "Let me call you from the plane, and I'll let you know the guys he mentioned. See what you think."

"Sure thing." His GM disconnected.

He knew why he still had nightmares, why he couldn't shake the guilt. It was because, while he'd never seen Booker again, Jaime *had* seen his friend's parents. He'd just never told anyone about it.

It had been harrowing.

It had altered his brain chemistry.

The three of them had been barred from the hospital,

but nothing could've kept Jaime away. He'd snuck up the stairs and made it all the way to the ICU. Even from the stairwell, he could hear Ms. Hayes sobbing, and when he'd cracked the door open, he'd seen Booker's parents clutching each other.

The mother was inconsolable, and the father had tears streaming down his face.

Jaime had frozen solid. In that moment, he'd understood the horror of his selfishness. He'd been so hell-bent on making sure his friend was alive, he'd disregarded the wishes of Mr. and Ms. Hayes. And right then, he knew he'd made things worse by sneaking in where he wasn't wanted. Silently, he'd stepped back into the stairwell, ready to close the door.

That was when he'd heard, "*You.*" It was the ravaged voice of Ms. Hayes, and it had stopped him in his tracks.

He could've run. Probably should have. All he had to do was keep going.

Instead, he'd taken a step forward, letting the door close behind him. To this day, he could still hear the snick in that hallway. He didn't remember everything she'd said, but there was one line that played on repeat in his mind.

If he dies, you'll have to live with that.

Two months later, he'd gotten the words inked around his biceps.

You'll have to live with that.

A reminder that his actions had consequences.

Apparently, he'd needed a second reminder six years later when a child wound up on his doorstep, the product from a hookup he barely remembered.

Since then, he'd been doing a very good job of behaving himself. That is, until temptation appeared in the form of a sexy baker.

Thank God, she's gone.

When he reached the foyer, he found the receptionist on a call. The relief he felt at seeing that shamed him. Because as much as he wanted to apologize to his friend, he got sick just thinking about the encounter.

The reaming he would get.

You ruined my life.

Why couldn't you have just dealt with your family issues by yourself, you selfish fuck?

He had his answer ready. He rehearsed it every night, the moment his head hit the pillow.

You're right. I was a selfish, reckless asshole.

I stole your dreams, and there's not a damn thing I can do to get them back.

I'm sorry.

I regret my choice to send that text every minute of every day.

But he did need to give his friend the chance to confront him, so Jaime waited for the receptionist to finish the call.

When he did, Jaime said, "Hey, man. Is Booker around?"

Another call came in, and the man held up a finger as he answered. "Elite Sports Management. How may I direct your call?" As he listened, he covered the receiver with a hand and said, "Sorry, he's out of town."

Jaime waved in thanks.

"Do you want to leave a message?" the man called after him.

Yeah. Tell him I'm sorry.

Tell him I'd trade everything I own to give him back his career in the NHL.

But life didn't work like that. So, instead, he said, "No, thanks. I'll catch up with him later."

. . .

Heading down 191 from the airstrip, Jaime was glad to be home. He didn't like being away from his daughter. And also, he liked his life on the ranch with his family a whole hell of a lot.

He didn't want to think about Grace or the way he'd left her, but it was for the best she'd gone home.

She'd been a test—and he'd failed in the worst way.

He'd fucked his friend's fiancée.

Yeah, they'd broken up. But he'd brought her to the ranch to give her an escape. Time to come to terms with the end of a fifteen-year relationship.

Not to complicate her life by having sex with her in a hotel bathroom. *Classy.*

Or her cabin. *Three times.* He closed his eyes when he remembered spanking her ass.

But even while shame burned through him, his dick went hard at the memory of how wet she'd gotten. How her ass had pitched higher, and the frenzy of need in her eyes.

That woman was fire.

But she was living proof that he had to manage his environment. Without temptation, he did just fine.

That woman—she was a juicy, ripe apple he couldn't resist.

When he'd left her, she was happy, sated. She'd been totally fine with a hookup. And if he'd walked out on that note, they'd have been cool. But instead, he'd gone cold. Like an asshole, he'd practically run back to his cabin.

But it's okay. Everyone made mistakes, and this one didn't seem to have any bad consequences. He would text her, apologize for being weird. He'd make it right. She deserved that.

And then, he'd get back on track.

Mid-morning, there wasn't too much traffic. Calamity had two shoulder seasons between the flood of winter and summer tourists, and this—late June—was one of them. As he drove through town, though, he noticed a crowd had gathered right off the town square.

He could've sworn he saw a golf cart with the Dupree Ranch logo.

What the fuck? The crowd shifted, and he got a clearer view. It sure as hell was.

What's our golf cart doing in town?

He pulled over, jerked the gearshift into Park, and got out. He didn't listen to much pop music, but he recognized the Lorelei Calloway song. Wait, wasn't Lorelei the artist-in-residence at the music festival this summer? He thought she might be.

And when the moon's bright
There's a party every night
So get up, get up, get up, get up
And dance, dance, dance, dance

He had no idea why the singer would have one of the ranch's golf carts and wagons. They bred bulls, so it wasn't like they needed the promotion, but maybe his parents had offered it as a favor to Brodie Bowie, who ran the festival at his Owl Hoot property.

Except...the crowd shifted again, and he saw *Grace* singing her heart out and... He had to wait until a couple moved away to see what she was doing.

Is she selling pastries?

As he approached, he saw Brodie, his wife, and their three children stuffing their faces with treats. Rosie's eyes rolled back in her head. "Are you kidding me?" she gushed. "What is this magic?"

Grace stopped singing to answer. "That's a Mont-Blanc. It's meringue, whipped cream, and chestnut cream." She reached into a basket. "Do you like chocolate?"

"Is that a serious question?" Rosie asked.

"Ha." Brodie slung an arm around his wife. "This woman is the queen of secret stashes. Luckily, I'm a smart man, and since I know all the locations, I keep her supply intact."

"That doesn't sound very secret to me." Grace was dazzling. Her smile, her pretty hazel eyes, everything about her radiated joy and happiness. "But if that's your thing, then, try this one. Underneath the custard is a layer of dark chocolate. I'm just trying it out, but it's been vetted by a ballsy six-year-old."

"What's ballsy, Mama?" the oldest child asked.

Grace grimaced. "Sorry."

Rosie waved a hand dismissively. "My children have three ridiculous uncles. They've heard it all." She accepted the fruit tart and took a bite. "There's something wrong with you. This is too good. This is…you're a sorcerer, right? You have to be. I've had a million fruit tarts in my life, but this one's out of this world."

"I don't think there's any magic to it," Grace said. "It's just the usual ingredients, but I do think we eat with our eyes first."

That comment turned Jaime's attention to the cart. Only a few pastries remained, but they were all adorned with tiny, colorful flowers and sprigs of greenery. Even for a guy who didn't like sweets, they were fanciful and appealing.

He didn't even realize he'd fixated on a lemon tart until it was lifted by a feminine hand and brought to his mouth.

"Go on. Taste it." Grace smelled of sugar and warm butter.

I'd rather taste you.

"Welcome home." She had a glint in her eyes that said, *Bet you didn't expect to find me here.*

Dessert was the last thing on his mind, but with so many eyes on him, he couldn't reject her offer. "Thanks." Thinking he'd play along for her sake, he took a bite.

He'd expected a mouthful of sugar like every other dessert he tried, but this... The flavor was fresh, tart, and bright. It was like sunshine in his mouth. "It's good."

"*Good?*" Rosie asked.

"Hey, man." Brodie reached out a hand. "Nice to see you."

Jaime gave a chin nod to the baby strapped to his friend's chest. "Growing that brood."

"Yeah." The big, muscular man gave a smile Jaime had never seen on him before.

While they'd gone to high school together, they'd run in different crowds. The Bowies were hardcore athletes, too, but where Jaime and his friends focused on hockey, the brothers were all about snowboarding and skiing. The oldest had won Olympic gold.

Like his friends, they'd been wild and untamed.

A total free spirit, Brodie was the last of the brothers to settle down. So, to see him this deeply contented with a wife and kids threw Jaime off his game.

"Where's your bakery?" Rosie asked.

"Duff Island." Grace accepted cash from a customer who made off with a Napoleon.

"Wait, are you talking about Rhode Island?" Brodie asked.

"Yes. Renzo's. Have you heard of it?"

"No," Rosie said. "But I'd assumed, since you were selling in town, you'd opened a bakery here."

"Oh, no. Actually, I was supposed to head back today, but I decided to stay a little longer. At home, I only get to make croissants and turnovers, and I guess I had a little too much fun playing around. I didn't know what to do with all these pastries, and I thought, well, I have to pay my parents back for the wedding that never happened." Her cheeks went red, and she looked at them sheepishly. "Sorry. I'm babbling. I'm supposed to be on my honeymoon right now, but my boyfriend—well, fiancé—stole from me and my parents, so I ran, and this guy"—she gave Jaime a grateful smile and a pat on his bare arm—"rescued me."

It was friendly. Nothing more. But its warmth spread through him, and he wanted more.

Fucking temptation.

"He was a groomsman, and he brought me out here. And I thought, Why not try to sell all this inventory? It won't make a dent in what I owe, but it's *something.*"

Rosie handed off her tart to the child standing beside her, reached out, and drew Grace in for a hug. "You've had a rough go of it."

Tears shone in Grace's eyes. He watched this brave, kind, spirited woman lean into a stranger and hated himself for being so cold. For being so consumed with his attraction to her that he didn't bother seeing her as a woman who'd gone through a trauma.

"It's all right. You're here now." Rosie held her close. "We've got you."

Grace pulled back, wiping under her eyes. "Look at me. I've kept myself so busy I haven't let myself feel anything. I just…want to pay my parents back, you know?"

"How much?" Brodie asked.

"Brodie." His wife nudged him.

"No, it's okay." Grace turned to sell another Napoleon. Pocketing the money, she said, "I don't mind. Um, I need seven grand for the wedding. The rest, what my ex stole... that'll take a lot longer. My whole family works in our bakery, so there's only so much money to go around. I figured I could get a head start selling what I made."

"You want to run a food truck?" Brodie asked.

"What?" Distracted by another sale, Grace pocketed the money and then turned back to Brodie. "A food truck? Oh, I can't do that. I have to get home. I only planned to take a week off."

"My family and I have a place called Owl Hoot here in Calamity," Brodie said. "Every summer, we run a music festival in an outdoor amphitheater, and we've got all kinds of food trucks around the perimeter. Only two of them sell dessert, and one of the guys just bailed because he broke his arm. Last year, he made fourteen grand selling churros and doughnuts, and this year, our ticket sales have more than doubled, so I can pretty much guarantee you'll earn enough to pay your parents back."

"Are you serious? And I can sell whatever I want?" The prettiest pink suffused her features, and her whole spirit seemed to blossom.

"No. You'd have to stick to what he sells, but you can sing your heart out."

"I thought you said it was a music festival?"

Brodie chuckled. "Yeah. So maybe don't sing when there's a band on the stage, but the rest of the time...go for it. We'll bill you as the Singing Baker."

Jaime wanted to tell her to take the offer. That if she had the chance to pay her parents back from a summer's worth of work doing the thing she loved, she should absolutely do it.

But he wouldn't say that because he didn't want her staying on his ranch.

Not when he'd have to see her perfect ass and that happy smile.

Hell, no.

"But wait, she can still make these desserts, too, right?" Rosie asked.

"I don't see why not," Brodie said. "You'd be making the fried stuff right there in the truck, so anything you bring in from home, you can sell for yourself."

"Am I sharing the profits with him?" Grace asked.

"No. He could use the income, so we'll lease the truck from him—and I'm paying for that since I need more dessert options. So, yeah. You'll keep one hundred percent of the profits. You should make more than enough to pay back your parents and pocket some change for yourself. Deal?"

"I have a million questions like where I'll stay and what my family will do without me, but I'm smart enough to say, 'Yes, please,' and 'thank you,' and figure out the rest on my own."

A clash of emotions rocked him.

A weird kind of elation that she was staying, along with a fear that he wouldn't be able to resist her.

And a fierce desire to see this woman succeed.

But he could manage the situation. Between him and the Bowies, they'd find a cheap place for her to rent.

Because she sure as hell isn't staying on my ranch.

Standing at the kitchen window in her tiny cabin, Grace looked at the mountains. It was breathtaking and vast and brutal and completely unknowable to her.

Everything here is different. The fresh, clean air, the adventure-seeking people, and the constant edge of danger. It wasn't just a stream—it was a rushing, frothing river. It wasn't just a mountain—it was a jagged block of granite that had been violently uplifted six million years ago.

She couldn't even contain her excitement—*I get to stay in Calamity and bake my pastries.* One summer. Eight weeks.

The only other time she'd done something for herself was when she'd dropped out of college and gone to culinary school. She'd felt tremendous guilt because her family didn't need her to learn anything fancy. They served what they served. That would never change.

We know our customers, honey.

That's the key to success, knowing your customers and giving them what they want.

She'd done it for herself. But just like the switch to culinary school, something in her spirit called to take this opportunity, to stay here in Calamity. Sure, she'd make the churros and doughnuts, but the idea that she could spend an entire summer baking pastries—the gorgeous, creamy mousses, the crunchy pâte à choux, and the elegant curls of chocolate she used to decorate...well. *I have to do it.*

Where will I live, though?

She'd caught Jaime's horrified expression of, *Oh, no. My hookup's going to be in my face every day?* She'd wanted to tell him right there in front of everyone not to worry, she wouldn't become some needy stalker. She'd rather eat a Twinkie than beg a man to want her.

Whatever. I'll find a place. Between the four Bowie

brothers, Brodie thought they'd be able to find a place for her.

So, okay. I'm doing this.

Time to call Mom.

This is going to suck. But before she could pick up her phone, someone knocked at the door. Expecting to see a little girl with blond hair, she reared back to find Jaime. His presence took up all the space in the doorway.

First, embarrassment hit. He'd come over to tell her she couldn't stay. What else could it be when he wore that steely expression?

But underneath that, a tiny bud of hope sprang to life. It barely had a pulse, but it beat with a yearning to be with him. A whole summer with Jaime Dupree.

And that just pissed her off. She had to stop with these stupid, fanciful ideas. "Don't worry. I'm leaving." She had a smile on her face because screw him. She was not going to stand there and listen to him tell her he'd had a great time but that he wasn't looking for something serious right now. "Brodie's got a place for me." At least, she hoped he did.

"No. He doesn't." He said it grimly, like it was the worst thing in the world. He motioned to get past her. "Can I come in?"

While she'd rather slam the door in his face, he did own the place, so she stepped aside. "Of course."

He took in the suitcase, the dishes on the drying rack, and the vacuum cleaner she'd left out.

She wanted to say, *See? I'm going.* But he'd just dropped some pretty terrible news. "Did he tell you that? Because he said he was sure they'd have somewhere for me to stay. If this is about money, I'm willing to pay rent. Ian might've emptied my savings, but I do have money in my checking account."

ERIKA KELLY

"It's not that. Rosie's family's in town, and security won't let them stay in hotels."

"Security? Are they famous?"

"She's a princess. Her parents are the king and queen of St. Christophe."

"You're kidding me. Rosie's a *princess*? That's the wildest thing I've ever heard." Although, now that she thought about it, the blond, slender beauty had a regal air about her. *Yeah, I can see that.* "Okay, well, I'll get on my laptop and start looking for a place."

"No, it's fine. These cabins are just sitting here empty." He let out a big exhale. "You can stay here. But—"

Oh, God. Here it comes.

"Look, I have to be honest with you." He sounded so tortured.

I know, I know. You had a great time, but you're not looking for a repeat of the other night.

Ugh. I really don't need to hear this.

This is exactly why I don't do one-night stands.

"I'm attracted to you," he said.

Wait, what?

He looked like he had hot coals in his boots. Like he needed to run far and fast to get away from the pain. "In a way I've never…" Roughly, he scratched the back of his head. "This is not normal for me."

Hold up. "What's not normal?"

"Me being this…drawn to a woman. I like women. Love them. But I've never…no one's ever…" He jammed a hand into the pocket of his worn jeans. "After a hookup, I don't think about them. Their scent doesn't fucking *linger*…" He scrubbed his face with both hands. "*Dammit.*" Finally, he looked at her. "Look, I can't explain it. The way you smell, it's like it connects with something in here." He smacked his

110

chest like the whole idea made him angry. "It doesn't make sense. It just gets me all worked up. I mean, even standing this close to you makes me want to—" With a harsh shake of his head, he put an end to his rant. "My point is that I can't be around you."

"You can't be around me because you're attracted to me?"

"Yes."

"Okay." *Werido.* "Well, like I said, I'll find somewhere to live."

"That's just it. There's nowhere you can afford to rent. Calamity's a small town, but in the summer, we have a million people coming through." He motioned to the window. "The Tetons, Yellowstone, the whole wild west thing. Anyhow, like I said, these cabins are just sitting here, so you're welcome to stay. Rent-free." He swallowed. "But it's best if we keep our distance."

"Because you get all worked up around me." It might be funny if he wasn't so upset.

"Exactly."

"That shouldn't be a problem. I'm up at three baking, and then I'll be working at the festival from noon till nine at night. Our paths won't cross."

Relief came out of him in a rough exhalation. "Okay, good. Good." And then, he turned and headed back out the door. At the threshold, he stopped. Glanced back at her. "I like you, Grace. But four days ago, you were supposed to get married."

"*That's* why you're all worked up over this? *Ian?*" *Whatever.* She didn't need to hear his excuses. "I'm not looking for a relationship. I'm not fantasizing about some future with you. I'm here to make money."

"Believe me, I know. It's not you I'm worried about."

And with that, he was gone, taking all his chaos and wild energy with him.

Leaving her with some facts.

I don't have to move.

I get to stay here.

And Jaime Dupree wants me so badly that he's freaking out.

Wow. Wow, wow, wow.

It helped to know it, considering she couldn't stop thinking about him. About his hands and his mouth. The way he'd taken what he wanted from her and given more than she'd ever thought to ask for.

But he was right. They couldn't get involved. She had an enormous job ahead of her—working at the festival plus baking. She didn't have time to sleep, let alone have some wild fling.

So, there you go. Everything's settled.

She grabbed her phone off the counter and called home. It only rang once before her dad answered.

"Grace?"

"Oh, hi, Dad. I thought I was calling Mom."

"You were, but I saw your name, and I wanted to say hey to my little girl."

He was so sweet, and it made her feel worse about what her ex had done to them. "I'm so sorry about all this. It's killing me that Ian stole your money."

"This is exactly why I answered the phone. To make sure you understand something. You've got no part of this. We were all blindsided. He knew how hard you worked for that savings, and he gambled it away. That boy is dead to us. You hear me?"

"Has he talked about paying you back? Is he going to do anything about it?"

"Sure, he has. But how do you think he's going to do that?"

"More gambling," her mom called in the background.

"His mommy called and said she'd pay us back." Her dad didn't like weakness, and Ian, an only child, had grown up the focus of his parents. "I told her, 'No, you pay Grace back.' He only got fifteen grand from us, but what he stole from my daughter took a lifetime to save up. I don't know how he can live with himself."

"I know. Me neither." And here was her opening. "But I've found a way to pay you guys back."

"You're not paying us anything. You didn't do this."

"Just listen. I have an opportunity to work at a music festival in Calamity. It's a food truck, and the owner made fourteen thousand dollars last summer."

"Who told you that nonsense?" Her dad's disbelieving tone reinforced his view that outsiders couldn't be trusted.

"The man who runs the festival. Dad, I can make real money doing this."

"Well, if you do it, you do it for yourself. Not us. You're the one who lost her savings."

Huh. He didn't seem to mind her staying. "I'm not going to argue with you. I'm telling you that the first seven grand I make goes to pay you back for the wedding." Anything extra would cover the rest of his losses. But… "You're okay if I don't come home?"

"Of course, I'm not okay. You think I want you out there all alone, so far from your family? What if you get a flat tire, and we're not there to help? What if you get attacked by a bear? And who the hell's gonna make croissants as good as you? But you're a grown woman, and you make your own decisions. All I ask is that you stay in touch, let us know you're all right."

"I will. Thanks, Dad."

Once she disconnected, she knew it was time. She had dozens of texts and missed calls from Ian that she'd ignored. She wanted this summer so badly, and she didn't want to head into it with baggage, so she hit the green Connect button.

It rang four times, and just when she was about to give up, her ex answered breathlessly. "Grace?"

"Yes."

"Aw, babe. I'm so glad you called me back. I was losing my mind. I'm sorry. You know that, right? I'm so fucking sorry."

In that moment, they were ten-year-olds racing their bikes on the Duff Island loop.

They were teenagers, and he was sneaking into her room to be alone with her, even though he'd come to visit her brothers.

The moonlit beach would always be associated with him because that was where they'd had their first kiss, their first gropes, and their first sex.

She'd cried over him, missed him, hurt him, loved him, hated him, wanted him, and avoided him. He'd been her best friend, her lover, and the man who'd broken her heart one time more than he'd healed it.

It was well and truly over. "Okay."

"Look, I know you. I know your voice. You're pissed, and I get it." He let out a huff of breath. "You're right. I have a gambling problem. I'll join a program if that's what it takes."

"Ian." She said it gently. "Getting help sounds like a good idea for you but don't do it because you think we're going to get back together." She weighed the next two words in her heart and knew they carried no doubt or hesitation. "We're not."

"Don't say that. I fucked up. I know that. You have every right to hate me. And when you come home, we'll talk. My parents and I worked out a plan to pay everyone back. Text me your flight information—"

"I'm not coming home. I'm staying in Calamity for the summer."

"What? No. You can't do that. What's your family supposed to do without you?"

"Hopefully, they'll be able to keep the woman they hired while I was supposed to be on my honeymoon. And if not, it won't be too hard to find a replacement. It's just muffins."

"Ah, come on. You're mad at *me*. Don't take it out on them."

"*Ian*. This isn't a spat. I'm not throwing a tantrum." *He doesn't get it at all.* "My parents don't have much time left to build a retirement fund. You understand that, right? How many more years do you think they can stand on their feet all day running a bakery? And if you include the wedding, you just wiped out *twenty-two thousand dollars* of it. So, trust me when I say this has nothing to do with you." *Nothing has anything to do with you anymore.* "It's all about paying back what you stole from them."

"Baby, I'm so sorry."

"I hope you are. But either way, it doesn't matter. What you've done is unforgivable. You betrayed my trust, and that's not something you can ever earn back. I'm only returning your call because I don't want to spend my summer seeing your name pop up on my screen. This is goodbye."

Chapter Seven

I want a tall man
A rich man
An absolutely fine man
I want the car
And the money
And the kisses just like honey

I want the world on a plate
Diamonds and a date
I want to drink the wine
And tell you that you're mine

IS THIS REAL LIFE? WHILE DIPPING SWEETENED DOUGH into the fryer, Grace belted out a sassy, fun Lorelei Calloway song. Since opening the pass-through window at noon, her singing had drawn a constant flow of business. *Yay!*

Everyone seemed happy to be outdoors on this gorgeous June day. And the biggest bonus—they'd come to her truck for a doughnut or a churro but the minute they saw her pastries, their eyes lit up, and their hands were all *gimme.*

Day one: having the time of my life.

Loads of people wandered the lawn of the amphitheater, going from one white tent to another. She hadn't taken a break yet to check out the vendors, but she could see stalls selling jewelry, metal sculptures, paintings, and topiaries.

The bands were scheduled every four hours during the day with the main show scheduled for seven o'clock on weeknights and eight on weekends. Tour buses parked behind her truck, so she had a chance to see the surprising number of famous musicians who came all the way out to this charming mountain town to play their music.

"Hey, Singing Baker," a customer called. "Save a chocolate macaron for me." The woman wore a baseball cap low on her forehead. She was pretty far down the line, and Grace had no doubt she'd be sold out by the time the woman reached the window.

"I'll make more tomorrow," she called.

The next customer came forward, a man in a large black cowboy hat. "Can I get two maple bacon doughnuts, please?"

"You got it." Grace didn't have a lot of experience with fried foods, but she'd gotten in touch with the truck owner, and he'd sent her his recipes.

"And can you please keep singing?" the man asked.

Grace laughed. "You bet I can. You got a favorite song?"

"Do you only sing Lorelei Calloway?"

"Pretty much, yeah. But that's because I used to be in a tribute band." She and Lorelei were both lyric mezzo-sopranos, so even as a teenager, she'd noticed how her voice aligned perfectly with the famous singer's.

"I can see that, seeing as you look just like her."

"I hear that a lot."

The woman whose arm linked through his, asked, "Can you sing 'Heart of a Woman?'"

"That's actually one of my favorites." It allowed her to use her four-octave range. With her tongs, she collected the requested doughnuts and launched into the song.

> *The heart of a woman is brave and true*
> *Consider yourself lucky if she gives it to you*
> *The heart of a woman is giving and kind*
> *So let me tell you something*
> *You better know your own mind*
>
> *Love her hard, love her strong*
> *Be the one she can count on*
> *Love her gentle, love her sweet*
> *The middle's where you'll meet.*

As predicted, she sold out of the chocolate macarons by the time the baseball-capped woman reached the front of the line. Grace was just finishing the last note of the song, singing her heart out, when she found herself looking into the eyes of the star herself.

It was Lorelei Calloway.

Grace just stared, jaw hanging open.

"You got lungs, girl." The singer grinned, but there was a hard edge in her eyes.

"Uh...thank you?"

"Why are you surprised to see me?" Lorelei asked. "Isn't this what you wanted? To meet me? Get my attention?"

"I...no." *What is she talking about? Get her attention how?* "If I had any inkling you were around, I would never dream of singing your songs." She was so confused. "What on earth are you doing in Calamity, Wyoming?"

Lorelei seemed skeptical. "I'm the artist-in-residence this summer."

"Are you serious?" She set down her tongs to smooth her hair. *I must look a mess.* "I can't believe this." Why had no one told her?

She cocked her head. "So, you didn't come out here hoping I'd see you and make you famous?"

"What? No. I'm a baker. I bake. My family owns Renzo's on Duff Island. I make croissants and…" She reached for the nearest basket. "Here. Have a cannoli." But the singer didn't take one. "I swear, even if you begged me, I wouldn't get on stage with you. I'd be mortified."

"You just said you were in a tribute band."

"Yeah, to make money. When I was younger, I wanted my own bakery, but now, I'm going to use it to buy a house or maybe to start a side pastry business. I don't want to be a *singer*. I love what I do."

"Yeah, I can see that." Lorelei gestured to the baskets. "Okay. But just so you know, I can't make anyone famous. It doesn't work like that."

"I really, truly don't want fame. I just want to bake." Grace wanted the earth to crack open and swallow her whole. In a million years, she wouldn't have imagined she'd find the biggest singer/songwriter in the world in Calamity. "Um, I don't have any more chocolate macarons, but do you want any of the other flavors instead? Or how about a Paris Brest?"

"A what?"

"It's an almond pâte à choux with vanilla cream inside."

"Mm, that sounds divine. But I don't eat sugar. I just wanted to bring some cookies to my crew. Man, your pastries are pretty." She waved a hand at the baskets, wiggling her fingers. "All those itty-bitty flowers and the leaves. It's art." She glanced behind her. "Well, I'll let you get back to it. I just thought you were trying to use me."

"Absolutely not. I promise I don't want to do anything but bake." She bagged up the Paris-Brest and the remaining macarons. "Here. Take this to your crew. And if you eat them when no one's watching, they have no calories. Trust me. I know."

Lorelei grinned. "Oh, I like you. All right, I'll be back for more tomorrow. My drummer's got the worst sweet tooth." She lifted the bag. "Thank you."

And with that, she dashed behind Grace's truck, across the parking lot, and up the stairs of a sleek black tour bus.

That was awful. *What do I do? I can't keep singing her songs.*

It didn't matter. She could just behave like every other food truck and sell her pastries.

But a seismic shift took place inside her, and she knew that was not the answer.

The whole point of being here is to make money, and if singing brings in the customers, then you bet I'm going to sing.

But the secondary reason she was here? To live her passion.

It wasn't like she'd ever get to do it again.

The Singing Baker it is.

It amazed Grace, one week into this gig, that she wasn't exhausted. In fact, she was more energized than she'd ever been.

At twenty-two, when she moved out of her parents' home, no one could believe it. Why live in a tiny apartment when she could be surrounded by her brothers, her parents, and all the friends and family who constantly dropped by?

At home, there'd always be a hot meal, a fresh batch of almond biscotti, and someone to talk to. All good points, and she adored her family, but she needed her own space. It was when she was alone, when her mind was quiet, that her creativity crept out from its hidey-hole and did a happy dance.

So, the tiny cabin? It let her imagination run wild. Even after a long day on her feet and a never-ending line of customers, she still looked forward to baking at night. The response to her pastries had been phenomenal, and every day she had to bake more and more to keep up with the demand.

She couldn't believe how much money she'd made in just seven days. She'd even upped her prices to try and slow down sales, but it hadn't worked.

It made her giddy to know she'd created something people loved.

Every night, as soon as she got home, she showered off the smell of fried food, grabbed a quick bite to eat, and got busy. Tonight, she planned on making a whole collection of lovely petit fours. Maybe in a woodland theme—each one could be a different furry animal. *Cute.*

Pulling into the driveway, she punched in the code, and the massive iron gate swung open, allowing her to pass underneath the Dupree Ranch sign. Heading up the long, winding road, she was pulled from her thoughts when she noticed flashlights arcing in big swoops around the property. She rolled down the window of the car Joseph had loaned her for the summer and heard, "Kinsley? Come on, girl. Where you at?"

"Kinsley!" a deep voice shouted.

Grace braked and cut the engine. As soon as she got out,

she caught up with the nearest search party. "Everything okay?"

"Kinsley took off again."

"Oh, no." She shoved her keys into her pocket. "How can I help?"

"You know the ranch?" one of the guys asked.

"No. I'm afraid I don't." With moonlight filtering through a cloudy sky, she could barely make out the silhouettes of a house, a couple of barns, sheds, and the row of cabins nestled against the tree line. Beyond what she could see lay the pure darkness of pastures, hills, and then the national park.

A chill ran down her spine when she thought of the little girl out there alone.

The man clearly caught the tension in her expression. "It's okay. We'll find her. She does it all the time."

"At night?"

He shrugged and took off, leaving her unsettled.

She couldn't just go back to her place and pretend like a six-year-old—Jaime's *daughter*—wasn't out there. She had to do something. Turning on her phone's flashlight, she scanned the immediate area. Her first thought was maybe Kinsley had gone for more pastries, so she headed to her place.

But she didn't see lights on at hers or any of the other cabins. *Where are you, Kinsley?*

Woodsmoke scented the cool, crisp July air as the search team called the little girl's name. Flashlights swooped like seagulls near the shore, and she got a glimpse of the barn door ajar, the metal lock dangling.

Is that normal? Wouldn't you lock up a barn at night? She had no idea, but what could it hurt to take a look? The soles of her chef clogs crunched over gravel as she hurried over.

122

Inside, she smelled hay, dust, and the earthy scent of horses. The clouds had shifted, allowing shafts of moonlight to cut through the windows, making a Harlequin pattern on the hay-strewn ground.

"Kinsley?" She hesitated to go in any farther.

"Shhh. Stella's tummy hurts."

Oh, thank God. She's here. Quickly, she fired off a text to Jaime.

Grace: Found her. She's in the barn. I'll bring her home.

"You have to turn the light off," Kinsley whispered. "She's having a baby."

Grace lowered the beam to the ground and headed toward the voice. She peered into the stall, and shock hit her nervous system.

She might not know much about ranches, but she figured standing behind a horse the size of a minivan was bad. The little girl was all of what? Fifty pounds? She'd be crushed by a thousand-pound horse.

"Hey, Kinsley?" She spoke softly, sweetly, to let the horse know she was there and wasn't a threat. "Can you come here, please?"

"No. I have to stay with Stella."

"If she's in labor, we need to call Joseph. He'll call the vet. There's no better way to help Stella than to get the doctor here." She looked at her phone to find the ranch manager's number.

"No. Don't call him." Kinsley had a hand on the horse's left rear flank, rubbing soothingly. "He'll get mad at me."

"I don't know a lot about horses, but I can see that her ears are pulled back. She looks nervous. I wonder what that means." *I think it means she's pissed and is about to go equine on you.*

"I don't know."

The horse stomped a foot and switched its tail.

Grace was done waiting. She stepped into the stall, whisked the little girl into her arms, and quickly got out. She set her down but kept a firm grip on her hand as they hurried out of the barn. "That was scary. Okay, let's get you home." As she headed to the nearest search party, she found her text chain with Jaime and tapped the microphone icon. "Hey, I've got Kinsley. I'm bringing her to Joseph, okay?"

Once the girl was in safe hands, she headed home. After the festival, she'd stopped at the gourmet store for supplies. So, as soon as she brought the groceries inside, she called her favorite person in the world and recapped what had just happened.

"What the hell?" her brother asked.

"I know. I couldn't believe it."

"The kid grew up on a ranch. How does she not know shit like that?" Romeo sounded as upset as she'd been, and he hadn't even lived through it.

But that was the thing about her brother. He was all swagger and badassery, but deep down, he was real, sensitive. Compassionate.

"I have no idea, but listen, Mom told me you punched Ian."

"Yeah. And he deserves a whole lot worse."

"He deserves something, all right. But it's not violence. That's not going to solve anything."

"That fucker was my best friend. He hurt my family... my *sister*. I take that shit personally."

"Fair point. In any event, it's over. And I'm going to earn enough this summer to pay Mom and Dad back."

"See? That's why I'm so pissed. You're thinking about Mom and Dad before yourself. You're a good person, and I want to punch Ian into next week."

Just the act of pulling out the heavy cream and vanilla beans kicked her imagination into gear. She needed to get to work. "Okay, listen, I've got to go. I've been on my feet all day—"

"Yeah, I know. We saw it."

"Saw what?"

"Mom was looking up Calamity, and there's a picture of you singing right there on the town's website. Here." He went quiet for a moment, and then her phone pinged with a text message. "Check it out."

She clicked on the link he sent her. There she was, leaning out of her truck to hand a little girl a cream puff. Her mouth was wide open, so she was clearly singing. "This is crazy." The headline billed her as the Singing Baker, just as Brodie had promised.

"I'll let you go but look at the comment section. People are lovin' you."

She scanned it. "I can't believe what they're saying."

"Right?" Her brother sounded proud. "Kickin' ass, as always. Love you. Talk to you later."

After she disconnected, she read some more.

Swear to God, she sounds just like Lorelei Calloway! But those pastries—they're the prettiest things I've ever seen.

She better not give up baking to become a singer. This woman knows how to cook.

I had a cannoli, and I'm telling you, that cream filling is like manna from the gods.

Forget the music festival—go for the food. Especially the Singing Baker! Her magical pastries are to die for!

Emotion flooded her. Sure, people loved Renzo's, but a

muffin was a muffin. To be celebrated for the gifts of her heart? It was *inspiring*. She couldn't wait to get to work.

She'd been dreaming of panna cotta, sandwiched between a pistachio crust and a rose jelly. She'd visualized bits of nuts and dried red rose petals sprinkled across the top. Doing a quick inventory, she saw she had all the ingredients—including the caster sugar, gelatin, dried edible flowers, and rosewater essence. *Awesome.*

Also, she wanted to do a strawberry tart with lemon mascarpone. Her mouth watered at the idea of that tart and creamy filling. She loved lemon anything.

Transported to a place of pure sensory pleasure, Grace got lost in the scent of warm butter, the taste of macerated strawberries, and the connections that fired between her taste buds and her mind as she anticipated which flavor would enhance another.

So, when someone knocked at the door, she jerked so hard, she knocked the carton of whipping cream to the floor. Who on earth could be stopping by this late at night?

At least I'm not singing, so it can't be a noise complaint.

Drying her hands on a towel, she called, "Coming."

Could be Joseph. Possibly Abby or Kate. *Oh, come on. You know exactly who you want it to be.* She was like a kid on Christmas morning who was afraid she wouldn't get the one gift she wanted more than anything.

But she did. She got it. Excitement exploded in her chest at the sight of Jaime filling her doorway with his bad boy energy, muscled chest, and broad shoulders.

"If you tell me my mixer's waking anybody up, we're going to have to move me into the Dream House." She was only joking, of course, but man, could she use a kitchen like that.

"Nah. You're good." He peered around her. "What's cooking tonight?"

"Do you want to see?"

"No. That's all right."

Why did this man deny himself the things he most wanted to do? It didn't make sense.

She noted the perspiration plastering his messy hair to his forehead and the taped stick in one hand and duffel bag in the other. "I thought you stopped playing hockey?"

"I did." He set his gear down on the welcome mat so he could swipe the damp hair out of his eyes. "I help out the forwards sometimes. Hey, listen. Sorry to come by so late, but I saw your light on."

"Of course."

"I wanted to thank you for finding Kinsley." A flash of guilt cracked through his stoic demeanor. "I was on the ice and didn't see my phone till I finished."

"Yeah, it was scary. I came home to a whole search party out there."

"Told you. She's always been this way. Gets a thought in her head and just goes."

"You need to embed a chip in her."

He smiled. "Believe me, we've thought about it." That sexy grin exposed three dimples. One under his left eye and two bracketing his expressive mouth.

He'd only grinned at her like this once before, and that was when they were in bed. And that simple thought was all it took to deliver a memory of his hand cupping her neck as he reared over her, thrusting, never taking his eyes off her. A shiver passed through her. *Would you stop it?* "Who was watching her tonight?"

"It's not my mom's fault." He reached for his stick, his tone going hard.

Crap. She'd been preoccupied with the naked version of him. "No, I didn't mean it like that. I was just wondering what happened that sent her to the barn."

He nodded, his shoulders relaxing. "I guess she overheard my mom on the phone talking about Stella going into labor."

"I nearly had a heart attack when I saw her standing behind that horse." She pressed a hand to her chest. "Scared the life out of me."

A bead of perspiration trickled down his temple, and he brushed it away. "Yeah, I'll bet." He glanced down at his sneakers. "She's too damn reckless." His gaze swung up until those intense gray-blue eyes found hers. "If I don't watch her like a hawk, she'll run wild. It's easy to get into trouble out here."

"I can't even imagine. With the animals and—" Her nose caught a hint of something just on the edge of overcooking. "Oops." She dashed to the oven and pulled out a tray of tarts.

"Everything okay?" He came up behind her. "They look perfect."

"They are." She tipped one up so she could see the bottom. "I caught them just in time."

"How did you know? I didn't hear a timer go off."

"Ah, well, my nose is a better judge than a timer. I can smell when something's ready."

He seemed confused. "You serious?"

"Totally."

He took in the cooling racks. "I don't know how you manage to bake all this in that tiny oven."

"It's not the ideal situation, but you won't hear me complain."

"You should use the Dream House's kitchen."

What did this man just say to me? "No way. You're saving it for your parents."

"It's sitting there empty now. Might as well give it some use." He didn't even seem uneasy about it.

"I don't want to ruin it for your mom."

"If she wanted to use it, she would. Even for family reunions, she still cooks at home."

Which brought up the obvious… "Why don't you and Kinny live there?"

There was that flinch of guilt again. How odd. What was keeping him from living in that gorgeous, empty house?

"Trust me, if I'm in there, then my mom will never move. Deep down, I think she's afraid we'll lose everything again, and she doesn't want to get attached to something that will be taken away from her. But in any event, you've seen the kitchen. It's got two of everything and plenty of room." He gestured to the cooling racks that covered every surface.

Even though the house didn't have enough furniture, the kitchen was complete. It would make her life so much easier to bake there. She nudged his sneaker with her bare foot. "I thought you wanted to keep your distance from me."

His gaze dropped to her toes, making her glad she'd put on a fresh coat of hot pink polish. "I've got no reason to be there."

"Yeah, but the more you let me into your world, the more time we'll spend together. You don't want that."

He held her gaze a little too long, and it gave her time to imagine being in his kitchen. Given their chemistry, how long would it take before things heated up between them? She could picture him coming up from behind, wrapping his arms around her waist and pressing his erection against her. His hands cupping her breasts. How soon before they'd be naked, going at it on the counter?

"Your choice." He gave a shrug like it was no big deal.

But she was better able to read him now. What she'd thought was disinterest was stillness. It was almost like if he dared move a muscle, he'd stir up emotions. This man was working very hard to restrain himself.

That must be exhausting. Well, he'd made an offer, and since he didn't live there, she couldn't reject it. "I'm not going to say no," she said. "But you were very clear with your expectations. You've been incredibly generous. I don't want to do anything that will make you uncomfortable."

He was acting so nonchalant it was almost funny.

Until she realized *what* he was suppressing—his feelings for her. But why couldn't he let himself have a little fun? It was just for a summer. Even as she thought it, though, she knew the answer. With them, it was explosive. And not just their sexual chemistry.

Their connection was crazy—such a rush of energy between them.

We could be so good together.

"I wouldn't offer if I didn't think it would work. I'm never there, so I don't see a problem."

"That's true. And honestly, I'm not in a position to be polite about this. I do need the space, so thank you. I appreciate it more than you know."

He rapped his knuckles on the counter as if to conclude their conversation. But he didn't go anywhere. "How's it going?"

"It's fantastic. But…" Her cheeks went hot. "You won't believe who's been coming by my truck every day." She paused. "Lorelei Calloway."

"No shit." He broke into a big grin. "She heard you singing?"

She nodded. "I'm mortified."

"Why? You have a great voice. If I closed my eyes, I wouldn't know the difference between the two of you."

"At first, she thought I came to the festival to get discovered. Can you imagine? She actually dressed up in disguise and waited in line so she could confront me."

"That kind of shit probably happens to her all the time. She's been famous since she was a kid. You explained your situation, right?"

"What? That I'm a runaway bride whose ex wiped out her savings so I'm spending the summer in a tiny cabin on the ranch of the groomsman I banged?" She laughed. "No, I didn't really get into all that."

A dark pink stained his cheeks. "Yeah, you could probably skip the runaway bride part. The banging's good, though. That'll get her attention."

She laughed, and there it was. All that energy came flooding in, hot and electric. *This is why he keeps the door locked so tightly. We're combustible.* "Her tour bus is right behind me, so I haven't been singing as much. It's too weird when she's the artist-in-residence."

"Hey." He leaned closer and cupped her chin. "Does singing make you happy?"

Mesmerized by the intensity of his gaze and his commanding tone, she could only whisper, "You know it does." *Slide that hand lower, scrape those calloused fingers down my neck. Reach into my shirt and cup my breast. Just like you did a week ago.*

Every single thing you did to me, I want you to do again.

Her body went up in flames.

She had to stop doing this. He'd made himself clear. He

didn't want a second round. Forcing herself back to the conversation, she said, "Even better, it draws the customers. You should see the line for my truck."

"I did."

"You've been there?" Had he come specifically to see her? A thrill ripped through her.

He shook his head. "You're on the cover of the *Gazette*. My mom drove around town and grabbed as many copies as she could find."

"For me?"

He nodded.

"Are you serious? That's so sweet. Why would she do that?"

"She likes you." His gaze cut away.

"I feel like there's more you're not telling me?"

"She worries about you. She knows how easy it is to lose your individuality when the family business is the sole source of income."

"She said that?" It hit her right in the solar plexus. The impact radiated all the way to her fingertips, making them tingle. No one...not one single Giordano had ever acknowledged the simple, obvious fact. Because it was a given. A way of life.

Just hearing the words, though...*losing your individuality for the sake of the family business...*

God.

Yes.

And she couldn't even say she'd realized it on her own, but it was absolutely true.

She was a team player, so she'd never gotten to become her own woman.

And that's why this summer matters so much. I'm coming into my own, finding out who I am.

"It was one of her biggest challenges," he continued. "Knowing they couldn't survive without our help but also wanting us to be true to ourselves."

"Abby credits you for finding a way to allow everyone to live their dreams but also stay here on the ranch."

"Yeah, well..." Contemplative, he thumbed his lower lip. "I wasn't the best role model, and my siblings were *not* on good paths. My parents had enough to worry about, so I tried to help them find...compromises, I guess."

"Abby said you sent her to art school."

"I didn't send her. That's what she chose."

"But your parents wouldn't have paid for it. They said it wasn't practical. So, you did. With your own money. And then you found a way for her to do art on the ranch."

"Well, we needed merch."

She doubted that very much, but she loved this side of him. The one that was kind, caring, generous, and sweet. *Oh, brother.* If she had a chance in hell of keeping this crush under control, then she needed him to get moody real quick. "That's funny because Abby told me you created the shop just for her. But nice try going with the whole badass mountain man thing you've got going here."

"I'm not trying to be anything." He chuckled. "I really am a badass mountain man." He turned his attention to the lemon tarts. "These are pretty."

In this cozy space scented with lemon and baking dough, she just felt so close to him, like she'd known him forever. "They taste even better." She picked one up and brought it to his mouth.

He reared back. "No, thanks."

"This again, really? Can't you just take one bite to see if you like what I make?"

"I'll like anything you do, but dessert's just not my thing."

"Because one lemon tart is like all the others."

"I'm sure yours are better, but it's empty calories."

"And you don't do anything unless it has a purpose."

He didn't answer, just held her gaze as if plundering the depths of her soul, looking for every piece of her. She got the sense that when this man committed, he went all-in. If he ever did tear down his walls, he would find out who she was and what she wanted and then, spend his life giving it to her.

She never knew until this moment how much she wanted—no, needed—to be that important to someone. That special. *Too bad it won't be him.* "Well, something's not adding up. Your mom said you had a wicked sweet tooth."

"I did. As a kid. But when you're dedicated to a sport, you learn to field the distractions so you can focus on what matters."

"So, in this plan of yours, is there no room to indulge yourself?"

"The less temptation, the better."

That was the second time he'd used that word. And it was all she needed to stop playing around with him. She set the tart down. "Okay. Well, I should get back to work. I need to double what I made today."

"If there's anything you need—"

"No." She'd taken enough from him. "You've set me up to make a ton of money this summer, I'm living here rent-free, you've loaned me a car...I'm all set. You don't need to worry about me anymore."

With a curt nod, he pushed away from the counter.

She regretted shutting him down like that, but it had to

be done. He said he wanted to keep his distance, and she chose to believe what a man told her.

"Better get home. Who knows what ideas got into Kinny's head today? I once read her a book about bats, and in the middle of the night, I heard her little feet hurrying down the hallway. I caught her before she got far, but she'd decided she had to go outside and see them for herself."

She walked him to the door. "I'll tell you, though. She was genuinely concerned about Stella."

"Yeah, I know. Like I said, she's not sneaky or rebellious. She's a good kid. I just have to get her impulsive nature under control. Get her to understand self-discipline."

"I'm not sure you can change her nature."

"I changed mine." He grew thoughtful. "Well, maybe not my nature. It's something I have to be diligent about. But honestly, my parents didn't rein me in. They let me raise hell, and I'm not doing that to Kinsley. I'm going to teach her self-control. Life will be a lot easier for her that way."

She thought about Kinsley standing behind a horse. "So, this plan of yours to change her nature, does that mean no horseback riding?"

"Exactly." He seemed relieved that she understood. "Can you imagine if I let her get near them?"

"Except she's growing up on a ranch where the primary mode of transportation is horses. And your mom's a riding instructor, so she could teach Kinsley how to handle them. I mean, I grew up on the ocean, and I can promise you, my parents introduced us to water safety from the time we were born."

"I can't risk it. Not when she's this impulsive."

"I guess you got hurt a lot growing up here, so you would know best."

He looked away, eyelids fluttering closed for a moment. "No. I was lucky."

There was something in his tone, but she couldn't quite figure it out. "But your friend did, right? Pretty badly."

He gave a curt nod. "Booker." Emotion darkened his features.

"So, you saw what happened to him and realized how dangerous it was, the stuff you guys were doing?"

"No, that's not it at all." He tugged on his scruff. "I *caused* his accident."

"I thought it happened when you went BASE jumping?" Unless he pushed his friend off a cliff, how could it be his fault? "Is he okay?"

"He went through some pretty intense rehab, but he's recovered. He's got a good career." He hunched a shoulder. "That's what I hear anyway. I haven't seen him since."

"Are you saying he blames you for what happened?" They all jumped together...how could Booker be angry about what happened?

"Of course, he does. He never played hockey again. I took that from him."

"You guys were teenagers, having fun together. I can't see how anything was your fault."

"Well, it was. I was a selfish prick back then, and I'm trying not to be. And I'm doing my best to make sure Kinny learns self-discipline before she gets herself—or anyone else—into trouble."

Moved by his outburst, she stepped closer. "I don't buy it for a second. I've known you all of a week, and I can tell you're the most generous man I know. And you're obviously a great father. Besides, even if it was your fault—which I just can't see—you can't punish yourself for something you did as a teenager. All kids are selfish."

"Maybe, but I took everything to the extreme."

"Oh, boy." More pieces of the Jaime Dupree puzzle fell into place. He was living a life of penance for what happened that night. "I'm a hundred-percent sure you were a boy full of energy with a lust for life. If your parents didn't try to tame you, it was because they loved your spirit. And trust me, I've gotten to experience it firsthand." She only meant to tease him about their hot night together, but electricity arced between them. "I really have to stop doing that."

"Doing what?"

"Bringing up our one-night stand." She tried to shake off the stream of desire, but it was like holding back the tide. It rushed through her. "All right. You're way too hard on yourself, but fortunately, there's a cure for it. Here." She picked up a cooled tart. "Your first indulgence in a decade. Try this. It's mango puree, and it's so good you're going to weep."

He cracked a grin. "Crying's for wimps."

"Trust me. One bite and all your troubles will melt away." She brought the round tart to his mouth.

"See, that's my point. I don't have any troubles. I make sure of it." But he caught her wrist and took a bite. His lips brushed her fingertips—all soft and warm. While he chewed, he looked right into her eyes, almost defiantly, like proving her food would have no impact on him.

But then, he made a dramatic show of buckling his knees and reaching for the counter. "Holy shit."

"It's good, right?"

"It's unbelievable." He gazed into her eyes so deeply, she almost heard, *You're unbelievable.*

Dear God, she loved the way he looked at her with a message that told her she was a marvel.

"Rosie's right," he said. "You're a sorcerer, and I'm leaving before you cast any more spells on me." This time, he turned abruptly and walked away.

Watching him go hurt. Because he'd given her something she'd never had before. And now that she had it, she knew she could never go back to a relationship like she'd had with Ian.

They could be so good together. If only—

Oh, no, you don't. You don't fall for a man's potential.

He thought he needed to suppress his passionate, balls-to-the-walls personality in order to be a good, responsible adult. But one day, a woman would come along he wanted so badly, he'd go all Hulk on the walls he'd built to protect himself.

He'd love her so wildly he wouldn't have the strength to restrain himself.

That'll be one lucky woman.

But it won't be me.

Chapter Eight

"Carissa got these black boots, Daddy, and they're so cool. You should see them. They're shiny. I'm going to invite her over. Can we go swimming?"

Jaime loved his mornings with his little girl. While they ate breakfast, she'd talk his ear off. "You mean here or the lake?" Now, just finishing, he stood at the sink rinsing their plates.

"If we go to the lake, she won't wear her boots, so I want her to come here and swim in the pool."

"She's welcome to come over, but why don't you just ask if you can see her boots? Why are we inventing a fake occasion?"

"What's a fake cajun?"

"Kinny. Do you want to go swimming or see her boots?" Like the idiot he was, he watched out the window, hoping for a glimpse of Grace. Why, he had no idea. She had one of the first cabins. She wouldn't wander this far into the woods unless she was specifically looking for him.

Look for me, Grace.

He had the strangest sensation of being trapped—and he

needed her to find him. To reach in and pull him out. *Find me.*

"I want to see her boots," Kinny said.

"Is she going swimming in her boots?"

"Daddy." With her milk mustache, his daughter cracked up. "You don't swim in boots."

"That's my point. You're making up a reason for her to come over instead of just saying, 'Hey, Carissa, can I see your boots?'"

His phone vibrated, and he saw his GM's name on the screen. He picked it up but only to shoot him a text.

Jaime: Getting Kinsley off to daycare. Call you in ten.

"Did I tell you we couldn't play outside yesterday?" Kinny asked. "It rained."

He supposed the boot conversation was over. "That's too bad."

"Yeah, first, we went outside. But then it got dark and scary, and it started raining really hard, and everyone ran inside. Except me. I stayed outside and watched the rain come down. Look." She got down off her chair so she could stand and tip her head back. "I did like this. See, Daddy?"

Watching, he mimicked her stance. "Like this?"

"Yes, just like that. So, I could see raindrops falling from the sky. I wanted to get it in my mouth to see what it tasted like, but it got in my eyes and made them sting. Like this." She raced over to him and attacked him with her little fingernails. "Does that sting?"

"It does. Is that what your eyes felt like with rain falling in them?"

"Yes."

"So, was it worth it? To watch it rain if you wound up getting hurt?"

She gave it some thought, then nodded with the sincerest expression. "Yes, Daddy. It didn't hurt that bad."

"Well, then, next time it rains, I'll look up at the sky, too. Just to see what it's like."

He pulled her lunch box out of the fridge. "Now, go brush your teeth."

As she skipped away, he called his GM. "I only have a minute. What's up?"

"I only want a minute. This is just a heads-up to let you know I put you on the reserve list."

"What?" He must've misheard. It made no sense.

"I don't like the report I got back from Korzak's PT."

"Okay, well, if he can't play, we'll bring someone up from the minors. But you can't put *me* on the reserve list. I'm the owner."

"There's not one player in the minors or on our own roster who's better than you, and we can't afford to head into this season with our top goalie injured."

"I don't play hockey."

"You get more time on the ice than most professional players. But that's beside the point. We've got sixty-three players on the list, and we're allowed ninety. It costs us nothing to have you there. All right, I've got to take this call. I'm sending over a contract. Sign it."

Jaime wasn't about to get all worked up over a situation that would never happen. Of all the goalies they could call up, it sure as hell wouldn't be him. He continued cleaning the kitchen until he heard Kinsley trample down the stairs.

"Ready," she called.

"Oh, it's you." He greeted her at the bottom, handing off her backpack. "I thought it was a herd of elephants."

"Daddy!" Her eyes lit up. "Oh, when I get home, will you read me The Large Family?" She loved the series about a family of elephants.

"You bet."

"All of the books? Every single one?"

"Like I'd leave one out?" His favorite time of day was when she got home. He always made dinner early so he could hang out with her, do whatever struck her fancy, and basically be the receptacle for the barrage of thoughts swirling around her beautiful mind.

Together, they walked down the driveway. A ranch hand drove by in a golf cart. He slowed to high-five Kinsley. Another guy jumped off his tractor to run over and give her a quick spin in the air. Miss Martha came out of the henhouse with a basket of eggs. She blew kisses and shouted, "Have a great day!"

His girl was loved. If he'd done anything right in his life, it was raising his curious, smart, big-hearted daughter.

The bus roared down the road, and he picked up his daughter and gave her a big hug. "I love you."

"I love you more, Daddy. After school, can I go to Gracie's house and have a treat?"

"I thought we were reading?"

"I have to have a *snack*."

"We have plenty of our own. Besides, Grace's going to be at work then."

"Can you ask her to leave me something?"

"I've got a better idea. Why don't we go to the music festival tonight and grab some dinner? For dessert, you can get one of her pastries."

"Yes." But then, her excitement withered. "Do I have to eat something good for me?"

"At a festival? Heck no. You can have a greasy burger or a slimy hot dog or anything that catches your fancy."

"Thank you, Daddy."

"You got it." He kissed her on the cheek and set her down.

As the bus slowed, the brakes squealed. When the doors whooshed open, Kinny climbed the stairs. She stopped midway and turned back to him. "I like Gracie, Daddy."

"Yeah. Me, too."

"I hope she stays forever." She disappeared into the bus.

Unease twisted through him. He stood there for a moment, watching the bus rumble on down the road. When it was out of sight, he started back up the driveway.

He had to be careful because Kinsley got confused.

A woman is nice to her, and she wants to keep her.

Well, we're not keeping Grace.

Dammit. It'd be nice to keep her.

He'd get to see that smile every day. Every morning, he'd come into the kitchen to watch her dancing with a whisk in her hand.

For one moment, he allowed himself to imagine a life like that, one so full and complete. Kinsley, his family, this ranch...and Grace. This feeling took over—one so unbearably happy that he smacked it down. There was no point in wasting his energy on something that would never happen.

As he approached his house, he saw a familiar black Land Rover. Cole Montgomery stood on his porch, stick in one hand, duffel bag in the other.

The hit of satisfaction had him quickening his pace. To have his friends back after ten years of feeling like he'd ruined their lives...it was the best. "You're the highest-paid forward in the NHL. What're you bothering me for? Bored of domestic life already?" Not even a year ago, his friend had taken over the care of two little girls. Lucky for him, the co-guardian wound up being the love of his life, and now, the foursome was a family.

"Hey, man, I left a tea party with chocolate chip cookies to hang out with you, so it won't take much to send me back home."

"I hear you. So, what's up?" He tipped his chin to the hockey stick.

"I want to work on my game."

Everyone, no matter their level, needed practice. It was too easy to fall into patterns, and once a player did that, the opposing team could anticipate his every move. "Gotcha." Jaime moved past him to get into his cabin. "Let me change." He gestured to the kitchen while he headed up the stairs. "Grab a coffee or whatever you want. There're some pancakes left in the skillet."

"Pancakes? Oh, man." Cole grabbed one off a plate and took a bite. "These are good. You got a recipe? Mine are shit."

"You've got to separate the eggs and the whites," he called from his bedroom.

"Since when?"

"Since you don't want shit pancakes."

As he pulled off his shirt and kicked off his jeans, he became aware of his friend's silence. He peered over the balcony to find Cole with his hands on his hips, looking around. "What's up?"

"Why do you live here?" Cole sounded confused.

"What do you mean? Why am I still on the ranch?" He could live anywhere, he supposed. Kinny would love Wild Wolff Village, which went all-out for the holidays, had an ice-skating rink, and cocoa and crepe kiosks. Plus, it had a full-time concierge service for the residents. Or he could live in town, but that got pretty crowded during tourist season. "My kid doesn't have a mom, so I'm trying to give her family. She sees her grandparents, her uncles, her aunt—one of them—every day. It's good."

"No, I mean, why in this tiny cabin? Why don't you build a house for you and Kinny?"

"Ah, man. I just built one for my parents. I need a break. Contractors and vendors are no joke."

"But it's so small, you and Kinny must be on top of each other. Don't you need some space? You don't even have an office."

"I have one at the stadium." As far as his daughter, he supposed when she got older, she'd want more privacy. "It's fine for now. It works for us." Once dressed, he came back down the stairs. Since he helped out at the Juniors', Renegades', and his own private rinks, he kept his gear in the car. So, when they headed outside, he grabbed his stick and bag from the trunk. "We'll work on your deception and your quick releases."

To an outsider, it looked like any other big red barn on a ranch, but it was actually a full-size skating rink.

Was it an indulgence? Yeah, of course. But every time he got called away to work with someone, it was time away from his daughter. So, it had just made sense—once he had the money—to build one here.

It cut down on travel time, massively.

He heard tires crunching on gravel and turned to see Grace pulling her borrowed car into the spot in front of her cabin. As soon as she got out, she popped the trunk, and both he and Cole jogged over to help unload her groceries.

"No, that's okay." She tried to block them, but she must've had fifty bags.

"It's no problem. I got it." Arms loaded, he pulled back from the trunk and tipped his head toward his friend. "Grace Giordano, this is Cole Montgomery. He's our new forward."

She flashed that dazzling grin, and Jaime was unreasonably jealous. "Oh, man, I can't imagine the hate mail you must be getting. How could you leave Boston? We're the most loyal fans on the planet."

"You're a fan, huh?" Cole grinned. "What's a woman from Beantown doing on a bull ranch?"

Jaime whacked him. "You want to get these bags inside so we can get to work? Or you want to flirt with a woman who isn't your fiancée?"

Cole gave him the strangest look but walked into the cabin. As usual, her pastries covered every surface in the cabin. "Whoa. You've been busy." Since there was no counter space, Cole set his bags on the floor. One bag was filled with nothing but egg cartons. "And you're making more?"

"Jaime's been kind enough to let me use the kitchen in the big house. That's why I bought all these groceries. Thanks to him, I'm going to be making even more."

"You run a bakery?" Cole asked.

"I've got a truck at the music festival this summer."

"My girls love sweets," Cole said. "We'll come by Saturday morning."

"Wait. Take them these." Grace stood on her toes to reach a high shelf. She couldn't quite grasp the cardboard takeaway boxes, so Jaime came up behind her.

Between the whiff of her shampoo and the heat of her skin, his head began to spin. It brought him back to the night of the gala, their naked bodies pressed together. *Fuck. This is not good.* He grabbed the boxes and handed them off to her. "Here." Looking into her eyes…it made him ache. It stirred up a longing that made no sense. They'd only had one night together. "Sorry. I should've given you a key. After I work with him, I'll come back and help you carry all this over to the house."

"That's okay. Joseph loaned me a golf cart."

"I'm coming back with the key in an hour. You can argue with me then."

She smiled, and it ripped a hole right through him. Longing flooded him. He turned and strode past Cole. "Let's go."

Once they got outside into the early morning sunshine, Cole said, "What the hell was that?"

"What?" The fog that had settled over the valley hadn't burned off yet. The grass glistened with dew, and a thin layer of white cloud hovered over the pasture.

"You and Grace."

Well, fuck. He thought he was ace at locking things down. It hadn't occurred to him that his attraction was that obvious. And if Cole picked it up, that meant Grace did, too. Which explained her frustration with him. He was confusing her. "She ran from her wedding, needed a place to get away. Brodie gave her a food truck, so she's staying in my cabin for the summer." It wasn't fair to her. He had to get a handle on things. For starters, he'd have Joseph give her the key. The more he stayed away—which had been the original plan—the better for them both.

"Bullshit."

Jaime let out an awkward laugh. "What does that mean?" As they passed the arena, a ranch hand dragged the dirt with a tractor, getting ready for his mom's riding classes. "Trust me, there's nothing more to it than that."

"How'd you get in the path of a runaway bride?"

He didn't want to tell the story. "You remember Ian Adler?" Because he'd look like an asshole.

He wanted to be better than that.

"No."

At the barn, Jaime punched in the code. The gears whirred and then the lock opened. "The Rhode Island guy who used to come out to the dude ranch every summer?"

"Oh, yeah." Cole followed him into the rink. "The one who kept inviting you sailing?"

"That's the one." He'd never been able to afford it. Only when he'd turned the ranch around did he finally go. That was when he'd gotten his first glimpse of Grace. "Well, she was the bride in that wedding I just went to. I was his groomsman."

"You hooked up with Ian's...ex-fiancée?" Cole sounded confused.

He dropped his bag. "Yes." He looked to Cole for a reaction.

But Cole was busy sitting down on a bench and kicking off his worn sneakers. "No wonder you look so torn up." He pulled out his skates. "You've got a thing for your friend's girl. Did she run because of you?"

"No. Of course not. Ian stole from her and her parents." Jaime sat beside him and pulled his skates out of his bag. "They've been together fifteen years, and she can't get past the betrayal. She's done with him."

"Okay, but what about you?"

"I'm done, too. Absolutely. I talked to him, and he admitted what he did. Doesn't seem to get how badly he fucked them over. Thinks they can get past it."

"That's not what I'm talking about. You obviously have feelings for her."

What could he say to that? He could keep fighting

himself, pretending it was a hook-up like all the others…
or he could get real. "I do. But nothing's going to
happen."

"Why not? She's here for the summer. And I saw the way
she looked at you."

"How's that?" He shouldn't be so on edge to hear the
answer. Because it didn't matter.

"The same way Evvie would look at one of those
pastries."

Yeah, he guessed he knew that. The way she responded
to him was part of the attraction, the thing that got him all
worked up. But Cole didn't need to hear it. "Can you blame
her?" He pointed to himself.

Tying his skate, Cole grinned. "The sparks were flyin'.
That's all I'm saying."

"Yeah, well, I'm a father. Would you bring random
women around Paisley and Evvie?"

"Hell, no." Cole grinned. "Hailey would kick my ass."

"I meant if you didn't have Hailey, asshole."

"Sorry, man. I'm not going to imagine my life without
her. But I will say, I've dated a lot of women in my life, and I
didn't feel jack shit for any of them. But with Hailey—I
knew."

It was like fitting a puzzle piece into the right spot, the
connection, the click…the sense of rightness. "Like I said,
she's leaving at the end of summer."

"I hear you, man." Skates tied, Cole stood. "If you're
coming up with excuses, then she's not your girl."

"I just told you she's not staying."

"I heard you. But I lived in Boston, and Hailey lived in
New York, and I can tell you right now, nothing would've
kept me from trying to make it work with her. I was not
letting that woman go."

"It's different. Grace has to go back to her family's business." Jaime grabbed his stick and followed Cole.

"Like I said, when you meet the woman you can't live without, you won't be saying shit like that."

For a solid hour, Cole fired pucks. Jaime was in the zone, guarding the net with everything he had, so he might not have noticed the shard of light in his peripheral vision. He would've blocked it out had it not been for Cole's reaction.

His friend's concentration broke, and his whole being perked up to welcome his family. Jaime had to set his stick down and watch.

His friend skated to the edge of the rink and stepped out, dropping to his knees as both daughters ran straight to him. His hand hit the rubber behind him to keep from toppling over, but then he was hugging them tightly, whispering in their ears, unable to hide his enormous grin. Hailey joined them, wrapping her arms around the trio. They were a ball of joy and love.

It knocked Jaime on his ass. He couldn't say why. He had that kind of love with his own daughter, so it wasn't jealousy.

And yet, how could he explain the ache in his chest as Cole got up, carrying both girls, and the four of them clung together, talking like they hadn't seen each other in a year.

Jaime didn't want to be married. And yet...this yearning...

He squeezed his eyes shut, willing it to stop.

Because he *did* want that.

He wanted a mom for Kinsley, and for him, he wanted the kind of trust and intimacy his parents had. Hell, he loved being a dad so much, he'd like more kids.

He'd just never wanted a woman the way Cole wanted Hailey.

And Cole was right. The timing *had* been terrible when he'd reunited with Hailey, and yet he'd flipped his life upside down for her and those kids. He'd left Boston, left the Brawlers, and started a new life—all for love.

So, maybe one day...when Jaime met the right woman.

He ignored the whisper from deep inside that said, *You already have.*

Because it was different with Grace.

She could never live in Calamity, and he could never leave.

This is ridiculous.

Jaime threw back the covers, got up, and slammed his window shut. Ever since Grace had moved in, the smell of her baking wafted in and woke him up. It had only gotten worse when she'd taken over the big house's kitchen.

Bullshit.

He couldn't sleep because he couldn't stop thinking about her. Wanting her. He could try to avoid her. He could remind himself a thousand times a day how impossible a relationship was with her, but nothing stopped his body from its wretched desire to be with her.

And all because he knew what it was like to run his hands all over her smooth skin and taste her mouth, her fingers, and the slick heat between her legs. To hear the sounds she made as he licked inside her and found that hard little nub that made her cry out.

To know the feel of her tongue licking his cock.

Fuck my life.

All he wanted was to avoid temptation, and what did he do? He'd invited it onto his ranch.

Mashing his face into the pillow while rubbing the heel of his hand on his dick, he squeezed his eyes shut.

Screw it. He got out of bed, checked on his daughter, and quietly went downstairs. Just to be safe, he pulled the old baby monitor out of the cabinet and plugged it in. Then, he stepped outside.

He'd done a lot of landscaping on the Dream House to make it feel isolated from the bunkhouse, the cabins, the barns and corrals. He'd wanted it to feel like an oasis, a retreat. Trees and bushes surrounded it, but if he stood right *here,* he could see through the foliage to the kitchen windows.

And there she was. Grace shaking her ass and swinging her glossy dark hair to the beat.

He found himself on the move, his need for her more powerful than his ability to resist. The closer he got, the better the view. This woman just seemed to love life. Fuck the wedding that never happened, fuck the savings gone in the tap of a button, and fuck losing the man she'd known for fifteen years.

Gracie Giordano was doing what she loved. This woman was *happy.*

No wonder her pastries taste so good.

And then, it struck him. *I used to be just like that.*

The revelation landed hard. He loved his daughter and his family more than he could say, and he sure as hell appreciated this life he'd worked so hard for.

But that kind of deep-down, unfettered happiness?

It had ended the night he stole Booker's dreams.

He knocked on the French door. As she swung around, she saw him standing there and jerked to a stop. *"Jaime."* Hurriedly, she came to let him in. "Why do you love scaring me half to death?" She pulled out the ear pods.

"Sorry." He followed her into the kitchen.

"Did I wake you?" As she pulled a cake pan out of the oven, she glanced at the clock. "I didn't think anyone could hear me."

"They can't. I can smell what you're baking." *I'd be aware of you if you were on the moon.*

"Oh, I see. So, now my cooking's too loud." She grinned. "Got it. I'll try to keep it down."

"I'm a light sleeper. You know, always got an ear out for my daughter."

"Yeah, the little sneak. And you left her alone?" She pretended to be alarmed.

He held up the monitor, aware it was a little over-the-top for four in the morning. His daughter slept soundly through the night.

She laughed. "Of course. Do you have invisible lasers pointing in every direction, setting off alarms like in some *Mission Impossible* movie?"

See, this? This kind of easy, fun conversation was deceiving. It seemed simple, just the way people chatted. But with Gracie, it was so much more. All his cylinders were firing, sparking, revving. There was a connection between them he'd never had with anyone else. "What a great idea. I'll get on it." He liked teasing her. "Trust me, for four years, I've slept with one eye open, ready to see the flash of her nightgown running by. She's always off on a mission."

"She doesn't get scared sleeping in a little cabin in the woods?"

Affection bloomed for his little girl. "Actually, she loves it because she gets to see the entire ranch. I built a balcony for her, and she likes to dress up like a princess and survey her land. You should see her with her plastic tiara and wand." He caught her grinning at him. "What?"

"She's a lucky girl."

"Oh, yeah. Growing up on this ranch…there's nothing like it."

"No, I mean to have you as a dad."

"I don't know about that. I mean, I try. But I have to make up for the fact that her mom's not around."

"And didn't want her to begin with. That must be a hard story to explain to a little girl."

"She'll never find out about that. The only thing she'll know is her grandparents loved her, and she's got my whole heart."

"Oh, I have no doubt her confidence comes from knowing how much she's loved. Does she ask about her mom?"

"She has, once or twice, but it's complicated. Kinsley's got no memory of her, and I'm not sure she's old enough to ask the kinds of questions an adult would want to know. But our family has a cemetery, so I made a headstone for her. We walk over there a couple of times a year so Kinsley can talk to her mom in heaven."

"That's really beautiful." And then she shook her head. "I can't figure you out. On the one hand, you're superhero handsome, but then, I think you're more like the biker version with the tats and the scruff and the growly voice. Most of the time, you're all hard and serious, and then, you tell me something like this, and I think, God, you're such a sweetheart. Like, who are you?"

"I'm a man trying to fix his past mistakes." He pushed off the counter, grabbed a glass from the cabinet, and poured himself water. "I'm a dad trying to raise my daughter to be responsible and disciplined. Luckily, I'm not in this alone. I've got my family here, and my mom and sister pick up the slack because I can't change the fact that she's never going to have a mother." It was a constant concern that flickered at the edges of his mind. It would have to impact her. He just didn't know how. "I have to hope what I'm doing is enough."

"I'm not sure anybody escapes childhood without some trauma. But anyone can see you're doing a great job."

"It's just so damn frustrating because I'm trying to get her to control her impulses, but it's not working."

"I don't have kids, but I've watched my parents raise four boys, and I can tell you they couldn't control anything. You know how the oldest is supposed to be the achiever?"

I sure as hell do.

"Well, Enzo didn't start that way. He was the one lighting bottle rockets in the alley. My parents had to bail him out of jail six times. It's a running joke in our family— we literally keep a tally on the whiteboard in our office. He turned it all around and put himself through business school, but that had nothing to do with my parents. And Romeo, he's the athlete. He's the one with all the swagger. He loves hard, plays hard, and works hard. Marco's the kiss- ass. The teachers love him, my parents think he can do no wrong, but guess what? He's the one sneaking out of girls' windows and forging notes to skip school. And the baby of the family, Rocco? He doesn't care what anyone thinks. He has this whole secret life none of us knows anything about. So, you see what I mean? I have great, really involved parents, and there was nothing they could do to control their sons. People are just born with a certain nature, and I'm not sure anyone can change it."

He noticed she hadn't mentioned herself in that long list. "And what about you? What's your nature?"

"I was the dreamer. My brothers were breaking their necks doing parkour, while I was on the beach making sand pies.

They were climbing trees, and I was decorating cakes at the base of them. While they were busy pranking each other, I was picking wildflowers and making designs out of the petals." She headed back to the oven to pull out a tray of profiteroles. "From what I can tell, Kinsley's a great kid. Which means you're doing a good job. So, maybe ease up the pressure you put on yourself so you can enjoy her instead of constantly worrying about her."

"Not as easy as it sounds."

"No, I know. My brothers put my parents through the wringer." She checked the bottoms of a few of them and then set the tray on a trivet. "They're just big into natural consequences."

"There's nothing that terrifies me more than that."

"Yeah, but the only way to become good at something is to practice. And the more experience we get, the sharper our instincts become. I mean, Enzo was really into skateboarding, but it took some serious falls and stitches before he figured out how to avoid getting hurt. But he learned through experience. Not because of warnings from my parents or advice from other skaters."

He could only offer a curt nod of acknowledgment because he knew if he gave Kinsley a skateboard, his fearless girl would try to ride it off the roof and into the pool or something equally reckless. "Kinsley's just…more."

"Well, you obviously know her better than I do, so just ignore me. Consider it the ramblings of a woman baking furiously at four in the morning." She headed to the fridge and brought out a carton of eggs.

Back to work, she pulled a whisk out of a drawer and opened a new bag of sugar. Her movements were graceful, her expression thoughtful, and for the first time in his life, he could see what he was missing.

He had a big family, lots of friends, and plenty of acquaintances. He had all the female companionship a man could want. But he didn't have the thrill of being with someone who excited him. Who stirred him up.

He told himself he didn't have the bandwidth to add a romantic relationship to his life, but really, he just hadn't met anyone who tripped his switches.

But Grace did. Not only did he like talking to her and get comfort from just being in the same room, but she made his blood hot.

Watching her triggered some primal instinct, some beastly roar from deep within that made him want to claim her, sink his teeth into the back of her neck, and make her part of his pack.

Being near her made him vital and alive.

He didn't know about the constant tension he held in his neck, his shoulders, and his back until he watched her crack eggs, separating the yolks from the whites. Her practiced movements soothed him. The whir of the mixer, the intensity in her eyes as if the entire world balanced on the sturdy peaks of her egg whites...he could watch her forever and not get bored.

The tumult in his mind settled, leaving him with the core of her message to him. "I know I hold her back. I just didn't think it mattered at her age."

"I mean, her grandma's a riding teacher, and I found her standing behind a horse in a stall." She set the mixer down and added vanilla to the whisked egg yolks. "But I've been here two weeks, so what do I know?"

"If I let her go, she'll...she could get hurt." He couldn't bear to see his daughter in pain.

She stopped working and gave him her full attention.

"You said she was curious. Did you mean to say she's a thrill-seeker?"

"No. She's not." Great question, though, because that was what he'd been. That difference seemed important. "But she doesn't assess risk well." *Or at all.* "She's impulsive." Sometimes, he felt so fucking helpless. "I just want to keep her safe."

"Of course, you do." She reached for his hand and gave it a gentle squeeze. "It's normal to limit her exposure to dangerous things until she's old enough to make mature decisions."

"Yeah. Exactly."

A clear liquid began to boil, and she checked the thermometer perched on the side of the pot. Quickly, she cut the flame and set it on a back burner. "But if she's not allowed to take risks, I'm not sure how she'll get enough experience to navigate the tough situations."

He got that. He and his friends had done a lot of risky shit before attempting BASE jumping. Years of pushing the limits had taught them to be wily and to trust their intuition.

He was denying Kinsley the opportunity to hone those instincts and to learn through failure. While he couldn't argue with Grace's logic, it made him deeply uncomfortable. Because if he took his eyes off Kinsley—if he let her go wherever her impulses took her…

A churning sensation hit his gut, the same he'd had while watching Booker fall from the sky. His memory played out the scene, showing him the moment his friend's body hit the ground, his legs crumpling—

Chapter Nine

JAIME'S HEART GALLOPED, AND AN ICY HAND CLOSED around his heart. The kitchen felt hot as an oven, so he moved to the French doors and threw them open.

But Gracie was right there. She stood at his side, her palm on his back. "Hey." Her voice was soft, unbearably sweet. "Are you okay?"

A kindness he didn't deserve. "Yeah. Fine." He wanted to leave, get the fuck away, but he couldn't move. "I'll let you get back to it." He was still in panic mode, his heart racing, his palms damp.

"Jaime." Her kindness poured all over his body, seeping into the cuts and slashes and gaping wounds. "Talk to me. What's going on?"

"Nothing. It's fine. I should get back home."

She stepped in front of him, cupped his cheeks with hands that smelled like pie crust, and forced him to look at her. And then, she smiled. Soft, warm, comforting. "You're a great dad. You're doing such a good job with her."

He shuddered. He wanted to draw her close, hold on to

her. He wanted her sweetness to wash through him, flushing out the jagged bits.

Somehow, she knew what he needed, because she took a step closer, winding her arms around his waist. "I got you. I'm here."

A cool breeze chilled the perspiration, waking him up. He held on as if his life depended on it. He didn't know why this happened to him, but when it did, he took inventory.

Kinny's tucked in bed, sleeping peacefully.

She's good. Everything's fine.

But nothing felt right at all.

Grace…she was pushing, prodding, loosening the locks he kept bolted. He didn't like losing control. What was it about her that unearthed all the doubts and insecurities, the fears and self-loathing? Nightmares he could deal with. They only impacted him. He could wake up, shake them off, and go on about his day.

But falling apart like this? When he had responsibilities? He couldn't afford to do that.

Still, he held on, taking strength from a woman who was a full nine inches shorter and a hundred pounds lighter. Only when something on the stove boiled over and sizzled did he pull away and release her.

But she didn't go anywhere. She gazed up at him with an expression that said, *Go ahead and fall. I'm here to catch you.*

And he'd never wanted to let go as badly as he did in this moment.

But he couldn't. He had a daughter to think about. Brothers, a sister, his parents, this ranch…

Irritated with himself, he pushed past her, headed for the burner, and turned off the flame. "Sorry. I fucked that up for you." He sure as shit didn't need to fall apart in front of this woman who was only here to make money this summer.

"It's nothing but a simple syrup. It doesn't matter." She turned her back to the counter and hoisted herself up. "I don't think you're upset about Kinsley."

The flashback lingered, and he didn't see the point in lying. "No."

"Who do you talk to?"

"I'm close with my family. We talk all the time."

"But not about Booker's accident, right? I get the feeling you're so ashamed of what happened that you don't talk to anyone."

The stab of truth had him looking away.

"You're working so hard to prove you're not that guy anymore, but have you stopped for a second to see the man you've become? You were eighteen when it happened. Ten years and a child change a man. Maybe you could give yourself a break."

She didn't understand. She couldn't. She'd never stolen someone's dream. "Yeah, sure. Good point."

With a dramatic sigh, she rolled her eyes. "You know, instead of keeping everything inside, you could talk to me. I'm a safe choice."

"Oh, yeah?" *There's nothing safe about you.* "How's that?"

"Because I'm leaving soon. You can bare your soul, tell me all your fears and worries, and then never have to see me again."

The idea of losing her gave his stomach a sickening twist.

"Look. This is the zone." She jumped off the counter, grabbed the whisk, and waved it like a wand. "The Soul Baring Zone. Whatever's said within this space evaporates the moment we breech the walls."

"Oh, we're breeching now?"

"No." She rolled her eyes. "We're not *whales*. We're friends who share our deepest, darkest fears. Go."

He shook his head. "You go first."

"Okay." She got back up on the counter. "I'm terrified I'm going to live my life doing the same exact thing. Making croissants, muffins, and turnovers." He opened his mouth to say something, but she held up a finger. "I love my family. I love my life on Duff Island. At some point, I'll figure something out. This is just me prying open the box that holds my deepest fears. Now that I know what passion is, I'm terrified I'll never find it again. After we had sex, I understood what was missing with Ian and the other guys I've been with."

Did she just mention sex as casually as a trip to the market?

And why did he like that so much? Because she didn't have hang ups. That night, she'd had zero inhibitions—and that was so fucking hot.

"Now that I know what it can be like, I can't believe I ever accepted mediocrity," she said. "Like, what's wrong with me?"

"Absolutely nothing. You didn't have anything to compare it to before you came out here. In the past, you dated ponies. Now, you've had a stallion." He grinned.

She whacked his arm.

"Okay, sorry. My point is...now that you know there's something more, you'll never settle for less."

She drew in a sharp breath, her chest rising, her shoulders pushing back. "I should get a tattoo of that. Because I don't want to go home, fall back into the routine, and then forget what it felt like to have something more." She tapped him with her foot. "Your turn."

One of the reasons he never talked about that night was because he didn't want anyone's judgment. It was enough to live with his own. But for whatever reason, he felt safe with her. And he found himself ready. "I dread seeing Booker. Hearing him tell me I ruined his life. It's one thing to think I did but to hear it from him? To see the disgust in his eyes when he looks at me?"

"Then do it."

"Talk to him?"

"Yes. Face him and apologize. Give him the chance to let you know exactly how he feels about what you did."

Last summer, after Kurt's funeral, he'd had his friends over for the first time in ten years. Booker had gone to the bathroom—and then left. Ghosted them.

Ghosted me.

"Go on," she said gently.

"I'm terrified every day because I know you're right, that we can't change who we fundamentally are. And that means no matter how hard I try, no matter how hard I fight my impulses, I'm going to fuck up spectacularly again. Only this time, it'll hurt Kinsley."

"When you say *fuck up*, what do you mean exactly? What did you do that night that caused Booker's accident?"

"I got some bad news," he began.

"Your parents were going to sell the ranch, so you gave up hockey to stay and help them."

"Right. And instead of dealing with it, I made my friends come over."

"Well, I mean, you didn't make them. You asked them to come over and commiserate with you. It was your last chance because everyone was leaving the next day."

"We'd already said goodbye. They were packed, ready to go. I never should've asked them to come over." *I never should've jumped.*

Why the fuck did I jump?

"Okay, but again, you're saying *fuck up* like there's some fatal flaw in you."

"There is. I'm selfish. I do what I want, and I don't consider the consequences."

"Wow, I'm not seeing that at all. In fact, I can't think of a single thing you do for yourself, and if you were genuinely selfish, that's all you'd be doing. And you wouldn't care. Is Kinsley selfish?"

He shook his head. "She's bold. She's not scared of anything, and there's no such thing as a stranger to her."

"She's a firecracker. And yeah, I can see how that'd be scary for you."

"The first time I met her, I picked her up from her grandparent's house, and she just latched on to me. She looked at me like, 'So, we doing this?' And from that moment on, she was my buddy. I took her with me everywhere." He grinned, remembering how she'd just *expecte*d to be in his arms at all times. As if she'd always been there.

"I love your bond. It's so special."

"Yeah. But now that you've brought it up, I can see how my overprotectiveness is going to get her hurt. I don't know how to let her loose in a situation where I can predict the outcome."

"Jaime." Her voice brushed over his skin like a soft breeze. "Is it an outcome or is it a worst-case scenario?"

"What does that mean?" A parent had to think two steps ahead to keep his kids safe.

"Well, you're super focused on what can go wrong, but are you taking the time to notice her strengths? Are you thinking about what she'd be good at? Instead of catastrophizing, maybe think about what she'd love to do. You say she has your recklessness, but maybe she has your athleticism, too. She told me she was good at sports, and when I asked her what she plays she said she was too little."

Embarrassed, he dropped his gaze. "That's what I keep telling her."

"Well, she's only six, so there's plenty of time. Has she asked to join a team or take lessons?"

"She's watched me play, so yeah, she wants to skate."

"You never know. She might be as good as her dad." Her lips curved in a teasing grin.

He wanted to kiss that sexy smile right off her mouth. Instead, he focused on the most intriguing part of that sentence. "How do you know if her dad's any good?"

"I peeked."

"You peeked, huh?"

"In the barn. While you were playing."

"And what did you see?"

"I saw the greatest forward in the history of hockey unable to get a single puck past you."

He chuckled. "Then, I got lucky. You chose the right moment to watch."

"Sorry, buddy. My family's die-hard Brawler fans. I know my hockey, and you're good. But look, maybe Kinny will hate sports, and she'll turn out to be a brilliant artist. Or a baker like me."

"Five minutes in a kitchen, and she'd turn baking into a science experiment. Light my whole house on fire."

"Not you jumping straight to the worst-case scenario."

Damn, he did do that. Caught, he held up his hands. "You're right."

When she flashed him that bright smile, happiness streaked through him.

Honestly, he hadn't noticed the darkness he lived in until she turned on the lights.

He hadn't understood the emptiness until she'd filled it.

"I have to assume it's because you saw what happened to your friend. With that kind of trauma, it's no wonder you're so anxious about Kinsley getting hurt."

"Yeah." He didn't want to talk about it, but in this moment—in the kitchen he'd designed to feel cozy despite its size—surrounded by fresh-baked desserts created by this woman who had such a hold on him—he couldn't hold back. "I keep reliving it. From the elation of a good landing, to being with my friends…and then, to the shock of watching Booker's body twist and jerk right before landing."

She touched him. Just a light hand on his arm. And it was the exact contact he needed to stay grounded.

"It's like a reel that plays on constant repeat somewhere inside me. It's torture." His vision blurred, and he blinked furiously. He would not cry.

What was it about Grace that brought everything to the surface? All the things he worked so hard to shove down and bury? Because he had good people in his life, people he could trust. People he could talk to.

But with her, there was a connection beyond the physical, beneath the obvious thud of his heart. Their unique chemistry bound him to her, and his spirit recognized hers as safe. As home.

She reached for his hand and drew him closer. Gently, she sifted her fingers through his hair. "We're still in the zone. You can tell me anything."

"I can't take it anymore. I can't." It all gurgled up to the surface and spilled out. "It's like there's this shadow lurking behind everything I do. And it's not even the nightmare itself. Most of the time, it's just a feeling that pops up out of nowhere. I can be playing hockey or at our Sunday night family dinner—it doesn't matter. It grabs me, and I seize up." He couldn't believe how good it felt to get it off his chest.

"Oh, anxiety. Yeah." She nodded like it was the most normal thing in the world.

But it wasn't. It couldn't be.

She smiled. "I get them, too."

"Them?"

"Anxiety attacks. What, you think you're the only one? Oh, come on. It's the most common thing in the world. What I do is make a quick assessment. Am I okay? Is the house on fire? Okay, good. Everything's fine."

"I do that, too."

"Yeah, see? They're manageable. The guilt, though…I don't know what to say about that. It feels like a choice to me. You refuse to forgive yourself for something that happened ten years ago, something that was totally within the playbook of what you guys did together. So, if you want to hang onto it, that's fine. But you're never going to live a full life."

Noise filled his head, and he went very still inside. His mind refused to process her words. But they hung in the air, hovering, pulsing.

And then, she sucked in a breath. "Oh. Of *course*. You don't want a full life because you stole Booker's. This is your penance. Wow."

"I don't know that I've ever thought that—"

"You don't have to. You live it. Oh, man. That is one big price to pay. Let me ask you something. What if *Booker* had sent that text? What if his team had pulled his contract at the last minute, and he'd asked you guys to come over and have a few beers? If he'd decided to jump that night, and you were the one who got hurt and had to give up hockey, would you hate him? Would you think he didn't deserve happiness?"

He answered without hesitation. "No."

"You'd forgive him?"

"Absolutely."

"Okay, then tell him that. Pretend I'm Booker, and I've just told you how much guilt I feel. What're you going to say to me?"

She thought this would be a life-transforming exercise. That she was offering a tectonic shift to his emotional state. She was wrong. "You're asking me to imagine a scenario I can't relate to. I wasn't drafted. Besides, I'd already lost hockey, remember? I had to stay home—"

"No, you didn't. Your parents didn't tell you to help save the ranch. It was a choice you made. Selfish teenagers don't make choices like that, by the way. But you did."

He appreciated what she was trying to do, but he couldn't do it. He couldn't pretend. "In any event, it didn't happen like that. It was me. I did it."

She wrapped her legs around his hips and jerked him closer. "Yeah, real clear on that. But you should treat yourself with the same kindness you'd treat a friend. And if you won't do it, I will. Here's what I'd say." Cupping his cheeks, she held his gaze. "Booker, dude, are you serious? I had no idea you were so messed up over this. Look, it sucked. It was a rough couple of years but look where I am now. I'm doing great. Besides, if I'd gotten news like that, if the Cavalcade had pulled my contract, you bet your ass I'd have asked you guys to come over and commiserate with me. It was our last night. You guys were all going off to live the dream we'd always imagined. Of course, I would've. And you know what else? We did what we always did when we got together. Only that time, things went sideways. But I'm okay now, so let it go. I've moved on. We're cool."

"I don't think you understand what hockey meant to Booker and his family."

"You're right. I don't. But I do know you're not responsible for how Booker processes what happens to him. You're only responsible for your decisions and choices. And you've made some damn good ones since that night."

"You have more faith in me than I do." He brushed the hair out of her eyes. "Why is that?"

"Because I don't know teenage Jaime. I know the man you are today. You're good and caring and hardworking and generous."

"And handsome?"

She smiled. "Oh, please. I'm not going to feed that giant ego."

"What? I'm just trying to get a clear picture of how you see me." He wanted to keep teasing her. Because the temptation to believe her was so strong it scared him.

Made him feel like a coward for thinking he could so easily slink away from personal responsibility.

"Okay, fine. You're handsome. And I get that you don't want to talk about this anymore, so let me just say one more thing. One day, you're going to look in the mirror and see the man you've become instead of the boy you used to be. And after that, you'll be free. You're going to fall wildly, madly in love with a beautiful woman, move into the Dream House, and have lots of gorgeous babies."

"Damn you, Gracie Giordano."

"What?" She gazed up at him with those big hazel eyes, her lush pink mouth, and all that thick, silky hair.

Shoving between her knees, he braced his hands on either side of her and dipped his face into her neck. He breathed in the scent that turned him feral. "What is this power you have over me?"

"It's funny you phrase it like that. I don't want to control you."

He leaned in close enough to brush lips over hers. "What do you want?"

"What I want, you can't give me."

She was right about that. She probably wanted a future. A family. Back on Duff Island, where she could raise her children surrounded by grandparents, aunts, uncles, and cousins. Screwing around with him was a waste of time.

Still…his kitchen might be big enough to fit forty family members, but when he was with Gracie, it felt like it was built for two. The heat from their bodies, the warmth in her eyes, and the bare skin of her arms and thighs…it made him so hard he hurt.

And it made him want to know her as well as she seemed to know him. Because maybe he had it all wrong. "How do you know I can't?"

Her lips parted, her gaze fixed on his mouth, and her eyes went sultry and hot. "Because if you could, you'd be doing it."

Dammit all to hell.

She'd just opened the floodgates. A fierce desire took hold, and he kissed her. Just the brush of soft lips and the swipe of his tongue inside her hot, slick mouth felt so good he thought his heart might explode.

She opened to him, her fingers fisting in his hair. She tasted of warm chocolate, and her scent promised a happiness he craved but didn't deserve.

But God, did he want it. Wanted her naked, grinding on him, and chasing her pleasure. He wanted her sighs and her lusty moans. He wanted to be alone with her under the covers, the kind of privacy meant only for lovers.

The deeper his kisses, the more desperately she clutched him, and the more she unknowingly coaxed the beast into play. It scared him enough to stop. His fingers flexed, digging into her flesh—and he had to force himself to release her. He tore his mouth off hers. "Dammit. I can't keep doing this." Mind racing, he backed away. I'm sorry." But her expression burned through his fear.

She was hurt.

He'd hurt her.

"I'm sorry." He scrambled to think. *Kinsley.* "I can't let my daughter get attached to someone who's going to leave." *Yes.* That was exactly right.

"Bullshit." She jumped off the counter and headed to the oven to pull out a cookie sheet of mini tarts. "You're one of those tortured guys who gets off on the drama. 'Oh, I want her, but I can't have her. Oh, the unbearable conflict of it all.' Well, guess what? There's no conflict because I'm removing myself from it."

"What're you talking about? It's the opposite. I avoid drama at all costs."

"No, you avoid *pleasure.* Or anything that will bring you happiness. Look, there's nothing to talk about. You don't want me enough, and that's fine. But I'll tell you something right now. I'm done with men who aren't on *fire* for me." She lifted one of her beautifully decorated pastries and shook it at him. "Now that I've had a taste of passion, there's no going back." She picked up the whisk. "Just keep your hands and mouth off me, okay? There won't be any hard feelings if you can do that."

Rooted to the spot, he watched her every move as a new energy charged through him. This woman had left her wedding, her family, and her job, to live on her own terms, to pursue a dream. She was so real, so true, and so fucking strong.

All these years, he'd been locked in his head, and this woman owned the key. If she could be brave, he could, too.

And honestly, he didn't think he had a choice. "I can't."

Distracted, she looked up from the stove. "Can't what?"

"Keep my hands and mouth off you. I want you too much." *Say it. Tell her.* "Gracie Giordano, I am on *fire* for you." In two steps, he had her in his arms. The relief he felt nearly dropped him to his knees, but their mouths fused, and as she grabbed fistfuls of his T-shirt, she hitched a leg around his ass. *Fuck, yes.*

Their tongues tangled, their hips rocked, and he bent his knees to lift her. She clung to him as he walked them to the kitchen wall and slammed her against it.

Pitching his hips forward, he thrust his cock right into the juncture of her thighs. Sensation roared through him. He couldn't kiss her deeply enough, couldn't get close enough—he was desperate for more.

With her hips grinding, swiveling, pressing against his cock, she gave out these restless, desperate cries, and he couldn't take anymore. He had to have her.

The moment he set her on her feet, he snatched the T-shirt over his head and started to yank down his pajama bottoms. Reason broke through the haze of lust, and he grabbed her hand. "Come here." Unlikely as it was that anyone would walk by at four in the morning, he wouldn't take chances. He led her into the walk-in pantry.

Pulling off his pants, he dropped to his knees. She was already shimmying out of her leggings, but he stopped her. "Let me." He unveiled her slowly, savoring the smooth peachy skin and the heady scent of her arousal. He pressed a trail of kisses up the inside of her thigh. When he had her naked, he said, "Put your foot on my shoulder."

Grabbing her ass, he licked inside the wet cove between her legs. He watched her while his tongue swiped the length of her until he hit her clit. He loved the shudder that went through her.

"Jaime." She grabbed his hair, crying out as he licked her into a frenzy. "God. *God.*"

He fucking loved it. Loved the way she tasted, the way she smelled, and the way her body responded to him. There was nothing like it. Nothing like her.

He should've known from the start this woman was too precious to keep at a distance. No matter the cost, he had to be with her. Had to. Even if they only had six more weeks.

As she began to buck and tremble, his tongue swirled faster.

"Yes. Like that. Oh. My. God." And then, she was jerking, pulling his hair, and crying out in the windowless room. When she came down off her high, she gave him a half-lidded, sexy smile. "Mm. Delicious." She watched the grasp he had on his cock, the tight slide of his hand up and down, and the way he ran a palm over the head. Her teeth sank into her bottom lip. "I need you inside me."

"Yeah, you do." He stood, whirled her around, and planted her hands on the wall. "You on the pill?"

"Yes, and we've always used protection."

"Same. Now, hold on. This is going to be hard and fast."

"Yes, please."

Yanking her hips back, he tilted her ass, grabbed hold of his cock, and slid inside her juicy, hot channel. Her back arched, as she took him all the way in. Deep. So fucking deep.

Just for one moment, he stayed right there, and the

strangest thing happened. Affection flooded him, and he wrapped his arms around her and kissed her shoulder. He just...really liked her.

Immersed in her scent, his cock buried inside her channel, he'd never felt closer to anyone. It was the purest form of happiness he'd ever felt.

When he pulled back out, her muscles clenched, like she didn't want him to leave, and something in him snapped. Punching his hips forward, he fucked her. Hard, fast. Jesus, she felt so good, so tight, so hot. He was greedy for more and more of her. Sweat drenched his body, his hair fell into his eyes, and he lost himself entirely in everything Gracie.

My Gracie.

Tension twisted him, lifted him off the ground, and he found himself caught between bliss and an urgent, straining demand for release. He didn't want it to end, but it reached an unbearable breaking point. And all it took was a wiggle of her hips, the way she rammed back on him when their bodies met, to send him soaring.

Wave after wave of pure elation rode through him. He held her hips tightly and pounded his release into her.

And when he finished, when he had nothing left, he rested his chin on her shoulder. Even when he couldn't catch his breath, a profound sense of peace filled him. "I can't feel my legs."

"That was intense." Releasing a shaky sigh, she turned within his arms. With both hands, she scraped the hair off his face. "Are you okay?"

He knew she didn't mean physically. She was remembering their first night together, and he'd have to make up for that. "I'm more than okay. I'm right where I want to be. I've chased a lot of highs in my life, but nothing's better than being with you."

"Sex with me is better than dirt biking? Is that what I'm hearing?"

He smiled, giving her a gentle kiss. "Better than boarding Corbet's Couloir. Gracie…" Emotion welled up, threatening to crash over him.

"Yes?" It came out a whisper, and he caught the vulnerability in her eyes.

She deserved so much better than what he'd given her so far. "I'm sorry for the mixed messages. I know on the outside I look like I've got everything under control. But inside—"

"I know. I see you now, Jaime. And, as long as you get it, why you pull away…as long as you don't do it again, we're okay."

He pulled her into his arms. "I won't. I've tried to keep my distance, but Jesus, Gracie."

"What?"

"Look at you. You're the most beautiful woman I've ever seen. You're…*fuck*." How could he describe the bond he felt with her? "This thing between us is so huge. I'm not strong enough to resist the pull." There was only one thing, and he wasn't sure she'd go for it. "Do you think we can keep it between us, though? The other day, at the bus stop, Kinny said she wanted you to stay."

"She did?" Her soft smile told him she was deeply touched.

"Yeah, so I know she's getting attached to you. But you're leaving in August, and I just can't do that to her."

"I understand. It's fine." She handed him his bottoms and shook out her leggings. "We'll have our little secret rendezvous." Dressed, she led the way out of the pantry.

She seemed fine with it, but he wasn't sure. He caught her around the waist and brought her up to his chest. "Hey, are we okay? I don't want you to think I'm hiding you."

"Well, you are. But I understand why."

After washing her hands, she got back to work, and he took in the organized chaos of her operation. "You can't keep this up. It isn't sustainable. You need help."

"I do, but every cent I make is going to my parents. Not to an employee. Besides, it's only for the summer."

He didn't need the reminder. Then again, maybe he did. "Two of my boys on the Juniors team are suspended right now. They can't get back on the ice until they complete fifty hours of community service."

At the stove, she stopped. "You're not suggesting they work for me, are you? Helping pay my parents back for the wedding that didn't happen is hardly philanthropic."

"Sweeping the locker room isn't much different. Do you want their help?"

"What did they do to get suspended?"

"Fighting."

"Oh, that's okay. I'll pass. I don't need testosterone-fueled teens working with me."

"It's not like that. I wouldn't suggest them if I thought they'd cause you trouble. They fought over a girl—Ben hooked up with Jeremy's ex."

"Oh. That sucks. Well, in that case..." She came over and wrapped her arms around his neck. "The timing's really good since I've just taken on this new project."

"Oh, yeah? Which one is that?"

"Project Summer Fling." She grinned.

But he didn't find it funny. "That's not what we are."

"That's exactly what we are. And the only way I can do this with you is to keep in mind that I'm leaving. Now, go on and get out of here. Let me get back to work."

He hated leaving her, hated walking away from how good she made him feel. He gave her one last, lingering kiss.

And then, as he headed out, he called over his shoulder, "I'll text you the address so you can stop by the rink and meet the guys. Make sure you're comfortable with them."

At the door, he turned back to see her one last time and found her watching him.

His heart grew too big for his chest. Her smile undid him.

This thing with her was thrilling.

And terrifying.

He could not fuck it up.

He couldn't hurt this beautiful, sunshiny woman.

My Gracie.

Chapter Ten

Today at the festival, Grace chose the most upbeat songs. Her smile stretched wider.

Because she didn't just get to make pastries this summer, she got to be with Jaime.

Joy!

She glanced up from her food truck to take in the well-lit meadow. Just like every other evening, it was jammed with people roaming the booths, picnicking on beach towels, and waiting for the next band to take the stage.

Her feet hurt, she was starving, but she couldn't remember a time she'd been more content. But Jaime was right. As much as she didn't want to accept more favors, she understood she couldn't keep up this pace. She needed help. She'd been slammed all day—hadn't even had a chance to take a bathroom break. So, yes, she'd go to the rink tomorrow morning and meet the boys. She'd be more productive *and* have time for really hot sex.

Everything was great…except the whole thing about hiding their relationship.

That didn't sit well with her. All morning, she'd wrestled

with his request, but it came down to one question: what would she do if she had a child? If she only had a few weeks with a man, would she let him meet her daughter? No, she wouldn't.

So, if that were the case, how could she expect anything different from him?

Well, she knew the answer to that. She just liked him so much and wanted to spend every free moment with him.

She wanted to taste desserts at Wally's and Harley and Lu's Emporium. She'd heard about the Homestead Inn's Dark Chocolate Obsession cake and wanted to try it. She wanted to ride the mechanical bull at Wild Billy's and hike deep into the forest until she saw a moose. She wanted to wander the stalls at the farmer's market. With Jaime. As her date.

But she'd see how it went. If it didn't feel right, if she started wanting more than a fling, then she'd end it. For now, it was fun, he was hot, and no one could get hurt because the festival ended Labor Day weekend. After that, she'd have no food truck and no reason to stay in Calamity.

Not to make excuses for him, but she really did understand the big leap he'd taken in allowing himself this one slice of pleasure.

Bagging up six doughnuts, she handed it to the customer. "Thanks very much. Have a great day."

The next person in line moved forward. "Hey, do you have any of those caramel chocolate cream puffs?"

"Sorry. I didn't make them this morning."

"But they're my favorite."

She laughed. "Fair point. I guess the longer I'm here, the more I'll figure this stuff out."

"Will you have them tomorrow?"

"Sure, I can do that." She lifted one of the baskets. "Can

I interest you in a—" Familiar laughter jerked her attention over to a group of people walking by. It sounded like Jaime.

Is he here to see me?

She started to smooth down her hair—*it must be a mess* —but remembered her hands were sticky from the powdered sugar she'd rolled the last batch of doughnuts in.

From this angle, she didn't have a clear view, so she wasn't sure it was him. But then, someone called his name, and he had to move closer to shake hands. Yep. It was him, all right.

Since he had the confounding appearance of a professional athlete who modeled *and* belonged to a motorcycle club, he stood out in any crowd. It was almost comical to watch him catching up with his friend as heads turned and people stopped talking to check him out. Because he had no clue. None.

If she had help, she'd run right into his arms. Well, she couldn't do that, but she could at least—

Whoa. A gorgeous red-haired woman came up and stood beside him. Grace froze, watching their interaction.

Are they *together* together? Like…on a date?

Would he do that to me?

He couldn't possibly talk to me the way he did last night and then show up with another woman the next day, could he?

Oh, she was with him, all right. A woman knows these things. From the way they stood so close together and the ease in their body language, Grace knew they'd had sex.

The redhead smiled like she was dazzled by him. With a crop top, jean shorts, and combat boots, she had an edgy vibe. She looked artsy, sexy, impulsive, and fun.

Everything I'm not.

"What's the closest thing you have to it?" the customer asked.

"To what?" Grace forced herself to look away. It hadn't occurred to her to bring up exclusivity. Not with the way he looked at her. Devoured her.

What the hell?

Is he like that with everyone?

She'd thought they were on the same page—that they both felt lucky to have found this outrageous chemistry and connection. Maybe in the bedroom, he let go... with everyone?

How many women is he seeing?

Is that why he's hiding me?

But she was jumping the gun, making assumptions. She was sensitive because she'd known all along she wasn't his type. That summer when they'd docked in the harbor, Ian made some crack about Jaime not liking wholesome women, and it had stuck with her.

Because that's me. I'm "wholesome."

And the red-haired woman was in a whole other league. She oozed sexuality.

Just like Jaime. From his growly voice to his athletic prowess, he reeked of dirty, raunchy sex.

She forced her attention back to her customer. "The closest thing to the caramel and chocolate cream puff, huh?" She glanced at her pastries. "How about this? It's a chocolate choux with a salted caramel filling."

"That sounds good. I'll take that."

"Great." She had to force herself to handle the transaction and not look up.

Don't check Jaime out.

But after she bagged up the treat, she couldn't help herself. She found the woman easily, thanks to the rhinestones glinting on her belt. It was dark, though, and while the lights lit up the meadow in some spots, it left shadows in others.

Jaime wasn't touching her, but the woman's familiarity left no doubt they were together.

Why would he act like he just had to have her, like she was the most special woman he'd ever met, and then parade another woman around her the next night?

I mean, he's right there. He has to know where my truck's located.

It hurt to see him so comfortable with another woman when he'd been nothing but uptight with her. Well, except when they were having sex. He certainly wasn't uptight then.

And isn't that all he wants from me? Sex in the middle of the night when no one else could see them together?

Wait, wait, wait. She knew him better than this. He didn't have a cruel bone in his body.

If she calmed down and paid attention, the sexual energy came from the redhead. Jaime was focused on his friend.

"I gave you a ten."

"Excuse me?" She snapped out of it, realizing she'd given her customer a twenty-dollar bill. "Sorry. Here." She reached into the till and brought out a five. "Enjoy."

"Thanks."

She had to shake it off. She got so much joy from her beautiful pastries. *That's why I'm here.* She had the opportunity of a lifetime. She wasn't going to freak out over a guy.

Well, of course, he wasn't just a guy. He was Jaime Dupree. Sexy, strong. An amazing dad and devoted son. Come on, he'd built a house for his parents so they could retire in comfort. He'd considered every angle of the aging process in the design. He listened when she spoke, and he gave her more pleasure than she'd ever imagined was possible.

So, okay. She *was* freaking out. Because she'd never felt this way for anyone, and she was scared he'd hurt her. But she couldn't let fear guide her. Hooking up with other women while seeing her in private was a dealbreaker, and she'd have to address it the minute she had time alone with him.

The next customer stepped up, and it took a moment for Grace to make sense of what she was seeing. "What on earth are you wearing?" She laughed at Lorelei's latest disguise of bright orange overalls, combat boots, and a hot pink boa around her neck. "You're just dying to get noticed, aren't you?"

"Oh, God, no." Lorelei flicked a hand toward the meadow. "Tonight, the Kitty Kat Rats are playing. Everyone's dressing up, so I totally blend in."

Grace hadn't known that. She'd been so busy, she hadn't paid much attention to the entertainment, but when she looked around, she could see the singer was right. "I have to get out more."

With a frown, Lorelei examined the pastries. "Shoot. I got here too late." She glanced up at Grace with a smile. "We had the best day in the Tetons, though. We saw a grizzly bear. Can you believe it?"

"No, I can't. That's amazing. The only wild animals I've seen are the bison in the reserve I pass every morning to get here." Yep. She was definitely taking Jaime up on his offer of help. She had to get out and explore the area.

She softened when she thought of all he'd done for her. Not once had he lied or faked anything. In fact, he'd been surprisingly honest.

Of course he wouldn't stand near her truck flaunting a date.

Lorelei's manager came up and peered into a basket. "Ooh, what's that?"

"That's a blackberry, lemon, and white chocolate tart." On top of the lemon curd sat a squiggle of creamy white chocolate and tiny purple and bright blue flowers. "Want one?"

"You bet I do." The older woman accepted the treat. "It's so pretty." She pointed to another basket. "Is that real gold on top of the chocolate ones?"

"It's edible gold leaf." And very expensive, so kind of dumb for her to buy it. But she was having so much fun experimenting that she couldn't help herself. It wasn't like she'd ever have this opportunity again.

As soon as she got home, she'd be back to churning out croissants, muffins, and turnovers.

Her spirits sank. *And here's the one negative of her summer.* What had once been such a joy—working in the family bakery—now felt limited. Stifling.

She didn't think a special rack in Renzo's would work, but maybe she could sell them to hotels. Or something. She'd figure it out.

"What should I get the guys?" Lorelie asked. But when her manager didn't respond, she looked up and followed the older woman's concerned gaze.

Grace turned to look out the window at the back of her truck. The bassist and drummer from her band were walking to the bus, laughing. Given how the bandmates were together twenty-four seven, it looked normal to her. If she *wanted* to look for something sketchy, she could say the two stood a little too close. Maybe they had a pinch too much comfort with each other?

"You better watch your back with those two," the manager said quietly.

"Oh, stop. They're my best friends." Lorelei didn't have a shred of doubt in her tone. "They're the only reason I've kept my sanity in this business." She turned back around. "Okay, you know what? I'm going to get one of those and one of those. And give me the purple one, too. Wait. Maybe I should try—"

"Hey, can you hurry up?" the woman next in line asked. "I want to hear the lady sing."

"Yeah, man," the man behind her said. "You have an awesome voice. It's even better than Lorelei Calloway's."

It took everything she had not to look at the pop star. Instead, she simply said, "Not by a long shot, but thank you."

Lorelei laughed. "You heard them. Start singing."

Oh, my God. In front of the biggest pop star in the world?

With everyone looking at her, what else could she do but launch into a song?

The moment her headlights flashed on the cabin, Grace got excited. She couldn't wait to see him. First though, she needed to shower off the scent of oil, get some dough proofing, and set up her mise en place for tonight's baking.

She doubted anything was going on with him and the redhead, but she had to bring it up. Because he'd never come to her truck. He hadn't even looked her way. It was just all so odd.

Her stomach grumbled at the scent of the Mexican food filling the interior of her car. She'd bought it on her way out of the venue, and the whole ride home, she'd been munching tortilla chips. Still, she was starving.

The second after she parked and cut the engine, she unwrapped the burrito and bit into it. *Oh, God.* Spicy ground beef, creamy, melted Monterey Jack and cheddar cheeses, and the heat of diced jalapenos hit her taste buds.

Grabbing her giant canvas carry-all and stack of empty baskets, she took another enormous bite and got out of the car. Mouth full, she came face-to-face with Jaime and a hockey friend. "Oh. Hi." With her stuffed cheeks, she must look like a squirrel storing acorns.

Meanwhile, Jaime looked like an ad for the NHL. Hair stuck to his forehead, his cheeks were rosy with exertion, and he held a hockey stick. He grinned at her. "Hungry?"

"Guh. I haven't eaten all day."

He relieved her of the baskets. "Yeah, I can see how that would be difficult in a food truck."

Preoccupied with chewing, she could only say, "Hey, I can't live off doughnuts and churros."

"And the food truck next to you? What does it sell?"

Finally, she swallowed. "Have you seen the lines for my desserts?"

"Hey. I'm Lou." She hadn't paid attention to his friend until the man reached out a hand.

"Sorry. Hi. I'm Grace." She glanced down at her chest to see crumbs. "I'm a baker." *And that explains tortilla chip crumbs how?*

"It's very nice to meet you." His grip was warm and firm. "Are you a Dupree?"

"Oh, no. I'm a friend. In town for the festival." She gestured to the cabin. "Jaime's letting me stay here." And tonight, if they were on the same page, he'd let her swallow his cock.

Her cheeks flamed as if the man could read her thoughts.

Hey, I've finally had good sex. Excuse me for being a little preoccupied.

"Nice," Lou said.

She got a little flustered. Was he talking about the blow job?

Thankfully, Jaime saved her. "She runs a food truck at the festival. Two of my Juniors are suspended, so they're going to earn their way back to the team by helping out the community."

She was grateful for the moment to get her head back on straight. "That's me. I'm the community."

"When are you going to stop by the rink to talk to the guys?" Jaime asked.

"Morning is best for me, but I don't want to interrupt practice."

"They're not on the ice. They're doing laundry and cleaning out lockers."

"You're making teenage boys do laundry for their teammates?" Lou asked. "Hardass."

"If they want to be good players, they've got to learn self-control."

"Can't argue with that." Lou smiled at her. "So, Grace. Where you from?"

"Rhode Island. Have you ever been to Duff Island?"

"Can't say that I have. You live on an island?"

"Yep. That's my life. Beaches, umbrella drinks, and flip-flops."

"And you've traded it for mountains, a sloshy, and hiking boots?" Lou asked.

"For a few months anyway."

"You'd never know it." He gestured to her jean shorts, Lorelei Calloway T-shirt, and kitchen clogs.

She wanted to die. These gorgeous men—and given

Lou's physique, she assumed he played on the Renegades—radiated badass energy, while she stood there with beans in her teeth and reeking of churros.

"Well, I should get in." *I need a shower, a gallon of water, and a power nap.* "By the way, what's a sloshy?"

"It's an alcoholic smoothie," Jaime said.

"You've never had one?" Lou seemed surprised.

"Nope. But it sounds right up my alley."

"Wait, how long have you been in town?" Lou asked.

"Three weeks."

Lou elbowed his friend. "What's the matter with you? You've got this gorgeous East Coaster living in your cabin and working her tail off, and you don't take her out for a sloshy?"

"She's busy *working*," Jaime said.

Lou stepped in front of his friend. "Excuse him. He's a savage. How about I take you out for a drink?"

"She's been on her feet all day," Jaime said. "She's exhausted."

Now, there's a side to him I've never seen. His tone was firm, possessive, and not open to discussion. *I like that.*

Lou broke out in a slow grin. "I see how it is. It's cool, man."

"It's not like anything." Jaime didn't back down. "Look at her. She's just getting home at nine thirty. She'll be up baking at three in the morning."

"All the more reason someone should take her for a night out on the town," Lou said. "What do you say? Can I take you out? Show you some of the sights?"

She waited to see what Jaime would do. He wanted to keep them a secret, but that was because of his daughter. No need to hide around the players, right? There was no way he'd be okay with her dating someone else.

Then again, if he were, she wouldn't need to have that discussion about the redhead. She'd have her answer.

His jaw went hard. He ground his teeth. But he didn't say a word.

Was everything he'd said to her a lie?

This thing between us is so huge.

It sure as hell doesn't feel like a fling.

Or was he that screwed up he'd rather her date someone else than claim her publicly?

She grew hot and flustered, but when he still stood there like a tree stump, she turned all her focus on Lou. "Sure. I'd love that."

"Awesome. What night works for you?"

"The festival runs seven days a week, so I won't have free time until I get my new employees trained up." She gave Jaime a shit-eating grin. "Good thing you suggested those boys."

"Cool." Lou pulled out his phone. "Let's trade numbers, and you can hit me up when you're ready." He turned to Jaime with a look that said, *Is this okay with you?*

Grace couldn't wait to see his response.

And honestly, after fifteen years of a man who didn't mind breaking up with her over and over again so he could see what else was out there, she wanted a man who cared enough to say, *No, it's not okay. I've got some issues, but I know how I feel about this woman, and I'm not giving her the chance to catch feelings for someone else while I pull my head out of my ass.*

She's mine.

A feeling of certainty filled her, and she knew without a doubt what she wanted and more, what she deserved. And that was not a secret relationship. She'd been willing to consider it, but now she saw it as an excuse for him to not commit to anyone.

Jaime lowered his gaze to his sneakers, wiped the back of his hand across his damp forehead, and then said, "I'll catch you later, Louey." With a lift of the baskets, he strode off toward his house. "I'll drop these on your porch."

His indifference hit her soul like a splash of boiling water.

She felt scalded. She meant a whole lot to him when he had a hard-on but not so much when he had a sexy redhead waiting in the wings. *Well, fuck that. I'm not going to shrivel up just because some guy doesn't want me enough.* "You know what? I'm here such a short time. Let's grab a drink right now."

Not that she didn't trust Lou, but after a quick shower, Grace drove herself into town to meet him at the bar. "So, this is Wild Billy's." She passed it every day on her way to and from the amphitheater—hard to miss with that neon sign of a bull rider on top.

She'd heard it was the biggest, wildest night spot in Calamity. Divided into three sections, it had a packed restaurant, a lively bar, and a mechanical bull that drew a huge crowd.

Lou sat across the café table from her, a flickering votive in the center. Legs stretched out in front of him, he sipped a frothy beer. "Most nights, there's a live band and some two-stepping." He glanced under the table. "Hope you wore your boots."

"That sounds fun, but no. Unfortunately, the only shoes I brought were meant for walking around Paris." And her chef clogs because she'd signed up for an all-day baking class.

He cocked his head. "You chose Calamity over Paris?"

"Well, long story, but…I was supposed to go there on my honeymoon."

His eyebrows shot up.

"Yeah. I ditched the groom five minutes before the ceremony."

"Ouch."

"Nope. We're not feeling bad for him. He did something awful. It's all on him."

"I'm sorry to hear that. How long were you together?"

"Fifteen years. On and off."

His thumb rubbed the condensation on his glass. "And how does Jaime figure into this story?"

"He was a groomsman. My ex sent him to find me."

He sat up, dragging his boots under the chair. "It just gets better and better. So, Jaime whisked you away to his ranch. Interesting. So, if you don't mind me asking, what's going on between you two?"

She would never betray Jaime's trust—even if he'd hurt her. "Not much. There's an obvious attraction, but neither of us is looking for a relationship."

"You wanna make him jealous? 'Cause I'm down to play."

She smiled. She liked this guy. "As great as that sounds, I'm not a game player. Like I said, I'm only here for the summer, and I'm working my ass off. I don't want drama. I just want to make money." A squeal had her glancing toward the mechanical bull where a woman was holding on for dear life. "And maybe have a little fun."

"Gotcha."

The waitress approached the table. "What can I get you guys? Another drink, or do you want some food?"

"I'm okay for now," she said. "But thank you." As the

woman filled their water glasses, Grace scanned the bar. She wondered if Lorelei Calloway ever played here, but before she could ask, her gaze snagged on red hair.

Alarm rang through her body. It was the woman from the festival, and she was standing right next to Jaime. *That fucker.*

So, he is hooking up with her.

In a black T-shirt and worn jeans, Jaime stood a head taller than the others, his smile so devastating she felt a rumble in her bones. God, he looked so handsome, so confident.

Why does he affect me like this?

It doesn't make sense. *He's just a guy.*

Yeah, a guy who makes his daughter French toast before school and reads to her in the hammock in his front yard as the sun goes down. She'd gotten a glimpse of them snuggled together, him pointing at pictures, and Kinsley giggling.

A guy who takes care of his family—Abby told her what he'd done for all of them, putting them through school, flying out to LA to get one of the brothers in rehab. He'd built that house for his parents.

He cared. He was generous. But really, it was his intensity that did it for her. He was a wildly passionate man.

Who suppresses it.

Let's not forget that.

Because he's not allowed to be happy.

And since I make him happy, he can't have me.

Which was sad, but it didn't change anything.

"You okay?" Lou asked.

Grace tore her attention away from Jaime and back to her date. The waitress had left, the water glasses were full… "Sorry about that. Yep. Fine."

"So, what do you do for fun back east? I can't imagine

there's much nightlife on an island. How far are you from the city?" Lou had high energy and was generous with his smiles.

He was trying to make this a good night out, and Grace appreciated it. It's just that she wasn't feeling it. She wished she could've stopped herself from developing real feelings for Jaime. *But look at him.* He had such a commanding presence, a charisma that drew people to him.

She could see how he'd have been the life of the party— before Booker's accident.

Oh, well. It is what it is.

She wanted to go home, get her hands in some dough, but she was the one who'd suggested they go out tonight, so she had to be there for Lou. "It's a little over five hours. But I don't really go out much since I'm up so early baking."

"That's no fun. While you're in town, we've got to get you out more."

"Yeah, I'd like that. But to be honest with you, I've never been much of a partier. I really love what I do."

For the first time, he dropped the perpetually upbeat façade. "I feel the same way." He tapped his fingertips on the scarred table. "I think hockey's always given me an excuse to get out of partying."

"What do you like to do instead?"

"You're gonna make fun of me." He gave her a shy smile.

"No, I'm not. Come on. I prefer to make lemon curd than go out. What you do can't be weirder."

"I like to learn languages. My dad had this globe in his office, and I used to hang out with him in there. I got obsessed with all the different countries—like how crazy is it that we can have so many cultures? How can there be so many different ways to live and eat and dress when we're all on the same planet?"

"Why would I make fun of that? That's fascinating stuff."

"So, while the guys are on their phones or talking to each other, I'm the asshole with headphones learning to speak another language."

"How many are we up to?"

He ticked off his fingers. "Italian, French, German, Spanish, and now, I'm working on Mandarin."

"And have you visited all those countries?"

"Yes, but not the way I want to." He drew in closer. "Hockey's pretty much dominated most of my life, but when I retire, I'm going to visit every continent and really get to know as many cultures as I can. I've been learning photography so I can write a book about it."

"Very cool. I love it. I think people like us are lucky."

"Like us?"

"People who're born with a passion. The ones who don't have it are restless. They tend to get into trouble because they don't have this burning desire to do something."

"Like hockey for me and making croissants for you?"

Her jaw went slack, and her body hollowed out until she was nothing but a heartbeat inside a drum.

The revelation hit so hard it rocked her world. It was like peeling a cloudy film off her eyes and seeing clearly for the first time.

"What'd I say?" Lou sat up, reaching out for her. "I thought you said you loved baking. Did I get it wrong?"

"No. Not at all." *I'm the one who got it wrong.* "Some people are fine making croissants all their lives because it gives them an income, or in my case, it connects them with family. It's enough. But other people need more."

I need more.

She'd suppressed her passion for the good of her family,

but she'd always yearned for something different. She'd ignored it because of the *culture* of the Giordanos.

It was an inherent, embedded fear that the world was dangerous and the only protection came from the strength of relatives. Outside the fortress lurked uncontrollable forces. Inside was safety.

But *she'd* never been afraid to leave. She'd craved different sights and tastes and experiences. And yet, as a good soldier, she hadn't wanted to hurt her parents or rock the boat.

"I like talking to you." He leaned across the table.

She would never know whether he'd intended to kiss her or confide in her because loud, raucous laughter caught their attention.

Jaime's group had become the nexus at the bar. The bartender lined up the shots—there had to be twenty glasses —and then lit the first one.

"Well, look at that," she murmured. "He does let go every now and then."

"Nah. He doesn't. Watch."

While Jaime laughed and was right in the thick of it, he didn't reach for a glass. Everyone knocked back their shots, except for him.

Lou watched for a moment. "He's a tough one to figure out. He's a great guy, takes his job seriously. He's really turning the team around. But he doesn't get too close to anyone. I hear he used to be a wild man, but I guess having a kid changes you."

The redhead pushed through the crowd to sidle up to Jaime. When he smiled down at her, Grace forced herself to stop paying attention. She looked away, but the image lingered in her mind, twisting her up, until she could barely breathe. "So, how do you like playing for the Renegades?"

"I love it. It's been hard to build a competitive team because of where we're located. I sure as hell wouldn't have even considered it, but once Cole Montgomery signed, other top players started paying attention. And now that I'm here, I can't imagine living anywhere else. I'll show you around. You won't believe this place."

"I'd like that." She didn't want to presume anything, but she should probably let him know where she stood. "Just…I need to get it out there. I'm only in town for a month and a half, so I'm not looking for a relationship."

He flashed her a cocky grin. "Oh, I know. I get it."

She didn't know what he was thinking, but since he seemed okay not dating, it didn't matter. "I'll be honest with you. I feel like I'm playing hooky from my real life, and I'm loving every minute of it. Actually, I feel like Cinderella, and at the end of summer, I go back to churning out croissants." But no. She wouldn't do that. Renzo's would have to hire someone else to do the basics. When she went home, she'd have a talk with her family. *The only way to keep me is to let me sell my pastries.* "So, all I want to do is bake and make money. I don't want"—she glanced at Jaime—"distractions. Even with fun relationships, someone inevitably winds up hurt. And that's just not where I am right now."

He seemed genuinely concerned. "I get you. I'll let you know when a bunch of us go hiking or have a barbecue or something. That sound good?"

"I would love that. Thank you."

"Cool." He did a double take to the bar, and his smile grew wider. "Took him long enough." He scraped back his chair. "Come on. Let's dance."

As she got up, she followed his gaze and found Jaime staring at her. Their gazes locked, and her pulse rocketed. The longing she found in his eyes matched hers.

But for her, it quickly turned to anger.

Your date is standing right next to you.

Do you think I can't see?

Do you think I don't care?

She broke away from the table. "Let's do this."

Together, they headed onto the dance floor. Honestly, she was devastated. The last place she wanted to be was in a crowded bar, but she'd asked Lou to come out with her tonight, so she'd get through a song or two.

Then, she'd go home and sleep until it was time to lose herself in the joy of baking.

It was a lively country song, and the dance floor was crowded, so it confused her when Lou reached for her hands. He placed one on his chest, and the other on his hip. And then, he swayed with her. She started to pull away, but he lowered his mouth to her ear. "I can see that he's hurt you, and I'm sorry about that."

She relaxed a little. His shirt smelled clean, and he wore an expensive cologne. "It's fine. We want different things."

"I don't know him well, but I hear he only does situationships."

She looked up at him. "What's that?"

"You know, you're not dating, but you hook up whenever you're in the same town. Jaime likes women who don't live in Calamity. You might live across the country, but you're staying on his ranch. That probably wouldn't work for him."

Then, he needs to keep the hell away from me. "Yeah, that's not my thing. Let's just dance." She started to back away, to get into the rhythm of the song, but a grin teased his lips, as he swung her away from Jaime.

He pulled her up close and wrapped his arms around her

as if they were doing a slow dance at the prom. His hands inched down her back.

"Lou." She tried to wriggle out of his hold, but he held her firmly. "What are you doing?"

He chuckled. "Trust me."

Chapter Eleven

JAIME FUCKED UP.

Badly.

He wanted to charge onto the dance floor, elbowing everyone out of the way, toss Gracie over his shoulder, and take her home.

But he couldn't.

Because he'd done this. He'd stood there like an asshole when Lou had asked her out. He could've claimed her. Could've said, *She's mine.*

Or, maybe less caveman, he could've said something as simple as *Grace and I are dating.*

Instead, he'd disrespected her.

He'd made Grace feel like she didn't matter. Like she was just someone to fuck in the middle of the night.

Opening up to her, confessing his feelings about how happy she made him, meant nothing when his actions told a whole other story.

Shame burned through him. It was bad enough he'd hurt her, but now, he had to endure the punishment of watching her with another man.

Well, fuck that. Fuck this shame, this guilt, this constant fear he lived with that something terrible was about to happen.

Fuck it all. He'd gotten lucky beyond measure when this beautiful, happy, passionate woman had crashed into him, and he wasn't going to mess it up.

"What're you looking at?" At nearly six feet in those heels, Maxine was eye level.

Unfortunately, she was blocking his view. Over the loud music, roar of conversation, he could only hear one thing: his blood pounding in his ears.

Because Lou was holding Grace like a boyfriend. Not like a couple on their first date.

This is torture.

"No way," Maxine said. "No fuckin' way."

"No way what?" He was distracted. Gracie didn't seem all that comfortable, but she wasn't pushing him away. *That should be me. I should be slow dancing with her, taking her on hikes, making her dinner.*

She cooks all day, works in her truck...and smashes a burrito on the way home.

Why am I not cooking for her?

Because I don't want her around Kinny?

What the hell *is wrong with you?* Kinny would be lucky to know a woman like Gracie. *Even if it's only for a few weeks, it will be the best thing that's ever happened to my daughter.*

"I never thought I'd see the day."

Now, he was just irritated. "Get to the point." He probably shouldn't talk that way to the woman who was responsible for seventy percent of his sales, but he'd known her a long time. She and her dad were the ones who'd given him guidance when renting the cabins hadn't gone the way he'd hoped. They'd helped launch his business. He owed her everything.

"Who is she?" Maxine asked.

"She's my heart."

He could feel Maxine watching him, but he couldn't take his eyes off Gracie.

"But she's taken?"

Determination kicked him into action. "She sure as fuck is." He launched off the bar and arrowed through the crowd.

He'd hurt his heart. The only woman he'd ever wanted.

Back home, she didn't sing. She didn't make her special pastries. Her family didn't see her.

But I do. I see her, and I want all of her.

Clamping a hand on Lou's shoulder, he pried him away. His friend grinned. "Oh, hey."

He gave the guy a menacing look—*don't fucking play with me*—before turning to Gracie. "Can I talk to you?"

She arched a brow. But he saw the slight quiver in her lips, and it just about broke him.

"Please?" He grated out the word he only ever wanted to hear come out of her mouth when he was close to giving her an orgasm.

"Will it be worth my while?" she asked. "Or are you going to waste more of my time?"

"Gracie." The two syllables came out a jagged-edged growl.

She blew out a breath and rolled her eyes. "Fine."

Reaching between them, he closed his hand around her wrist and pulled her out of Lou's arms.

The idiot threw his head back and laughed. "The guys are going to love this."

But Jaime didn't give a shit what he said. He cupped Gracie's elbow and fast-walked her to the long hallway that held bathrooms, a utility room, and an office. He crowded her against the wall. "I'm sorry."

"You hurt me."

"I know. Dammit." He smacked the wall with the palm of his hand. "I wasn't thinking when I asked you not to tell anyone about us."

She shook her head. "That's the point, isn't it? You have these knee-jerk reactions, and I'm telling you right now, I'm not here for the drama. You either get your shit together, or we're going to be people who wave as our cars pass each other in the driveway."

"No." His firm tone was louder than he'd intended, and she flinched. "That'll never be enough. Gracie, I think about you all the time. I can't sleep at night for wanting you." He had to dig deeper though, find the truth, and pull it out by the roots. "Last night was better than anything…it was…" Frustrated, he exhaled roughly. "I'm so fucking crazy about you. But right after I said I wanted to be with you this summer, I got…"

"You got what? Say it. Talk to me."

"I got scared. I have so much good in my life, it feels… dangerous to add more." *Yes, that's it. That's what it feels like.* "But you're the most amazing person I know, and I disrespected you by trying to hide us. I'm sorry. I still want to be careful with Kinny—"

"Of course."

"But you're no one's secret. You're mine, Gracie. And I'm going to make you feel special every minute of every day. You've got a smile that brings me to my knees, and *I* want to put it on your face."

"You've got a shitty way of going about it."

"I know that. And I'm sorry. But if you'll give me a chance—"

"No." She ducked under his arm. "You crossed a line when you brought a woman to the festival and stood right where I could see you. I didn't want to believe you could be so cruel, but I guess you're more messed up than I realized. If your intention was to push me away…congratulations. You succeeded."

"What woman? I don't know what you're talking about."

"The same woman you brought to the bar."

"Are you talking about *Maxine*?"

"I don't know her name. And I don't care."

"That's my broker."

"Well, you've definitely slept with her."

"Oh, hell, no. I have *never* slept with her. She and her dad are the biggest distributors in the country. She's the most important business relationship I have. And as far as flaunting her…I wanted to show off your pastries. I never got to your truck because I ran into another client, a local rancher, and by the time we finished, I had to get to the rink."

As she searched his eyes, he needed her to believe him. Needed her to trust him.

Wrapping his arms around her waist, he hauled her up to him. "I used to think I was an adrenaline junkie, that I got my high jumping off cliffs—but now I see I was trying to feel something. And I only know that because I met *you*. This is the feeling I've missed, that I've been chasing. It's you, Gracie. You've pulled me out of a dark and lonely place, and I never want to go back."

"I feel the same way."

"I'm sorry I made you feel small. I'm sorry I tried to hide you. I will get on that stage right now and tell the world we're dating. I want them to know how much you mean to me. I want them to hear you sing and taste your éclairs. I want you to shine, Gracie. I want you to be everything you can be, and I want all your dreams to come true. I just want to be by your side while it's happening—even if it's only for the next six weeks. I'm a broken man, but your belief in me, your fucking *smile*, is piecing me back together again. Please forgive me. Please give me another chance."

"I don't need a stage. I just need to know you're in this with me, and you're not going to let your fears keep getting between us."

"I'm fighting them, Gracie. With everything I have. And it's all because of you."

He feasted on her. There was no other way to describe what Jaime was doing.

Stretched out on her bed, moonlight streaming through the window, Grace gripped his silky hair, holding him tightly to her. Not that he gave any indication of wanting to be anywhere but between her legs, but she didn't want him to ease up the pressure or swirl of his tongue.

Never in her life had she felt so luscious, so adored...so sexual. In Jaime's care, she was a goddess. A sensuous, tempting woman. Everything about her seemed to drive him wild.

It released her. Freed her. She lost her inhibitions and her sense of time and place. In bed together, they existed on a whole other plane. She lost her boundaries, and they flowed into each other.

As he held her ass cheeks in the palms of his hands, his tongue sent her soaring, spiraling, to the point she could barely stand the streak of intense pleasure. Her back arched as she cried out, "*Jaime.*" On the edge, she rocked her hips, ground them against his face, and when he growled, when one hand left her bottom, slid up her stomach and cupped her breast with rough desperation…when he squeezed lustily, she went wild.

"More. I need…" Fisting the sheets, she slammed herself against his mouth.

This man threw himself into the things that mattered. He was the best goalie, the best team owner, the best son, the best dad…and dear God, the very best lover.

"So good, Jaime. So, so good." His hair brushing her thighs, the urgency of his sounds and grip, and the scent she would forever associate with this exact moment—when she was her most physical, sensual self—shot her straight into ecstasy.

At the same time her body seized up and spasmed, her spirit soared. It was unlike anything she'd ever experienced, and it was beautiful and perfect, and she never wanted to come down.

He didn't stop, kept licking her, pinching her nipple, and she twisted with each aftershock. Finally, she let out a satisfied moan, and her body calmed down.

Jaime reared over her. "You're so fucking hot." He kissed her. Hungry, carnal. His big hand cupped her chin, spanning her jaw, as his hot, slick mouth covered hers, sucking, licking. Ravenous.

God. His passion.

It's for me.

I *do this to him.*

Even when she thought she had no more to give, he whipped her into a frenzy. She clutched his back, reached for his muscular ass, and jerked him down to her, trapping his hard cock between them. "Give it to me now. *Now.*"

Angling his hips back, he lined himself up, and pitched

forward. Her body went electric, every cell screaming, agitated, awake, and fully alert.

He fucked her savagely. Tucking his face into her neck, he bit down, one hand sliding under her bottom to lift her, lock her in place, giving her no room to move as his thrusts got shorter, tighter, wilder.

His head reared back, and he released a shout so loud, it filled her tiny cabin with unadulterated lust. "Goddammit, Gracie. God-motherfucking-dammit." One last hard thrust into her, and then he slowed. He slid in and out leisurely, as if savoring every last moment. And then, he fell onto his back, rested an arm across his forehead and said, "Fire. That's what we are. Fire."

Grace had two perfect weeks before her world flipped upside down.

She paced behind her cabin, phone to her ear. "I can't believe it." Panic sent her pulse beating out of control. "Everything's been so perfect. I thought I had another month. I don't...I don't know what to do. I have to go home, right? I have no choice." Without a job...without an income...she couldn't stay.

"Grace, slow down," her brother said. "You gotta catch me up here."

She stopped moving and took a breath for the first time since Santos had entered the food truck that morning. Oddly, breathing in the pine and the earthy scents of ranch life calmed her. "The guy who owns the truck. He's back."

"What about his broken arm?"

"It's in a soft cast, so he feels like he can handle it. Either way, he has no choice. It's his only income, and he has a family to feed."

"Okay, that's fair. Man's got bills. He's got a right to take his business back. But he's got to cut a deal. More than half the profits come from your fancy pastries, so he can split things fifty-fifty."

"He won't. I tried. But he did offer to pay me twenty dollars an hour."

"Dude." Romeo let out a disgusted huff. "Come on. Let's be honest here. Sure, the guy needs an income, but he only came back because he heard about your success. And that's because of your singing and fancy pastries—not his fuckin' doughnuts. He can do better than pay you hourly. He's got to give you a stake."

"I've worried about this exact thing all summer." Every time Brodie's PR team filmed her singing and showed off the long line waiting for her desserts, she'd get this twist of worry that Santos would see it and take it away from her.

Well, it happened.

"So, what're you going to do?"

"There's no negotiating with him. I tried. Bottom line, he'd rather go back to his normal income than split profits with me. So, that's it. I'm done. Without a job or an income, how can I stay here?" Her heart squeezed so hard, she had to close her eyes, lower her head, and breathe.

Jaime.

I can't lose him. Not yet.

God, she'd never known this kind of happiness.

Please don't take it away from me. Please.

"Romeo." It hurt to swallow, so she took a few more deep breaths, waiting for the knot of tension in her throat to ease.

"I'm here." He said it softly, gently. He knew. "You gotta make it work."

"Who's going to hire me for four weeks? And I can't live

off the money I earned. It's all going to Mom and Dad." Besides, her family needed her.

Her choice to live here was totally self-indulgent.

Her brother went quiet. "You willing to give up, just like that?"

"No, but I can't stay in town while I wait for Jaime to have some free time. Besides, Eliza can only work in the summer. She has to go back to her classroom soon. There's no one to bake after she goes."

"Let me ask you something. If you don't come back, does Renzo's go out of business? Or can we hire someone else to make the croissants? Because if you're not somewhere where you're special, then, Grace, you're in the wrong place."

Yes. Yes, yes, yes. Every time Jaime looked at her, he made her feel like there was no one else on this earth who could compare to her. But it was all so confusing. It wasn't like Jaime wanted her to *move* there. *It's a summer fling. That's all.* A spectacular one, but still. The boundaries were clear.

Of course, it wasn't just about Jaime. It was the joy of baking her pastries. Every time someone bit into her profiteroles and their eyes rolled back in their heads, and they moaned with pleasure, she knew she had something special. "What're you saying? We all work for the family business. Don't you want to?"

"Yeah, I do. I've got a good gig here. But I'm not like you. I don't have something I'd rather be doing. I do my job and then I fuck around with my buddies. That's enough for me. Is it enough for you?"

"No. It isn't."

"Then do it. Stay in your outlaw town."

"And do what?" Excitement came barreling in. "I don't have a truck."

"You think your success comes from that dude's truck?

No, man. It comes from you. Get a card table. Do whatever you need to make the pastries you've always dreamed about."

"Mom and Dad aren't going to like this. You know what they say."

Friends come and go, lovers break your heart, but family is the one constant you can count on.

"Yeah, and that's because Lorenzo came to America by himself. He left a big, multi-generational family in a small town to come to a huge city in America where he didn't know anybody. He had to start from nothing, and it was ingrained in every generation to stay together at any cost. But times have changed. And Grace, what's the cost to you?"

Romeo was right. They could hire someone to do what she did. Her family loved her, but she wasn't doing anything unique there.

She was special here. In Calamity. *I mean, come on, frickin' Lorelei Calloway stops by every single day.*

I'm on the cover of the Jackson Hole Gazette.

Here, I'm celebrated. At home, I'm a cog in the wheel.

"What do you want?" her brother asked.

Oh, she knew exactly what she wanted. She wanted to stay here and bake and sing…

And get every ounce of loving she could get from Jaime.

She glanced over to his very lived-in cabin. The hammock on the lawn, the swinging rocker on the porch. The colorful hanging flower baskets. Kinny's bright beach towel slung on the banister after running through the sprinklers.

The idea of leaving them was unthinkable. "I want to stay." She was protecting herself when she called it a summer fling. She knew it was more. Jaime knew it, too. "I need to."

"Then, do what you've gotta do to make that happen."

"You don't think Mom and Dad will be angry?"

"You're still doin' it, man. Look, I love having you a block away from the bars so I can crash on your couch. But you're more worried about Mom and Dad than yourself. Isn't it time to change that?"

"Yes."

"Get yourself a truck, Grace. I love you, but if I see you in the kitchen at Renzo's, I'm gonna stuff you in the bow locker."

She now had mild claustrophobia thanks to her idiot brothers locking her in that tiny storage pod on the boat. But she grinned. "I'm not five anymore. I won't fit."

After disconnecting, she went back into her cabin. She didn't know the first thing about food trucks. But Brodie Bowie did.

Grabbing her keys from the counter, she headed to Owl Hoot.

Grace was practically floating as she entered the rink later that day. *I get to stay.*

She couldn't wait to tell Jaime. Of course, he didn't know what happened. She'd wanted to come to him with a solution and not a problem. *And I have it.*

She'd met Brodie at his house, explained her situation, and he'd immediately directed his assistant to find a truck and get it delivered to the amphitheater as soon as possible. He wouldn't hear of her leaving.

As they'd talked, she couldn't help noticing the meadow of flowers outside their family room window. She'd been blown away by the beauty. Apparently, his wife was a perfume maker who grew her own lyantha, the distinguishing ingredient. Rosie was kind enough to offer her a space to grow her own edible flowers.

Good people.

Of course, Grace hadn't accepted the extremely generous offer since she wouldn't be staying long enough for her plantings to come into bloom. But as she'd stood in that meadow, children laughing on the nearby swing set, the mountains rising up so abruptly, the granite peaks glittering in the sunlight, she'd had a profound sense of rightness. A longing for a life she knew in her bones fit her.

She wanted to live here. With Jaime, Kinny, and a whole passel of blond-haired babies they'd make together. She'd have own her own bakery and live in a home with a spectacular view of the Teton mountains.

As she headed toward the ice, she reined herself in. She was getting way ahead of herself.

Ah, dreams. Those nasty suckers wrap around your heart like vines and squeeze.

Besides, how could she even consider raising children two thousand miles away from her family? Her parents wouldn't be right down the street. Her kids wouldn't grow up with her brothers, aunts, uncles, grandparents, and cousins.

That's not going to happen.

Anyhow, she'd come to meet the hockey boys, so she headed toward the cluster of players. People sat in the bleachers, most looking at their phones, some watching the action on the ice. It looked like several classes were going on at once. In the center, coaches led kids in a figure skating class. At either end, teams gathered around the net doing hockey drills.

And of course, in the sea of moving bodies, Grace spotted Jaime right away.

He blocked the net on the far end of the rink. Teenage

boys worked him hard, as they lined up to fire off a row of pucks.

Not one got past him, of course.

He liked to say she'd only seen him at the right time, but she knew better. It was every time.

A woman came up to her. "And that's why they call him Goose."

Who's she talking about? "Are you talking about Jaime?"

"Yep. Back when he played for this same team, he was known for shutouts. Which meant the other team had a big goose egg. Zero goals."

"That makes sense. He's good." *Oh. Ick.* She'd sounded a little swoony there.

The woman checked her out. "Are you dating him?"

Yep. It was that obvious. "Yeah. I am."

"Really?" The woman checked her out—a full-body scan from Grace's hair all the way down to her chef clogs.

Grace raised an eyebrow. *Excuse me?*

The woman laughed and waved her hands. "Sorry. Oh, my God. I'm so sorry. I didn't mean—well, no, I did. I totally did. He's got a reputation, and I was wondering— never mind. I'll stop talking."

"What kind of reputation?"

"He owns a professional hockey team, he's gorgeous, he's a powerful athlete. He's basically the most eligible bachelor in Calamity—and yet he doesn't date."

"Well, maybe I'm safe. I'm only in town for the summer. I'm Grace, by the way."

"Alice. My son plays on the Juniors team. Well, he's suspended right now."

"Oh, that's why I'm here. To meet the boys."

"Well, you're in luck. I'm Dipshit number one's mom."

"And I'm the baker he might be working with."

"Glad to meet you. Helen couldn't be here. She's out of town, but she's Dipshit number two's mom. Come on. I'll introduce you." She pointed. "That's them, sitting on the penalty bench watching their teammates get ready for their season."

"Oh, that hurts." Grace followed the well-dressed woman.

"Jaime said you were hesitant to work with them, so I'm here to assure you they're good kids. Helen's Dipshit thought it was a brilliant idea to date my son's ex-girlfriend after they broke up. It was Jeremy's first heartbreak, and so when his best friend and teammate betrayed him, he lost it. They held the *conversation* on the ice."

"Hard to fault him."

"Well, I'm his mom, so I've got to teach him a better way to deal with his anger and pain. I mean, I wanted to knock Ben out, too, but did I throw a punch?" She laughed. When they reached the penalty box, Alice rapped on the Plexiglass. Her son turned around, spied Grace, and popped up. His friend—sitting at the opposite end—stood, too. "Guys, this is Grace, the lady you'll be working for. She wants to know that you're responsible and hardworking and won't let her down." She gave each a pointed look. "This is her business. It's how she earns a living, and she can't afford to have her employees show up late, play on their phones, or chat with their buddies. Can you reassure her that won't happen?"

"Yes, ma'am." The taller one reached out a hand. "I'm Jeremy Witmer, and I've worked at Bliss Ice Cream for the last year. I also mow lawns. I can get references if you need them."

The teen held her gaze the entire time. He was well-spoken and had a good, caring mom. "My hours are unusual. I start baking at around three or four in the morning. And I work in the truck from noon until about nine at night. It gets hot in there." *Wait. New truck, new situation.* "Actually, it won't be that bad because I'm not frying anything." *I'm totally free now.* "We're only selling the pastries I make that morning. We'll have drinks, too."

"I'll work as many hours as you want." Jeremy cut a glance to the rink with a tortured expression. "The sooner I get back on the ice, the better."

"And what about you?" she asked the other teen.

"This is Ben," Alice said.

He was stockier and a bit more closed off. Still, he held her gaze. "I'm not going to let you down. I want to play hockey."

"And just so you know, Coach made it clear, if they mess up with you even once, he's resetting the clock." Alice gave the boys a pointed look. "And that will drop them down to the third line. Basically, they'll miss out on the entire season."

"That's not going to happen," Jeremy said.

"Okay, great." Joy clutched her heart and sent her soaring. For the next month, she got to make her pastries, live on a ranch in Jackson Hole surrounded by mountains, and have help so she could get out and explore a little. And be with Jaime. *How is this my life?* "I should have a truck by tomorrow, so if you're ready to get to work, come by at six in the morning."

Seemingly satisfied, Alice hitched her purse higher on her shoulder and turned to sit down.

But Jeremy said, "I thought you start baking at three?"

"I do. But I'd never ask you guys—"

"I don't mind," Jeremy said.

"I don't, either. I'm grounded." The other boy hunched a shoulder. "It's not like I'm staying up late this summer."

Jeremy glared at his former friend, and it looked like he was stopping himself from saying something like, *Whose fault is that?*

"Are you guys okay?" she asked them. "Because I've been doing this by myself and can absolutely continue to do so."

Jeremy stood straighter. "No. I'm fine."

"Yes, I believe as individuals you're both fine." She wagged a finger from one to the other. "But the hostility between you isn't going to work."

"She's right." Alice nudged her son. "We talked about this. I'll remind you about your priorities."

"I know, Mom. I get it." Jeremy turned to her. "I want this job, and I won't let you down."

"Same," Ben said.

"Okay, we'll give it a shot. I'll trust you until I can't. I'm going to head out now, but I'll let the ranch manager know you'll be there at four. I'm the first cabin, so you can't miss it. It was nice to meet all of you." It was time to leave, but she couldn't help casting one more glance at Jaime.

He'd stopped playing to talk to a couple of boys. Masks up, they listened raptly to what he said. She wouldn't interrupt him, but she wanted nothing more than to run out onto the ice and throw herself into his arms. She wanted to kiss him senseless.

Instead, she turned to leave. That was when she noticed a little girl spinning and flapping her arms on the rubber flooring. *Oh. It's Kinsley.* Grace cut a look to the rink and saw she was imitating the movements of the figure skaters.

She headed over, and when the girl finished her routine, Grace clapped her hands. "You're a really good dancer."

"I know." She came closer. "Do you have any yummies with you?"

"I'm afraid I don't. But if you tell me your favorite treat, I'll make it for you."

"I like everything. But mostly, I like how pretty your stuff is. It's like you're a fairy or something."

"That makes me so happy. Thank you. Are you waiting for your dad?" He'd said he needed to take Kinny shopping today.

"Yes," she said it dismissively, still focused on the ice. "That's Lacey. She's got a pink dress. That's the one I want. I wish I could be in that class, but Daddy says I'm too little."

Oh, Jaime. "How old are those kids?"

"Sixes and sevens."

Exactly Kinny's age. Of course, she wouldn't point out the obvious.

Kinsley watched the kids with intense focus. "I can do that."

"Yes, I saw. You're a beautiful dancer."

Her gaze was trained on the kids as though memorizing their moves. "I'm good at that. Daddy says I'm too young, though." Kinny looked up at her. "But I want to."

"I'll bet you do." *Should I talk to him? Or leave it alone?*

But before she could decide, Jaime noticed her. Guarding the net, he popped up, yanked off his mask, and gave her a look that sent a flashfire through her body.

And then, he came for her.

Chapter Twelve

WHEN JAIME LOOKED OVER TO CHECK ON HIS daughter, he found her talking to Gracie.

The sight of her never failed to blow through him like a gust of wind at the top of a summit. "I'm out of here. Got a date with my daughter." He pulled off his mask and skated to the edge of the rink, waving to his two favorite girls.

He meant to say hello to Gracie. He meant to contain all this wild energy coursing through him. Because he really did believe Kinny shouldn't get too attached. It was okay if she spent some time around her, just not too much.

But the draw of her was so strong he didn't stop. He kept moving. Tossing his gloves onto the rubber mat, he gripped the wall and leapt over. Affection for this beautiful woman overwhelmed him, and he picked her up, hugging her so tightly her feet came off the ground.

Without thinking, he found himself kissing her. One hand cupped the back of her head, the other arm wound around her waist, and he fed the hungry beast that couldn't get enough of her.

"Daddy." Kinny's delighted shriek had Gracie pulling her mouth away.

Arms slung around his neck, she smiled at him. "Hi."

He didn't know he had bindings around his heart until they broke free. "Hi." For the first time in—well, maybe ever—he had room to breathe.

"Put her down, Daddy."

When he did, the boys on the bench started clapping. "Way to go, Goose," one of them shouted.

Exhilarated, he laughed. He lowered her feet to the floor, but he didn't let go. He didn't ever want to let her go. "Did you talk to Jeremy and Ben?"

"I did. It's all set. They start in the morning." She glanced at the boys. "They're coming over at *four*. They said they want as many hours as I can give them."

"Oh yeah." He gestured to the ice. "They're behind. They'll have to work hard to get a place on the front line."

"I'm not sure what they'll be doing yet. My dad always says to focus your efforts on the thing only you can do and hire people to do the rest. So, I'll do the baking, and they'll do prep work, load the van, work in the truck…stuff like that."

"Makes sense." He couldn't help himself from kissing her again.

She kept it brief, tucking her face into his neck. "You claimed me."

He clutched her. "I did. Is that okay?" Even now, after all the time they'd spent together, his blood still felt carbonated around her.

"I'm not the one who wanted us to be secret."

Ah, hell. "I hate that I did that to you."

"Forget it. It lasted all of three hours. My point is that I know this is hard for you. You didn't want Kinny to know. And now she does."

When she heard her name, his baby reached up and tugged on his jersey. "Come on, Daddy. I've been waiting so long."

"I know you have. You've been very patient. And now, we can finally go home and nap."

Kinsley giggled. "*Daddy*. I'm too big for naps. You promised to take me shopping."

"Did I? I thought we had a date to clean out the chicken coop? And weren't we going to wash my car after?"

"No. Stop joking around. I have to get my dress."

She'd been so patient. "All right, angel. We'll go."

Kinsley looked up to Gracie. "Will you come, too? Please?"

In his arms, he could feel Gracie's body stiffen.

I did that.

I made her feel unwelcome. He'd drawn a line, a boundary around him and his daughter, keeping Gracie out.

She wriggled out of his hold and took a step back. "I think this is your special time with your daddy. Where are you going?"

"I'm getting a dress for the dance," Kinsley said. "And I need you to come 'cause you know what pretty is."

"I do?" Grace seemed confused. "I'm not sure I have the best sense of fashion. I live in chef's clothes."

"You make pretty things, so you can find me a pretty dress."

With a worried expression, she looked to Jaime as though he might find a way out of the situation. But he didn't want to do that. He wanted Gracie with them.

Hang on. Was that selfish of him? He'd done a good job keeping his two worlds separate, but now that he'd kissed her in public… He had to think ahead to the consequences. After Grace left, after his daughter got attached—

"It's okay." Gracie pressed her hand on his arm. "I have work to do." She looked down at Kinny. "Sorry, sweetie."

No. He wasn't going to shut her out anymore. "I want you to come with us."

"You do?" she asked.

"Absolutely. She likes your style." *That's not why you want her to come, asshole.* "And we want you with us."

"Okay, well, I'd love to come."

"Really? You can?" Kinny clapped and bounced with excitement.

"Sure. What kind of dress are you looking for?"

"A princess one." She reached for Gracie's hand. "And after we find one, Daddy will get us ice cream cones."

"I love ice cream. It's one of the few desserts I can eat without analyzing it."

"Let's go, let's go." Kinny grabbed his hand, too.

"Give me two minutes to take off my skates and get dressed."

"Oh, Daddy. You're killing me here."

He burst out laughing. "That's what my mom says. All the time." He kissed his daughter on the forehead. "Two minutes." When Kinny went back to watching the figure skating class, he sat on the bench and untied his skates. "Is this okay? I know you have to work."

"Actually, I don't." She sat beside him. Watching him carefully, she said, "Santos came back."

"What're you talking about? The *truck owner?*"

"Yep."

"What does he want?" He'd seen her success. Of course, he had. "You don't have to give the truck back, do you? Because that's bullshit."

She smiled, unconcerned. "Yes, he wants it back."

What was he missing here? "He can't have it. You've committed to a summer here. He can't take away your business."

"He absolutely can. I was only borrowing it. But also, he needs the income. You can't fault him for that."

"I sure as hell can. You've got to make a living, too. You counted on this income. It's the only reason you're here."

"Well, he did offer to pay me to stay on."

"*Help* him? You're the hit of the festival. You're all over social media. You put his truck on the map."

"He knows. Look, it's—"

Kinny swung around. "Can we go now? What if the store sells out of all the dresses?"

"Hm, someone's catastrophizing." She gently nudged him. "I guess you're right. She *is* just like you."

Oh, shit. That was a terrible thing to impose on her. He'd have to watch himself.

Kinny tugged on his jersey. "Daddy, you promised."

"Have I ever broken a promise to you?"

With tremendous gravity, she contemplated the question. "No."

"And I won't now. But let me finish talking to Gracie about this. It's important." He reached for her hand. "So, where do things stand? How much did he offer to pay you? Because if it's any less than you've been making—"

"It is. It's twenty an hour."

"Is he out of his mind? You're the Singing Baker. That's the draw. That, and your pastries."

"I know." She didn't seem even slightly worried. In fact, she seemed to be enjoying this.

"I told him it wasn't worth it. I can make more working at Renzo's."

His stomach dropped so fast he grabbed the bench. "You're leaving?" *No.* He wouldn't let that happen. "You're happy here. You're the most popular vendor at the festival. You can't leave." Resolve had him on his feet. "I'll get you a food truck."

"That's a great idea." She stood up, too. "And Brodie had the same one."

"What're you saying?"

"Brodie's finding me one. He doesn't want me to leave." She laughed.

"Well, good." He looked down at his socked feet. "That's good."

"Yep. But it won't be ready until tomorrow, so I'm free this afternoon."

"Cool. Cool. Well, then, let me change, and we'll go." Only after he started off for the locker room did her smile make sense. He called back to her, "You had fun with that."

"Sure did."

He's holding my hand.

It was nothing really, just a gentle clasp. Both their hands rested on her thigh. And yet, with his daughter in the back seat, it was everything. Especially after the way he'd kissed her in front of everyone at the rink.

His SUV smelled of new leather and something minty. It was huge and badass and fit him perfectly. As he drove, she kept sneaking glances at the way his round biceps flexed and popped, and his worn jeans hugged his powerful thighs. She loved his strong, calloused hand on the steering wheel.

In the back seat, Kinsley hummed, and when he punched the accelerator to turn onto 191, the engine roared.

He caught her watching him and grinned. "You're picturing me naked right now, aren't you?"

"Oh, my God." With a disdainful sniff, she stared out the windshield. "Your ego has no bounds." And then, she said, "Of course, I am."

He chuckled.

"Well, look at you. Can you blame me?"

"Nah. I get it all the time."

She shifted to face him. "You get women asking to see you naked all the time?"

Smiling, he glanced in the rearview mirror. His daughter was still in her own world, oblivious to their conversation. "We all have our gifts."

She rolled her eyes. "Okay, heartbreaker." She'd never seen him so relaxed, so...content. "I can't believe you're being so chill about me coming with you. I thought you'd freak out." She kept her voice low so she wouldn't draw the girl's attention.

He feigned offense. "Men don't freak out."

"This one does." She muttered it to be funny.

But he didn't laugh. He took it very seriously. "I *want* her to know you. Even if she only has you for a month, she's damn lucky." He cut her a look. "I'm sorry it took me so long to figure it out."

"It's okay."

"Daddy, Gracie says I should be in the figure skating class. She says you should let me."

His eyebrows flew up to his hairline.

Grace touched his arm. "I didn't say that."

"She says I'm not too young," Kinsley said.

"Oh, brother." Grace lowered her face into her hand. "I swear, I never said it."

"No, it's all right," he said. "This is on me."

"Can I, Daddy? Can I be in the class?"

"Yeah, sweet pea. You can."

"I can?" In her excitement, her legs started kicking the back of Grace's seat.

"Yes. I'll sign you up today."

"I get to skate?"

His pained expression told him how hard it was to hear Kinny's disbelief. "You do. As soon as we get to the first store, I'll do it."

"Yay. I get to skate. Thank you, Daddy."

"You're welcome."

And this was why Grace had taken a chance on him. Yes, he was damaged. Yes, he'd hurt her. But he was trying so hard. And he was winning. He was truly overcoming his fears. "Good job."

"It's past time. I just know her. I know she's going to try triple axels when the rest of the class is learning figure eights."

"Too bad they don't have like...I don't know, *coaches* on the ice or something to keep them in line."

He grinned. "I get it. I get it." But his hand flexed on the wheel.

"I doubt she's the first spirited student these coaches have ever seen, but if you're worried, talk to them. They'll keep an eye on her."

He squeezed her thigh. "I like that you call her spirited. It's a much better way to describe her than reckless." He flashed her a grateful smile. "Thank you for giving me another way of looking at it."

"Daddy, can I have my own skates?"

"Yeah, of course."

"I want white ones. And I want a pink skirt. And I want pink socks. You know what the girls wear?"

"I do."

"Can we get it now?" Kinny asked.

"Sure thing."

"Thank you, Daddy. Thank you so much."

"You're welcome, sweetie." His eyelids squeezed shut. "I hope I don't regret this."

"You'll be fine." She gave his thigh a squeeze.

What could possibly go wrong in a beginning figure skating class?

"What in the world?" Sunlight filtered through a canopy of pine trees. As they passed under a stone and wrought iron arch that said Wild Wolff Village, Grace sat forward. "Did we just drive through a magical portal? Am I in Europe?"

"Feels like it." Jaime cocked an elbow out the window. A warm breeze tousled his hair, and he looked so damn handsome, she wanted to crawl onto his lap and make out like drunk kids at a frat party. "This place used to be a dude ranch just like ours, but about twenty years ago, they turned it into a ski resort. Everything you see is owned by the Wolff family." As they approached the town square, he tipped his chin toward the commercial area. "They lease out all the stores and restaurants."

They parked behind the lodge and then walked into town. Cobblestone streets, window boxes bursting with colorful flowers, and iron benches only added to the European feel of the village. A trolley rumbled by, its bell clanging.

The town square had an ice-skating rink, a clock tower, and kiosks that sold crepes, cocoa and coffee, and ice cream. *I could sell my pastries here.* She didn't dare voice it out loud. It was impossible since she had to get back home. But she could see herself in an apron selling pastries and espresso drinks.

An image hit, filling her with a rush of happiness. She needed to decorate her new truck, and she knew exactly what she wanted. She'd paint it magenta and then string a wreath of light pink peonies all around it. *This is going to be so much fun.*

And now that Jaime didn't mind her spending time with Kinny, her summer would get that much fuller. They'd sit together in the bleachers watching her figure skating class. Or maybe he'd be on the ice with the Juniors at the same time. He'd skate over to the wall and give her that sexy look and motion her over. Give her a kiss. Kinny would call out, *Daddy,* as if she was embarrassed but secretly loving it.

It was throwing off family vibes, and she was there for it.

"You all right?" Jaime interrupted her absolutely psycho reveries.

Which was a good thing. The more carried away she got, the more it would hurt when she had to leave. "Yeah. Of course. I just love this place so much."

Besides, the only planning she needed to worry about was decorating her truck and the pastries she'd sell now that she had help and more time.

Except…she knew she was lying to herself. She'd accepted her life on Duff Island. It was all she'd ever known, and Ian was an obvious part of it.

But this one with Jaime? It was nothing she'd ever imagined but everything she craved.

Because here, all her senses fired up. She felt alive, vital, and free. *Creative.*

As they walked along the street, Kinsley kept up a steady chatter of conversation that jumped from one topic to another. Still rattled by how very much she wanted a life that wasn't possible for her, Grace distracted herself by peering into windows of high-end boutiques filled with clothing, shoes, purses, and electronics. They passed fancy restaurants, a diner, and several bistros with outdoor seating.

"You're awfully quiet." Jaime reached for her hand. "What're you thinking?"

That you may have taken big steps, but you can't handle the future I'm imagining with you.

Oh, hold on now. If he couldn't, that was on him. She wasn't going to dim her light or pretend to be someone she wasn't. If he got spooked, then she was wasting her time with him. "You know, even though I grew up making sand cakes, went to culinary school, and spend my free time imagining the kind of pastries I could make, I never got *invested* in it."

"In what? What do you mean?"

"I guess, since it was never a possibility, I didn't waste my time dreaming about owning a bakery. It was drilled into me that no one wants 'that fancy stuff.' But out here, people love what I do. I have return customers who say, 'I only came to the festival to get one of your tarts.' I mean, *Lorelei Calloway* buys one every single day. For herself. And she hasn't eaten sweets in ten years."

"Yeah, that's pretty cool."

"And look at this place. Wild Wolff Village—I mean, this is everything I ever imagined. I wanted all of this." She gestured to the old-world elegance of the storefronts and cobblestone streets.

"On the website, you can apply to lease one of their buildings, but I know the Wolff family, so I could get you a meeting with them. Though I doubt you'd need an introduction. Everyone knows about the Singing Baker. You'd probably jump to the top of the waiting list."

She stopped walking. Letting go of his hand, she stared at him, studied his expression. Did he know what he just said? The implication of it?

"What're we doing?" Kinny asked. "There's no dresses here."

"Hang on, sweetie." Jaime cupped Grace's chin, his thumb brushing across her cheek. "Did I misunderstand?"

"That's what I'm wondering. You just offered to help me start a bakery in your hometown."

She saw it then. The frisson of tension that rippled across his features. He didn't say a word, and she gave him the space to work it out. What they were contemplating was huge.

A trolley whirred past. The scent of grilled meat filled the air. Kinny dropped to a crouch to examine something on the sidewalk. And Grace teetered on the precipice.

If he could get me to the top of the list…would I actually want to stay?

Would I leave Renzo's?

Excitement flowed through her with such force it threatened to lift her off her feet, but her mind raced with thoughts reminding her about family, history, loyalty. Renzo's, Renzo's, Renzo's.

But I'm not abandoning my family.

I'm claiming me. My best self.

Why would I go back home and suppress all that makes me happy? Why would I do that? I'll always be a Giordano.

"Are you serious about this?" he asked. "I don't want to ask my friend if you're not."

A profound sense of rightness filled her being. "I'm sure."

His fingers sifted through her hair until he cupped the back of her head. "You don't sound sure."

"I know. I know. But that's because I'm so scared of stepping outside the lines my parents have drawn. I'm just not sure they can stuff me back in the bottle, you know?"

"I do know."

There was a glint in his eyes, and she was too afraid to name it. She needed him to say it. "That would mean I move here."

"It would be hard to commute from Rhode Island."

"I need you to be serious right now. Do you get what we're talking about?"

He let out a shaky breath that was somewhere between a laugh and a sigh. "Gracie." His gaze swung away as he bit his bottom lip, but when it came back to her, it was filled with a burning need. "I want you to be happy. I can't think of anything worse than you going back to a life of making muffins. And if you tell me you want this"—he made a sweeping motion up and down the street—"then I'll call my friend so fast your head will spin. Because the idea of you leaving me…it keeps me up at night. It's like a clock inside me. I can hear every minute that ticks by. I don't think you understand what you bring to my life. I just don't think you get it." He gripped both her arms. "Swear to God, I do *not* want to go back to a life without Gracie Giordano."

The breath left her lungs, her legs turned to rubber, and the only thing keeping her tethered to this earth was the intensity of his gaze and the firmness of his grip. "We're doing this?"

"It's a huge decision. You need to give it some thought. But for me, it's a yes. There's nothing I want more than for you to stay."

Jaime stood in the middle of the boutique. It was an explosion of frilly, frothy, white fabric.

A pink velvet ottoman served as seating for the bride's entourage and no more than twenty gowns filled the racks with their tulle, silk, and feathery glory. "These are wedding gowns."

"Yep." Grace spoke quietly, her arm slung through his. "Custom. We're talking twenty thousand dollars a dress."

"Then why did my mom suggest this place?" He pulled out his phone to check the list she'd sent. This shop was the first. "They're supposed to have princess gowns for little girls."

"I'm sure they have flower girl dresses. It's the perfect place for what Kinny wants."

Of course, the minute he'd stepped inside, his daughter had gasped and raced to the other end of the shop. She was currently lost in clouds of tulle.

"Let me get some help."

He watched Gracie head to the counter. In her white shorts and flowy blouse, she was the sexiest woman he'd ever seen. Every time he looked at her, his gut tightened with lust. It had been that way from the moment she'd sat across from him on the plane.

Only now, there was another layer. Friendship, a companionship unlike anything he'd ever known.

And—miracle of all miracles—she wanted to stay.

He'd jumped right in—told her to do it. And he didn't regret it. Not at all. But he had to wonder if they'd both moved too quickly. Shouldn't they give it more thought?

He just didn't want to still be that reckless fucker who pursued his own interests without a thought for the people who might get hurt by his actions.

Because he had to consider one simple fact: he wouldn't

leave his family to move to Duff Island. So, how could he expect her to do it?

Fortunately, Gracie's laughter tore him out of his wretched thoughts. She crouched beside Kinny at a rack of little girl-size dresses. He ached with affection for her. For the life his daughter would have with Gracie in it.

He might not deserve all this goodness, but he was going to take it.

If she wanted to be with them, he was abso-fucking-lutely going to take it.

Gracie caught him watching and waved him over. When he got there, she said, "I think Kinsley found one she likes." She stood, pulling the dress off the rack.

Eyes wide with awe, his daughter pointed to the beaded tulle ballgown with a pink satin belt. "I love it, Daddy. I love it so much." She gazed up at him. "Can I have it?"

"Isn't it too much for a dance?" Jaime asked, though he knew he would buy it. Even if she just wore it on her balcony to survey her kingdom.

"No. It's perfect. I want it so much, Daddy. Please, please, please." She was bouncing in place, barely able to contain her enthusiasm.

In his irrational attempt to keep her safe, he'd denied her so much in life. Adventure, experience, physical challenges. "Why don't you go try it on? See if it fits." He couldn't deny her this.

"Let's go, Gracie." Kinny took off to the dressing room.

They followed, but on the way, Gracie checked the price. With a horrified expression, she mouthed, "Four hundred dollars."

He nodded. *It's fine.*

"What kind of dance is it?" Gracie asked.

"It's the annual Rancher's Ball. My dad's the president of the Wyoming Rancher's Association, so we have to go."

"This dress might be a little much."

"She's not the kind of kid who asks me to buy her stuff." *In fact, she's just the opposite—she asks for so little.* "I don't mind doing it."

Gracie raised her eyebrows. "Okay." At the dressing room, she lifted the heavy velvet drape to let Kinny in, and then let it drop closed behind them.

He went to sit on the pink tufted ottoman. Next to him, a woman said, "I'm surprised to see a groom in a bridal salon, but I guess the times have changed. Back in my day, we cared about all those rules—don't let the groom see the wedding gown before the wedding. But your generation's got its priorities right."

Before she could go on, he said, "Sorry, I'm not the groom. I'm just here to get my daughter a dress."

"Oh, I thought that was your fiancée. I should learn to keep my mouth shut. Last Christmas, my daughter-in-law walked in the door. She had a little pooch, and I knew they were trying to have kids, so I said, Yay! Congratulations! Why didn't you tell me? My daughter-in-law gave me a look that made me shrivel up inside. Turned out she wasn't pregnant. She'd just gained weight." The woman rolled her eyes. "My bad."

"No, it's fine."

"I saw the way you looked at her. Maybe you *should* marry her." The woman laughed.

A vivid image popped into his mind, and in that one instant, he could see his life laid out for him.

Gracie's cheek dusted with flour, her hips swinging to the beat in their home.

Home.

Me, Kinny, Gracie. He didn't know if Grace wanted more kids, but he sure as hell did. He wanted them with her. He wanted kids with her bright, fierce, compassionate, and fun spirit. Her creativity, and her zest for life.

A curtain whisked open, and a young woman stepped out in a massive gown. She had a huge smile for her mom, who stood up. "Is this it? Is this the one?"

Her daughter nodded.

"Mazel tov. You found it." As the clerk led the woman over to the dais for a fitting, the woman turned to Jaime. "We've been to three states, thirty shops, and she's tried on hundreds of dresses. When you know, you know."

A voice inside his mind said, *I know.*

It was both a thrilling and an unnerving thought. He got up and paced to the window. Gazing out at the foot traffic, the horse-drawn carriage clopping along the cobblestone road, he could only marvel, *Do I really get a life this fucking beautiful?*

"Daddy?"

He spun around to find Gracie and Kinsley stepping out of the dressing room. Those two together, the happiness shining in their eyes, sealed it for him. He headed over.

Yes, dammit. I can have this life.

Once he reached them, he bowed. "Princess." And then, he asked Grace, "Excuse me. Have you seen my daughter? I thought she went into that dressing room with you, but I'm obviously mistaken."

Kinsley's smile stretched across her face, lighting up her eyes. "It's *me*, Daddy."

"No, that's not possible. You see, my daughter's a little girl. Not a princess like you."

Gracie curtsied. "Sir, may I present Princess Kinsley Dupree?"

Clapping a hand over her mouth, Kinsley giggled.

The clerk joined them. "Oh, look at you. That dress fits perfectly."

"I'm a princess."

"Yes, I see that. And is this your prince?" She gestured to Jaime.

"He's not a *prince*." Kinsley giggled like the idea was absurd.

"Wait, how come I'm not a prince?" he asked.

His daughter flicked her hand toward him. "Princes don't look like that. You're the Beast."

Chapter Thirteen

WITH ONLY THREE WEEKS LEFT IN CALAMITY, GRACE was literally living every dream she'd ever kept stuffed deep down inside her.

She made luscious, gorgeous pastries for a living. She was in the most passionate relationship of her life, and she lived in this magical mountain town where the people were wild at heart.

And she *might* get to stay. Jaime had reached out to Wild Wolff Village, but his friend was out on paternity leave. The assistant said she'd let him know Jaime called.

All of it was good. Better than good. Except one thing.

I don't have the money to lease a space like that.

So, even if they offered it to her, she couldn't afford it.

Damn you, Ian. That was the whole point of her savings.

She could try to get a loan. Because, if the opportunity came her way, she'd do everything in her power to make it happen.

But there was another thing, one that was harder to manage. Because this happiness came at a terrible cost. It was a betrayal to her family. In their eyes, they'd given her time off to recover from her failed wedding and fully expected her to come home.

She had no idea how to tell them she wanted to live here.

"Weren't you going to take your dinner break?" Jeremy asked.

"Yep, I sure was." Even though the boys were doing a great job, she still wasn't used to having help. Fortunately, they'd both had experience working sales counters, so she didn't have to worry about that. She reached for her insulated bag. "All right. I'll be back soon."

With two hours before the next band took the stage, all the vendors were crazy busy. She headed out into the cool evening air and sat on a picnic bench in the woods. As she unzipped her bag, she took in her pretty food truck. Every time she looked at it, she got a little skip in her heart. What Brodie had delivered was white, scuffed, and dented. With no time to wait for a vinyl wrap, she'd painted it magenta—a color that would catch anyone's attention in the crowded meadow. Out front, she'd set up a big chalkboard so she could switch up her daily offerings. She'd draped fairy lights across the top and strung together a garland of big pink peonies that spilled down the sides and around the pass-through window.

As she bit into a chicken salad sandwich, she remembered her lemonade and made a quick dash back to the truck. She'd only cracked the door open when she heard the low voices of the boys.

"You dumped her," Ben said. "You didn't even like her."

"It doesn't matter." Jeremy's tone was flat. "You don't touch your friend's ex. How do you not know that?"

"Guys?" She stepped inside and pulled her bottle from the refrigerator. "I know this is hard for both of you, and it seems like you two really need to have it out, but not here, okay? Now is not the time."

"Sorry." Jeremy nodded curtly, as Ben exchanged a box of truffles for a twenty-dollar bill.

She really did feel bad for them. Relationships were a hard road to navigate—and it never got easier. "It's all right. I get it." She returned to her table. Awash in the sounds of the crowd as they waited for the next act and the chatter from the tour bus area behind her, she ate her sandwich, sipped her lemonade, and then she put everything away and pulled out her phone. Ian had been reaching out through direct messages, texts, calls, and email. He said he had something important to tell her, and he sounded excited. If he'd found a way to get her money back, she'd listen. Otherwise, forget it.

She hit Connect.

"Grace?" He answered on the second ring, sounding as friendly as always.

Which would be easy for him. What consequence had he suffered? He could live without her—he'd proven that countless times.

"Yep." She'd keep it brief. "What's up?"

He was quiet for a moment. "I hate to hear you sound like that."

"Like what?"

"Cold. Like I'm a telemarketer."

"And you can't think of a single reason why? Not one? Look, unless you have a way to pay me back, I don't want to talk to you. So, I'd really appreciate it if you'd respect that." A woman took the stage, speaking to the crowd.

"I do." He drew in a breath. "I've been trying to work this out all summer, and I think I've finally found a way."

Easy applause rippled across the meadow. People shouted and whistled.

"My parents are going to buy a building in Newport."

"Okay. Cool. I don't know what this has to do with me." She was more curious what was going on in the amphitheater than in Ian's family's life.

"It's in a prime location. You can have a bakery on the street level and an apartment on top."

Whoa. He'd said the magic words. *You can have a bakery.* "What're you talking about?" A zing streaked from her chest down to the soles of her feet.

"We're giving you the entire building rent-free until you and your family recover what I took from you. And you keep all the profit."

"You realize this is your parents cleaning up your mess, right?" Six weeks ago, she might've been excited. But now, she almost didn't want the option.

She didn't want a reason to go back home.

"I do. But it's the best thing I can come up with. And it's good because it's an upscale neighborhood, so you can open a Renzo's *and* sell your pastries. It's the best of all worlds."

"I appreciate the offer." The audience was chanting. Weirdly, it sounded like *Singing Baker, Singing Baker, Singing Baker.* "But I don't know—" *If I'm going to come back or not.* Yeah, that wasn't something she'd tell Ian. That conversation went to her parents. "I'm not sure I'm comfortable with the idea of your parents buying me a building. I have to think about it."

"I figured you'd say that. Just know I'm sorry for stealing from you and your parents. I can't explain it other than to say I got carried away. I guess, you know, I got greedy, and I lost myself. I *will* make it up to you however I can." He went quiet, and she could almost feel his remorse from thousands of miles away. "I hate myself for what I've done."

She was surprised, but it did help her let go of some of the anger and resentment. "Well, I appreciate that."

The truck door flew open, and Jeremy jumped out, missing the stairs completely. "Why aren't you going?" He pointed to the stage. "She's calling you."

"Who's calling me?"

"Lorelei. Can't you hear her?"

"Why's she calling *me*?"

Jeremy looked like he wanted to throttle her.

"Okay, okay. Ian, I have to go."

"What's going on?"

"I have no idea." She grabbed her dinner and hurried to the truck.

"Grace Giordano." Lorelei's voice boomed through the speakers. "Get your golden pipes up here."

"She's been calling you for ten minutes." Jeremy snatched her insulated bag. "It's *Lorelei Calloway*."

Ben poked his head out the door of the truck. "Why aren't you going?"

"Because I don't know what she wants from me. Why would *I* go on stage?"

"She wants you to do a duet." Jeremy waved frantically. "Go."

"She wants me to sing?" *What on earth is she thinking?* Just as she started off, Ben called, "The apron!" *Oh.* Shaking her head, she untied it and pulled it off. "Be right back. Oh, and take the chocolate caramel tarts off the chalkboard. We're all out." Grace wove in and out of the picnic blankets and stadium chairs. With so many people, she had to move carefully while keeping up her pace.

"Here she is," someone called.

And from that moment on, the crowd was clapping and nudging her along.

This is ridiculous. I'm not singing with Lorelei Calloway in front of all these people.

As she neared, someone directed her to the stairs at the side of the stage. They already had a mic stand set up for her.

Oh, my God. Oh, my God.

She'd loved her tribute band. It was a blast. But never, not once, had Lorelei been in the audience.

The singer greeted her with a giant smile, and the audience roared its approval.

Grace leaned in close. "What're you doing?"

But the superstar faced the audience, ignoring her. "Ladies and gentlemen, here she is. The Singing Baker."

The response was deafening. With the lights practically blinding her, all Grace wanted to do was go back to her truck and surround herself with her pretty pastries and happy customers.

But nope, that wasn't going to happen. Lorelei made a settle-down motion with a hand. "As the artist-in-residence, I've had the super fun job of inviting the talent to the festival this summer. I was going for a whole range of bands—from the unknowns who've tagged me in their songs all the way up to the superstars. But one thing I hadn't considered was a tribute band."

Another wave of applause.

"As you all know, the Singing Baker sings my songs. And a lot of people are saying"—she hitched a thumb toward Grace—"she's *better* than me."

Grace lunged for her mic. "It's not true. I'm not. I'm totally not."

Amid the loud boos came a few claps and shout-outs.

God. Stop. Just stop.

"So, we're going to have a face-off to figure it out once and for all. Who's better at singing my songs, me or the Singing Baker?"

The crowd went wild. It was clear Lorelei truly meant this event as something fun. There wasn't an ounce of resentment or negativity in her.

And why would there be? She had fifteen Grammys. She was beloved globally because her lyrics were smart, romantic, and real, while her melodies were evocative and moving.

No one was her competition. It had to give her all the confidence in the world.

Well, what could she do but play along? Grace pulled her mic off the stand. "Takes some mighty big lady balls to throw down when *everyone's* been saying I'm better than you." She got a lot of boos for that, but even more laughter and applause. The singer's shocked expression made Grace laugh. "But you asked for it, so let's do this."

"All right, here's how it's going down," Lorelei said. "We'll trade off each verse and then duet the choruses and bridges. Think you can handle that?"

"Pssh. I could do it in my sleep."

"Oh, you think so?" Lorelei glanced to her band. "You ready, guys?" In response, she got a drum roll and a guitar riff. "Hit it."

The drummer rocked the beat, and then Lorelei busted out her chart-topping Grammy-winning song that utilized her entire four-octave range.

He said no
And I said yes
And that's the way it goes
With heartbreak

Luckily, Grace had the same range. Together, their voices joined together for the chorus.

Could you ever love me
The way I want?
Could you ever ever ever
Be the man I need?
Or are we destined
To fly in different time zones
Circle the globe
In different directions
Soar past each other
In different altitudes
And never once collide

The hairs at the back of her neck stood up from the glorious alchemy. She didn't need to be in the audience to know their voices melded together perfectly.

Next, it was her turn. She jumped right in, very aware that Lorelei had given her the verse that would best showcase her voice.

I moved on
And he came back
And that's the way it is
With heartbreak

They joined again for the chorus.

Could you ever love me
The way I want?
Could you ever ever ever
Be the man I need?

Or are we destined
To fly in different time zones
Circle the globe
In different directions
Soar past each other
In different altitudes
And never once collide

Grace stepped back, lowered her mic, and let Lorelei have the high notes, riffs, and runs of the bridge. No one but her could handle it without shredding their vocal cords.

I don't know. I don't know. I just don't know.

It was haunting. It made you ache. Since Grace wasn't singing, she could step out of the spotlight and scan the audience. She could only see the faces in the pit, but everyone there was mesmerized. When she landed on Jaime, her heart nearly jumped out of her chest.

Their gazes locked. *How are you here?*

He just smiled and lifted Kinsley out of her seat and onto his lap. The little girl was clapping and bouncing in place. Grace waved, nearly losing her place in the song. She recovered, but nothing could keep the smile off her face. Happiness filled her to bursting.

Finally, when the last note rang through the meadow, when the singers lowered their mics, the amphitheater went eerily quiet.

A breeze shifted her hair and cooled the perspiration. Just as she cut a look to Lorelei to see what might be wrong, applause split the silence.

"Right?" Lorelei said. "Isn't she amazing?" She made a

sweeping motion to Grace. "Ladies and gentlemen, the Singing Baker."

But Grace wasn't going to take credit for what just happened. "And the one and only, the writer, composer, and singer herself, Lorelei Calloway."

The pop star gave the audience a few moments to shout and cheer, but then she got the crowd to settle down. "All right. Before we go on, let me say one thing. I'm sure you know this vote is all in fun, but I really did want to give some stage time to Grace. She's got an awesome voice, but more importantly, she's about the nicest person I've ever met. And if you do like her voice better, feel free to show her with your applause. Don't worry about hurting my feelings. Want to know why?" She reached for her boyfriend's arm. "Because I've got all the love in the world. As many of you know, I've been with Landon since we were fourteen years old. And Cissy, my drummer?" She motioned for her friend to stand. "She's been my ride-or-die since First grade." She introduced the other members of her band. "These are the people who know me. Without make up, in a bad mood… when I feel sorry for myself…they're always there. That's why I can take anything the media or the trolls throw at me. So, go on and let us know. Does Grace have the better voice? Clap if you think she's better than me."

Grace teared up at the more than respectable response. Her tribute band was always a hit, and she'd been complimented on her vocals many times. But tonight was different. Jaime was watching, and he was beaming with pride. She didn't know how he'd managed to come see her performance, but she loved it.

Taking the mic, Landon slung an arm around his girlfriend's shoulders. "Now, go on and vote for Lorelei."

The audience responded with a thunderous applause and a deafening cry of adoration.

Lorelei reached for Grace and lifted their joined hands in the air. "Sounds like a tie to me! Now go on and buy her yummy pastries. If you haven't tried one yet, trust me. This woman's magical."

Notching the mic back into the holder, Grace waved to the crowd and headed down the stairs.

Jamie was waiting for her, wearing the biggest smile she'd ever seen, and Kinsley, in his arms, threw herself at her. The three of them hugged and laughed.

"You were so good, Gracie," Kinny said.

Riding high from the performance, she kissed the girl on the cheek and held her close. "The best part of the night was having you there to watch me."

"You were fantastic." Jaime kissed her on the mouth.

"Thank you. It was completely unexpected but incredibly fun. How on earth are you guys here?"

"My sister has tickets for the show tonight, and she texted me the minute Lorelei started calling for you. The only reason we got to see you is because it took you so long to get up on that stage."

"I thought I heard them chanting my name, but it made no sense, so I kept ignoring it."

"Daddy was reading to me. Auntie Bay-Bay called, and Daddy shouted and picked me up, and we ran out the door."

It was the first time Grace noticed the little girl was wearing a nightgown and slippers.

"That's hilarious."

"Worth it. So, are you going to give up baking to become a world-famous singer?" Jaime asked.

"Not a chance." She had everything she could ever want right here.

And that undercurrent of fear she'd been living with?

Gone.

Because right then, she knew she couldn't compromise.

She'd found true happiness, and there was no turning back.

Grace didn't have much time, but she couldn't miss Kinny's first figure skating class. The little girl was so excited, her dad could barely get the laces tied on her skates.

"Come on, Daddy. Hurry." With her gaze riveted on the ice, she couldn't sit still.

"Almost done." Jaime squatted in front of her, trying to keep her legs from kicking out while working the laces. "They have to be tight. You don't want it loose around your ankles." Finished, he stood. "All set."

Kinny made a dash for the rink, but her dad caught her shoulder. "Hang on." He got eye level with her. "You listen to the coaches, okay? Follow their instructions."

"I know, Daddy. I *know.*" She pulled away and wobbled her way to the center of the rink.

Jaime came back to the first row of the bleachers and sat beside her. "That went well."

"She's excited. You finally let the racehorse out of the barn."

"She needs to calm down." He tracked her every movement. "Look at her. She's wired."

She wondered if he'd be better off not watching. "What time's your meeting with Ross's agent?"

"Twenty minutes, but I'll take the call from here."

"From an ice-skating rink?" Around them, a few parents

worked on their laptops, a couple of moms chatted, and two little kids played a computer game side by side.

He broke into a grin. "Okay, fine. I'll step into my office." When Kinny tried to spin and landed on her butt, he flinched. "Probably for the best."

She chuckled. "I'm going to bet you never fell. You probably hit the ice-skating like Connor McDavid."

He turned to her, eyebrows raised. "You really do know your hockey."

"Please. Sports are huge in my family—but only Boston teams. We're a loyal bunch." She checked the time on her phone.

"You've got to go?"

"No, I can stay about twenty more minutes, but I want to get back in time to help the boys pack the van. I'm not sure hockey players understand how delicate my éclairs are."

That got his attention. "What've they done?"

There he went again, sliding into warrior mode. "Nothing. They've been great." It was funny because it annoyed her when her brothers were overprotective, but with Jaime it made her feel like he'd go to the ends of the earth to make sure she had what she needed. "But they're still learning how I like things done."

"All right, but you let me know if they mess up."

"If they mess up, I'll talk to them. But thank you." As Jaime tracked his daughter's every move, Grace couldn't stop grinning. "I actually love when you get all clan warrior on me."

"Oh, yeah?" He wrapped an arm around her shoulders and drew her up against him. "Cole's dad's got some kilts. I could put one on tonight."

"It's less about the costume than the attitude, so I think we're good. But real talk, does he wear underpants under it?"

Jaime laughed. "Sorry. That's something I'll take to my grave."

It was the big joke in the media whether Trevor Montgomery, star of the Clan Wars franchise, went commando under his kilt, so everywhere he went, people jokingly tried to get a look. "So, you do know. At least tell me this. Does he wear a kilt around the house?"

"No. That's for show." He kissed her cheek. "I like being with you. We fit."

Pleasure spread through her, hot and fast, but she kept her attention on the ice so he wouldn't see how much that simple statement affected her.

He chuckled.

"What?" She pretended to be irritated with him.

"You like me."

"Oh, is it feeding time again? That ego of yours is voracious."

His fingers brushed across her cheek. "You know I can read everything on your face, right?"

"I hope so. It's important to see how much you annoy me." But she couldn't conceal her grin. Or the goosebumps his gentle touch elicited.

"Yeah, that's not what I'm seeing. You like it when I pet you with my words."

"I don't like being petted at all. I'm not a farm animal." Still, she wouldn't look at him. "But yes, sometimes I need to hear that you're in this with me."

"Oh, I'm deep in this with you. And I'm sorry if I don't say it enough. I don't want you to have a single doubt about the way I feel about you. Mostly for selfish reasons." He stroked her again. "Because I like when you turn pink." He cupped her chin and forced her to look at him. "Your mouth goes soft, and you let out this shaky little breath. Same thing you do after I kiss you senseless."

She squirmed on the hard bench. "Is it warm in here?"

"Not sure if you know how an ice-skating rink works, but there's a frozen element to the whole thing." He rubbed her bare arm. "No, I think it's me that gets you hot and bothered."

"Yes, well, your body heat's basically sourced from the sun, so you might want to scoot over a few feet. Give me some space."

"I'll give you everything you want but don't ask me for space." He closed the gap between them. "I can't stand being apart from you." His nose brushed the hair away from her ear. "If I could keep you in my bed, I'd do it. Do you know what my favorite part of the day is?"

"When you're balls deep?"

His head tipped back, and he barked out a laugh. "Nope."

"Hm. That might mean we're doing it wrong."

"Four a.m. You, me, the kitchen. Watching you bake, talking to you. I like it best when it's just us. That's my favorite time of the day."

All her defenses melted like candle wax. One hand on his cheek, she kissed him, gently, softly, even though she wanted so much more. "It's my favorite time, too. And I love when you say we fit. I love that you touch me all the time." Then, she whispered in his ear, "I love how hard you go in bed because it makes it feel like you're desperate for me."

He swallowed. His features didn't go pink. They went dark red. "Good." He swallowed again. "Good. That's how you should feel."

"It is, isn't it? Wow." The truth hit square in the center of her chest. "All this time, I accepted the kind of watered-down love Ian gave me. I'm one of five kids, so I guess that's all I knew."

"You deserve everything, Gracie. And if I don't give it to you, you need to tell me. We have to promise we'll always talk to each other."

"I promise." She reached for his hand. "And the same goes for you. Because you deserve everything, too."

There it was. That flinch of pain, that…uncertainty.

And that's what scares me. Deep down, he doesn't believe he gets to be happy.

What do I do about that? Do I trust he'll work through it? Do I leave my family, my life on Duff Island, and take a chance on a man I'm absolutely, one-hundred-percent falling in love with…but who I know might push me away?

She didn't have answers. She would just have to take the leap. Speaking of which… "Hey, so, I talked to Ian today."

He tore his gaze from his daughter and looked at her with concern.

"He and his parents came up with an idea to help us recover the money we lost."

"The money he *stole* from you."

She smiled because…warrior. *That's hot.* "True. But anyhow, his parents are going to buy a building in Newport so we can open a second Renzo's—and since it's in an upscale neighborhood, I can sell my pastries, too."

He watched her carefully. "How do you feel about that?"

She tried to cover her disappointment. It was just hard to see him go from warrior to…blasé when it came to her whole damn future. If he wasn't going to get riled up at the idea of her opening a bakery two thousand miles away, then what were they doing?

Then again, to be fair, they weren't talking about her leaving. They were only talking about the offer Ian made.

Calm your ass down. "I don't know why his parents should pay for his mistakes."

"If we were talking a thousand bucks, I might agree with you. But it's your life savings. And I'm pretty sure his parents will get something out of it, too."

"They're not. He said we won't have to pay rent, and we could keep the profits."

"Right. But I'm saying the building probably has other usable space that will cover their mortgage with the other businesses."

"Oh, good point. I hadn't thought of that." She smiled. "You're smart for a jock."

"I'm not a jock."

"Says the guy who puts in more hours on the ice in a calendar year than a professional goalie."

"Not even close." His brow furrowed as he watched Kinsley wander away from the other kids to try some more daring moves. "Dammit."

"What? What's she doing?"

"Ever since she watched the Olympic figure skaters, she's been dancing around. You should see her in the backyard. She holds her arms across her chest and tries to spin, or she's racing across the yard with her arms wide open—" His jaw snapped shut as his features went hard. "That's it." He popped up.

"*Jaime.*" She grabbed the back of his shirt. "Don't embarrass her."

"She's going to break her neck."

"Seriously? That's your starting point? The *ER*?"

He lowered his head and let out a huff of breath. "Fuck. You're right. I know you're right."

"She's going to fall. That's a given. But it'll teach her what to do and what to avoid." Of course, she knew it wasn't a boo-boo that scared him. It was the reel playing in the back of his mind, watching Booker hit the ground. "I remember when my brother got into an accident."

"Enzo?"

She loved how he listened well enough to remember what she told him. "Yes." She squeezed his hand. "He was in the passenger seat when he got T-boned. The truck hit maybe a foot away from where he was sitting. He says he saw it happening in slow motion, but the truck hit so hard, it dragged the Jeep all the way across the intersection."

"Jesus."

"Yeah. It was so upsetting that he had a hard time sleeping at night. His grades fell. It was awful. My parents sent him to a therapist who said something that stuck with me. He said trauma can make it feel like you have a hundred problems. You can't sleep, you can't eat, you can't concentrate…and each issue has a consequence. You get bad grades, make mistakes, lose friendships. So, it feels like your life is spinning out of control, and you have no idea where to start to fix things, when really there's one issue. And how much more manageable is it to see that you've got one problem with many faces?"

"Did it help your brother?"

"It did. He didn't have to fix ten problems. He just needed to deal with the accident and the trauma it caused. You're a good man, Jaime. I don't know what it will take to make peace with what happened that night, but you have to figure it out."

"Everyone says I should talk to Booker." Watching the ice, he hunched a shoulder. "It's his life I fucked up."

"The thing is…I'm not sure there's anything he could say to relieve you of this guilt because no matter what, he didn't get to play hockey. And that won't change. So, you could look him in the eyes and apologize. You could let him have a go at you, tell you you're a miserable son of a bitch who ruined his life…but will that set you free?"

"No."

"If he says he's happy as a clam, he's found his true calling in life doing whatever he's doing now—"

"He's a sports agent."

"Okay. If he says he loves being an agent, will that set you free?"

He let out an uncomfortable laugh. "I don't think so."

"So maybe the only forgiveness you need is your own. Maybe you need to let go of a choice you made when you were a teenager and trust the man you are today."

When Kinny attempted to spin and landed hard on her ass, Jaime tensed.

She laughed. "In the meantime, maybe you shouldn't watch her lessons."

Kinny got up, rubbed her butt, and then skated off. She attempted some kind of crazy move—like she was trying to leap and then spin. Jaime's fingers fisted, but the coach skated over and picked the little girl up off the ice. As he got her back on her blades, he knelt in front of her and had a conversation. Kinsley listened intently.

"Well, look at that." She said it smugly, playing with him.

"Fuck it. You're right. Let's get out of here." He stood, reaching for her hand. "Come on. I'll walk you to your car."

She could tell he was lost in thought, so they didn't talk on their way out of the rink. Outside, the bright morning sun had her fishing around in her purse for sunglasses. "I love the air here. It's so fresh and clean."

"Think you can live without salt water and sailboats?"

"I think there's something here I can't get anywhere else in the world."

He backed her up against her car and put his hands on her hips. "And what is that thing, Gracie?"

She gave a long, dreamy sigh. "The sloshy. I had one on my date with this hockey player I met, and it was delicious."

"Is that right?" He was dangerous in so many ways, but none so wicked as that sexy, playful grin.

"You have the best smile. I want to lick it like an ice cream cone."

"Well, then, it's good you like ice cream because I'll need you to do a lot of licking." He framed her cheeks with his hands and kissed her. Deep, sensuous, the kiss lifted her out of her body and sent her floating. His mouth was soft, warm, and slick. His tongue teased hers into play, and she wanted to climb him like a tree.

She was in a parking lot, though, and so she gently pulled away. "If I didn't have to get to work, I'd want you in the back of my car so I could lick you somewhere else."

"If I didn't have a conference call in five minutes, I'd let you."

Chapter Fourteen

It was four in the morning, and Jaime threw back his covers. Eager to get to the Dream House and see Gracie, he headed into the bathroom to wash his face and brush his teeth.

When he caught his reflection in the mirror, his daughter's words popped into his mind. *You're the Beast.*

She had her princess dress, but she didn't have a prince. And she sure as hell didn't want to take the Beast to a dance.

Worse, she had a dad who held her back. Jumped straight to worst-case scenarios when all she wanted was to throw herself into the things she loved. He'd never have seen that if it hadn't been for Gracie.

I want to be better for my daughter.

I want to be her prince.

Determination took hold, and he grabbed his razor and shaving cream. First, though, he trimmed his beard. After he made it more manageable, he squirted the cream onto his palm, rubbed his hands together, and then lathered up his face. He worked until he removed every last trace of the scruff he'd worn for a decade. Finished, he dried himself and rubbed his now-smooth jaw.

But he still didn't look like a prince. Not with hair that brushed the collar of his shirt and was as messy as if he'd been riding his motorcycle on the Gallatin Road.

You're more one-percenter than Hallmark hero.

He couldn't believe how badly he wanted to be Kinny's and Gracie's hero.

Cut it.

Dropping the towel in the sink, he left the bathroom. He didn't keep scissors in the cabin because he didn't want Kinny to get a wild hair up her ass and start cutting clothes, furniture… her bangs. *That's ridiculous.*

What have I been doing to this kid?

He turned on the baby monitor, grabbed his end of the device, and headed out of the cabin. He was so eager to get the job done, he nearly broke into a jog. When he burst into the big house, he heard the music and breathed in the scent of bread baking. A rising sense of purpose flowed through him.

Ten years ago, he'd barricaded himself inside this mental cave, the four walls nothing but movie screens replaying Booker's landing. Then, she'd crashed into him, this bright, sunny woman with a passion for baking—*a passion for me.* Just by being herself, she'd drawn him into the sunlight.

I need her.

He stalked into the kitchen and, as always, came to a hard stop. The sight of her was like taking a hockey puck to the chest. She was the dream he'd never allowed himself to have.

This morning, she was wearing black leggings and a cropped white T-shirt. It revealed a slice of her abdomen, and he flashed back to the night before when he'd had her naked, his mouth, his tongue, his fingers exploring every inch of her.

Fuck, but she was responsive.

As much as he wanted her, she was working, and he was on a mission. He'd leave her alone.

He pulled open a drawer and sifted through the ladles and spatulas. *No scissors.* He tried another one. It had corn on the cob skewers, a whisk, measuring cups and spoons.

Where the fuck are they?

"Jaime." Her hand landed in the middle of his back, and when he looked up at her, her eyes went wide. "Oh, my God. What have you done?" She laughed. "I almost didn't recognize you. I mean, you were hot with all that facial hair, but without it?" She made a gimme motion. "Come to Mama."

"I'm glad you like it." He moved to the next drawer. No luck. He slammed it shut.

"What're you looking for?"

"Scissors."

"Over here." She gestured to the knife block. "Is there anything I can do to help?"

Her scent triggered his libido, her voice catapulted him back to her bed—their bodies grinding, hands caressing— and her nearness cranked his need for her. "I don't want to interrupt you."

She'd decided she was a one-woman show in the kitchen, leaving the boys to load her van and work long hours in the truck. She didn't have time to be involved in his grooming issues.

He crossed the kitchen and pulled them out. "Thanks."

"Sure." She went back to piping cream. "Well, if you need help cutting the tag off your jammies, let me know."

It made him aware of his pajama bottoms and T-shirt. "What do you mean?"

"I can only assume you're having a sewing emergency." She glanced at the clock. "At four-thirty in the morning."

"No. I need a trim."

"Okay, so, there's a predawn *hair* emergency?"

Lowering his head, he cursed himself for being such an asshole. He chuckled. "Yeah. That's it."

She plucked the scissors out of his hands. "Unless you're cutting the fat off raw chicken, you might want to use the ones actually designed for hair. Come here." She led him into the laundry room.

It was a huge space. In addition to the industrial-sized washer and dryer, he'd asked the contractor for a large folding table, built-in hampers for colors, whites, and delicates, and closet space. Everything his mom might like.

Grace handed him a black case. "Here."

He unzipped it to find a clipper, comb attachments, and scissors. "I didn't even know this was here." He took what he needed, stepped around her, and put the bag back on the shelf.

"I only know because when your mom and sister glammed me up, Abby trimmed my hair. She wanted to give me 'soft layers around my face.'"

"I hope you stopped her there. You should see the cuts she gave her dolls." He lifted the scissors and comb. "Well, I'll let you get back to it."

She followed him into the kitchen, but before he could leave, she said, "You need me to do it? Kinda hard to do it yourself."

"No. It's fine."

"Mm-hm." She stepped in front of him, sifting her

fingers through his hair. "Why don't you tell me what's going on?"

Just that simple touch had his blood churning. "Nothing." His gaze fell to her lush mouth. Only hours ago, it had been fastened around his very hard cock.

"You're being weird."

"Yeah, I guess I am. But..." He pulled at the ends of his hair. "It's a mess."

"A sexy mess. But again, where's the fire? Why now?" She wrapped her arms around his waist and pressed her cheek to his chest. "Put it this way. When you can keep your hands off me, I know something's off."

He grinned. She always disarmed him. "Trust me. If I didn't know how much work you have to do by yourself right now, you'd be bent over, holding on to the counter to keep from being fucked into the cupboard."

When she laughed, her eyes sparkled, and her whole face lit up. "You're right. I do have a lot. Still, you're going to do a lousy job if you cut your own hair." She grabbed a chair and brought it to the sink. "Sit."

As soon as he plunked down, she slung a dish towel around his neck. Tipping his head back, she scooped handfuls of warm water onto his scalp. "You going to tell me what brought this on?"

Over and over, slowly, sensuously, her fingernails scraped through his hair, until his body started humming. "I was thinking about what Kinsley said the other day."

"That you're the Beast?" When he nodded, she said, "Yeah, I wondered if that would bother you." She turned off the water and guided him to straighten. Using a second towel, she blotted his hair, then combed it through.

"It's our first dance." With everything he had, he loved his little girl. "She deserves a prince."

"Oh, Jaime. You sweet, clueless man. Don't you know that in every way that matters, you already are?" She combed a section of hair, held it in her fingers, and snipped. "I wish you could see yourself the way everyone else does." She glanced at him. "You know, maybe this trim will help." She lowered her hand. "Every time you look in the mirror, you see the reckless eighteen-year-old boy. Now, you'll see the man you've become."

He liked that very fucking much. "In any event, she lives on a ranch, and there aren't many opportunities to dress up. I want it to be perfect for her."

"You have a good heart. She's a lucky girl." She was at his side, her chest close but not touching his shoulder, her breath warm on his ear.

He wanted to wind his arm around her waist, bury his face in her belly, and lick a path to her breasts. He wanted the lush feel of her mouth on his, her silky hair, and the quiet, urgent moans as their hips pressed together, shifting, rocking.

But he had to stay focused. She was doing him a favor and needed to get back to work. "I got some good news."

Snip, snip. Strands of dirty blond hair fell to the floor.

"Tell me." That soft, sensual voice.

Fuck, but she turned him on. "Ross LaRoux's coming out here."

"Really? Congratulations." She took a break to give his shoulder a shake. "This is fantastic. What about that salary cap?"

"His agent said Ross's only ever been part of a winning franchise and likes the idea of being part of a team that's building. He thinks if we bring him out, have him bond with the guys, we might catch his interest. To be honest, we're getting close to the deadline of the free agency period, so I think it means Ross's not excited about other teams. Which gives us a shot."

"I'm so happy for you." She went back to work. After each section, her fingers glided through his hair, and it stirred him up. "When's he coming?"

"He'll be here Sunday." For Cole and Declan, he had to get this done. Whatever it took, he had to sign Ross.

"You really want this guy."

"Oh, yeah. He's the best goalie hockey's ever seen."

"That's not what I hear."

He shot her a look. What did she mean?

"Stay still or you'll have a bald spot. I keep hearing you're the best goalie the world has ever seen."

"That's bullshit. People feel sorry for me, so they say shit like that."

She'd made it all the way around him, and now she stood facing him. "Feel *sorry* for you? You own an NHL team. You have a thriving ranch. A close family. You're more handsome than a movie star. And you think anyone feels sorry for you?" She shook her head. "You're ridiculous."

That just made him want to cup her ass, jerk her onto his lap, and grind her all over his cock even more. "How am I ridiculous? You don't even know the talent out there."

"I'll tell you what I know." Trimming the sections around his face put her tits right at eye level. They jiggled with each snip. "Cole Montgomery comes to *you* to work out. He doesn't ask the Renegades' goalies. Also, I've watched you in the barn, and the only time I saw a puck get past you is when I lifted my shirt."

He was thrown back to that moment when he'd spotted her standing next to Hailey and the kids. Cole's fiancée was getting the girls settled on a bench with snacks, and while they were distracted, Gracie had flashed him.

He grinned at the memory. "That was a dirty move."

"You like me dirty." Her eyes went half-lidded, and her tongue peeked out and moistened her pink lips.

That's it. He grabbed her ass and jerked her forward. The moment she climbed onto his lap and straddled him, he yanked off her tank top. When he peeled the cups back, her plump breasts spilled out, filling his hands.

She arched her back. "Yes."

Pushing them together, he licked each nipple, then sucked one into his mouth. With his hands still on her ass, he worked them both into a frenzy, and she let out a needy moan that drove him out of his mind.

He couldn't take any more. Lifting her, he carried her to the guest bedroom, kicked the door shut, and laid her out on the bed. Hovering over her, he took in her sleepy eyes, her pink lips swollen with his kisses, and her glossy, dark hair sprawled all over the white pillowcase. "Gracie, you came out of nowhere and rocked my world. And now I can't live without you."

She shut him up with a hungry kiss. The world narrowed to her hand at the back of his neck, the hot, slick slide of her tongue, and her hips slamming against him and grinding all over his hard, aching cock.

He didn't know sex could feel like this. He didn't know he was capable of this much emotion. This woman split him wide open and revealed layers he might never have uncovered.

He licked a path down the column of her sweetly scented neck, scattered kisses across her collarbone, and worshipped her gorgeous, plump breasts. Her back arched, and she grabbed a fistful of his hair.

Sitting back on his heels, he pulled down her leggings, watching as she unclasped her bra and tossed it aside. And there she was, laid out before him like the most decadent feast. He'd taste every inch of her. Starting where he left off, he lavished attention on her breasts, cupping them, squeezing them, and sucking on her nipples.

Moving down her torso, he licked a fiery trail, scattering butterfly kisses along the way. His fingers parted her curls and glided through her slickness. When he circled her clit, she shuddered.

Parting her thighs with his shoulders, his tongue followed the path his fingers had just taken. He loved the way her legs wrapped around his back, encircling him, caging him, as though she feared he would run.

But there wasn't a single impulse, not one excuse left, for him to do that.

If she wanted to stay, then he was the luckiest son of a bitch on the planet. He couldn't *believe* he'd kept Kinny from her.

I love her.

I love this woman.

Emotion overflowed, and he channeled it into his mouth, his tongue, and his hands. Showing her through touch what she meant to him. Her sunshiny smile, her sweet scent that roused something embedded deeply inside him, and the way she listened to him...*saw* him.

Saw him and still liked him.

How was it possible? His hands slid under her ass, lifting her, as his fluttering tongue licked her into a climax that made her spasm, twist, and writhe.

She reached for him, dragging him up till they were face-to-face. "I need you." She yanked down his pajama pants. "I need you so much."

He fisted his shirt at the back of his neck and yanked it off. Then, in one swift move, he got up and kicked away his bottoms. He needed to be inside her. Needed to fuse with this woman who made him whole. Climbing back onto the bed, he settled between her thighs. "I'm gonna give you everything." She brought him so much happiness, he wanted to make her delirious with pleasure.

Her lips were pink and wet as a fresh raspberry, her skin had a healthy blush, and her chest rose and fell as she struggled to catch her breath.

"You're so fucking beautiful." He kissed her sweetly, letting her know if she needed to get back to work, he was fine. He just wanted to be near her, to feel her heat and hear her heart beating against his.

But she reached between them, grasping his cock in her warm hand, and a primitive yearning took hold. With a tight grip, she pumped, the palm swirling around the head —just as she'd seen him do to himself—and it felt so obscenely good, he dropped his head into the crook of her neck. When the pleasure peaked to a point he could no longer take, he pushed her hand away and lined himself up at her opening. Staring deeply into her eyes, he watched them go all sultry and hot as he slowly eased himself inside.

She was so tight, so wet, he had to clamp down on his urgent need to fuck her. He gave her body a minute to adjust to him. Slow glides in and out had them both panting. Their locked gazes allowed an intimacy he'd never experienced. It was like he could see all the way through to her soul.

And in it, he saw beauty. Acceptance.

Love.

Forgiveness.

He saw his salvation.

It didn't take long before she grew restless. Her hips shifted impatiently, and she gripped his ass, begging for more. And then, he was fucking her hard. With his hands braced on the mattress, he drove her up the bed. Her palms flattened on the headboard, her cheeks flushed, her eyes rolled back in her head, and she was making these insanely sexy cries and moans, and when he didn't think he could last another minute, he lifted her hips until he found the exact spot and rhythm that made her scream. Her hips hiked off the mattress, and she rode out her orgasm as he drilled into her.

It wound him up so tightly that when he exploded, he saw stars behind his eyes. Clutching her hips, he slammed home, and one climax after another had him driving into her in hard, fast pumps.

Bliss.

That's all. That's it.

He'd entered a state of pure bliss.

And even when his body temperature cooled, and he rolled to the side, gathering her in his arms, the feeling stayed with him.

And he knew, if he didn't screw this up, it could be this way forever.

The scent of fresh flowers and melting candle wax filled the Owl Hoot Resort and Spa ballroom. On the dance floor, grown ups in fancy clothes danced with children. Some shuffled, the kids standing on their shiny shoes while others went all-out spinning and dipping their princes and princesses.

Holding her little hand in his, Jaime felt a swell of love for his little girl. It was hard to believe she'd only been with him for four years. She was his whole world now, and he couldn't imagine a life without her.

Kinsley took the clear plastic cup filled with pink punch and drained it. She did everything with gusto. With a stained upper lip, she reached for his hand. "Come on, Daddy. Let's dance."

In her fluffy princess dress, she led the way onto the dance floor, an undeniable look of pride in her eyes. He'd never seen that before, and he wondered if it had anything to do with his shave. As soon as she found an empty spot, she started shaking her booty and swinging her arms. He smiled because Kinny wasn't the type to step on anyone's shoes.

And so, what else could he do, but match his princess's energy, letting go with some moves of his own? They danced with abandon until a slow song came on.

She reached her arms up, and he lifted her. "You having fun?"

She nodded and kissed his cheek. "Thank you, Daddy. I love my dress."

"I'm glad." As she mindlessly rubbed his clean-shaven jaw, he asked, "You like me without a beard?"

"It feels nice."

He held her close as they swayed to the beat. "I shaved because I wanted to look like a prince for you. I want to make you happy tonight."

"You always make me happy, Daddy." Her tone suggested he should already know that.

"You feel like a princess?"

She wrapped his arms around his neck and squeezed. "I *am* a princess."

"Yes, you are. Do you like your figure skating classes?"

"I love them." She pulled back to look him in the eyes. "Gracie wants me to skate." There was something imploring in her eyes, as if she needed him to believe her. "She thinks I'm really good."

"You are good, Kinny." Why would she think otherwise? For some reason he couldn't figure out, she wasn't buying it. "I always knew you'd be good at skating because you've got great coordination. You're strong and flexible." Still, she seemed uneasy. "What is it?"

"You wouldn't let me skate."

"Right, but—" *Oh, shit.* He'd never considered the message she received when he came up with excuses. He kept saying she was too young, and he thought she'd believed him since that was what she repeated to anyone who asked.

Setting her down, he knelt right there on the dance floor. One hand on her waist, he cupped her chin. "Sweetie, look at me. You're a very good athlete. The only reason I didn't let you skate was because I was afraid you'd get hurt."

"Because you think I'm bad at it."

"No. No, no." How did he explain? "I'm a good athlete, too. And when you're really good at something, you get a little too sure of yourself."

"What's that mean?"

"It means you take risks you're not ready for. That's what I did. I took too many risks, and I'm afraid you'll do the same thing. But that's my problem, not yours."

"But I am ready. I'm good." Tears filled her eyes. "I'm really good, Daddy." Her lower lip wobbled.

His heart snapped clean in half. Regret stung like lemon juice on a cut. "Kinny, listen to me. You're a very good skater. You're strong and confident and you're perfect just as you are. I should have let you skate and ride horses and all the things you want to do."

"I can ride horses?" Her eyes went wide with hope.

"Yeah, princess, you can. Daddy made a big mistake. I've been standing in your way, and I'm not going to do that anymore. When you tell me you want to do something, I'm going to move heaven and earth to make sure you can do it. Because, baby, you're magnificent. You're fierce and smart and creative and strong, and there's nothing you can't do if you decide you want to do it. And if I say no to you, then—"

"Gracie will let me do it?"

He barked out a laugh, drawing the attention of the families nearby. "Yeah. That's exactly right. Gracie will have a word with me, remind me I'm making choices out of fear, and she'll encourage me to let you do it."

"I love Gracie, Daddy. I want her to stay."

"I do, too, Kinny." *You have no idea.*

"Can she?"

So, here it was, the moment he'd feared from the beginning. His daughter had gotten attached to a maternal figure who might not stay. "I hope she does. But she has a job and a family somewhere else, and they need her, so she might have to go home."

"We need her, too, Daddy."

"Why? Because she convinces me to let you take figure skating class?"

"No, because she makes us happy."

"You are so right." But he needed to set his daughter's expectations. "I don't know if she's going to stay." His friend Rhys still hadn't gotten back to him. He had a new baby, so it was totally understandable, so he'd left a message with the leasing office. "If she has to go home, at least we've had her this whole summer. I think we're pretty darn lucky we got to know someone as great as her."

But damn, I want her to stay.

. . .

Jaime stood beside his GM, arms crossed over his chest, watching the action on the ice. He tensed when the forward fired a puck…and Mr. Zero blocked it. *Yes.* The other players went wild.

"Ross LaRoux is in the house." Jaime pumped a fist. "Good energy. Just what we need."

"Fuck, man," Darren said. "He's almost as good as you."

"He's the missing piece. With him and Cole, we're bringing home the Cup." He watched Ross block another puck. "I've got to get Ross." They had him here. Now, they needed to convert his interest into a commitment. "You've spent time with him. How's it look?"

"He keeps it close to the vest. Hard to tell." Darren seemed worried. "With most of the guys on vacation, he's not getting a true idea of what the team looks like."

Most families took as much time together as possible before the season started. "True." Fortunately, Cole was trying to give his girls stability, so they were around and doing lots of bonding at home. "Just means we have to work a little harder. He leaves day after tomorrow?"

Darren gave a tight nod.

"Okay." Jaime took off.

"Where you going?" There was something in the GM's tone that stopped him.

"I'm going to call his agent."

"This is my job," Darren said. "You know that, right? It's why you hired me."

Shame sent a rush of heat through his body. "I do."

"If you don't trust me to get the job done, then why am I here?"

"I do trust you." He glanced at the ice. "But I owe it to

Cole and Declan. They took a chance on this team, and if I don't get Cole a goalie at his level..."

"Then what? What happens if you don't get Ross? You think Cole's going back to the Brawlers? He didn't come here for you. He came for his family. Regardless, it's not your responsibility. It's not on you. Now, if you don't think I can—"

"I do. I'm sorry. Do you want to make the call?"

"No, you've got the relationship. I just want to know if this is how it's going to be going forward. Because if this is the level of involvement you see for yourself, then I'm not sure I'm the right guy for you."

"It's not. After we sign Ross, I'll back off. You're a great GM. You've turned the team around." Darren was right. It wasn't his responsibility. He had to get that through his head.

"Yeah, okay. Talk to Sam. Let me know how it goes."

"On it." Jaime headed into the tunnel and locked himself in his office. He fell into his seat and dialed the agent.

Sam answered on the first ring. "Hey, man. What's up? I'm heading into a meeting, so I've got thirty seconds."

"What's it going to take to sign Ross? Bottom line?"

"Are we back to this again? Look, he could play for anyone, right?"

"Yes."

"But he's with you right now. Why do you think he's in fucking Wyoming?"

Jaime got up and paced to the bookcase. "Because of Cole. Because he wants to take a team from the bottom all the way to the playoffs."

"Come on, man. You're looking at this all wrong. Ross's

got money, he's got trophies, he's got endorsements out the ass. What can Wyoming offer him that no one else can?"

He scrambled to think. "Calamity's a great place to live."

"Yeah? How would he know? He's looking at the rink and the four walls of his hotel. He came out there because all anyone talks about is fucking moose, but he hasn't seen one. He wants to go fly fishing, board a glacier—though, straight-up, I'll kick your ass if you get him hurt. He hasn't even seen a bull. Why the hell haven't you taken him to a damn rodeo? *That's* why he's there. Think you can show him a good time?"

The thought of taking Ross snowboarding made him break out in a cold sweat. He hadn't done anything reckless in ten years.

How badly did he want this goalie, though? He thought about Gracie, how he'd almost missed out on being with her, and about Kinny, how he'd caused her to doubt her self-worth. All because of this damn fear that held him frozen in time.

He was done with that shit.

"Yeah. I can do that."

Chapter Fifteen

WHOP WHOP WHOP. OVER THE THUMP OF REVOLVING blades, Jaime high-fived Cole and Declan.

Back together again.

It almost felt surreal. It had been ten years since they'd done anything like this.

Originally, they'd planned on boarding an easier glacier. With the season starting, no one could afford an injury. But they'd seen Ross's expression, and he wasn't into it. Turned out, he'd grown up in Michigan and had played as hard as Jaime and his crew ever did.

He wanted a good time, and who better to offer it than the three of them?

So, they'd rerouted to the Red Sentinel Couloir, a massive, steep, avalanche path. Now, they hovered over it while the pilot cleaned snow off a peak. Once he finished, they'd each take turns jumping off the chopper.

Ross went first. He landed on the peak, then reached back into the helicopter for his board.

Jaime shot a look to his friends. A lifetime of adventures,

of shared experiences had solidified their ability to communicate without words.

This is risky.

We shouldn't be doing this.

But then, Declan broke into a grin. *We got this.*

Cole followed. *This'll be fun.*

He needed that. Needed the muscle memory of not just his body but the positive, powerful energy they created as a unit. A smile broke through, flooding him with happiness. He laughed. He wanted this. He wanted it so fucking badly.

He'd *missed* this. Fuck the fear, the nightmares, the ravaging guilt.

"Let's carve some tracks, boys." He was the next to jump out of the helicopter.

After his friends jumped out and joined him and they'd all gotten their boards, Jaime gave the pilot a thumbs-up. Despite the icy air and the snow kicked up by the blades, he felt hot, excited, and ready to go.

They buckled their boots onto their boards and lowered the visors on their helmets. It was blindingly bright up here. The four of them lined up, unable to contain their giant smiles.

And then, Jaime inched his way to the drop. With a sixty degree fall line, the adrenaline pumped through him, fueling the beast that got off on these thrilling rides. With a holler, he took the plunge.

Elation hit the moment he caught air.

The one thing he knew was that confidence kept people alive.

The moment you entertain doubt, you lose focus. And that's how accidents happen.

So, he walled it off and let himself have a great fucking run.

It might be nine in the morning, but the ranch was long into its day. Grace crossed the dew-laden grass to get back to the big house. Arms loaded with baskets, she stopped for just a moment to take it all in.

Kate was already in the corral teaching a private lesson, and a battered pickup truck, the bed filled with workers, rumbled nearby. In a million years, she could never have imagined living on a ranch in Wyoming, falling for a single dad, and turning her fantasy sand cakes into reality.

I'm just so stinking happy.

Sure, there was fear that her parents would flip out, read her the riot act, and demand she come home. She could pretty much predict what her mom would say.

Family stays together.

What sacrifice is Jaime making for you?

Friends come and go, lovers break your heart, but family is the one constant you can count on.

But he wouldn't break her heart. How did she know that? Because he'd done the unthinkable. He'd snowboarded on a glacier.

And, after the day they'd spent shopping, she now got to snuggle in the hammock with him and Kinny, participate in their movie and popcorn nights, and even stay long enough to read bedtime stories. He'd brought her into his family.

All of that meant one thing: he'd stopped punishing himself.

He was free.

Ducking through the trees, she crossed the lawn and the slate patio, moving around the gorgeous pool no one used, and headed through the French doors.

She stopped when she heard angry voices.

"Because you're a shit friend," Jeremy whispered harshly.

She waited in the dark of the vestibule that smelled of new wood and varnish.

"I said I was sorry." There was a new level of anguish in Ben's voice that just about killed her. How long did he have to keep paying for his mistake?

"So? You made your dick a priority over friendship. That's it. There's nothing more to talk about."

She needed to get the baskets loaded, but she hung back, giving them a moment. Sunlight poured into the mudroom, showcasing the pretty hall tree, and for one startling moment, she could imagine the hooks lined with raincoats in all sizes. Boots shoved under the bench.

It was just so damn sad that a house like this would go empty while Jaime lived in that tiny cabin.

A spark of fear ignited in her core. Maybe Jaime wasn't free, after all. If he were, wouldn't he have moved into his dream house?

"I get it now." For the first time, Ben's voice held no defensiveness. "How I fucked up. I get it."

"Then, why'd you do it?"

"Because she's hot. Because I could never get a girl like that."

"Well, I hope it was worth it because you lost me as a friend."

She hurt for these boys. They were only seventeen, learning life's lessons. A shoe scuffed on the wood floor, bottles jangled as the refrigerator door opened, and one of them blew out a breath.

"It wasn't, okay?" Ben said. "It sucked. I pretty much knew right away it was a mistake, but what could I do? If I didn't follow through, she'd have made fun of me at school."

This time, the quiet went on too long, so she moved

forward and peered into the kitchen. The boys were gently moving the pastries, organizing them, and she appreciated their care.

"She smells funny." Ben said it cautiously, as if he wasn't sure how the comment would land.

The boys stared at each other, and in the mounting tension of their silence, Grace wondered if she should intervene. Break it up.

"I know." Jeremy asked, sounding genuinely confused. "What was that?"

Relief cracked Ben's features, and for the first time since she'd met him, he relaxed. "I don't know. But Laney says her whole house smells like it."

"All right." Jeremy finished loading the last basket. "I think that's it. Should we see if Grace needs help with the baskets?"

"No. She asked us to wait here. If she needed our help, she'd have told us to come with her."

"True," Jeremy said.

Both boys stared at the screens of their phones.

And then, Ben said, "It won't happen again."

Never looking up, Jeremy said, "Yeah. I know."

She was just so relieved for them. Moving into the kitchen, she set her load on the table. "Looks like you're all set. I appreciate you guys so much—you jumped right in, and you're doing a terrific job. Let's fill the baskets, and then you can go ahead and load the van."

By the time she'd sent the boys off to the festival grounds and returned to clean up the kitchen, she found Jaime leaning against the counter eating a croissant fresh out of the oven. He wore worn jeans that barely contained his muscular thighs and a gray T-shirt that did nothing to hide his ripped obliques, chiseled abs, and broad shoulders. "My God, you're hot."

Still chewing, he lifted his shirt to give her a peek.

Heading straight for him, she took the invitation and licked a path from his belly button to his nipple. Hands on his chest, she got on the tips of her toes and kissed his mouth. "Since when do you eat my pastries?"

"Since I've got a woman that wears me out every night." He released a long-suffering sigh. "I'm starving."

"Poor baby." Smiling, she threw her arms around his neck. He smelled so good—like soap and warm man. "I could ease up on you, if that would help."

"The hell it will." He tossed the croissant onto the counter and wrapped her up in a tight embrace. "The boys are out early."

"Today's the Blue Fire concert, so we're going to be slammed. I made double batches of everything."

"Cool. You're going to make a killing." He seemed unusually relaxed.

"Fingers crossed."

"Hey, so, I got a hold of my friend at the Wild Wolff Village. Rhys?"

"Oh." She took a step back. She had a lot riding on this. Until she figured some things out, she wouldn't tell her family about her decision. *I might not get to stay.*

He nodded. "He's out for the next month to be with his family, but he said he'd talk to the leasing office manager."

"I'm as scared as I am excited."

"What's got you scared? Break it down for me."

"What if they give me a space?" She pressed her hands together. "And I can't afford the lease?"

"I'll—"

"No. I know you want to help, and I appreciate it, but I

have to do this on my own. I can't take a lease unless I know I can afford it. Can you imagine if anything went wrong between us, and I was stuck—"

"No." He reached for her, lifting her and setting her on the counter. "I can't because it's not going to happen. You think I'm going to fuck up the best thing that's ever happened to me? To my daughter? Not a chance. We'll figure this out. Whatever comes our way, we're in this together."

A ring of fire blazed the mountain peaks as twilight settled over Jackson Hole. In his private box in the pit of the amphitheater, Jaime watched his daughter playing with Cole's girls and Hailey and Gracie chatting away.

Cole unwrapped his arm from his fiancée's shoulders and turned to face Jaime. "He sign yet?"

"Yep. One hour ago." Just one more piece that had fallen into place. For the first time since Kurt had formed this team twenty years ago, they had a winning roster.

The only reason their former coach had bought a hockey team in the first place was so the four friends could play together. The Dream Team, he'd called it. And now, finally, it was happening. It might not be exactly how Kurt had envisioned it—only Cole played hockey, but with Declan as coach and Jaime as owner, it was close enough.

While talking to her friend, Gracie's fingertips gently caressed his thigh. She flashed him a quick smile.

I have everything.

It didn't seem right that one man could be so happy.

The only missing piece was Booker…

But he shook it off and clapped a hand on Cole's shoulder. "You're going to get your cup."

His friend watched the three girls play together, totally ignoring their dinner. Paisley and Kinny got on like they'd known each other forever. "It's not like I sat around thinking of us as adults...getting married, having kids. In fact, I didn't think that was in the cards for me. But right now, with our two families hanging out, it just feels right. I hate that Kurt died, but I sure appreciate the way he brought us back together."

My family.

Me, Kinny, and Gracie.

Jaime sat up straighter. "I want her to stay. I lo—" No, Gracie got to hear those words first. Besides, he didn't need help with that part of the equation. "She's the one for me, I know it. But she's sacrificing a lot to be with us. I don't want to be a selfish prick."

"You're only selfish if you push her to do something she doesn't want." He gave a chin nod to where Gracie brushed hair off Kinny's forehead, making her take a bite of the cheeseburger she'd ordered. "Does she want to make the move?"

"Yes, absolutely. She's got some concerns, though, about the viability of opening a bakery here whereas at home, she's got a space for her business and an apartment. Both free of charge."

Cole watched him carefully. "Is that the real problem? Her choice between opening a bakery in Rhode Island or one out here?"

"No." He let out a frustrated laugh. "It's like...I live with this sense of impending doom, you know?" He kept his voice low. "Like one wrong move, one wrong decision, and something terrible will happen. And right now, it's almost too good to be true. Like a trap. Like if I take one step deeper into this life, it'll all blow up."

"And what does this blowup look like to you?"

His jaw snapped shut. Words got scrambled in his mind, but the images came front and center. Kinny cracking her head on the ice, his mom getting kicked by a horse...

Booker coming in for a landing.

Fuck.

"Hey." Cole set his hand on the back of Jaime's head. "Listen to me. What do you think? You put a ring on that woman's finger and the Yellowstone Caldera's gonna blow? Hot gas and magma will come shooting out, covering the earth, wiping out civilization?" He let him go.

"Yeah." He kept his gaze trained on his daughter. "Something like that."

"I get it. I lived with the same guilt."

Lived. Not live with. Past tense.

If Cole can get there, can't I?

"Makes you feel like you don't deserve the good stuff. But it's not true. You can have her. You can have all the things you want. Because punishing yourself isn't going to get Booker back to playing hockey." Cole looked him right in the eyes. "What happened that night isn't a life sentence."

"Grace says I think Booker's keeping score. Like if he sees me being happy, then I'm not paying penance."

"Grace is a smart woman. Listen to me. You get to have this life. It's yours for the taking. The question is—do you have the balls to grab it? To spend every day for the rest of your life earning it?"

Jaime sat with the questions for a few minutes. Really let them sink in. "Fuck, yeah." And suddenly, he knew what he had to do. For all of them. "Hey, can Kinny have a sleepover with you guys tonight?"

"Yeah. Sure."

Then again, he didn't want to do this in his cabin or

even the Dream House. He wanted to go somewhere special. "If Grace can take off the time, you think Kinny can spend two nights? I want to get out of town."

"No problem. Go for it."

"The only hitch is that Kinny's got her figure skating class the day after tomorrow."

"We can get her there. No problem. I'll bring the girls in case Paisley wants to join."

"Perfect time for her to watch. They've got an exhibition that day."

"Cool. You got any idea where you want to take her?"

"Not yet."

All he knew was he had to make it good. This was the kind of question a man only asks once.

Ass perched on a stool, Jaime tipped back his bottle of water and enjoyed the show. Gracie was making the clerk describe every pastry in the case.

"And what's this one?" With her knees bent, she tapped the glass.

"So, that's a shortbread crust, dulce de leche cream inside, and a chocolate raspberry mousse."

"Oh, that sounds good. Let's try that one. You don't happen to know what kind of shortening the pastry chef uses, do you?"

Jaime chuckled. He might as well settle in. *She'll be at this for a while.* He checked his phone again. Reception had been spotty for this half of the trip as they crossed the mountain range back into Wyoming. Last he'd heard, Korzak's ankle wasn't going to be good enough to play, so the GM had made the call to keep him out of exhibition games.

Now, they had to decide which goalie to bring up from the minors. A big part of him wanted to be there for that—he had Cole and Ross to think about. Their second goalie not only had to be damn good, but he had to start working with the team right away.

That was what he'd hired Darren for. *Let the man do his job.*

Besides, the festival ended in four days, and he needed to make sure Grace knew he was fully invested in them, that she wasn't giving up her family and job for an unknown future.

That he loved her so completely, he couldn't stand to think of a life without her.

"Yes, that's it." Her voice broke through his thoughts. "Just those. Thank you."

Good. She'd made her decision. He stood, shoving his phone in his pocket.

"You want to eat these here or take them to go?" the clerk asked.

"To go, please."

While the woman boxed up the treats, Gracie sashayed over to him with a huge smile. "This is so fun." She threw her arms around his neck. "I can't believe you arranged all this."

"It wasn't that hard." He'd researched bakeries in a hundred-and-fifty-mile radius. Calling it the Pastry Loop, he'd mapped out a trip from Calamity to Idaho Falls down to Montpelier and back up to Calamity. So far, they'd visited twelve shops and had tasted a wide variety of desserts.

"It's not about the level of difficulty." She went back to pay, and then, hand in hand, they left the store. "It's the fact that you did this for me." Digging into her bag, she pulled out her sunglasses. They covered her eyes…but not before he saw them glistening.

"Hold on." He pulled her to a stop. "Are you crying?"

"No. Of course not."

He tipped the glasses up to her forehead. "You sure are." He held her face in his hands as if it were a delicate bird's nest. "What's going on?"

"No one's ever done anything like this for me."

"Like what? Go on a road trip with you?"

"It's not that." A Jeep passed by, the music blasting, kayaks latched to the roof. "Come on."

They climbed back into his SUV. The scent of sugar and butter filled the car, and he turned on the air-conditioning to keep the pastries fresh. "Talk to me." He pulled away from the curb and joined the light morning traffic in this tiny mountain town.

"You know how it goes in big families. There's one big party for all the December birthdays, and your parents can't go to everyone's games and recitals, so they only show up every once in a while." She gazed out the window, those damn glasses back in place. "You know that feeling where you're in a recital, you're up on stage, and you keep looking for them in the crowd. You don't even hear what's going on because you're so focused on spotting them. You don't give up hoping they'll be there until you're off the stage, and everyone else is getting hugs and bouquets, and you're just standing there all alone feeling like an idiot."

He could picture his sunshiny girl scanning the crowd, body tense with anticipation and hope, and he wanted to hug the loneliness right out of her, let her know he would wear a neon shirt with bells and flashing lights so she could always find him in an audience.

I will always be there for you.

He turned off Main Street to make the long winding trek back to their remote cabin.

"But I guess, if I'm honest, none of that matters as much as the fact that no one cared about my interest in making pastries. I used to bring my mom sand cakes decorated with shells and seaweed. I had a lemonade stand where I sold lemon squares. Everyone knew what I loved." She turned to him, and he nodded. "But no one ever asked me to make them anything. I mean, come on. At least ask me to make the Bûche de Noël for Christmas, right? And here, you've planned this trip for me." She lifted the bakery box.

He couldn't drive, not when she was practically weeping, so he pulled off the dirt road and parked inside a copse of trees. Cutting the engine, he felt cocooned in this cool, covered space. He pulled off her sunglasses to look into hazel eyes filled with affection.

For me.

She set her hand on his arm. "You just make me feel so special."

"You are special. You're so special." Should he do it now? He had a whole thing prepared, but should he just go for it?

"I think…I think I love you." She blinked back tears. "Is it too soon to say that?"

"No. God, no." Yes, he'd do it now. Fuck the rose petals and the candles. Fuck his plans.

But her mood changed, and she broke into a smile. "Do you hear that sound?"

With the windows open, he heard birds trilling, leaves shushing in a gentle breeze, and the ticking of his engine. "What do you hear?"

"This fig tart begging to be tasted." She opened the lid and lifted out the pastry, taking a small bite. "Oh, my God.

Oh, my God. Oh. My. God." She brought it to his mouth, her hand underneath in case a slice of fresh fig fell off.

He enjoyed the sweet flavor, but it was nothing compared to the utter joy of watching her eat. "It's good."

She picked up a profiterole. "Let's try this one." After taking a tiny bite, she seemed disappointed.

"Not good?"

"Hm. Something's just not right. Here." With a teasing smile, she swiped the filling and painted his lips with it. "Let's try it this way." As she licked the whipped cream off, she clutched the back of his head and shifted over, straddling him. "Mm. So much better."

He chased her lips for more kisses, but she sat back.

"It makes me wonder…" She picked up the box and sorted through the pastries. "How much better would it taste here?" She pulled his T-shirt up and off, flinging it into the backseat. Then, she set a strawberry slice on his collarbone and sucked it into her mouth, licking the juice off his skin.

"All summer long, you've been trying to get me to taste your goodies." He grabbed her hips and settled her over his hard cock. "I'm hungry now, Gracie. Real hungry."

"I thought you said this trip was all about me?" She smoothed dulce de leche cream over his nipples and then lapped it up with her pretty pink tongue.

"Fuck, Gracie. Give me that cream, and I'll make it *all* about you." He couldn't resist squeezing her ass cheeks. "Pull up your shirt. Let me see your tits."

As soon as she sat up and yanked it over her head, he filled his palms with her lace-covered breasts. Now would not be a good time to ask her, but all he could think about was the ring waiting in his pocket. He pushed her breasts together and jiggled them, loving the wobble and bounce.

"Tonight, I'm gonna fuck these." He could see it, too. See his slick cock gliding through that deep valley.

Her lids lowered, her mouth went all pouty and soft, and she reached for a cannoli. "I always wanted to make this for the bakery. I mean, we're Renzo's. We should be making Italian desserts. Let's taste it." She swiped a finger through the cream and held it out to him. Grabbing her wrist, he sucked it into his mouth, licking it clean. "I like that. Let me try."

"I'm not finished." She got off his lap and unzipped his jeans. "There's one place I haven't tried." That warm, feminine hand wrapped around his cock and pulled it out.

"Shit. Fuck." Even through the fog of lust, even though he needed to be in her mouth, he had to keep her safe, so he glanced out the windows and rearview mirrors. When he didn't see any sign of life, he braced his feet on the floorboard, lifted his ass, and lowered his jeans.

She took her time slathering cream all over his dick—tugging and twisting—and then, she started lapping at it.

Lust crashed through him, and he stretched out his legs, curling his toes. She licked like nothing had ever been more delicious. "Jesus, Gracie."

Once she'd cleaned every trace of whipped cream off him and her fingers, she sucked his entire length into her mouth and held him there, her tongue flicking back and forth right under the head.

He clamped his hands on her head, holding her in place, completely lost in the hot, slick sensation of her mouth. She grasped him at the base and jacked him in tandem with sucking. Her tongue flicked just under the head, and the pressure was so intense, he jerked back, slamming into the headrest.

Slowly, the rhythm picked up, until she was working

him hard and fast. Hands twisting, tongue sucking, she put him in a state of arousal that left him moaning and ready to explode. The pleasure was so intense, he never wanted it to end.

When the tension grew unbearable, his hips punched, and he came so hard he went soaring into a state of euphoria. She kept sucking, coaxing more explosions out of him, until he nearly lost consciousness.

When she let him go, she sat up with a very satisfied expression. "Now, that was really good cream."

He burst out laughing. "Okay, vixen. It's my turn." He pulled up his pants. "Get dressed. I'm taking you back to the cabin so I can defile all your pastries."

Her eyes flared with delight. "Lucky me."

This woman was everything. She was fresh and beautiful, filthy as fuck in bed, kind, generous, fearless—he couldn't wait to put a ring on it. He backed out of the wooded area and continued up the road. Weirdly, while the mountain town didn't have good cell reception, the cabin did. He hadn't talked to Kinny since last night, and he wanted to hear about the exhibition. Since she'd only had two lessons, she had to sit it out. He knew it would be tough for her, but he also figured it would encourage her to take the next class and get better at her sport.

He thought about what Gracie had said, about searching the audience, and vowed to never miss any of his daughter's events. "I like being with you."

She was busy putting the box into a large canvas tote. "I like being with you."

"You're the most passionate person I know."

She set the bag on the back seat. "We do have amazing chemistry."

"No, I mean in every way. When I watch you baking,

I'm floored at the joy it brings you. You dropped a tart the other day, and the filling splattered all over the place, but instead of being upset about losing one of your products, you were bummed because you like the way it'd looked."

"It was an especially pretty one. But honestly, I don't have time to get upset about anything. I have so much to make."

"But that's what I'm saying. Anyone else would break under the pressure. You thrive under it."

"Yeah, well. I get to do what I love."

"You're amazing." He reached for her hand and brought it to his mouth, kissing the back. The moment they reached their rental cabin, his phone rattled in the cupholder. "We got reception." But then, it vibrated again. And again. *Shit.* He hit the brakes and grabbed it.

Bluetooth picked up a muffled sound, as if the caller had dropped the phone.

And then, his daughter's voice filled the car. "Daddy, everyone gets to dance. How come I can't? Where are you? Why aren't you answering? I want to dance, too. Please, Daddy? Please, can I do it?"

"Dance?" Grace asked. "What's she talking about?"

"The exhibition." His answer was curt as he waited for more. So many messages had come in, he'd lost count. He had a sickening feeling they were not just from his daughter.

The second message started. "Today's the *last day* of class. It's my only time to dance with them. I just have to. *Daddy.*"

"And I told you you could take the next class," he said out loud, though she obviously couldn't hear him.

In the third message, Kinsley sounded panicked. "Daddy, where are you? It's almost over, and Coach Molly says I can't perform without your permission. Tell her I can do it. Tell her, Daddy."

"Shit." His palms went clammy on the steering wheel, so he wiped them on his jeans. "What have you done, Kinny?"

He noticed Gracie remained quiet. Normally, she would reassure him, tell him he was catastrophizing. But this time, she agreed. Something bad happened.

They waited for the next message. "Hey, Mr. Dupree. It's Molly. Kinsley really wants to get out there. I can't let her do it without your permission. I know we talked about this, but the three kids who just started want to hold hands and skate out there. Let me know if that's okay." She paused. "We've got about ten minutes left."

The next message came from Kinny. No longer panicked, her tone was confident. "I'm going to do it, Daddy. Gracie wants me to."

There was a moment where time felt suspended. Rationally, he knew his daughter had to be fine. It was ice-skating. Really, what could she have done? Attempt a triple axel?

And yet, with multiple messages remaining...he knew. He just knew.

Cole's wife came in hot on the next message. "We're on our way to the hospital. I'll call you once we get there."

Hospital?

What the fuck?

Jaime gripped the steering wheel so tightly his knuckles turned white. Jerking the car into gear, he swung around and tore down the road. Dust kicked up, and gravel knocked against the metal.

"She's okay," Grace said. "You know she's fine. She's six, and it's just ice-skating."

"I don't know that. It's Kinny."

"The worst-case scenario from a six-year-old ice-skating

exhibition is a broken bone, and you know they grow back stronger."

"It could be a compound fracture. Multiple breaks held together by pins and multiple surgeries."

"She's not the goalie of the Brawlers, Jaime." Her voice was soothing. It wasn't the least bit patronizing.

Still, he didn't want to talk. He wanted to hear the next message. "Hey, it's me." His sister Abby sounded frazzled. "Hailey called. Mom and I are headed to the ER. I'll call you when we're there."

Jaime couldn't wait another second, so he stopped listening to the messages and called his sister. When it went to voicemail, he shouted, "Dammit." But then, he left a message. "I'm on my way home. We're about forty-five minutes from Afton, so I'll have better connectivity soon. Call me and tell me what's going on." He tried his mom's number and then his dad's. No one answered. He stopped leaving messages.

He drove in silence, glad Grace didn't engage him in conversation. He didn't want to hear how everything would be all right.

Because neither of them had any answers.

He'd known, though, hadn't he? All along, he'd had this foreboding, this sense that something was going to go wrong.

And it had.

He'd let himself get caught up in what made him feel good and stopped thinking about the consequences.

You selfish son of a bitch.

Chapter Sixteen

PREOCCUPIED WITH WORRY, GRACE HAD A HARDER time getting her pastries made the next morning. Which was frustrating because the sooner she finished, the sooner she could get to the hospital.

The moment she got the van loaded and gave the boys instructions in case she was out for most of the day, she took off.

Now, racing down the hallway, punching the call button on the elevator, she kept checking her phone. Nothing from Jaime. Not a word. They'd kept her overnight because of the swelling. Had it gotten worse? Was it better? Why wouldn't he tell me?

The moment she entered the room and saw the little girl in bed, IV tubes connected to her tiny hand, tears burned the backs of her eyes. But she plastered a smile on her face and held out the bouquet of flowers she'd picked up. "Hey, guys."

Jaime glanced up from his phone.

And terror struck her heart. She hadn't seen that hard, flat expression in a long time. Not since those early days.

Oh, no. Please don't do this. Don't shut down.

She wouldn't let him. She'd grab his hand and pull him back. This one little incident would not send him back into that cold, lonely cave. First, though, she gave Kinny a kiss on the forehead. "How's my sweet girl?"

"My arm hurts."

Jaime popped up. "I'll get the nurse." He was out of the room before she could even react.

Oh, boy. That wild look in his eyes scared her. "I'm so sorry you fell, sweetheart." True to form, Kinny had attempted a spin and taken a hard fall, fracturing her forearm. It wasn't a bad break, though.

She reached for the hand that didn't have a needle in it. "Oh, your fingers are so cold." She cradled it inside her cupped ones and blew warm air on it.

"I can't feel anything, and Daddy's scared I'm going to have surgery."

"Did he tell you that?"

"No, I heard him talking to my grandma."

She tried to ignore the pinch of hurt that he hadn't told her.

It's not about me.

Except it was kind of about her because if they were going to be together—essentially, as a family—he should be coming to her, confiding in her. She'd cut him some slack, though. After all, hadn't everything played out exactly how he'd feared? He'd wanted to keep his daughter in the bubble for this very reason. Of course, he felt guilty.

Or angry. *Maybe he blames me.*

He has to. I'm the one who pushed.

Dammit. She had to talk to him. *I have to know what he's thinking.*

This is killing me.

When he came back, he gave a flick of his hand. "She's got enough painkillers in her through that thing." He went around to the other side of the bed and kissed his daughter's cheek. "I'm so sorry, baby."

In her mind, she could hear the rest of that unspoken sentence play out. *I never should have put you in that class.*

Yes, you silly boy. You should have.

All kids get hurt.

Especially the ones who've been sealed in bubble wrap their whole lives.

With a flourish, she presented the box she'd tucked into her tote bag. "I have something for you." She'd tied a pretty pink and purple bow on it. "Ta da."

Kinny's eyes brightened. "What is it? Which one did you bring?"

"I brought you three profiteroles. One has a caramel crunch top, the other's strawberries and cream, and the third one's—"

The little girl jerked up. "Nutella?"

"Hey, hey. Lie back." Jaime checked the IV port and drew the blanket up to her chest. He took the box from Grace, opened it, and then handed it over. "Here you go."

Kinny bit into one, the creamy brown filling squeezing out. "It's so yummy. Thank you, Gracie."

"You're welcome."

"I got an idea." Wide-eyed, she looked to her dad. "Instead of a birthday cake, can I have these?"

"You can have whatever you want." But he seemed confused. "You just want, like, a platter of cream puffs?"

"Actually, I can make a croquembouche, which is a tower of them." Grace loved the idea. "So, it'll look like a birthday cake, and we can put some candles in it. How does that sound? Here." Knowing the little girl had no idea what she was talking about, Grace pulled out her phone. "Let me show you." When she found an image, she showed them the cone-shaped tower of shiny cream puffs.

"I love that," Kinny said.

"Is that okay with you?" Grace asked Jaime.

"Anything my princess wants."

"I want to have a pool party." Kinny looked so tiny in that bed Grace couldn't stand it. She wanted her home and chatting about what happened in daycare that day and playing with leftover dough. It was horrible to see her in pain.

"It might be a little cold in September," Jaime said. "Why don't we wait and see what the weather's like?"

"But I want a princess swimsuit. Can we get one?"

"You bet we can," he said.

"We should probably start looking now," Grace said. "I'm not sure we'll find them when the weather starts to change."

"I want to go with you. Can I, Daddy? Can I go shopping with Gracie?"

Perspiration beaded on his forehead. "We don't even know if we're going to have a pool party. Let's not worry about swimsuits. Right now, I want to get you home. That's all I'm thinking about."

He was losing his cool, and she'd never seen that happen. "I'm going to see if I can find you milk to go with those treats." She kissed Kinny's forehead again before smiling at Jaime. "Walk me out?"

It was the flash of annoyance that tore a corner of her heart. Sure, he didn't want to leave his daughter alone. *But it's me.*

She started to lead him down the hallway, but when he resisted, she had to explain why she'd made him leave his daughter's side. "She heard you tell your mom she might need surgery."

"She *what?* How?"

"She's got owl ears." She tipped her head. "Come on, let's get a little farther away." They found a quiet corner near the stairwell. "When do you think she'll be able to go home?"

"They're still watching the swelling. Her fingers are numb, so if it's compartment syndrome, they'll have to do surgery." He tugged at the collar of his T-shirt, even though it wasn't anywhere near his throat, and looked like he wanted to climb out of his skin and run screaming.

"Hey." She reached for him, but he held up both hands. The rejection stung like a slap to the face.

"I'm sorry. I'm just…I can't right now." His furtive gaze landed on a bench by the door to the stairwell. "Can we go back? I need to be with her."

"Jaime, I'm worried about you."

He shoved his hands into the pocket of his jeans. "Look, I know I'm overreacting. I know that." His troubled expression told her he had more to say, so she waited, her whole body on edge.

Because she couldn't read him, and he wasn't talking. She was afraid he'd go back to sheltering Kinny, and that would be awful. For all of them.

"But I also know I stopped listening to my gut," he continued. "And that's never a good thing."

Here it is. "I wondered if you'd blame me."

"I don't blame anybody but myself, and you're definitely not the only one who's tried to get me to let her do things." He grew agitated. "But I know her. Kinny's a mini-me. If she's on a balcony with a pool below, she's going to want to see if she can jump."

Don't tell me that's *why he hasn't moved into the Dream House.*

"I know that about her, which was why I wanted to wait until she had a little more maturity, so she could make better decisions."

How was she supposed to make better decisions without experience? But she wasn't about to get into that conversation. "I'm here. You know that, right?"

"Yeah. Sure."

"Please don't shut me out." Not with the festival ending in two days.

He gripped the back of his neck, his gaze wandering to his daughter's room. "I'm just trying to focus on Kinny right now."

"What does that mean? Are you saying there's no room for me? Because you're certainly acting like it."

"No, of course not. My daughter's in the fucking hospital. Her fingers are numb, and my mind is racing, thinking it happened because I—"

"Stopped controlling things."

He had a terrible look in his eyes. "I ran off. Left her in someone else's care."

So you could do something selfish. Yeah, she got it. "This didn't happen because you went away for two days. It didn't happen because you weren't watching her. This is just life. Nobody gets through childhood without scrapes and bruises."

"I know that." He was ramping up again. "I get that it's just a broken arm, that it's part of growing up. But I didn't follow my gut, and in hockey, when you don't follow your intuition, you fuck up."

"You didn't fail Kinny by letting her take a beginning figure skating class. Every kid falls at some point, but they get better at it. If she *is* your mini-me, then you can count on her intelligence, her agility, her…" Clarity hit with a punch.

Stop it. Just stop trying to convince a man to want you.

Because that's what this comes down to. You're trying to help him heal, so he'll be free to love you back.

Spooked, she backed away. "I'm going to ask the nurse to get her some milk, so I'll let you get back to her." She started off.

"Grace." His tone held urgency.

Yeah, she heard that. Grace. Not Gracie. *Dammit.* "What?" She would hear him out, but nothing he said would matter. He was stuck in an endless cycle of guilt and penance.

"Look, I'm sorry, but you've got to give me a break here. My daughter's in the *hospital.*"

Time is the one thing we don't have.

And I'm not waiting around for someone to choose me.

Other than the first time Ian had broken up with her freshman year, she'd never been this devastated. And it was not lost on her that ending a fifteen-year relationship hurt less than losing Jaime.

At least in both situations, she'd known they were truly over. There was no overanalyzing, no wondering if she should give it another chance. Because she knew she couldn't stay with a man who walled himself up every time something triggered him.

She wasn't making light of Kinny's accident or the trauma Jaime endured from witnessing Booker's fall. It was simply that he wasn't ready for a relationship. She'd seen it in his expression. He'd crawled back into his cave.

Fear got hold of her lungs and held them in a vise, making it difficult to draw a breath. Because this time, she'd lost something truly spectacular.

After leaving the hospital, she'd known there wasn't a chance she could head to the amphitheater and sing. She needed to get away. But where? Where could she go?

Since Jaime hadn't had a chance to deal with the overnight bags they'd left in the rental cabin, he'd gone and paid for another week, figuring he'd drive out there later. But she needed the road trip, so she called the place for directions and told them she was coming.

She tried listening to her favorite songs but was too distracted, too wound up. The thought of leaving Jaime and Kinny, this town she'd come to love—no, the future she'd decided to claim for herself—didn't sit right. She knew she'd found something special here. Something she'd never find again.

For most of the ride, she'd picked apart everything he'd said, analyzing every shift of emotion across his handsome features, and it had her spiraling. So, with twenty minutes till she reached the campsite, she called her brother.

"Hey, what's up? Haven't heard from you in a bit."

"It's been a wild couple of days." She'd gone from the highest of highs—the most beautiful relationship she'd ever had—to quite possibly the lowest. "Kinny got hurt. She broke her arm."

"Oh, shit." Her brother got it, of course. It wasn't too hard to piece it together. "Ice-skating?"

"Yep."

"You're not blaming yourself, are you?"

"I mean, a little." The mountain road was remote with scary switchbacks, and only the occasional truck flew by. But she didn't really see much of the view. Jaime's expression, the way he'd said, *You've got to give me a break here*, held her mind hostage. "I pushed him to do something he wasn't ready for. In any event, it looks like I'm coming home."

"Wasn't that always the plan? Wait, you're not cutting it short because of some guy, are you?"

"No. I'm working to the end of the festival." She had a lot to catch him up on. "But Jaime and I had plans for me to stay."

"No shit? When did this happen?"

"We've just been getting so much closer, and he's like a whole other man from the guy I first met. He was so sure about wanting me to stay that he called his friend at the ski resort I told you about to see about leasing a space."

"Slow the hell down. You're opening a bakery there? You said it was way too expensive."

"It is. But…I don't know. I was willing to take out a loan or *something*. I've got credibility right now because of the festival. It just…it seemed possible." She slowed to take a sharp turn. "But then Kinny got hurt, and now, I don't know what we're doing, and I…I think I got a little carried away."

"Holy fuck, Grace. You're talking about owning your own bakery? In *Wyoming?*"

"Yes. I want it more than anything. I know Mom and Dad aren't going to understand, but I can't go back to making croissants and muffins. I just can't. And I don't want to leave Jaime and Kinny. I love him, Romeo. I love him so much." All these emotions had been trapped inside her, and it felt good to let them out. "But now, he's pulling away and—"

"Grace. I want this for you. I do. But you're not flipping your life upside down for a guy who can't make up his mind. He's either in, or you're out."

She sat up a little straighter. The cloud of confusion started to clear. "You're right."

"If a guy wants you, nothing's going to stop him. No commitment issues, no fears. Nothing. You know this."

"I do."

"And if he wavers? You walk."

"You're absolutely right."

"Now, opening a bakery's a whole other conversation. That's not contingent on a relationship."

"Well, there isn't a space, and it's a long waiting list."

"So? Open it somewhere else."

"There's already a gourmet food store in town that has a good bakery. There're also pastry chefs at the Homestead Inn and Wally's—those are both fine dining." But none of that even mattered. "The place I want is Wild Wolff Village. And I can't stay here without a job."

"Well, you can. You can run a food truck, build up some cash until something opens... There are options."

"That's really hard to justify when Ian's parents are offering to buy a building for me."

"They did it."

"Did what?"

"They bought the building."

"Oh." That pretty much sealed her fate, didn't it? If she stayed here, it would take years to save enough money. It didn't make sense if she had an opportunity waiting for her at home.

Suddenly, she missed her family fiercely.

In that moment, she understood what her mom kept telling her. *Boyfriends come and go, but family's forever.* "Well, then, I guess that settles it."

"What? No. That's on them. There's no obligation for you to take them up on their offer."

"True." But it delivered her dream on a platter, and if she didn't have an option in Calamity, she'd be a fool to stay. She was so distracted with her thoughts she nearly passed the brown sign with yellow lettering that announced the campsite entrance. "I miss you guys anyway. I better go."

"Okay, but you don't have to make any decisions right now. You've still got—what?"

"Forty-eight hours."

"Ah. That's why you're flippin' out. You think when they take the truck away, they take your reason for staying there. But I doubt Jaime's thinking about the timing. He's focused on his kid. If you tell him you've got a decision to make, he'll probably snap out of it."

"You're right." She pulled to a stop in front of the rental office. "Thanks, Romeo." She really loved her little brother.

It only took a moment to show her ID and grab the key before she was back in the car and heading to the cabin. She was glad she'd talked to her brother, but he hadn't seen Jaime's expression.

You've got to give me a break here.

Maybe she could do that if she didn't have to leave in two days.

Then again, that's not really the point. Instead of leaning on me, he's shutting me out. I can't be in a relationship where I'm inside the circle one day and outside the next.

She parked and got out of the car, breathing in the dusty, pine-scented air. Luckily, she didn't have any memories of this place, or it just might kill her to be back without him. Jaime had left her in town to do some window-shopping while he'd checked them in. He'd been worried they'd give away their cabin if they showed up too late.

She inserted the key in the lock, turned it, and stepped inside.

It took her a minute to make sense of what she was seeing.

Wilted rose petals littered the floor, unlit votive candles rested on every surface, and wood was stacked in the fireplace. Had they given the cabin to someone else? But no, she saw her suitcase on the bed.

He'd done this for her.

Oh, Jaime.

You sweet, romantic man.

God, she loved him. She'd never loved anyone like this before.

And she knew she never would again.

On her way across the room, she grabbed a handful of petals and inhaled their scent. She found two champagne flutes on the kitchen counter, each with a raspberry at the bottom of the glass.

She almost didn't want to let herself think it, but had he planned on *proposing?* She could see it so vividly. The fire in the hearth, him getting down on one knee—

Wait, would he do that? Or would he kiss her senselessly and then blurt it out? *Marry me, Gracie. Marry me and make me the happiest man alive.*

Yes, yes, yes. If he were on a knee, she'd hurl herself at him, knock him back, and scatter kisses all over his face.

But then, her fantasy came crashing down when she remembered the way he'd looked at her when she'd entered the hospital room. He was annoyed to see her.

Could he really go from setting up a romantic proposal to pushing her away in the blink of an eye?

No. She knew him better than that. They were *both* overreacting. All those messages he'd gotten, one after another, building up to what he'd feared the most... He was living his deepest, darkest fear: if he stopped doing penance, if he allowed himself to be happy, something would go terribly wrong.

But it struck her that she might not be all that different.

Look at the guilt you feel for wanting to stay in Calamity.

What about the happiness I'm not allowed to have?

God, it's so true. She'd never thought about it like that before, but her family culture didn't encourage personal happiness. It was about survival, and the way to be safe was to stay together, work together. It was insular.

She remembered Uncle Sal. Well, the story of him anyway. She'd never met him. He hated the ocean, hated the sand, and hated the bakery. He wanted to be a rock star, so he'd run off with a tourist to seek his fame and fortune and, after three failed marriages and a career in car sales, wound up dying alone. The only time anyone brought him up was as a cautionary tale.

In the Giordano mindset, if you abandon the family to pursue your own happiness, you'll perish.

I don't want to become another Uncle Sal story.

I want my family to still love me, even as I pursue my own dreams.

Maybe if Ian's parents hadn't bought a building for her, it would be one thing. But they did, and that would make it impossible to justify staying here and working some random job.

She'd rushed to blame Jaime, but she had some ownership here, too. She was wrong to expect him to be one hundred percent healed when she was still very much trapped in the Giordano mindset.

He'd come so far this summer—was it so bad he'd failed

his first test? Maybe all he needed was to see that Kinny would wear a cast, heal, and get back to skating.

And really, did she think she could charge into his life and ask him to heal himself on her timeline?

She hadn't been fair. She needed to give him space.

He'll get there.

Right?

Please let him get there.

Chapter Seventeen

It was the last day of the Owl Hoot Summer Music Festival, and Grace was sick.

Anxious, nauseous…she wanted to be alone in her cabin, under the covers, and stress-eating.

Because even though Kinny was back home—she hadn't needed surgery, and she was doing great—Jaime hadn't come to visit her while she baked. That was their special time together, when they were in the zone and opened up, sharing all their random thoughts and feelings. He had valid excuses, of course. They had to onboard the new players—not just Ross but the new goalie they'd brought up from the minors. With exhibition games starting soon, both players had to get up to speed quickly.

They were competitive for the first time, so there was a lot riding on it.

Because of Cole. And Declan.

Yeah, lots of valid excuses.

But no touches. No kisses. And she was starved for them. Scared witless that he really had gone from planning a proposal to shutting her out of his life.

Because this is it. The last day. Tomorrow, Brodie would come for the truck, and Grace would have no job, no income, and absolutely no reason to stay in Calamity on the Dupree Ranch.

This summer, she'd made more money than even Brodie had expected. Since she had a little left over after fully paying her parents back, she'd officially begun to rebuild her savings.

The mid-August sun was hot, and Grace was thankful for the breeze floating through the pass-through window. Jeremy was on his break, and Ben had run to the van to grab more tarts from the cooler, so she was alone when Lorelei showed up next in line.

"Well, look who's here," Grace said. "I thought you were in the studio till five."

"I got my part done early, so now, I'm going to surprise my boyfriend with a little afternoon delight."

"Did I need to hear that?" Grace made an exaggerated grimace. "No. No, I don't think I did." This would be the last time she'd ever see Lorelei in one of her ridiculous disguises. "Nice beret. I hear most of Paris shuts down for August, so welcome to America."

"Oui, oui. Merci. Je voudrais un…" She tapped her chin with a red fingernail, frowned, then batted her hand. "Oh, forget it. I suck at accents."

"That's because you're the most real and honest person I've ever met."

Lorelei froze. "Are you soaping my ass right now?" She had a wary expression. "Because in my world, people only say stuff like that because they want something. Are you sure you don't want me to take a selfie with your or have you sing on my next number one hit song?"

Grace laughed. "I'm positive. I meant what I said. You're awesome."

"Well, thank you. That's genuinely the nicest thing anyone's ever said about me."

She'd never see the singer again, so she might as well go for it. "I never understood how you stayed so true to yourself in such a difficult industry. But now, I know. Even if you baked croissants for a living, you'd still be a happy and confident woman. It's just who you are."

"Okay, you need to stop. This is getting embarrassing for you. But since we're signing each other's yearbooks here, I can tell you the real reason you've got such a long line. It's because you've got this light inside you, and it draws us to you. Which is probably why your pastries taste so good. Now, as you know, I have an agenda here, so I'll take everything you have that's filled with whipped cream." Lorelei winked. "If you know what I mean."

Oh, dammit. She was thrown back to the afternoon in Jaime's car, licking the cream off his body. That was such a great day. The whole trip he'd planned…*God.*

Come back to me, Jaime. Please, come back.

But she was at work, so she had no choice but to slap on a smile. "For all that's holy, Lorelei, spare me the details." But she got to work boxing up the filled pastries.

"Hey," a person in line said. "Save some for us."

The singer whipped around. "That's not how lines work. If you're at Target, do you tell the person ahead of you not to buy the last lavender face mask?" She swung back to Gracie. "Sheesh." And then, in a lower voice, she said, "Do you know I've gained five pounds this summer?"

"Well, if you're eating all those pastries, then I'm not surprised," the same person said.

"Do you have bat ears?" Lorelei shouted. "And they're not all for me."

"Guys, I have plenty more." As Grace started boxing up the treats, she noticed the singer's eyes narrow. "What?"

Lorelei didn't answer. Her features were pulled tight in concentration as she stared in the direction of the woods and the tour buses.

"Here you go." Grace tried to hand the box over, but Lorelei didn't take it.

Stark emotions played across her features. Blatant shock faded into a desolation so vast Grace's bones went cold. Setting the box down, she turned to look out the window on the other side of the truck.

Lorelei's boyfriend and best friend were coming out of the woods. Landon leaned back and brushed the dirt off the drummer's bottom.

Grace's stomach lurched, and she felt sick. *Lorelei's supposed to be in the studio right now. She got done early and wanted to surprise her boyfriend.*

I have to help her.

But when she turned around, Lorelei was gone.

For the next two hours, Grace fretted. She and Lorelei obviously hadn't exchanged numbers, and they didn't have the kind of relationship where it would be appropriate to go knock on the bus door and check on her. She had no way to find out how she was doing.

"What looks good today?" she asked the next customer.

"Can I get that one?" he pointed to a basket.

"The Paris Brest?" She felt so damn bad for the singer and wished more than anything she could help in some way.

"Yes, please."

"You got it." As she grabbed her tongs, she heard a knock at the door and tipped her head toward it, asking Jeremy to see who was there. For one moment, she wondered if it was Lorelei. But of course, that would never happen. She handed over the treat and shoved the five dollars into the till.

"It's Brodie Bowie." Jeremy sounded awed. The Bowies, she'd learned, were a pretty big deal in Calamity. Kind of like royalty.

Worried, she wiped her hands on her apron and motioned for Ben to take her place at the window.

When she stepped outside, she found him with Jaime. Even after all this time, all the things they'd done together, the sight of his tall frame, handsome face, and muscular body never failed to send her pulse racing. She held his gaze, found the same yearning she felt mirrored in his eyes, and wondered, *Are you here for me? Are you back?*

But no. He still wore that same flat expression. Which meant he was back to suppressing his emotions.

She had to accept it. Their relationship was well and truly over. "What can I do for you?"

Brodie turned his back on the meadow and in a low voice said, "Lorelei's gone."

"What do you mean by *gone*?" It was an hour before the final show of the festival, the big Lorelei Calloway concert everyone had been waiting for all summer long.

"She took off."

"But she'll be back, right?" *She's never cancelled a tour date in her life.*

"No. But the show's got to go on."

Those fuckers. How could they hurt the woman who trusted them so completely? Who loved them with all her heart. "You're confusing me. You're telling me she's gone but the show's still on?"

"Right. The band's here. They're ready to go. They just need a singer."

And why was Jaime just standing there? What did he have to do with this?

"We just heard from her manager," Brodie said. "Lorelei wants the show to go on. We just need you to take her place."

Both men stared at her. "*Me?* Are you out of your mind? No way. No. Not a chance."

"No one else can do it, Grace." Brodie held firm. He wasn't pleading, he wasn't even nervous. He just knew what had to be done and was here to accomplish the task. "I've got two thousand people in the meadow and a camera crew from *Entertainment Today* filming. I've got to give them a show."

"No one can replace Lorelei Calloway."

"Except you. You know the songs, and you've got the vocal range. Besides, everyone knows the Singing Baker." Brodie glanced over her shoulder.

She followed his gaze to the stage where roadies were setting up the equipment. The pink drum kit could be seen from a satellite.

"Yes, but I'm not her. I'm a novelty item. A fun sideshow if you happen to be at the festival. Trust me, no one"—she gestured wildly to the meadow—"came to see a pastry chef perform. They'll come at me with pitchforks."

"They came to be entertained. And you're the only one who can do that." Brodie looked her right in the eyes. "I'll pay you ten thousand dollars to do it." He wasn't playing.

Oh, damn. She sure could use that money. "You don't get it. It's not just about singing her songs. The reason those people are here tonight is because Lorelei sings from her heart. She lives the lyrics, and the melody is part of her. No one can take her place."

"She asked for you." Jaime finally spoke.

And it irritated the crap out of her. "What are you doing here?" What business was it of his?

"I'm the one her manager contacted. She figured you'd say no, so she asked me to talk to you."

"Well, she was wrong." *You don't have that influence over me anymore.*

"What will it take?" Brodie asked.

"This isn't about money." How could they not see that? "I can't do her songs justice. I'll get booed off the stage."

"Would you do it for a hundred and seventy-two thousand dollars?" Jaime asked.

That fucking fucker. He knew the exact number that would motivate her.

A horrible feeling settled in her stomach, weighing so heavily it nearly buckled her knees.

The only reason he'd make sure she got her money back was to appease his stupid guilt.

This is his send-off.

Thanks for a great summer. Here's a token of my appreciation for the good time.

But of course, she knew him better than that. He wasn't cruel. Just messed up.

It was an apology for hurting her. An acknowledgment that he wasn't ready for a relationship and a loving gesture to make her whole again.

As if money could even touch what he'd given her.

But she did need it. It would give her the freedom to make the choice that was right for her. Not Ian. Not her parents. Not even Jaime.

She looked him right in the eye and said, "You know I will."

The tour bus looked nothing like Grace had expected. She'd imagined dark paneled walls, tinted windows, polished tables, and a modern kitchen. Instead, the interior was pure kitsch. The banquette was pink, the appliances cherry red, and the floor a black-and-white parquet.

She met with the band at the white Formica table to go over the playlist. The bass player kept scraping his fingers through his hair and the drummer's red-rimmed eyes were focused on the screen of her phone.

She hated them for betraying Lorelei. It took every ounce of willpower she had not to lay into them for hurting the kindest, most real woman she'd ever known. The only reason she kept her mouth shut was to preserve Lorelei's dignity.

The manager stomped heavily up the stairs, taking in the lot of them. The betrayers squirmed under her evil grin. "Ready?"

"It's not going to work," the drummer said.

"Sure, it will." The manager's smile broadened. "This is what the boss wants, and this is what she'll get. Check your contracts if you have any questions about who's in charge." She gave them a moment to quiver under her hard stare. "So, I'll ask again. Are you ready?"

With the phone pressed tightly to her ear, Grace stood just offstage while Brodie tried to hype her up to the audience. "They're going to leave. They're going to boo and break out into fights, and then police will swarm and the entire meadow's going to be cleared out."

"That's one possibility," Romeo said. "*Or* since they know all about you and already love you, they'll chill out and have a good time."

"And here she is, ladies and gentlemen," Brodie called. "The Singing Baker!"

She tensed, listening to the response.

"So?" her brother asked.

"It's mixed. There's booing, but there's clapping, too. I just know the Mini Callows are bawling their eyes out."

"Maybe. But the only way to win them over is to get out there and perform for the ones who're clapping. Sing your heart out, Grace. You got this."

"Thank you, Romeo. I don't know what I'd do without you." As she disconnected, she thought about Lorelei somewhere out there hurting. Everything the singer believed to be true had been turned upside down.

And so, for her, Grace would deliver the performance of a lifetime. She strutted out onto the stage and grabbed the mic. "Thank you, Brodie, and thank you, Calamity Falls! I might be a poor imitation of the great Lorelei Calloway, but in her honor, I'm going to give you the best I've got. Now, let's bring down the house with my favorite song, 'Light Up the Dawn.'"

The band launched right into it, and Grace closed her eyes. She'd done this a million times. It might be the largest venue and the only media presence she'd ever had, but she'd block it out and just do her thing.

And then, she did it. She opened her mouth and sang the song, just like she'd done a million times before. Only this time, she put in a little more energy, so she didn't let Lorelei down.

It didn't take long to win them over. At no point did she check to see past the lights—it didn't matter if the meadow had cleared out. She was going to get through this set. She lost herself in lyrics she'd memorized years ago but still resonated with her, and she let herself dance, move, and sway to the melodies.

Maybe they'd turned the cameras off, loaded the vans, and driven back to the airport muttering, *Fuck this. Nothing to see here.* But she could see bodies in the pit, so she knew she was performing for someone.

And really, when it came right down to it, she was singing for herself. It was the best therapy in the world because she sang with her whole body and used every ounce of stamina and strength to push the words out.

Because tomorrow, she'd have to pack her bags and leave this town she liked so, so much. Leave the man and little girl she'd fallen madly, wildly, thoroughly in love with.

It wasn't painful.

It was gut-wrenching. It was her soul screaming that she was making the biggest mistake of her life. That she was meant to live here. She was meant to be a mother to Kinny.

Yes.

There. She'd said it.

I'm meant to bake Christmas cookies with her as we shake our butts to holiday songs in the big, warm kitchen. To read her books before bed and wash her hair in the tub. And I'm meant to ease her dad through all the difficult choices that are hard for him to make but are in Kinny's best interest.

And she was meant to spend her life loving that beautiful, generous, deeply sensitive man who couldn't live with the consequence of one decision he'd made ten years ago.

She sang and sang, and when she took a break, she

looked at the set list to remind herself what came next, and through it all, she decided she couldn't leave Calamity without giving it one more shot.

She had the money now. It bought her freedom, time, and options.

Tomorrow, she would talk to Jaime.

Because maybe she'd read it all wrong. Maybe he really was preoccupied with onboarding his goalies right before the season started and with Kinny going from a sling to a cast.

Maybe he'd be shocked to hear she was leaving.

Maybe he would beg her to stay.

After the show last night, people had crowded around her. Brodie and his wife, Abby, Jeremy, Ben…so many excited faces, so much excitement about the "phenomenal" performance. Lorelei's manager had sent a text message.

Leslie: I couldn't stay for the show—had to take care of my girl—but I watched it on **Entertainment Today** *and the clips on social media. You stepped in when Lorelei needed you, and we can't thank you enough.*

She'd tried to text back, but it had neither shown as delivered nor read, so she assumed she'd been blocked. Lorelei and Leslie had put the festival behind them.

Now, it's my turn.

Last night, Jaime had hugged her. He'd kissed her cheek. He'd praised her, but he hadn't asked her to stay. Hadn't even brought up her plans at all.

She stared at her empty suitcase. She'd opened her drawers, pulled shirts and dresses off hangers, but she hadn't actually packed anything.

Half of her wanted to run over to his cabin and demand he tell her what he was thinking. She was deeply hurt. She was angry. How could a man go from wanting to spend his life with someone to letting her go in the space of four days?

The other half understood. He'd seen his friend's body twist in the sudden gust of turbulence. He'd witnessed Booker hit the ground, and the scene replayed in his mind on repeat.

She thought he'd gotten past the worst of it, but if he could discard her so readily, he hadn't.

He doesn't want me enough to fight off his demons.

What about Kinny's croquembouche?

Her heart ached for all she'd lost.

Well, if she couldn't make the birthday cake, she could at least give the little girl a special present to remember her by. As she dusted off the beloved Renzo's red apron her great grandfather had worn, she wondered for the hundredth time if she was being too hasty.

Jaime was at the rink right now, at a team practice to help the new goalies acclimate to the players. She could head over and talk to him, at least give him a chance.

Her phone blared with Lorelei's "My Mama" song, and an unexpected wave of affection crashed over her. She grabbed it. "Mom?"

"Grace, sweetheart. I want to talk to you."

The dire tone had her plunking her ass on the arm of the couch. "What's wrong? Is Dad all right?"

"He's fine. Why would you ask such a thing?"

"You sound so serious. Not to mention, you rarely call."

"Oh, come on. You know I don't like the phone. Besides, I'm busy. How on earth can I run Renzo's and be on the phone with every cousin, kid, and uncle?"

"But I'm not every cousin, kid, or uncle, Mom. I'm me."

"Where is this coming from?" Her mom's tone softened. "You're my baby girl."

"I know. I'm not feeling all that great right now."

"Are you sick? I don't want you traveling when you're not well. Can you stay a few more nights in that cabin? Or I can get you a hotel. You want me to get you a hotel?"

"No, Mom. I'm not sick. Thank you, though. What's going on? Why did you call?"

Her mom gave a bitter chuckle. "Well, hang on. Let's make something very clear. I do love you, Grace. Very much. Now, why aren't you feeling great?"

She'd always been open with her mom. The only reason she hadn't told her about Jaime was because she knew it would make her worry. Her mom's greatest fear was having one of her children leave the family, and what was a stronger motivator for that than falling in love? "I fell for a guy. Pretty hard."

"Yeah." Her mom sighed. "That's what I figured. Why else would you stay away for nearly three months?"

"Because I love what I do. Because I'm celebrated here. I've loved every minute of it."

"I know, hun. I've seen the Calamity website. I saw your performance last night."

"You did?" She'd been so overwrought she hadn't thought to look. "I don't want to know the reviews. The Mini Callows are going to light me on fire."

"There are always going to be haters, but you'd be surprised at how much they loved you. Let's just say it's safe for you to scroll when you get to the airport. Now, tell me about this boy."

"Well, first, he's Ian's friend. He was one of the groomsmen."

"That ranch boy?"

"Yes. He's amazing, Mom. And he's got a daughter." She heard her mom's sharp intake of breath. "And that's why I didn't tell you. I knew you'd spend the whole summer worrying I'd never come home. But it didn't work out."

"That's why I always say it. Friends come and go, boyfriends break your heart, but family is always there for you."

"Yeah. I get it now. I do."

"I'm sorry he hurt you. But that's what happens. Love has so much power over us that we get carried away. We forget that friends and boyfriends aren't tied to us. Not the way family is. We're a tribe, forever connected. We look out for each other no matter what. It's in all of our best interests to band together."

But what if Jaime's the one? Then what?

"As soon as you come home, I'll make pasta e fagioli, your favorite comfort food. I can't take care of you two thousand miles away. And imagine if you'd had children with that man. You wouldn't have all of us to help raise them."

"Yeah, I know. I thought the same thing."

"Now, this brings me to why I called. I talked to the Adlers, and they told me about the building they bought for you. They want you to open a Renzo's, but your dad and I talked about it. You ran away this summer so you could do this thing you love—"

"I ran away from my wedding. I stayed here to make money to pay you back the money Ian stole." *And because I fell in love.*

With a man who doesn't feel he deserves to be happy.

"But if you were happy here, you wouldn't have done that. And hear me when I say, I want you happy, Grace. If you're happy, you'll stay. And so, the bakery is yours, sweetheart. It's not a Renzo's. Elise has agreed to stay on, so you can bake to your heart's content in Newport."

"You don't mind me not working in the bakery?"

"I mind you being two thousand miles away from me. Two hours and a ferry ride, I can handle."

This was huge. Something her mom never could have done three months ago. "Thank you. That means the world to me."

"I'll see you tonight, right? Text us when your flight lands. We miss you, sweetheart."

"I miss you, too." Grace ended the call and got up. With a renewed purpose, she set the apron in the suitcase and finished packing.

She tidied up her cabin and left a note for the Duprees.

And then, she walked out of the cabin and closed the door behind her.

Chapter Eighteen

Jaime could barely lift his fork. Did he have the flu?

He was pushing too hard, he knew that. Between caring for his daughter and onboarding the goalies, he hadn't had a minute. He hadn't even spent time with Grace.

During last night's show, he'd gotten a text from his mom saying Kinny was grumpy. He'd taken that to mean she was in pain, so he'd stayed to watch Grace's performance —wouldn't have missed it for the world—but then, after a quick hello, he'd hurried home.

After the family dinner, he'd head over to her cabin.

And yeah, on some level, he knew he'd been avoiding her. He'd seen how much he'd annoyed her with his overreaction. But it wasn't like he could snap his fingers and make the anxiety go away. He just needed time. A few days to pull his shit together.

How did he explain what it felt like to be back in that hospital, right near a stairwell? No, it wasn't exactly where he'd encountered Ms. Hayes. But it didn't matter. It threw him back to the woman's anguished cry, that finger pointing at him, telling him it was all his fault and that if her son died, he'd have to live with it.

It had a grip on him. Because this time, it was his daughter in the hospital. And while he hadn't put her there, his anxiety couldn't differentiate between the two experiences.

His mom reached for the mashed potatoes and slopped a good pile on her plate. "Did you hear what happened to Steve and Mel's little boy?"

Kinny, trying to cut a green bean with the edge of her fork like the adults were doing, wound up losing control, and the utensil went skittering across the table. Vegetables flew off her plate and onto the floor.

"No. What?" Abby didn't miss a beat and kicked them toward the dogs, who immediately hoovered them up.

"He pulled a Jaime." His mom smiled at him fondly.

Which confused him. It sounded like something awful had happened to the kid, so why was she smiling?

"He thought he could fly. Took his kite up to the ridge and jumped off." She shook her head. "Mountain boys. Always trying to conquer gravity. It's amazing anyone lives to adulthood."

Sometimes, it amazed him that his family could speak so casually about what happened that night. To this day, no one had held him accountable.

"Is he all right?" At least Abby sounded concerned.

"It's not a vertical drop, Abs." His dad held out his hand to show the angle of the mountain side.

"Oh, he took a tumble." His mom chuckled. "Rolled until a rock stopped him. Well, maybe it was his head that stopped him when it hit the rock. Knocked him out cold, but he's totally fine."

Everyone laughed.

"I remember when I tried to beat Martha, the goat, in a head-butting contest," Abby said.

"I was there," his dad said. "Saw the whole thing, and I was the one who watched you get six stitches. Bet you never took on a goat again."

"Nope."

"Why didn't you stop us?" Jaime blurted.

The laughter died, and everyone stared at him.

"Stop you from what?" His mom sounded genuinely confused.

"Running wild. Doing whatever I felt like doing. Why didn't you stop me?"

"I don't understand what you're saying. Did you want me to put a tracker on you so when Cole got the bright idea to skate on the frozen Snake River, I could drive over and demand you come home?" His mom looked at his dad as if he might know what Jaime was talking about.

"No." He was frustrated. They had to know what he was asking. "Before it got to that. You never grounded me or taught me self-discipline."

"You sure about that?" his dad asked. "Didn't everybody have to be home for supper? Didn't you have to get your homework done before you could play hockey?"

He couldn't argue with that.

"We did that to give you structure," his mom explained. "The consequence of not coming home on time was missing hockey. And since that was unthinkable to you, you were never late. I don't know a better way to teach self-discipline."

"Okay, but I took too many risks, and I was a shit role model."

"Daddy." Kinny gave him a stern look.

"Sorry, sweetie. You're right." He didn't need to lose it in front of his kid.

Abby's chair scraped back. "Hey, I forgot to bring over the ice cream I made this afternoon." She reached for Kinny. "Come over to my place and help me?"

Kinny's fork clattered on the plate, and she dropped to the floor. "What kind of ice cream?" she asked, as they crossed the kitchen and headed out the back door.

"You were a responsible young man," his dad said. "You had good grades, you were a great sportsman, you did your chores around here. You did a hell of a lot more than most kids your age. I'm not sure how much better of a role model you could be."

"You're a great brother," Nash said. He was closest in age to Jaime, but they'd never done the same things. His brother was into riding—horses, bulls, it didn't matter. He loved ranch life. "You were always there for me."

"Son, we live in the mountains," his dad said. "We raise prize bulls and train horses. This is Calamity. We've got rapids and glaciers, high winds, and hail the size of baseballs. Do you think homebodies live here? We chose this place to raise our family and thank God we did because you had a hell of a good childhood. And I know what happened with Booker gave you a scare, but Jesus, son, let it go already. It's done. Everyone's moved on."

"Broken bones come back stronger, and stitches give you character. It's nature's design." His mom reached for his hand. "There's nothing wrong with you. You're perfect just as you are." And then she pointed her fork at him. "And so is Kinny."

Everyone's moved on except me.

And that meant Gracie would, too.

He couldn't live with that. He didn't have time to get his shit together, not with the risk of losing her. "Hey, can

Kinny spend the night?" He threw his napkin on the table and got up.

"Of course."

"Thanks for dinner, Mom."

"Where you going?" his dad called.

But he was already out the door. It was only in the twilight race across the lawn, the soles of his boots crunching over the dirt road, and the bats swooping overhead, that the fog in his mind finally lifted.

And in the clearing, he saw Grace. How he'd neglected her. Cast her aside while he'd gone paralyzed. He could accept he had more healing to do. He could accept he was a work-in-progress.

But he couldn't shut her out.

He needed to see her. Fall to his knees and apologize.

And ask for her help. *If it ever happens again, please shake me. Remind me we're in this together.* Because he needed her. Couldn't live without the sunlight she poured into his dark spaces.

When he made it to her porch, a chill gripped the back of his neck. There was an emptiness that didn't feel right. The energy felt different.

Something's wrong.

Somehow, he knew not to knock. He turned the knob and walked right in. In the shadowy darkness, it hit him. He didn't even need to turn on the lights.

She's gone.

Fear seized him, held his entire body captive.

The festival's over.

She must've given her food truck back.

Over the last two days, he'd been as cold and emotionless as a boulder. He'd given her nothing but excuses.

He dropped to his knees. Weighted by the unbearable sense of loss, by the unsustainable fatigue of carrying guilt, shame, and anxiety, he let it all crash over him. Just gave it free rein.

He stopped fighting. Stopped trying to control his emotions and just surrendered.

Of course, he'd lost her. And not because he didn't deserve her, but because he'd let her go. He'd let the most beautiful, passionate, creative, kind, giving, loving, intelligent, generous person he'd ever known go. There was no one like Gracie.

And he'd let her fucking go.

Because I can't get out of my own head.

I choose to carry this burden. I walk through life with it on my back.

She doesn't need my shit.

Kinny doesn't need my shit.

How does it make amends with Booker? How does it even the score?

It doesn't.

It doesn't do a damn thing but wear me down and give me less to offer the people I love.

A revelation hit, bringing in a tide of new energy.

If I want to make up for what I did, then I need to be a better man.

It's as simple as that. No matter how badly someone fucks up, the only way to earn forgiveness is by making better decisions.

Which is exactly what I've been doing. So, if I can throw off the cloak of shame, if I can step out of the shadow of fear, then I'll be all right.

I just need to be my best self. Nothing more, nothing less.

Just like that, the weight dropped. Because it was

manageable. It was doable. Whereas punishing himself, denying himself happiness, was a lifetime battle that wore him down to a hard nub.

He got up, turned around, and started out—but something on the kitchen table caught his eye.

He flicked on the light, and the stark emptiness lashed across his heart.

This room used to be filled with her bright sundresses, her colorful T-shirts, and the mess of whisks, cookie sheets, and bowls from her constant experimenting.

He grabbed the piece of paper from the table and started reading.

I'm not sure who's going to find this but thank you for welcoming me to the Dupree Ranch. This was the best summer of my life, and I will always remember it—and all of you—for the freedom it gave me to become my truest self.

    Sincerely,
    Grace

Stupidly, he brought the note to his nose and inhaled as if it carried her scent. It didn't, of course. And he didn't want a memory of her. He wanted her real and alive and vivid and smiling.

I have to get her back. I have to.

It's not too late. It's been four days since…

Fuck. Since he'd planned on proposing.

The cabin. He'd forgotten all about it.

The rose petals, the candles, bath salts, and champagne.

He'd never checked out, so they must've tossed it all away.

At least he'd kept the ring with him. With six pink

diamonds surrounding the larger one in the center, he'd designed it to look like a flower.

Determination sent blood pumping through his veins.

He'd put that ring on her finger, and he'd get his family back.

Because he did deserve her.

And he would spend the rest of his life earning her love.

On his way to Duff Island, Jaime stopped in New York City to deal with some unfinished business. Something he should've done years ago.

He stood on Delancey Street amid the New York City rush hour traffic. People swerved around him, everyone hurrying to get somewhere. The lowering sun glanced off the steel and glass building, nearly blinding him.

Whatever anxiety he used to feel when thinking about this confrontation was gone. In fact, he wanted to catch up with his old friend. He wanted to look him right in the eye and apologize. But not out of shame so much as the need to set things right. He wanted to know how Booker was doing, whether it ground away at him to support elite athletes instead of being one.

He waited for a break in traffic and then jogged across the street and entered the new and upscale apartment building. At the concierge desk, he stopped. "Hey, I'm here to see Booker Hayes. I'm Jaime Dupree."

"Is he expecting you?" The concierge reached for the phone.

"No, he's not." *And he might send me packing.*

"Jaime Dupree is here." He listened. "Yes. No problem." He hung up and directed Jaime to the elevators. "Twenty-seventh floor. Number 2712."

"Thanks, man." With every step he took, he grew more confident. He'd rehearsed this conversation for years. He welcomed it.

As soon as the elevator doors closed, and he was alone, his entire being remembered Grace. Her dazzling smile, her gentle fingers, and her wicked tongue. He missed her so damn much.

Every inch of his body craved her touch.

I need her.

I need her, and I'm going to win her back.

The doors opened, and he headed down the hallway. Would she forgive him? It hadn't been that long. But he knew it had nothing to do with the length of time. It was the fact that he'd stopped coming to visit her at four in the morning. He'd pulled his affection.

For four days, he'd let her feel unimportant.

He would fix it.

She hadn't responded to his texts or calls, so he wouldn't bother sending another. He would see her in person.

With a firm knock, he took a step back from the door and squared his shoulders. It wasn't like Booker would see him and take a swing. It was more the hatred, the disgust, that he needed to brace for.

But it wasn't Booker. An older woman answered the door. "Jaime?"

It was like stepping off the edge of the world, plummeting through space without a parachute.

He'd prepared himself to see Booker. He could handle anything the man would say since he'd anticipated it for so long.

He was wholly unprepared for his friend's mother.

"Look at you, all grown up. Come in, come in." She

stepped back, swinging the door wider. "It's so good to see you."

He flashed back to the hospital. Standing in the stairwell and hearing her gut-wrenching sobs. Watching her turn to look at him, recognition hardening her distraught-ravaged features. Her eyes narrowing on him. Her voice shaking with rage as she shrieked, "If he dies, you'll have to live with that."

But he pulled himself out of the past and took a step forward. "Ms. Hayes." He moved like his limbs had been placed in the wrong sockets.

"Was Booker supposed to meet with you? Because he's had a last-minute trip to the West Coast. Some crisis with one of his football players. You know how it is." She ushered him into the foyer of a sleek, modern apartment. A corner unit, it had two walls of windows. "Well, how are you? I hear you own the Renegades now."

He stood there like a statue. "Yes, ma'am. Actually, we're all owners—Booker, too—but the others aren't ready to take on the job yet."

"Yes, I heard." She gave him a compassionate smile. "I'm sorry for your loss. I know how much you boys loved Kurt." The effort to hold up a one-sided conversation seemed to wilt her smile. "Booker will be sorry he missed you."

Talk, asshole. "He didn't know I was coming. I probably shouldn't have surprised him, but I didn't want to give him an excuse to turn me away."

"Oh, he wouldn't do that. He misses you boys."

"I saw him last summer after the funeral. He left before we could talk."

"I'm sure he had another meeting to get to. That man is a workaholic." She touched his arm. "Do you want to sit down?"

"No, thank you." It struck him that the person he needed to speak to all these years wasn't Booker after all. It was the woman standing right in front of him. Only now that he had a child of his own did he understand her emotional state in the hospital.

Kinny had a broken arm. What this woman had gone through was on a whole other level. When she'd seen him, she didn't know if her son would live.

"I'm sorry for what I did. If I hadn't sent that text, Booker would be playing hockey right now." The lines on her forehead tightened. Was he upsetting her? "He'd definitely be giving Cole a run for his money. At the very least as Sexiest Man Alive."

His attempt at humor failed. Instead, she looked concerned. "Apology accepted. I won't pretend it wasn't a terrible time for us. But now, it's my turn. Please, sit down." She led Jaime to a set of chocolate-colored leather couches.

Before he even sat down, he launched into his apology. "I'm sorry I put you through that trauma, and I hate myself for ruining Booker's career in hockey." It felt so damn good to get it out. To say it to the woman he'd nearly destroyed with his selfishness. "I wish I'd left it at just a bonfire. I wish I'd never jumped. If I could go back in time, I swear to God—"

"No." She popped up. "No, no, no. Let me explain something. I'm a city girl, born and raised. When my husband took the job in Calamity, I thought it would be so much fun to live in a charming little town. What I didn't expect was the women wearing hiking sandals with their cargo capris. They had kayaks strapped to the tops of their Subarus. They didn't want to meet for coffee. They wanted to hike. They wanted to ski. I didn't do any of those things, and Booker…" With a smile, she shook her head. "He was a rascal from the start. That boy was always climbing the furniture, trying to ride our dog…he was full of energy. And it turned out Calamity was the best thing for him and the worst for me."

He didn't know where she was going with this, but she had a story to tell, and he would listen.

"That day in the hospital, I couldn't tell you what I wore. I don't remember whether it was sunny or raining. The only thing I remember is thinking I'd lost my son." Her features flinched as though witnessing a gruesome crime scene. "That will stay with me forever. But now that I'm talking to you, I remember when you saw us at the hospital. We'd only just gotten there. We hadn't talked to the doctor yet. At that moment, there was a very real chance my son would die."

"I know." He lowered his chin, shame washing through him. "I'm so damn sorry."

"Jaime, honey." The kindness in her tone had him looking up. "What I'm trying to say is Booker might not have wanted to jump that night, but he would've done it on any other one. How many times did my son lead the way? If it hadn't been you sending that text, it would have been one of the other boys."

"Not the night before he moved to LA to play with the Cavalcade."

"You're not hearing me. It was what you boys did when you were together. Do you understand? It was the basis of your friendship. In the beginning, when he first started playing with you boys, I grounded him, I tried to get him to play an instrument. I put him in Boy Scouts. But he didn't want any of it. Nothing would've kept him from doing the things you did. He was an adrenaline junkie. I used to say, 'That boy's got a death wish.' I'm a homebody and a city girl, so I didn't understand any of it. But let me tell you something, that night was the end for me. I couldn't take it anymore. And that's why we moved."

"I can understand that. I put my parents through hell." Wait, had he, though? After talking to them the other night, he couldn't really hold on to that false belief anymore.

"But if you want my opinion, as far as hockey, I think what he loved about it was playing with you boys. *That* was the joy for him. I'm not entirely convinced he would've loved it on his own."

"He would've. It's hockey. It's the greatest game in the world. There's nothing like it. The speed, the strategy. There's no other truly team sport where you can't win unless you do it together. No, he would've played, and he would've been one of the greats."

A slow smile spread across her features. "I think you're the one who should be playing. Why aren't you? Weren't you considered a phenom?"

"Oh, I...I own the team."

"You didn't ten years ago."

"No, but I had the ranch. And a daughter."

"Don't professional athletes have families?"

"Yes, ma'am. But that ship has sailed for me."

"Okay, well, you know what else he's great at? Negotiating. He loves it. Jaime, I don't know what would've happened if he hadn't gotten hurt that night. I do know that the average career in the NHL is four and a half years because their bodies get broken down."

"True."

"His passion used to be running around with you guys and defying the laws of nature. But now, he's found a new way to challenge himself as a sports agent." She got up, moved around the glass coffee table, and sat beside him. Her hand settled on his arm. "Thank you for coming over to apologize. It shows what a good man you are, and I'm sorry you've been carrying this guilt all these years. But you can let that go now, Jaime. He's fine. He's thriving. And we hold no ill will for anything that happened that night."

Never had she appreciated moving out of her parents' house more than the day after leaving Jaime Dupree. Because that first morning home, she couldn't get out of bed.

Her mom would've whisked the curtains open, her dad would've asked her to help him bake a ricotta cake to take to their second cousin on his brother-in-law's side, and Grace would've gone along with it.

Because that was what she did. She went along with it.

That day, though, she'd just felt heavy, like someone had covered her in a thick wool rug.

And she knew she only had herself to blame. She'd known from the start Jaime was wounded. For a few weeks there, he'd pushed past it to be with her.

It would've been easier if she could have chalked up the attraction to chemistry, good sex. But it was so much more. Together, they were magic. Apart, they were...well, it was almost like they needed each other's energy source to become fully alive.

But whatever. Even if he snapped out of it and came begging for another chance, it wouldn't matter. He just wasn't healed in a way that would make it safe to give him her whole heart.

Except...that was a lie, wasn't it? She'd already given it to him.

Whatever. She had to stop obsessing.

Eventually, she'd quit wallowing. She'd gotten out of

bed, showered, and headed into Newport to see the building the Adlers bought. It was gorgeous, roomy, elegant…the perfect choice.

But ultimately, she hadn't accepted their offer. His parents hadn't stolen from her—Ian had. Besides, she had the money she needed to start her own bakery. And she didn't see the point in living in Newport. It would just mean unnecessary travel time to get to family birthday parties, graduations, and anniversaries. If she lived in another state —like, say, Wyoming—she wouldn't be able to attend every single gathering, but when she was only two hours away, she'd feel obligated to come to everything.

Besides, she loved Duff Island, so she'd talked to a realtor and, only a few days later, found a gray clapboard building in an ideal location.

And so, here she stood, on her final walk-through before she made a formal offer and put down her earnest money.

Outside the window, bikes lined up, ready to rent for the end-of-summer tourists. People walked by licking ice cream cones, pushing strollers, and peering into windows of the various shops along Anchor Street.

Upstairs, she had fifteen hundred square feet of recently renovated living space. A nice kitchen, a bedroom, and windows that overlooked the ocean.

She loved the idea of coming down to bake before dawn and then going back to bed. Especially in winter, when she wouldn't have to trudge through a blizzard.

A toilet flushed upstairs, and a moment later, her brother's flip-flops smacked on the wood floor. As he made his descent, his muscular legs appeared, then his blue and white board shorts, and then he was there, all tan skin and wind-tousled hair. He flashed his heartbreaker smile. "So, we doing this?"

She rolled her eyes. "I don't own it yet."

"Yeah, so?"

"So, you don't use the bathroom."

Romeo's grin widened. "Oops." He rested his hip against the counter. "You like it?"

"I do."

"Then, you should definitely buy it. I'll even help paint."

"How did you know I'd want to paint?"

"White counters, white café tables and chairs with pink-striped cushions, pale pink walls, big white vases with pink flowers…do I have it right?"

He'd described everything she'd ever dreamed of, and now that it was within her reach, shouldn't she be way more excited?

Why wasn't she? "I haven't imagined any pastries since I've been home." It had only been four days, but still. It was like someone had shut off the spigot.

"What?"

"When I was younger, that's all I dreamed about. Lemon curd and chocolate mousseline. I would lie in bed and wonder what it would taste like if I put coconut milk in the whipped cream. What if I flavored it with coffee? But that all stopped when Ian and I got together." And she'd gotten carried away in all her firsts. "And then I had culinary school, and then I was working full time. It came back to me in Calamity. Like, right away. That very first night, when I should've been crying about the wedding that never happened, I was imagining pastries."

"Well, baking's your therapy."

"It is. Jaime thought it was hilarious that he stopped at the grocery store after we landed, thinking I'd get milk and yogurt and deli meat or whatever. Instead, I got butter and eggs and baking sheets." She glanced around the beautiful space, the sunlight pouring in through the windows, the view of the harbor right there, colorful windsocks whipping in a strong breeze. "Something's very wrong with me because I get to live a dream I never thought could come true. And yet…now that I'm here, in this perfect space with the money to do it, I feel like I'm settling."

"That's because you are."

Stunned, she could only stare at her brother.

"You don't want this." He tapped the counter. "You don't want to be here."

"Yeah, but I mean, if I have to be here, this is the perfect place. I won't find better."

"Why do you have to be here?"

"Are you serious? I told you the situation in Calamity. There's no space available in Wild Wolff Village." She couldn't bear the idea of running into Jaime and Kinny. He would heal. At some point, with such a loving family and great friends, he'd finally conquer his demons. And then, he'd allow himself to love and be happy.

And it won't be me.

No. She couldn't do it. It would kill her to see him with another woman. But she couldn't let herself think about it. "Besides, now that I have the money, I'm not going to waste it on a food truck. No, this is fine." Decided, she headed for the door. "Let's buy me a building."

She made it all the way to the realtor's office. The hot August sun would've been sweltering if not for the ocean breeze. Water lapped against hulls and sailboat sheets banged against masts.

These were the sounds of her childhood. The briny smell in the air, families biking the seven-mile loop, and the sense of endless summer were everything she'd ever known.

Until Calamity.

The mountains and meadows, glacial lakes and wild animals. The bison preserve, the bike paths that cut through forests, cowboy boots and pearl button western shirts. It was a whole other world. She'd barely begun exploring the trendy shops downtown, the living museum of Owl Hoot, the upscale ski resort—

Wild Wolff Village.

A sense of rightness swelled inside her. *That's it.* That magical, European-style town was the only place in the world for her bakery. "I don't want fine."

"Yeah. Didn't think so."

"I don't have to settle for anything. I'm the Singing Baker, and what I make is special." *Maybe it'll hurt to see Jaime with someone else but that can't stop me from living the life I want.*

"Damn right." Her brother threw an arm around her shoulder and gave her a shake. "That's my big sister."

Right there on Anchor Street in the middle of the busiest time of day, she pulled out her phone. Stepping under the realtor's awning, she did a quick search for Wild Wolff Village's leasing office.

Once she found it, she hit Call. As it rang, a group of college-age girls walked by—loud, laughing, and very clearly checking out her brother. One of them slipped a phone number into the pocket of his shorts.

Grace rolled her eyes, but he just grinned. "Who're you calling?" he asked.

"The only place in the world where I want to open my own bakery."

"Paris?" His eyes went wide. "You're calling *Paris*?"

Used to his teasing, she smacked his muscular chest.

And then, right before she gave up, a woman answered. "This is Marni. How can I help you?"

She'd expected a more formal reply. "Oh, I thought I was calling the Wild Wolff Village leasing office."

"You are. I'm the manager. No one's at reception, and the phone was ringing, so I picked it up. What can I do for you?" The woman sounded in a hurry.

Well, she got the manager. She had to shoot her shot. "My name is Grace Giordano." She went with the best angle she had. "The Singing Baker."

"No kidding? I *devoured* your pastries this summer. And your voice, my God. You're really something."

"Thank you."

"So, what can I do for you?"

"I'm standing outside a realtor's office on Duff Island, ready to buy a building for my bakery, and the truth is, I don't want to open it here. I want to be in your village." Marni started to speak, but Grace wasn't ready for rejection. "I know you have a long wait list for your shops, but I'd be willing to start with a kiosk. With the momentum from the festival, I think it'd be beneficial for me and the village."

"Are you done?"

She gazed up at her brother, so scared of hearing they had seven thousand people on their waitlist or that there was an ordinance for the number of food sellers or some other excuse.

"You got this," Romeo whispered.

"I'm done if the answer's yes. If you tell me no, then I'm going to have to keep trying to convince you."

Marni laughed. "That won't be necessary. We'd be foolish to pass up a chance to have your posh pastries in our village. You fit right in with our clientele."

"I can have a kiosk?"

"No. I'm afraid there's a limit to the number of food carts we can have in the town square."

"Oh, then, what are you thinking? Pastry chef at the lodge?"

"We have one of those. But with the digital market surging, our bookstore can't sell enough paper and hardbacks to stay in business. They've just given their notice. Today. *This* morning. So, before I pull out the waiting list to see who's next—"

"Give it to me."

"I can do that, but do you want to hear the rent first?"

"Yes."

"It's fifty-five hundred a month."

Grace's heart sank. She mouthed the number to her brother. But a fierce sense of purpose took hold. "How big is the space?"

"Oh, it's huge. It's been here since the beginning when bookstores were a thing."

"How about I split it with them? We don't even need a whole wall between our spaces."

"That's actually a brilliant idea because it's got a large, underused kitchen. I think you'll make her day. She's really sad about closing."

"So, this is happening?"

"I'll bring it up with her, see what she says. I also have to do my due diligence, but I feel good about this. How soon can you get out here?"

"I can be there tomorrow."

Marni laughed. "A woman of action. I like that. Come by my office as soon as you get back in town. Let's see if we can get this done."

Chapter Nineteen

With her phone pressed to her ear, Grace stood on the slate patio behind the Bowie's bunkhouse. Sunlight played hide-and-seek with the mountain as clouds sailed across the August sky.

Am I really here? Did I just make this my life?

Sage scented the air. "You have to come out here." Her brother would love it.

"Yeah, I'll visit."

The patio hosted a huge grill, a firepit, and outdoor tables and chairs.

She'd considered driving to Calamity, so she'd have her car and a trailer of her belongings, but the priority was meeting with Marni and securing her spot in the village. She'd wound up only bringing two suitcases with her, but her parents would ship everything else.

Were they happy with her decision? Hardly. She'd probably never forget the look of fear in her mom's eyes as she'd walked away from her at the airport. But she'd make sure to text and FaceTime with her regularly so her mom could be assured she wasn't losing a daughter.

"So, what's it like?" Romeo asked. "Are there lassos and spurs and shit lying all around?"

Grace smiled. "Not even close. It's actually amazing. It hasn't been an actual bunkhouse since this place was a working ranch. Now, they've turned it into an awesome man cave. It has game tables and an industrial-size kitchen. The guys rent it to a film studio for a cooking show, but that's only in April. They said I can have it as long as I need."

She'd left the French doors open, so when bottles rattled, she whipped around to find a little girl rooting around in the refrigerator. "Oh, someone's here. Let me call you back." As she headed inside, she checked but didn't see any adults. *Is someone else staying here?* "Hey, there. What'cha looking for?"

"I'm thirsty."

The girl had to be about the same age as Kinny, and she got a twist in her heart for what she'd lost. For a while there, she'd imagined taking a role in her life, being a mother figure. The three of them becoming a family.

Of course, Jaime had texted her. Emailed. Left voice messages. He'd even flown all the way across the country, rented a car, and taken the ferry to get to Renzo's. Sure, she'd loved his pursuit. But it didn't matter because he hadn't really changed. The next time his daughter got hurt—or anyone close to him, really—he'd shut down again.

Besides, she was focused on her bakery now.

She came up behind the girl. "I haven't gone shopping yet, so you won't find much in there." But when she peered in, she found a fully stocked refrigerator.

"That's okay. My daddy keeps lots of stuff here."

Uh oh. "Do you live here?" Maybe Brodie thought the place was empty when he'd offered it to her. He had three brothers, so they might not keep track of whom they let crash here.

The girl grabbed a squeezable yogurt. "No."

"Any idea where he is?"

"No," she said. "That's why I'm looking."

"Are you lost?" Grace was so confused. "Who are you with?"

"Mommy's at the restaurant." She stood on her toes but still couldn't reach the can of soda on the middle shelf.

The moment she headed for a kitchen chair to drag it over, Grace stopped her. "Hang on a second. I'll get you something to drink. But first, I need to know who brought you here." The Bowie ranch was comprised of thousands of acres. Wildlife roamed everywhere—particularly around the more remote parts like this bunkhouse.

"Nobody. Can I have a soda?"

"Does your dad let you drink them?"

She looked away but didn't answer.

Well, there was only one thing to do. She'd have to drive the little girl to the main house. But just as she grabbed the car keys to her borrowed car, a tall, extremely fit man raced inside.

"*Ruby.*" He pressed his hand to his heart. "Jesus. You scared the crap out of me." He snatched the girl off the floor and enveloped her in his muscled arms. "What are you doing?"

"You said you'd be right back, but you didn't come. So, I went looking for you."

"Baby. Sweetie. Come *on*. You've got to stop doing this. Don't I *always* come back? Every time I go out, don't I always come back to you?"

"But why can't you take me with you?"

"Because I was working. I had to train someone. I told

you—very clearly—that I'd be gone an hour and a half. An hour to train, fifteen minutes there and back."

"And it's been six hundred thousand hours," Ruby said.

Grace stifled her laugh.

"It's been an hour and a half. Plus, the extra terrifying minutes I spent trying to find you. How did you get here?"

She hunched a shoulder. "I went looking for you. Can I have a soda?"

"First of all, no. You ran off. I'm not rewarding you with junk food. Secondly, the love of my life doesn't put crap into her perfect, growing body. Now, come home with me, and we'll have a snack in our blanket fort."

"Okay, Daddy."

Once the man finally relaxed, he turned his attention to Grace. "Hey, sorry about that." He reached out a hand. "Will Bowie."

"Grace Giordano. Your brother said I could stay here until I got on my feet."

"Yep. The Singing Baker, right?"

"Right."

He smiled at his daughter. "Remember the cream puffs?"

Ruby nodded enthusiastically.

"Chef Giordano made them."

She was impressed he knew to call her chef. But then, hadn't the little girl mentioned her mom worked in a restaurant? "Do you like cream puffs?"

Ruby nodded with total sincerity.

"If you promise to never leave your house without an adult, I'd be happy to make some and bring them to you."

"Could she, Daddy? I want them."

"You heard what she said. Only if you promise not to take off on your own."

With a solemn look, she pressed her hands together. "I promise so hard. I promise, promise, promise."

Tires rumbled across gravel, and a car came to a stop.

"Then, I sure will." Their family was kind enough to let Grace stay here and loan her a car until she got herself situated. *It's the least I can do.*

Out front, a car door slammed.

"All right, well, I apologize for barging in. It won't happen again." Will looked at his daughter. "Actually, that's not a promise I can in good faith make."

Grace laughed. "It's okay. Don't worry about it."

"Let me know if you need anything," Will said. "Ruby and I are going to head home." He was so tall and muscular that he blocked the doorway. "Hey, man. Good to see you."

She couldn't see who'd just shown up. Brodie, maybe? Checking on her?

"What brings you out here?" Will asked.

"I'm looking for Gracie."

But she sure as hell recognized that voice. Adrenaline crashed her system as if she'd pounded ten energy drinks all at once.

"You found her." Will jerked a thumb over his shoulder. "We'll get out of your way."

And then, the two large men switched places. Will walked out, and Jaime stood before her.

It had only been a week, so no, she hadn't forgotten what he looked like. But it would never change, would it? She would always get that hitch in her breath, the tumble of nerves in her stomach, and the swell of affection at the sight of him.

The look in his eyes mirrored her own reaction. She knew they both felt the magnet that pulled them together because it came from deep within their souls. It was undeniable.

And in a perfect world, one where he hadn't witnessed his friend's accident, they would live happily ever after. But life didn't work like that, and he couldn't seem to break free of the self-imposed shackles.

So, instead of running into his arms, throwing her arms around his neck, and giving into her agonizing need to be with him, she held her ground. "Well, I guess you finally caught up with me."

"You had to know I'd never give up."

Three months ago, she'd put off having her "closure" conversation with Ian. She never imagined she'd have to do the same thing with Jaime. "How did you find me here of all places?"

"It's a small town. Rhys told me you'd signed the lease." He stuttered out a laugh. "I missed it."

"Missed what?"

"That moment when you found out something had opened up."

"Actually, I called them. I got lucky because the manager happened to answer the phone." She glanced down. It hurt to think of every other milestone he'd miss. He wouldn't be there for the opening of her bakery. "It sucks. It really does." He seemed so integral to her dream coming true. She looked him right in the eye. "I love you."

Hope burst to life, brightening his features.

And it sucked that she had to quash it. "You're an amazing man, and I'd wanted a future with you and Kinny, but it's not going to happen. You're just not ready, Jaime."

"Ready for what?"

"To give me the kind of love I deserve. The past owns you, which means you're not free to have a future with me."

"I am." His tone was so emphatic, it startled her. "I talked to Booker's mom the other day, and I get it now. Punishing myself doesn't make his life better. The only thing I can do to make up for what I did that night is be a better man every single day of my life. Which I'm already doing."

Um, what did he say? Could he really be having his breakthrough?

"And it made me think about what you said. What if the situation had been reversed and I'd been the one who couldn't play hockey, who'd had to endure a year of physical therapy? I'd be pissed. I'd be frustrated. But...it would have nothing to do with Booker. If anything, I'd blame myself because it's what we did together. There was nothing new. Sure, the timing sucked, and I shouldn't have done it that night, but I wouldn't be blaming Booker. That's just not where my head would be. And really, if you think about it, the only thing I can do about it is make better decisions. So, that's the grace I can give myself. To do better. Every day. And you know what makes me better?"

"Me?" She laughed.

"Yes. You. Us together. As a family." He took a step closer. "I love you, Gracie. I love you so damn much that I can't sleep without you. I can't think. I can't eat. I don't want to do life without you. I'm sorry I shut down after Kinsley got hurt. I wish I'd reacted differently, but that was the first time in ten years I'd allowed myself to be happy. And it just felt so...decadent, and I was greedy for more and more. It doesn't make sense, I know, but when my daughter wound up hurt, it felt like my punishment. Like I'd let myself be selfish again, and look what happened? But I get it now. I get it, and I'm sorry." He reached for her hands. "I know you didn't move here for me, but could I be one of the reasons you stay?"

"No." She might've shoved him for the way he reared back.

"Okay." He let her go. "Okay. You don't trust me yet. I get that. What if we start over? Can I ask you on a date? All I want is the chance to prove I've changed. That I won't hurt you again."

"I'm glad you see things more clearly. I think that's great. But what exactly *has* changed?"

"What do you mean? I just told you."

"You see things more clearly, but are you doing anything differently? Are you still living in that cabin? Is the Dream House still empty?" She hated to see this powerful, muscular man deflate. But he needed to understand why she couldn't get back with him. "Are you still playing hockey inside a *barn?*"

"What's wrong with that? I built that rink so I wouldn't have to leave Kinny all the time."

"You want everyone to have these great lives, but what about yours? You say you built that house for your parents, but they don't want it. It's yours, Jaime, and it's sitting there empty. Everyone says you're the best goalie they've seen, and yet you hide in a barn. You get one shot at this life, so you'd be a fool not to go for it. The only one stopping you from living your dreams is you. And as for me, I believe you love me. I do. But no matter what you say, you're still living a life of penance. And in the end, that's going to blow up all your relationships."

Jaime stood with the GM and Declan behind the players' bench. How ironic that their first exhibition game set them against the LA Cavalcade.

The expected pinch of regret he always got knowing Booker wasn't playing for them didn't hit this time. Talking to Ms. Hayes had melted the core of him that had frozen the night of the accident. Knowing she didn't hate him, that Booker's life had turned out well, had enabled him to catch up to the present.

A present that didn't have Gracie in it. Right now, anyhow.

Because he would not accept losing her. They were each other's person. He knew it. Had no doubt about it.

She may have jammed a knife into his chest and twisted when she rejected him, but she'd been right. Words didn't mean shit. It was his actions that would prove he'd changed.

"Oh, fuck." Declan was on the move.

"What happened?" Lost in his own thoughts, he'd missed the play. Now, he could see the team gathering around the net.

"Byron's down." The GM watched, his body tense.

This can't be happening. "What's our curse with goalies?" First, Ross had pulled a groin muscle during warm-ups, but now the new guy was hurt? Exhibition games were basically a way for teams to warm up and give coaches a chance to make roster decisions, so a minor injury wasn't an issue.

But it definitely set expectations among the teams. And they wanted the Cavalcade running scared.

As the trainer hurried onto the ice, Byron remained on his knees, head lowered. "Shit. I hope he's okay. What the hell are we going to do if he's out?"

"Let's wait and see," Darren said.

They didn't have to wait long. Declan came back over. "He took a shot to the collarbone."

"That hurts like hell." Jaime knew it firsthand. "So, what now?"

The GM glanced at the player's bench. "We could put Richie in."

Declan shook his head, watching as the trainer skated the goalie off the ice. "Nah. It's LA. They'll crush us. We're not starting off like that."

"Then what?" The GM sounded irritated.

This is a shitty start to the season. He'd wanted to put together the best team, to make it worth Cole's while, but…*it is what it is.* He'd done everything he could.

"Look, we've got Cole, we've got Ross," Declan said. "We're trying to make a statement here. We're not putting in someone who hasn't shown us he's got what it takes. We have to intimidate LA. We have to put in the best." He gave Jaime a chin nod. "Suit up."

He had no idea what his friend was talking about. "*Me? What for?*"

"You're putting Jaime in?" For some reason, Darren didn't find the idea ridiculous. He sounded okay with it.

Which was just wild.

"You've watched him help out the forwards," Declan said. "How many pucks have gotten past him?"

The GM broke into a smile. "Good thing I had you sign that contract."

"Guys, shut up. Come on. We have a decision to make." They stared at him like it had been made. "You can't put me into an NHL game."

"We're playing against a team that hasn't missed a playoff in a decade," Declan said. "You bet your ass I'm putting you in."

A chill skittered down his spine. "That's not…no." He couldn't play. "The game's livestreamed."

"So?" Darren asked.

It was their confused expressions that cleared his vision.

This was what Gracie was talking about. He played hockey in a barn so Booker wouldn't see. That was the source of everything. He couldn't have what he'd stolen from his friend.

And if Booker saw him playing…what would he think?

He thought about Ms. Hayes, how she'd described her son—as the rascal, adrenaline junkie—and then, it all came rushing back. He'd lost sight of who Booker really was. The boy he'd grown up with, the teenager he'd had extreme adventures with.

And he knew right then exactly how Booker would react if he was watching this game and saw Jaime Dupree hit the ice and skate over to the pipes.

His friend would smile.

"You got your gear in the trunk of your car?" Declan asked.

There it is. That familiar energy rushed in. "Yes." He was pumped. He was ready to go.

He was itching to get on the ice.

Because he knew without a doubt, there was nothing the Cavalcade's forwards could give him that he couldn't block.

I am the best goalie for the job.

"Hurry up." Declan gave him a shove. "Go."

You better be watching, Booker. "Yeah, man. Give me fifteen minutes." *Because you're going to love this.*

And then he took off.

Because tonight, he'd live his dream.

Jaime had played regularly for twenty years. Between the college team, the Juniors, and the professional forwards he'd worked with, his muscle memory knew how to react to any situation.

But he'd never played in an NHL stadium.

You got this.

You've been training your whole life. You're ready.

Play your game. Stay focused. Get the job done.

Here we go. The centers lined up next to the ref, and the puck dropped.

Time to dial in.

The puck was flying around, and he never let it leave his sight.

Lefty coming down my off side dot lane. He's looking cross ice. His blade is open.

Jaime's gaze cut across to see who he was passing to. It was a righty.

Hips open. Stick tickling the ceiling, it's wound up high. He wants the one-timer.

There it goes. The puck shot across.

Jaime slid over and made the save.

Fuck, yeah.

The rebound shot across, and Jaime tracked it down the left side. One of their guys grabbed it off the wall and started moving towards the net. Out of his peripherals, he saw another skater on his right.

It's a 2v1.

Only four seconds.

Let the defenseman take the pass away and focus on the shooter.

The guy shot it on the ice.

This is it. Jaime made a pad save. The rebound kicked it out to the other player.

Get across and take away everything low. Make him beat you.

He stretched out and made the save right before the buzzer blared.

The crowd roared and got to their feet. The Renegades swarmed him. Cole cupped the back of his helmet, shouting something Jaime couldn't make out.

I did it.

I fucking did it.

I just won my first NHL game.

Chapter Twenty

As she walked along the side of the house, Grace could hear the squeals and shrieks of laughter from the backyard. Her heart could barely stand being a guest at the party she'd hoped to help plan.

But it's fine. I'm fine. It was a beautiful day. Early September in the mountains was cool enough to need a sweater but still sunny and lovely.

She walked carefully. If she dropped this croquembouche, it would be the last straw, and she'd cry. Because she'd gone all out—it wasn't just a tower. She'd designed it to look like a castle.

And because she missed Jaime more than her own family. More than Renzo's.

But him? The jerk had moved on. When she'd gotten his text message a week ago, she'd nearly thrown her phone against the wall.

Jaime: Hey, are you still down to make Kinny's birthday cake? It's all she can talk about.

How could he act so blasé toward the woman whose heart he'd shattered? She could only assume he'd gone back to being that emotionally flat guy she'd first met. She'd spent countless nights trying to figure out why he'd reach out to her like that. Was it a test to see how she felt about him? Was he inviting her to the party? Finally, she'd faced the truth.

He wants a cake, you idiot. That's it. He was making his daughter happy.

She could've told him to go screw himself, but she loved that little girl, and she wouldn't let her have a store-bought cake when she knew just what would make Kinny happy. So, she'd done it. She'd made a fabulous princess cake with turrets and a working gate with isomalt chains.

Since she'd moved here, their paths hadn't crossed—he was busy with exhibition games, Kinny had started first grade, and Grace was designing her space while it was under construction—so today would be the first time they'd seen each other since that day in the bunkhouse.

As she neared the backyard, she grew nervous. It would be unbearable to see him having fun while she'd been curled up at night crying her eyes out—but also, she wondered how his family would treat her. Did they think he was a jerk for not holding onto her?

Did they think about her at all?

It didn't matter. She'd found a lovely townhouse to rent in Wild Wolff Village—a professor from the University of Western Wyoming was on sabbatical—and her bakery opened next month. If the Duprees ever stopped by, she'd be happy to see them. She had no issue with them.

For today, she'd drop the cake off and leave.

But just as she reached the freshly mown lawn, Kinny spotted her. Her whole face lit up, and she shouted,

"Gracie." She raced over, the skirt of her flouncy pink dress fluttering, her eyes sparkling, and her cheeks bright pink. "You came."

"I did." When the child slammed into her, she had to brace, holding the cake up high and balancing it so it didn't shake or topple over.

"Where have you been?" Those little arms banded around her thighs. "I've missed you so much."

She wished she had a free hand so she could hug the girl. "I've missed you, too, sweetheart. Do you want to see your birthday cake?" She lowered the cake to give the little girl a better view. "What do you think?"

Kinny's awed expression was answer enough. "I want to live in it." She gazed up at Grace. "I love it so much. It's the best birthday cake ever."

"Grace?" Abby hurried over. Her eyes went wide when she saw the cake. "Oh, my goodness. This is stunning." She smiled at Grace. "Thank you. This is amazing."

"It's my pleasure."

"I hear you're moving here. You're going to open a bakery in the village?"

"I *have* moved here." Kids came rushing over to see the profiterole castle. "And yes, we open next month."

Abby glanced at the house. She seemed confused. "Did I miss a step?"

More people came to see the cake, and it edged Grace out. She wanted to leave before Jaime saw her. "I don't know, but I just came to drop off the cake." She lifted it. "Where would you like it?"

"I've got a table set up just for it."

As they headed off, Kate, Jaime's mom, came over. "Would you look at that? It's a masterpiece." She kissed

Grace on the cheek, giving her a warm squeeze. "It's so good to see you."

"It's good to see you, too." But she really did need to go. There were a lot of guests, but Jaime was bound to see her. "How about I just hand it off to you?"

"Oh, I'm not touching it." Kate held up both hands.

What choice did she have but to follow Abby to the table covered in a princess tablecloth and strewn with plates, forks, candles, and napkins? Grace set it down carefully. "Okay, here you go. Have a great party." She took a quick glance at the festively decorated backyard and noticed the big playset. It had a slide, a rock wall ladder for climbing, and three swings. Something looked different about the pool, too, and she realized it now had a slide.

Had Kate and Trace finally moved in?

Not my business. She needed to go. But just as she turned, her gaze landed on Jaime.

This time, a quiet explosion rocked through her at the sight of him. The party sounds muted, and everything but him became a blur. He looked at her like this moment was a homecoming. Like he'd waited years for her return.

Like the weight of the world dropped off his shoulders.

Holding her gaze, he threaded through the crowd.

She wanted to bolt. She would have—if she wasn't distracted by the fact that there was something different about him. She couldn't pinpoint it until he stood before her.

"Hi." He had an air of confidence, that's what it was. He was lighter, happier. Freer. He wasn't wearing his unreadable mask.

"Hi." She'd never felt awkward around him before, but his easygoing presence unnerved her. "I brought the cake."

"Thank you. It was nice of you to do that."

"I wouldn't let her down just because we didn't work out."

"Oh, but we did."

"Excuse me?"

"We worked out spectacularly."

"Why would you say something like that?" She flared up hot and fast. After all her suffering without him, how dare he be so aloof? "Is that all I was to you, a summer fling? 'Thanks for the great sex. Oh, hey, can you make a cake for the daughter you're never going to see again?'"

"Gracie. My Gracie. You were never a fling. You're an awakening. Do you remember what I said?" He leaned in, his lips just a brush away from her cheek. "I'll never give up." He reached for her hand and towed her across the patio and away from the crowd. "And I meant it. Come on. I want to show you something." In the shade of a tree, he finally let her go, but only to free his hands so he could cage her in against the other side of the house. "But before I do, I need to tell you something. I listened to everything you said, and I'm doing all of it. Why? Because I'm in love with you. I want you in my life and in my bed. I want to sleep next to you every night and wake up with you every morning. And in case it isn't obvious, there's no one else Kinny wants to be her mom. We are magic. We are spectacular, and I love you."

With him standing so close, with his sexy mouth and the burning desire in his eyes, she couldn't think, couldn't speak.

"Now." He lowered his arms and took a step back. "Come take a look."

As he veered away, she noticed a cut on his jaw. She reached for it. "What happened?" Oh, it looked ugly. "Did one of the kids hit you with a puck?"

"No. I got it in a game. It's fine."

"What game?"

His handsome features cracked into a huge grin. "I signed a contract with the Renegades."

"I'm totally confused. You're the owner."

"Not anymore, I'm not. Both of our goalies were injured, so Declan put me in. I gave it up."

"You gave up the team? You're not making any sense. You don't just sign a contract to play in the NHL."

"Sure, you do. They pulled me from the reserve list, I played a good game, so now I'm on the roster."

"You got on the ice and played in an NHL game?" Oddly, her voice sounded flat when she felt nothing but a sparking, crackling happiness. "Just like that, your life changed, and now you're living the dream?"

"Not yet. But I'm getting there." He gave her a look that left no question as to what the missing piece to that dream looked like.

Me.

It looks like me. But it was too scary to contemplate, so she reached up and touched his jaw. "No more Goose, huh? Too bad. I guess you'll need a new nickname."

"I sure as hell don't. I haven't let a puck in yet." He pointed to his scar. "Blocked this one with my face."

She couldn't help laughing. "Okay. This is crazy. But if all three of you are Renegades, then who owns the team?"

"We're working on that. Cole's going to retire at the end of this season, so he'll take on the role then. In the meantime, our attorney's handling things."

"But…isn't there only one other person who can be the owner?" *Booker.*

"Yep." Again, he reached for her hand and brought her over to a tilled section of the property. Surrounded by a fence, it had an arched gate.

"A garden plot?" *But no one lives here.*

"Yes."

"Did your mom finally retire? Is she going to take up gardening?" *And why are you showing me?*

"No, it's for you. For your edible flowers. Your costs are high enough leasing in the village and buying the equipment. I figured it might be cheaper to grow your own, but if you don't like gardening—"

"I do. I love the idea, but I don't live here, Jaime. No one does." That's when she noticed a towel slung over the second-story balcony railing. "Oh. I wondered about the playset. So, your parents finally moved in? I'm not going to garden in your mom's backyard."

"What if it was yours? What if you lived here with me and Kinny?"

She took a closer look at the towel and saw the princess. "Wait. *You* live here?"

He reached for her hands. "Yes. Kinny and I moved in."

She was floored. Absolutely gobsmacked.

"I've left the decorating to you, in case that's something you want to take on." He brought her palm to his mouth and kissed it. "You were right. I *was* living my life like Booker was watching, making sure he didn't see me too happy. And you know, it worked for a while because I could live in that cabin forever. I could live without the NHL. But Gracie...I cannot live without you. *You're* the game changer."

She melted. Her blood went hot, and her bones turned to jelly. Mostly because she believed him. His easy demeanor told her he wasn't fighting demons anymore.

He'd won.

And was he really talking about her moving in? And growing *flowers?*

"Jaime." His name came out a whisper, and her knees went weak.

"I moved into the Dream House, and I'm a goalie in the NHL. But those things mean nothing if I can't be with you. I'm sorry for hurting you. I'm sorry it took me so long to get my head out of my ass. But I'm here now, Gracie, and I'm free to love you with all my heart. I can't promise to never mess up, but I can guarantee I'll never stop listening to you, working with you, and loving you with everything I am. I will wake up every morning with no other thought than to make you and Kinny happy. Will you please give me another chance?"

She'd spent so much time imagining him coming back to her and saying these things that she almost couldn't believe it was real. But then, he was everything she knew he could be. "Of course, I will. I'll give you all the chances you need. As long as I know you love me, and that you'll always fight for us—"

"I will. I will never stop fighting for us."

Tears spilled down her cheeks as she fell into his arms. "I thought it was over. I thought I'd lost my one and only chance to feel this kind of love. I thought…I mean, I knew you loved me. I just didn't think you could get over your past."

"I'm a work in progress, but I have the best motivation in the world. I want to give you everything, Gracie. And I'm going to."

"The only thing I want is for us to be a family. Because I love Kinny, too."

He hugged her so tightly she could scarcely catch her breath. "I'm so glad you're back. Nothing has been harder than living without you."

She pulled away. "I went to the cabin and got our stuff."

"Yeah, I saw you left my overnight bag in your cabin. I figured you noticed…"

"The rose petals and champagne, yes. I've been wondering all this time what your plans were?"

He broke into a slow, sexy, sly grin. "That must be hard for you, the not knowing."

"Jerk. You just got me back, and you're on shaky ground. I'd be a little more careful if I were you."

"Oh, but you don't like me to be careful." With a grip on her hips, he yanked her against his chest. "You like me filthy." And then, he kissed her.

His love and affection and lust…all of it came crashing over her. It swept her away and made her feel so very, very loved. She was just so relieved, her heart so full.

She tucked her face into his neck and pinched his side.

"Ow. What was that for?"

"I just want to make sure this is real."

He tipped her chin so he could look into her eyes. "There's nothing more real than my passion for you, my love for my daughter, and the promise I'll make to love and protect you and to let both of my girls fly."

Epilogue

PALE PINK AND WHITE STRIPED WALLPAPER. *CHECK.*

White picture frame molding. *Check.*

Glossy hardwood floor. *Check.*

White café tables and pink-and-white striped cushioned chairs. *Check.*

Grace stood in the middle of the large, airy room, taking inventory.

It's really happening.

I'm opening my own bakery.

She'd spent a little more than she should have to make her space as gorgeous as possible. It was, after all, located in Wild Wolff Village. But also, she really wanted her customers to settle in and stay a while. The ambience needed to be inviting, the seating comfortable, and the playlist conducive to concentration *and* conversation.

The pièce de résistance was the logo Abby made for her. It adorned the storefront and the wall behind the counter.

The Singing Baker Patisserie.

This is it. This is exactly what I wanted.

With half the wall open to the bookstore, she and its

owner had decided to share some expenses. Since they envisioned customers reading while lingering over coffee and a slice of opera cake, they'd splurged on dark pink velvet club chairs. Plate glass windows with cushioned seating let sunshine stream in, and the vases bursting with peonies added the perfect fresh and sunny touch.

Jaime came up from behind and hugged her. He gave her arm a pinch.

"Ow. What was that for?"

"You've got this look on your face like you're not sure if this is real, and I'm making sure you know it is. You did this." He nuzzled her neck. "Congratulations."

She laughed and turned around within the shelter of his arms.

"I love you." This man made her feel so cherished.

"I don't think I have words for the way I love you. Because it's passion and affection and friendship and lust and…It's just so much more than I ever thought the word meant. You give me the space to become the woman I'm meant to be…you just make me so happy." She got up on the tips of her toes. "But you can save the pinches for other parts of my body tonight when we're alone."

His gaze went heated. "I can do that."

She cupped his cheeks. "I love you, Jaime Dupree. I love our life together."

Kinny and her friends Ruby and Posie sat at a table working with the cookie cutters and play dough she'd made to keep them occupied. The Dupree family was here, and the Bowie brothers had brought their entire crew, kids and all. So many people had come to celebrate the opening of her bakery.

She had such a full and beautiful life…the only thing missing was her family's involvement. She knew she'd hurt her mom, and her dad was busy—as general manager, he took on more than anyone else for Renzo's—but she couldn't help thinking they could try a little harder to stay in touch with her. It just felt like, if she wasn't right there with them, they forgot about her.

If her parents were trying to teach her a lesson, that she would come to regret leaving the safety of her family, they could forget it. She loved her life here, and she hoped one day, they'd make an effort. If they wanted her in their lives, they'd have to do something different to fit her in.

"Ready to flip the sign?" Jaime asked.

"One second." She kicked off her chef's clogs and stood on a chair. "You guys?" The room quieted down. "I'm going to try really hard not to cry, but I'm incredibly grateful to all of you for being so supportive, for treating me like you've known me forever, and for stepping in to be my family."

"We love you, Grace," Kate called.

"But me, especially," Abby said. "Because I've always wanted a sister."

"Believe me. Me, too." She took in all the beautiful faces smiling at her. "So, thank you. For everything. You've all earned free pastries for life."

They all laughed and clapped, and Jaime held onto her hips and lifted her off the chair. He hugged her tightly, and she knew everything had aligned to bring her to this moment.

"Now, are you ready?" he asked.

"So ready."

As soon as he set her down, she slid into her clogs and headed to the door. When he didn't follow, she turned back to him. "Aren't you coming?"

"This moment's all yours."

A crowd had already gathered, though she couldn't see

them through the temporary gauze curtain Knox Holliday had hung to make sure no one could see the beauty of her bakery until the opening.

So, she turned the sign over, opened the door, and started to say, "Welcome," when she saw a whole bunch of familiar faces.

"Mom?" Tears sprang. She fell against her dad's chest. "Dad." She drew out that single syllable until she was bawling as they both embraced her, hugging her tightly. "You're here. You came to my opening."

"We wouldn't miss it, sweetheart," her dad said.

"You gonna let us in or what?" Romeo's voice had her pulling away to see that all her brothers had come.

"What are you doing here? Who's taking care of Renzo's?"

"Hey, sis." Her brothers took turns hugging and kissing her.

"Where's the chow?" Marco asked.

"You got anything other than cake in here?" Rocco asked.

And then, they pushed past her to get inside.

They moved to a corner of the bakery so the rest of the crowd could get in. "I can't believe you all came out here," she said.

"We wanted to share this day with you," her mom said.

"I thought you were angry, that you were trying to teach me a lesson or something."

"What? Where do you get these ideas?" Her mom scowled. "If I haven't been in touch, it's because we've been busy making some changes, and we have you to thank for that."

"Me? What did I do?"

"We've done the same thing for generations, and we

never bothered to question it. But you made us think. When you moved away... Oh, I was scared. I was so angry."

"She was hurt," her dad said.

Her mom just shrugged. "Can you blame me? How can I protect you from two thousand miles away?" She cut a look across the bakery, and Grace turned to see she was looking at Jaime.

"I don't need your protection, Mom. I just need your love. I need your support."

"I know that now. Your dad and I were taught to fear outsiders, and we passed that along to you guys because we didn't know any other way. But you changed all that. We see how happy you are, how in love you are with this very good man—"

"How do you know he's a good man? You've never met him. You haven't even talked to him."

"Oh, but we have," her dad smiled. "Why do you think we're all out here?"

"*Jaime* did this?"

"He sent a few emails, just to show us pictures of the progress of the bakery," her mom said. "We started talking. He's a good man, and he loves you very much."

Now that the bakery was full of customers, the kids abandoned their dough project and began chasing each other. It was beautiful chaos.

"One thing I want you to know is that we made a mistake not letting you make your pastries," her mom said.

"Okay, who are you and what have you done with my parents?"

Her mom batted a hand. "Oh, stop."

"We've been so busy, so focused on keeping our business sustainable for the family, that we didn't see what made *you* special, and now—" Her dad gestured around the bakery.

"We do. You could never have anything like this at Renzo's, and we don't want to hold you back."

"So, we've made some changes." Her mom looped her arm through her dad's. "Your dad's stepping down as general manager."

What?

"What's the point of Enzo going to business school if I'm just going to keep doing things the way they've always been done?" her dad asked.

"So, he'll become the CEO," her mom said proudly. "And he's free to make the changes he thinks are best."

Her brother had so many ideas that no one was willing to implement. "What about you guys?"

"Well, we've bought the building you were looking at, so Marco can open a café—"

"That'll sell Renzo's baked goods," her dad said.

"Are you serious?" Her brother had always dreamed of owning a bar and bistro.

"Hey, you're not the only one who gets to follow her heart," her mom said.

"And what's your heart, Mom?"

Her mom looked startled. "Oh, I don't know. No one's ever asked me that."

"Maybe now, you'll have the time to find out."

"I do know one thing," her mom said. "We've worked so hard all our lives that we've missed out on getting to know our children as individuals. We'll have grandchildren soon, and we don't want to make the same mistake. So, maybe that's where I'll find my heart."

"We'll still work," her dad said. "We'll just hand more responsibility to others."

"Which gives us time to visit you," her mom said.

A crash had dishware rattling, and the room quieted for

a moment. Kinny had slammed into the antique whitewashed armoire that showcased local products and packaged baked goods. Grace bolted, but another parent got there first, picking her up and smoothing her dress.

"Are you okay?" the woman asked. "Where's your mommy?"

Grace hated when people asked that question—it hurt little girls like Kinny who didn't have moms.

But the little girl—with her hair a mess from playing, a streak of dried dough on her cheek—looked around the room, her gaze landing on Grace. She pointed. "Right there."

She could hear her mom's sharp intake of breath, she could feel the heat in the room from the crush of customers, and she could smell the butter and sugar that permeated her lovely space, but her entire being was focused on getting to that little girl who'd stolen her heart.

Hurrying over, she dropped to her knees and enfolded her in her arms. "I love you, Kinny. I love you so much."

Little arms wrapped around her neck, the cast a bulky weight.

"Are you okay, sweetie?" she asked. "Did you get hurt?"

"Yes. I hit my head."

"I'm so sorry, sweet pea."

But Posie shrieked, "Fairy cookies!" And then, Kinny forgot about her boo-boo and took off, leaving Grace with the feeling she'd just been given the greatest gift in the world.

Her parents watched her with warm smiles. "I take that back," her mom said.

"Take what back?"

"We already have our first grandchild."

Grace got up and threw herself into her mom's arms.

Her dad came over, and the three of them hugged, and she just felt so…safe in their love.

When they pulled apart, all of them had watery eyes. Jamie joined them, handing her a water bottle. "Everything good?"

"I hear you've been talking to my parents."

"I think we'll go take a look at those pastries." Her dad chuckled and steered his wife toward the display case.

"I sent them pictures so they could see the progress of all this. But yes, we've been emailing."

"And you flew my entire family out here."

"The team was coming back from an away game in New York. It was no big deal—" He saw her arched brow and stopped talking. "Yes, I flew them out here. I knew this day wouldn't be complete without them."

"I have never felt more seen, more understood, and more loved in my entire life. Never stop loving me, Jaime Dupree."

"Not possible." He gave her a lingering kiss. "You're the love of my life."

Thank you for reading TRULY, MADLY, DEEPLY! I'll bet you're wondering about that pretty diamond ring burning a hole in Jaime's pocket. Well, don't worry—I got you! You can read the swoony proposal free! Use the QR code below to get your copy!

For more about the four hockey friends, start with THE DEEPER I FALL, about a grumpy, tatted hockey player who falls head over heels in love with the spoiled princess he's forced to live with for a month. This one's Declan's book!

Do you subscribe to my newsletter? Get on that right now because I've got an EXCLUSIVE novella for my readers in 2023! You'll get 2 chapters a month of this super sexy, fun romance! #rockstarromance #surprisepregnancy #forcedproximity

We've created a recipe book for you! Ten fabulous pastry chefs contributed their luscious recipes.

Lee Ruocco of SweetAddictionFix.com
Fran Costigan of @goodcakesfran
Michal M. of Badolina Bakery and Café
Jean-Philippe of Oui Pastries Glasgow
Chef Nate of the French Kitchen
Manuella Mazzocco of Cooking with Manuela
Rebecca Blackwell of ofbatteranddough.com
Monique Polanco of Peaches 2 Peaches
CJ Cheyne of Oui & Si in Philadelphia
Angelina of Angelina Italian Bakery

Aim your cell phone camera at the QR code to get links to the recipe book, the bonus scene, and all the places you can find me!

https://linktr.ee/erikakellybooks

Need more Calamity Falls, where the people are wild at heart?

KEEP ON LOVING YOU
WE BELONG TOGETHER
THE VERY THOUGHT OF YOU
JUST THE WAY YOU ARE
IT WAS ALWAYS YOU
CAN'T HELP FALLING IN LOVE
COME AWAY WITH ME
WHOLE LOTTA LOVE
YOU'RE STILL THE ONE
THE DEEPER I FALL
LOVE ME LIKE YOU DO
TRULY, MADLY, DEEPLY

Have you read the Rock Star Romance series? Come meet the sexy rockers of Blue Fire:

YOU REALLY GOT ME
I WANT YOU TO WANT ME

TAKE ME HOME TONIGHT
MORE THAN A FEELING

Look for Booker's story coming soon! Grab a FREE copy of PLANES, TRAINS, AND HEAD OVER HEELS. And come hang out with me on Facebook, TikTok, Twitter, Instagram, Goodreads, and Pinterest or in my private reader group.

Read an excerpt from THE DEEPER I FALL

Excerpt of The Deeper I Fall

PROLOGUE

Ten Months Ago

TONIGHT, SERAPHINA MAUD CRUTCHLEY WAS A superstar.

She didn't feel like one very often. Rarely, in fact. But at this moment, with the spotlight trained on her as she stood in the middle of the ballroom surrounded by every single luminary in London's elite, she felt a wild mix of emotion: pride, certainly, but also the teensiest sense of imposter syndrome.

Honestly, she didn't know what to do with all the attention, so she smiled and kept her focus on the stage.

"The Lumley Foundation has hosted this ball for over a century." The CEO, in his black tailcoat and white bow tie, addressed the crowd of glittering donors. "Thanks to the addition of Phinny to our team, we've seen our donations quadruple. With her sparkling personality and boundless compassion, she is most certainly a bright star among us. Thank you, Phinny, for putting together such a spectacular array of auction items." He gave her a nod, and the audience broke into applause.

Her stepfather squeezed her shoulder, and her mum whispered in her ear, "I'm so proud of you, darling."

It was the most glorious moment of her life. Thanks to the blinding light in her eyes, she couldn't see the audience, so she just waved her appreciation. When the applause didn't die down, she began to wonder what was going on. The acknowledgment was lovely, but surely, she hadn't done anything *that* exceptional.

She supposed scoring a reclusive billionaire's superyacht for a week was quite a coup, but still…

This response is a bit much.

It was only when the spotlight turned away from her that she discovered the reason for the crowd's enthusiasm. Cameron Lumley had taken the stage. Shaking the CEO's hand, he grabbed the microphone. Then, her elegant, handsome boyfriend flashed his movie star smile. "Good evening."

Even though his family ran the foundation, he had no reason to be on stage right then. He might not run events, but he sure was an impressive sight. His custom-made suit hugged his broad shoulders and muscular thighs while his commanding presence captured the attention of everyone in the room. "On behalf of my family, I'd like to thank you all for your support this evening. As you know, the charity is my life's work, so it's only fitting that the woman who owns my heart now plays such a central role in it."

Surprise jolted her.

I own his heart?

They'd been together a while, but they hardly had some grand love affair. Not even close.

What's he going on about?

Her parents moved to stand on either side of her, enormous smiles stretching across their faces.

Cameron extended a hand. "Darling, please come up here."

She almost shouted *Why?* She didn't need to get up on stage. The band should start playing, and the patrons should go back to dancing. That was the order of events.

Her mum took the champagne flute out of her hand. "Don't just stand there."

With all eyes on her, what choice did Phinny have? But while her brain sent the signal to her legs, they refused to cooperate. A wave of nausea hit, and she went hot all over.

Her stepfather set his hand on the small of her back and gave her a nudge. "Go on now. Don't embarrass us."

That got her moving. As the crowd parted, she made her way to the steps. On some level, she knew what was happening, but her mind was racing, and she couldn't think clearly.

Please don't do this.

We're nowhere near ready for this. They'd grown up together but had only begun dating during their last year at university.

Casually dating.

Cameron stood center stage, while the CEO reached for her hand and helped her up the stairs. It was hard enough to move in her ball gown and shapewear bodysuit, but with her legs shaking, she moved like a newborn foal.

Which was fitting since her heart was positively *galloping.*

"Darling…" Cameron reached for her hand, kissing her palm.

And then, he dropped to a knee.

In the middle of the grandest charity event of the year,

her boyfriend—emphasis on *friend*—was about to propose. "I have loved you my entire life, but it was only when I saw you coming out of Trinity Hall that I knew it was time to start our future together. Every day has gotten better, and I can't wait to spend my life with you. Seraphina, will you do me the honor of becoming my wife?"

With the audience's collective gasp, the air was sucked out of the room.

She couldn't breathe. Blood roared in her ears, and her vision blurred around the edges.

In the silence, she had the strangest sensation of floating. She could picture herself grabbing a handful of helium balloons and drifting off the stage, out the window, and sailing over the rooftops of London.

Cameron's smile faltered, and it jerked her back to the moment. She couldn't embarrass him. "Yes. Of course, yes."

Relief washed over his handsome features, and he stood to his full height. He wrapped an arm around her and faced the ballroom, raising their clasped hands as though she were a trophy.

In the middle of the audience, Phinny found her parents. She'd never seen them so happy.

But why? The moment felt surreal. She'd never gushed about him to her parents. Never once talked about marriage or babies or any kind of future with him. They were two people from similar backgrounds who had fun together. *We're just dating.*

Marriage?

Standing on that stage, she felt like a paper doll cut out.

With a tug, she was led back down the stairs. Immediately, well-wishers swarmed them. His family, their friends…everyone was gleeful.

And it was all a lie.

Because she couldn't marry him.

Flee. It wasn't a thought so much as an alarm that rang through her body. She wrenched her hand out of his grip and made her way out of the ballroom. When she saw a sign for a powder room, she ducked inside and locked the door.

Oh, God. What is happening?

As she ran cold water over her hands, she looked up at her wild-eyed reflection. Her pulse pounded violently. Why had he proposed publicly? Now, calling it off would create a scandal.

It didn't have to be like this.

A hard rap jerked her attention from the mirror.

"Phinny?" *Cameron.* "Open up."

Angry that he'd put her in a terrible position, she opened the door, grabbed his wrist, and pulled him inside the lavender-scented bathroom. "What was that?"

His eyes flickered with hurt. "What do you mean, what was that? It was a marriage proposal."

"But why? Cameron, we're not ready for that."

"We've been dating for three years. When did you think we'd be ready?"

"I don't know." *Never.* "We haven't talked about it."

"What on earth do you think we've been doing all this time?"

"We've been *dating.*"

"Yes, on a course toward marriage. Why else would I be exclusive with someone if not with the intention to marry her? Why are you acting like this came out of nowhere? You can't pretend you didn't know it was the path we've been on."

She couldn't argue his point, and it flustered her. Because, really, it uncovered a truth that would only hurt his feelings. *I don't love you.* "I can't possibly get married now. I haven't done anything with my life."

His jaw snapped shut like he was trying to contain his anger. "Whatever you want to do, what better way to do it than as Cameron Lumley's wife?"

Obviously, that made perfect sense. Marrying into one of the wealthiest families in the United Kingdom would afford her any opportunity her heart desired. And it wasn't like Cameron cared what she did. That wouldn't change once they got married. He'd still go off with his mates on trips, and she'd go clubbing with hers. Sometimes, they'd do the holidays together, while other times, they'd be with their own families.

She knew exactly what her life with him would look like because that was the kind of marriage his parents had. And she didn't want to wind up like his mum, spending more time with her wine than her husband.

She pulled off the engagement ring. "I'm sorry, but I'm not ready to get married."

He just stared at her as though waiting for her to laugh and say *Gotcha. Of course, I'll marry you, silly!* "Are you serious?"

"Quite." His presumption that she'd just fall in line with some plan he'd never voiced irked her. "Cameron, come on. Do you even love me?"

"Of course I do." He seemed calmer as if they could now settle things. "I like you better than anyone else we know."

Well, there's a ringing endorsement for marriage. "And I like you. But I need more time."

"How much time?"

"I don't know."

"Are we talking about a few weeks?"

Weeks? "I'm twenty-four. What's the rush?"

His expression shuttered. "Waiting these three years has cost me nearly two million pounds."

She flinched as if he'd flicked cold water at her face. As soon as he married, he'd tap into his trust fund. With each child he added to his family, the monthly allowance would go up.

Quite the incentive to keep the Lumley line going.

She'd known that. So, why did it sound so ugly to hear him say it out loud?

He must not have liked her crestfallen expression because he reached for her elbows and bent his knees to look her in the eyes. "Darling, there's no one I'd rather spend my life with than you. You make me laugh…you make me happy."

"Well, yes, because I don't require anything of you."

He chuckled. "Most definitely, that's one for the plus column. But it works both ways. We give each other room to live our lives. Trust me, that's a good thing. We'll never grow restless or resentful."

I want more.

And what a bombshell revelation that was. She'd just been going along, having fun, not questioning anything, and she'd given no thought to where she was heading. Now that he'd forced her to think about it, she had to accept she hadn't done a damn thing with her life.

She couldn't say what she wanted to do exactly, but for the first time, she felt something missing. Something between the phases of parties, clubs, and shopping and getting married and popping out babies. "I need more time."

The smile vanished. He straightened. "No."

Fear sliced through her. She might not be ready to marry him, but she'd never contemplated a life without him. Like her parents, he was a major cog in the machine of her world, and she didn't know how to operate without all of them. "No, you won't wait?"

"I have waited. Three years is more than enough." He softened. "Look, you'd make a smashing stylist. Or you and your mum could open a boutique. Once we're married, you can use a portion of the extra fifty thousand pounds a month to do whatever you want. It doesn't matter to me, but we either get married now or it's done."

"It's done? Or we're done?"

"We're done. If you're not ready to marry me after three years, then I've got no reason to believe you'll be ready by four years or even five."

"I can't imagine my life without you, but I can't marry you because you've run out of patience with me. I'm sorry, Cameron." She took in the proud jut of his chin and the look in his eyes that screamed *Are you seriously going to walk away from me?* She liked him very much. They'd had a lot of fun together. But she didn't love him.

And so, she walked out the door.

Cut from her mooring, she felt adrift…uneasy. She hustled toward the exit as though the manor were on fire. The tight silk liner of her dress and the five-inch stilettos hampered her progress, though, as people rushed toward her, eager to share the happy occasion.

She couldn't talk to anyone right then, so she hurried on. Pulling out her phone, she tried to text her parents' driver, but her trembling fingers kept tapping the wrong pads, making her delete and start over.

"Seraphina?" Her mum glided along the hallway.

"Where are you going?" her stepfather asked. "We've just opened the bubbly to toast your wonderful news. Let's find Cameron. Come along."

The moment her mum reached her, the smile faded. "What's going on?"

Phinny handed over her phone. "Can you please ask Fergus to come 'round?"

Her stepfather snatched it. "We'll do no such thing. All of our friends are here to celebrate with you."

"There's nothing to celebrate." Phinny let out a tight breath. "We're not getting married."

"Of course, you are." Andrew's eyebrows shot up. "Don't be ridiculous."

When she'd met him as a little girl, she'd called him by his first name, but since she couldn't pronounce Andrew, she'd wound up saying Dewzy. For the first time since he'd come into her life, that term of endearment didn't fit. At this moment, when he cared more about his reputation than her feelings, he was purely her stepfather. "I gave the ring back. I'm not marrying him."

"Seraphina." Her mother sounded appalled.

"I told him I needed more time, and he said he wouldn't give me any."

Clasping her wrist, Andrew led them to an alcove. "You've known each other your entire lives. How much more time could you possibly need?"

"There are things I still want to do."

"Like what?" her mum whispered harshly. "You want to shop more? Travel more? Have more spa days? What exactly are you so eager to do?"

Like a can on the road flattened by a tire, Phinny's spirit compressed under the weight of her mum's words. She'd never considered herself frivolous. She'd been living the only life she'd ever known. "I don't know. But I would rather find out than get married to a man I don't love."

Her stepfather had always indulged her, and in return,

she'd tried very hard to please him. So, to see the tick in his jaw, the color flood his cheeks, truly upset her. "What on earth do you think we've been doing, Seraphina?"

"What do you mean?" A sickening feeling rolled through her.

"You don't have a proper job, you live in an apartment we own, and you use a credit card we've given you...why do you think we've been supporting you all this time?"

The great beast of fear loomed over her like a dark, menacing shadow. "I—" Her mind went blank.

"We've supported you because you were going to marry Cameron," her mum said. "And Lumleys do philanthropy, just as I've done. Just as you've been doing. *That* has been our expectation. If we thought for a moment you had no intention of marrying him, you'd have been polishing your CV and applying for jobs your last year at university. You'd have been paying your own bills upon graduation."

"Now, go and find your fiancé," her stepfather said. "And get things back on track. Or the locks to your Knightsbridge apartment will be changed by morning."

"What?" She could barely process his words. He couldn't possibly mean to throw her out onto the streets?

"Darling, please." Her mum patted his arm.

Oh, thank God. Her mum would always take care of her. They were a team. Her parents were upset. She understood that. But they'd never make her marry a man she didn't love.

But then her mum's features hardened. "Let her make some calls, see which of her friends will allow her to sleep on their couch until she gets a job."

About the Author

Award-winning author Erika Kelly writes sexy and emotional small town romance. Married to the love of her life and raising four children, she lives in the southwest, drinks a lot of tea, and is always waiting for her cats to get off her keyboard.

erikakellybooks.com

facebook.com/ErikaKelly

twitter.com/ErikaKellyBooks

instagram.com/erikakellyauthor

goodreads.com/Erika_Kelly

pinterest.com/erikakellybooks

amazon.com/Erika-Kelly/e/B00L0MLWUY

bookbub.com/authors/erika-kelly

Printed in Great Britain
by Amazon

46343682R00223